Engn

SIMON KEWIN

Engn, Copyright © Simon Kewin 2013

STORM
CROW
BOOKS

ISBN: 978-1-9993395-8-6

For my parents

Finn looked out over the fields of lights beneath them. "What's the point of it all, though? The machine is so vast and confusing and … pointless. I told you about the valves not functioning. Why do people go to so much effort doing things that simply don't matter? Why are more and more people being brought here?"

CONTENTS

I

The ironclads lifted Finn and heaved him into the moving engine. He kicked and bucked, skinning the knuckles of his left hand on the hatch as he tried to stop himself, but it was no good.

"No!" he shouted again. "Please, no!"

Any one of the ironclads could have lifted him, and there were three of them, one holding his legs, one on each arm. They flung him inside. He cracked the back of his head on the metal floor as he landed.

"No!"

His voice boomed in the enclosed space. The interior of the moving engine was dark, a cylinder of curved iron plates riveted together. It smelled of smoke and oil and rust, the stifling air hot in the back of his throat as he breathed it in.

The master stood behind the ironclads in the circle of light of the hatchway. He wore his familiar grin. "Shackle him, too. He'll travel the rest of the way to Engn in there."

The ironclads paused for a moment while they received their instructions. Finn saw his chance. The thought of being locked inside the moving engine was too much. He would rather die. He scuttled forwards to the opening and leapt to his freedom. But one of the ironclads seized his leg. Finn half fell to the floor. Screaming from rage and fear, he kicked and kicked at the ironclad who held on to him.

"Get him!" the master shouted. "Throw him back inside!"

While the other two ironclads tried to grab hold of his flailing arms, Finn put all his strength into one more kick. He caught the ironclad squarely in the face. They were protected by their metal masks, of course, but he heard the muffled grunt of pain as his kick caught the ironclad's nose. The grip around his shin lessened and he pulled himself free. Scrambling and tripping, he ran from the moving engine, from the ironclads and their master.

He had to get away. He wouldn't let them take him, as they'd taken the others. Connor and Shireen and the rest. He'd be like Diane. He didn't know the valley around Fiveways, but a stand of conifers, a finger of the woods that covered the upper slopes of the whole valley, lay not too far away. He bolted that way. He would be safe there. The woods were his territory and their horses would be no good among the trees. He could run and hide, and they'd never see him again. He'd live free and safe in the wilds; he'd hunt and fish and never have to face the ironclads again.

The blow on his back sent him sprawling to the ground before he had chance to react. He tasted mud. Turning over, he saw the master, astride his horse, standing over him, an amused look on his face. In his hand he held a thin metal staff with a bulbous club end. He held it ready to strike Finn again.

"Do you want to run some more, boy? I can play this game all day."

Finn scrambled to his feet, spitting mud and grass from his mouth. A sharp pain thudded across the back of his shoulders, but nothing appeared to be broken. The ironclads approached in a line off to one side, wary of him bolting again. Blood poured from beneath the mask of the one he'd kicked. He couldn't outrun them out in the open, not with their horses. He glanced uphill again, towards the trees, the welcoming darkness beneath them. They were his only hope. Could he get that far? Maybe, maybe not.

"Let me go," he said. "If you take me to Engn you'll regret it. Everyone there will regret it."

The master laughed, shook his head. "You know, I think we'll take the risk."

"I'm serious," said Finn. "When I get there, I'll fight. I'll…" He stopped himself. He'd nearly blurted out his great secret. But of course, he had to think of Connor.

"Fight back all you like, boy. It won't make any difference. Now get into the engine."

"You'll have to catch me first."

Finn turned and sprinted for the trees. He slipped and skidded on the sloping ground. He threw himself forwards, scrabbling with his hands. He was close now. He could hear the hooves of the master's horse as it cantered up behind him. But only a few more strides. Once in the trees, he'd run until he found the paths and glades he knew. Or head up the valley beyond Ironoaks where they'd never find him. Safe.

This time the blow was to his head. He must have blacked out for a moment because he had no memory of falling. The next thing he knew was the solid ground beneath his back and the grip of the three ironclads as they picked him up and carried him back to the moving engine. His vision swirled and he thought he was going to be sick. Weakly, he kicked and writhed, but it was no use.

This time two of the ironclads, reaching inside the cramped metal tank, pinned him on his back. The metal floor burned against his shoulder blades. He tried to wriggle free, desperate now, but their grip was unbreakable. As they held him, the third ironclad reached inside for a chain anchored to the inside of the machine. He clamped it around Finn's ankle, pinching his skin in the process.

"Well," the master said, peering over the ironclads' shoulders, "now we have you. And there's really no point trying to escape. If I were you, I'd sleep all the way to Engn. We'll be there in a week. You'll need the rest."

The ironclads released Finn and stepped back. He scrambled to his knees. There wasn't room to stand properly. He grasped the door frame, ready to pull himself out, back into the light, despite the chain around his leg.

"Move your fingers, boy."

The master held the metal door, ready to slam it on Finn's fingers. The grin on the master's face told Finn that he would do it, too. Finn pulled his hands back and the master heaved the iron door shut. The whole engine clanged around him like a cracked bell. Finn's head rang with the sound of it. He cowered to the back of the machine and sat there. He was alone in the darkness.

Sounds from outside the moving engine became immediately muffled. He heard voices, the master giving more orders to the ironclads, but he couldn't make out what was being said. The machine thrummed and throbbed; he could feel it in the bones of his chest. The air turned to smoke; it was warm and bad, as if it had already been breathed by something. He had been eaten by a metal beast. The darkness around him felt solid, a smothering blanket.

Nothing happened for a moment, and Finn began to think they'd left him to die inside the moving engine, ridden off without him. Then the furnace within the machine roared back into life. The moving engine twitched once then jerked forwards, sending Finn tumbling to the back of the cage, where he bashed his shoulder hard.

He sprawled on the floor. With a repeated *whoosh* sound, the breathing of the beast, the engine trundled forwards. Finn wedged himself into a corner to stop himself being jolted around. He curled into a ball, pulling his knees up to his chin. His face was wet. Blood or tears? He tasted some on a finger. Just tears. The metal floor was hotter here; he was near the furnace that powered the moving machine. He called out, a shout rather than words, but it was lost in the roar of the engine. He pounded the walls with his fists, again and again, but the engine trundled and jerked onwards, ignoring him.

He tried to think clearly, control himself. The air became thicker and warmer still. It scoured the back of his throat, making him retch and cough. With each bump in the road he jolted from side to side.

A line of small square holes ran along the curved side of his prison, only big enough for him to poke a soft fingertip through. He put his mouth to one of them, hoping to suck in fresher air from outside. Gritty flecks of rust came off on his lips. The metal tasted of blood. The hole was too small to pull in much air. He coughed again, the rust peppering the back of his throat. For a moment he couldn't breathe at all. Panic rose within him like the waters of a flood. He lost control of himself again, throwing himself at the walls, screaming ragged screams.

Finally, sobbing, breathing in gulps, he stopped. He crawled back into his corner.

His head hammered with pain. He shut his eyes, trying to calm his breathing. Perhaps he would be rescued. The wreckers would ambush them, set him free. Over and over he saw it, the ironclads fighting and dying, the master dying, the smile cut from his face. The door of the moving engine thrown open wide.

But no ambush came. Exhausted, rocked by the jolting of the machine, Finn's eyes dropped shut. He slipped in and out of a half sleep, vivid images coming to him, shocking him awake again. It was just as dark when he opened his eyes. He became more and more confused about where he was, what was real. Again, his mind fled the confines of his roaring prison, taking him off to happier places.

He was a young boy again, reliving his earliest memory, sitting with his sister Shireen in the clearing in the woods in the summer, the heat of the sun beating down on the top of his head.

She must have known what was to happen to her that day, some word of warning on the line-of-sight. His older sister, almost a grown-up herself, would never normally play with him for a whole morning. He was delighted to have her to himself.

"Close your eyes, Finn," she told him. "You mustn't see where I'm taking you."

She led him along twisting pathways in the oak woods on the slopes behind their house. He tried to work out where she was leading him but soon lost his bearings. Leaves tickled his face. The ground was soft beneath his feet, but dry. He longed to open his eyes, just for a moment, the slightest crack. But that would break the spell. He reached out with his foot to feel what was beside him on the path. He knew these woods as intimately as only a child could. Each mound and tree root and bush. Yet he could feel nothing with his outstretched toes, as if they were walking some unknown path with sheer drops on either side.

Her hand was damp in his, but the air was wonderfully cool under the leaves. The sun outside was unbearable. It was like creeping too close to the furnace in their father's workshop, the heat crashing into you like a cymbal being struck. Each day burned hotter than the last. The world became a shimmering cauldron by day, sticky and airless by night. In the garden, plate-sized pink flowers exuding a cloying smell had rampaged out of the beds to envelop everything. No one had the energy to cut them back. It was too hot to move, too bright to see. But among the shifting shadows of the great branches you began to wake up again.

"Here," she said. "Sit down here, Finn. You can open your eyes."

They were in a clearing he didn't recognize. They'd walked farther than he'd ever dared go on his own. His mother said he had to stay within sight of the house when he went out to play, but he was okay with Shireen.

He could see nothing beyond the green wall of trees and the darkness crowded behind them. The leaves lolled as they waited for a breeze to save them. A lone bird sang, rare in the heat. His sister smiled, her face full of bright, crisp detail. Sunlight through the treetops made her brown hair glow with gold sparkles. She sat down next to him. The bark of the old log was rough on his hands.

"This is my favourite place, Finn," she said. "I come here to sit, sometimes. No one else knows about it. I wanted to show it to you."

Finn looked around, expecting to see faeries like those in the books she read to him. Tiny figures with flowers for hats and clothes of red or blue or orange.

"Oh."

"Will you come here too, Finn? From time to time?"

"Why?"

"Just to sit. To think. To remember."

He shrugged. "I'll try. I might forget."

She smiled at him. "Not to worry. Just every now and then. You could play here with your friend. With Connor."

Finn said nothing. Connor wasn't his friend. Connor scared him. The Baron's son was a year or two older and much bigger. He could already ride a pony and had his own fishing rod, which he was allowed to use in the river. Finn had seen him haul a shining, writhing trout from the river a few days ago. Connor had placed his finger and thumb into the fish's gulping mouth and broken its neck with a simple movement, red blood staining its gills. Finn, hiding behind bushes, had crept away, his heart beating wildly.

"Would you do that for me, Finn? Come here?"

"You'll have to show me the way."

"You'll be able to find it yourself. When you're a bit older."

Finn accepted her word. Of course, he was aware that one day he would grow up like his sister. Right now, the fact was unimportant, impossibly remote.

"Okay."

They sat together for a long while, neither of them speaking, Finn waiting to see what would happen next. He closed his eyes.

He heard a distant sound, something like a trumpet playing a single, drawn-out, falling note, but very far away. He had never heard anything like it before.

"What's that?"

His sister sighed. "It's nothing important, Finn. It means we should be getting back. Give me your hand."

She stood up then bent down to kiss him on the top of the head, as his father did when putting him to bed.

At the edge of the trees she let go of his hand and pushed out across the yellow fields. Finn, following, squinting in the light, could only look down at his feet, the dust of the ground, as they trudged home.

The ironclads were waiting for them at the house. Something like horses, four of them, were tethered outside. Finn wasn't sure if they were animals or machines. He could see they had brown tapering legs, muscles twitching as flies landed on them, but their bodies were all bulky metal plates and silver studs. Their eyes were lost inside shining metal hoods, but they bridled and whinnied like any real horse.

"Why are they here, Shireen?"

His sister didn't reply. Ignoring the horses, she walked inside. Finn followed. He could feel a greater heat coming off the beasts, as if a furnace blazed inside them rather than a beating heart. Looking up at them, they were as big as the house.

Inside stood three figures dressed in metal like the horses. They had guns strapped across their backs, each barrel gaping as big as the mouth of a fish. They clanked as they turned to see who had come in. Finn knew all about them. The ironclads filled his stories and games. They were the monsters, the nightmares that would come and take you away if you were bad. They pursued you in your dreams until you jerked awake with a scream.

Over by the empty fireplace, his mother and father stood in conversation with a fourth visitor. This one wasn't an ironclad; he was dressed in simple, purple robes but with a metal belt round his waist like the armour of the others. His hair was shaved off. His skin looked very soft and pink. Finn smiled at the adults but none of them saw him.

His mother, he could see, had been crying. She turned away so he wouldn't notice. His father stood head and shoulders above everyone, his expression unreadable through his bushy, black beard. One of his great tree-trunk arms was held around his mother's shoulders.

"Shireen," his father said in a low voice.

His sister bowed her head and crossed to stand with them. She grew taller as she walked across the room, becoming an adult as Finn watched. He went to sit in a corner, as far as possible from the ironclads, and played with the wooden figures his father had carved for him. There was an old rug there, red and brown, laid on top of the flagstones. Over the years it had moulded itself to the contours of the uneven floor, forming slight valleys and mountains that often played a part in Finn's games. His mother had painted bright, smiling faces on the figures. He loved their smooth, shiny bodies. They rescued Peg, the smallest, from an underground dungeon, evading the roaring monsters that pursued them.

When the game was over, and all his toys were having a great party to celebrate Peg's safe return, Finn looked up. The ironclads had gone. His sister had gone. His mother and father stood looking out through the open door.

With the departure of Shireen, the heat of the summer finally broke. Storm clouds the size of mountains billowed up from the south, bringing with them sudden cold winds and lashing rain. People stirred and began to hurry once more, dashing from building to building between downpours, working with urgency to repair gushing gutters and gather swelling crops.

The day she had been taken, hours after she had gone, Finn had followed the trail left by the ironclads, down the lane between the fields, straying as far from home as he dared. Now, a week later, venturing down the lane again, he lost track of them, the hoof prints washed away by the rains.

Unable to go on after his sister, not wanting to go back home, Finn kicked stones around in the dirt. He picked some up and hurled them farther down the lane to see how far he could get them. More rain clouds gathered on the horizon, but it was dry for the moment. He wished Shireen was there to take his hand and lead him home. He poked a stick into the great puddle the rains had formed in the sunken corner of the field, stirring it up into a squelching, muddy soup.

Three Tree Hill was nearby: a small rise in the ground around which the Silverburn curled in a loop. Three vast oaks stood in a line upon it, their outstretched branches crossing through each other high above his head, as if they were interlocking their arms. It was Finn's greatest ambition to climb one of those oaks and work his way from branch to branch across to the other two without ever touching the ground. He decided to try again now. He shinned his way up the nearest trunk. Branches and knurs in the wood gave him all the toeholds he needed. The hard part was the leap between. The branches were never that close together when you climbed up high. The gulf of air down to the hard ground made him dizzy when he looked. From the second tree, he knew, there was a drop from a higher branch to a lower that was again possible, but the boughs weren't exactly under each other and you had to get it just right.

He stood up there for long minutes, holding one of the smaller branches to steady himself, imagining himself making the leap. A breeze blew on his face, ruffling his hair. He could smell the green of the tree. His knees jerked once or twice as they thought about actually jumping, but still he held on tight. He knew he could do it; he had measured out the distance on the ground and made it easily. Still, up there, it was a different thing.

Finally, he worked his way back to the trunk and climbed higher. There was a point where a branch curved off like a horse's neck forming a natural seat. He leaned his back against the trunk of the tree, perched far above the ground. Two smaller branches formed arms for him to hold onto. This was *his* secret place. He loved it up there, especially now it was summer and the leaves hid him from the world. He was flying above the land. When the wind blew more strongly, whipping the branches to and fro, making the whole tree sway, he was in the rolling crow's nest of a ship from some story, sailing across the fields to distant lands. He loved the feeling of being alone. He loved looking down on people walking along the lane, unaware of his presence.

Most of the leaves were still on the trees, although each gust of wind sent a fresh flock gliding to the ground. Through the gaps he could see the river, rattling down stony waterfalls, then the fields and the hills of the valley in which he had spent his whole life. He turned his head to look down the lane, the way the ironclads had taken Shireen. He could just see the chimney of Turnpike Cottage. Somewhere beyond that, over the line of those blue hills, lay Engn itself. He had once climbed to the very top of the tree, onto slender branches that bowed under his weight, to see if he could see over the peaks to the great city.

He wondered how far away she was now. He wanted to shout to her, in his loudest voice, to tell her he was there. But he knew she wouldn't hear him. Instead he plucked leaves from the tree and sent them floating down to the distant ground.

He saw someone coming towards him across the fields on the other side of the river. Someone striding through shoulder-high corn as if swimming in water. At first, he thought it was her, escaped, miraculously returned. But the hair was the wrong colour, the walk wrong. Whoever it was hadn't seen him. They kept stopping and looking from side to side, but never up into the trees.

Finn peered forwards, gripping the branches tight. With a jolt of alarm, he realized it was Connor. The older boy had a catapult in his hands. He stopped to fire stones at birds that clattered from the corn as he disturbed them. Finn wasn't allowed a catapult. He had been promised one when he was ten. But Connor appeared to be an expert already. A clump of crows wheeled up in alarm from a beech on the riverbank, voices grating. One of their numbers flopped to the ground in a flurry of feathers. Connor fired again, trying to hit one of the crows in flight.

With slow movements, Finn edged his way back down the tree, trying not to make the branches sway. Perhaps if he could move around the trunk, keep it between himself and the older boy, he could run away without being noticed. He could hear the hungry *thrum* of the catapult now, and Connor's laughter as he hit another target.

Finn missed his footing and landed hard on a lower

branch, making it wave in the air like a flag. A squirrel, disturbed by the commotion, shot around the trunk, past Finn's head and out along one of the branches. Perhaps it had intended to leap across to the next tree, too, but it chose the wrong branch. It ran out as far as it could, body and tail flowing in a perfect arc, but stopped at the end with nowhere to go. It sat up on its hind legs, head flicking around. A stone from the catapult cracked through the tree, barely missing it, knocking aside leaves with a *click* and sending them spinning downwards. The squirrel didn't understand. Another stone cut through the branches, striking it in the head with a soft crunch.

It cartwheeled to the ground. Through the leaves, Finn saw it hit the grass. It lay there twitching, legs running uselessly in the air, head ruined. Finn hung between branches, very still, hoping that Connor would think the squirrel had made all the noise.

"Are you stuck up there?" Connor shouted. "Do you need help to get down too?"

Finn's heart hammered. He was a long way from home and there was no one to help him. The worse thing was, although the river was between them, it was easy to cross there by leaping from stone to stone, especially with the waters so low. He knew he didn't have long before Connor would be at the foot of the tree, aiming his catapult up at him.

In a desperate hurry, face flushed with heat, Finn thrashed from branch to branch, making no effort to conceal his whereabouts. If he dropped to the ground Connor would see him, but if he could make the leap to the second tree he might be safe.

Another stone drummed off the trunk.

Finn stood back on the outstretched bough for a moment, excitement and terror flaring inside him. Before he could stop himself, he leapt into the open air. He hung there for long, long moments, aware of the ground beneath him, sucking him down. Then he landed on the other branch, bashing his left shin into it but managing to grasp a smaller branch to struggle on properly. He was across. He crouched there for a moment while his heart raced away, unable to believe what he had just done.

"I'm coming to get you!" Connor shouted.

Finn crawled his way along the branch, more careful now, not wanting Connor to know where he was, not daring to stand up. He reached the trunk of the second tree, then began to climb. Connor hadn't fired any more stones for a while. Crossing the river.

In some ways the drop didn't seem as bad as the leap; leaves not too far below hid the ground, giving the illusion of a solid surface to catch him. But if he missed the branch of the third tree the drop would kill him. Break his legs or his back at least. He sat with feet dangling in the air, trying to judge how hard to push off. The first drops of rain patted through the leaves around him. The best thing to do was to land feet-first on the branch of the third tree. He had to do it.

With a gasp he pushed himself off. Instantly he was falling, not flying towards the branch as he had imagined. He hadn't pushed off hard enough. His feet missed completely. Twigs smacked his face, catching him in the eye. With outstretched arms he managed to catch the branch as it rose past him. He clung on, swinging there, his feet running uselessly as he tried to gain a foothold. With a grunt, he swung his legs up to lie along the branch like a cat.

"I can see you!"

Connor sounded gleeful, but also distant. Finn guessed he was still over by the first tree, peering up through the leaves.

Finn pulled himself along the branch, breathing heavily and sobbing at the same time, then began to climb down to the ground. His legs felt wobbly but they knew the sequence of branches perfectly and he didn't slip again. He dropped to the ground and hid behind the third trunk. He could hear no running footsteps and no stones whistled past his ear. He had done it.

He ran, directly away from the trees, out across the field so Connor wouldn't see him, then around the bottom of the mound and so back to the lane. He didn't dare look back.

He arrived home, panting and wide-eyed, his shin bleeding where the skin had been scraped off.

His mother, meeting him at the door, squeezed him very hard. She smelled of fresh bread and summer flowers. She held him at arm's length to look at him.

"Where have you been? What have you been up to?"

"Nothing," he said.

"Look at you. You look like you've been dragged through a hedge backwards."

He slipped from her grasp into the house, where delicious smells of cooking awaited.

It was two weeks before he dared venture so far from home again. This time he saw no one else. He had the oaks of Three Tree Hill to himself once more.

II

The wind hammered at the windows. Finn sat with his parents at the table one evening, eating hunks of fresh bread and slices of cheese. They also had a bowl of bright red apples, windfalls from their little orchard. The log fire blazed and cracked, occasionally sending brilliant sparks shooting out onto the floor. When they did his father leapt up to pluck them off the rug and toss them back into the fire before they could do any damage. They never seemed to hurt his fingers.

"Winter's coming on," said his mother. She gazed off to the side, as if she could see through the walls into the gloom outside. "Soon be time to turn the lights on."

It was dark when he went to bed now. Shireen used to read to him as he drifted off to sleep. In the summer it was light enough with just the curtains open, but in the winter they would sit under the flickering incandescent globe in his room, huddled together under the blankets as she read.

"Waterwheel will need re-caulking," said his father. "I'd better strip down the generators before winter, too."

"That's supposed to be Matt's job," said his mother.

His father grunted in amusement. "Best do it myself."

He waved towards Finn with a triangle of the bread.

"Finn? Want to give me a hand tomorrow?"

Finn felt reluctant. He was supposed to be learning to do all the things his father did, but he knew how it would go. His father would grow cross with some technicality of the task at hand and Finn would just be in the way. But he'd probably be able to wander off eventually without his father minding. And, if he was lucky, there would be time for a game of chase or hide on the way.

"Yes, Father."

His mother picked up one of the apples, assessed it for a moment, then bit into its shiny skin.

"Nice and sweet," she said. "Time we got them in. Without Shireen to help I'd better get started soon."

The wind rose again, rattling the door this time, hissing through the gap underneath.

"Why did they take her?" asked Finn. "The ironclads."

His mother looked at his father. They had been waiting for him to ask.

"Finn, it's a sacred duty to be called to work upon Engn," said his mother. "Few are taken."

"But I want her to play with me. Will she come back?"

"No, love. You are called for life."

"Can we go and see her?"

"No, no. That isn't allowed."

"But you went once, Father. You told me about it. You said there were huge wheels as big as the setting moon. And chimneys far higher than any trees. It was bigger than our whole valley and at night it sparkled with light. It made the ground shake even from miles away. You said it was wonderful."

His father put down the bread he was chewing.

"Yes, I said all that, and perhaps I shouldn't. But no one is permitted to go so near now without being taken by the ironclads."

"What's *permitted*?"

"It means you're not allowed to go there."

"Why?"

"That's the way it is. Engn is a forbidden place."

Finn thought about this. They said the great machine spread farther across the land every year. How big would it eventually be? Would it reach them, there in the valley? They ate in silence for a time.

"When I'm bigger, will I be taken too?" asked Finn.

His father looked hard at him. There was anger in his eyes, but his voice was soft when he spoke. His anger wasn't with Finn.

"No. You will not."

"How do you know?"

"They don't take more than one from the same family," his mother said. "It wouldn't be right."

"Finn, I promise you," said his father. "You won't be taken. I won't allow it. Now eat up."

They ate the rest of their meal in silence. When he'd finished, Finn scrambled up the wooden ladder to his bed, to read to himself.

Winter came early that year. The soil froze to stone and was then buried under snow. Each morning brought a fresh fall, covering up the tracks and marks of the previous day as if the whole world had been renewed. The air was as sharp as knives on Finn's cheeks when he went outside to play.

He chewed his breakfast, deciding what to do that day. A sudden pounding at the door made him gasp and look up. His mother, scrubbing a pan at the kitchen sink, caught the look of alarm on his face. His father, scowling, crossed the room from the fire he was tending to haul open the door. In a great plume of windblown snow, Matt Dobey stepped into the room.

The lengthsman was dressed in thick, inside-out furs that inflated him to twice his normal size. He stamped snow from his boots and pushed back his hood to reveal his familiar smile: eyes wide, expression exaggerated, the smile of someone perpetually addressing young children. He reminded Finn of one of the cows on the farm: large, docile, bemused. He was bald like a baby, the dome of his head shining. His soft face resembled the formless lumps of dough his mother slid into the oven each morning.

"Well, any more of this and we'll be stranded in our own homes," he said brightly. "Hello, young man. Grown again, I see."

Finn smiled, excused from replying by a mouthful of bread.

"Sit down," said his father to Matt. "I'll be ready soon."

Matt sat in the fourth chair: the one they kept at the table but which no one used. He rubbed his hands together and blew into them.

"Where are you going today, Matt?" His mother stood at the kitchen door, drying her hands on a cloth. "Not far I hope?" She was thinner these days, shadows under her cheeks. Now when Finn hugged her, the soft bulk of her body was turning to bones.

"Old Mrs. Hampton has a broken connection," said Matt. "Been without light nearly a week."

"She didn't say anything."

"Then the path up to the Switch House needs clearing. Mrs. Megrim keeps telling me how dangerous it is. If I don't get around to that today, there'll be trouble, eh?"

"Well, she's not one to stand any messing, Mrs. Megrim."

"Best get on with it then," said his father. He shrugged his way into his own furs. He kissed his mother on the cheek and tousled Finn's hair as he walked past. "Back in a couple of hours."

The men left on a blast of chill air. His father often

grumbled about how useless Matt was at mending the roads and keeping the electricity flowing, but when they were together, they were the best of friends. It was strange. Finn could hear their laughter fading as they trudged away from the house.

When his breakfast was finished and he was bundled up in enough clothes to satisfy his mother, Finn followed them outside. The snow had stopped falling. The sun lifted over the hillside, sparkling off the fields and roofs, gold glints in the perfect white. Finn scooped up a handful of snow, his fingers tingling with the cold of it. He crushed the snow into a ball and hurled it as far out into the field as he could, where it landed with a satisfying *crump*.

It was, he decided, a perfect day for sledging.

The previous winter, his father had built the toboggan for him: polished wood, light and strong. He pulled it by its cord across the garden. The explosion of summer flowers was long gone. The garden was a plain of white apart from a few bony sprout stalks like sheep's spines, writhing out of the ground.

"Stay away from the water!" his mother called after him.

He looked back to see her framed in the doorway of their stone house. The double lines in the snow made by the sledge led all the way back to her feet. Finn smiled and waved to her before pushing on out of the garden.

A line of wooden posts, each topped with a stylized bolt of lightning, led away towards the river. These marked the line of the underground cables that carried electricity from the waterwheel. Lines of posts ran throughout the valley, up to each building. His mother and father had told him many times never to dig anywhere near them.

He followed the posts now. Each day there was more ice on the water of the millpond and he wanted to see if, today, it had finally frozen all the way across. The snow was deep, covering his leather boots completely, cracking underfoot with each step. Apart from the footprints of birds, lines of scattered letter Y's and W's, the snow was untouched. He was the first person in the whole world to walk in it. He almost felt like he shouldn't.

Water gurgled down the leat that powered the wheel, but otherwise the world was completely silent, the air muffled, like being under blankets. Nothing moved. The pond had frozen over more, but there was still a circle of open water in the middle, like an unblinking eye staring blankly upwards. His father had explained that water froze from the surface down, that even if it froze right across it would still be flowing beneath the surface. Finn skidded stones across it. The ice echoed with a weird metallic sound. He tried to make the stones stop on the very lip of the ice, then tried to hurl them directly into the water without touching the sides.

When that game was exhausted, he picked up the cord of his sledge again. He had tried with it yesterday but the slopes had been too gentle. He'd sunk into the soft snow. He needed somewhere steeper.

He crossed the footbridge, fanged with icicles, and began to climb up into the woods. The paths had all vanished, of course, the whole land rubbed clean of detail, but he knew exactly which way to go, knew which trees the trails wound around. He worked his way up the sides of the valley, the snow deeper and deeper all the time. The only sounds were his own breathing and the shush of the sledge behind him. Occasionally a branch, warmed by the sun, dropped a line of snow near him with a soft *wumph*.

Then he stopped. He thought he'd heard something else too: someone moving through the woods behind him as he climbed, the sound of something pushing through the undergrowth. He could hear nothing now. Perhaps it was just his own echo bouncing off the trees. Everything sounded strange in the snow. Small birds hopped around in the high branches, spots of black against the blue sky. Nothing else moved. Wild animals roamed the high woods, of course – black bears and wolves – but none had ever been seen close to the village.

He wondered again where Shireen's glade was, whether it was nearby. He had often tried to find it. It wasn't anywhere nearby, anyway.

Shrugging, he set off, angling up the slope to make the ascent easier. Each step was an effort now, more of a leap, the snow up to his knees. He waded forwards for a time then, abruptly, stopped again, whipping round to see if he could catch a glimpse of a pursuer. This time he caught a clear flicker of movement behind him: a detached shadow melting into the trees.

Someone was definitely there. Tall – a person, not an animal. These were *his* woods. Now that Shireen had gone no one else came there. He didn't like to think of sharing them with someone else. Could it be an ironclad? They came for him in his dreams most nights: clanking machine-men that kept on coming no matter what you did to stop them. If you smashed them into pieces, the fragments crept towards you. You could never rest. Had they followed his trail to find him, alone and helpless out in the woods? Had they been out there all along, waiting for him?

He was nearly at the upper edge of the woods now. Above him, the hill grew steeper and became the flank of the mountain. He had planned to find a long slope there to sledge down. Now he only thought about hurrying back to the river. Whatever followed him wouldn't dare pursue him all the way home. He considered hopping onto his sledge. The ground here was steep. But if he lost control and crashed into a tree, his pursuer would surely catch him.

Instead, he strode back into the woods. In a few minutes, he was panting heavily, lungs burning from the climb. If he didn't run, his pursuer might not realize Finn had spotted them. There was a place lower down where the trees thinned out and the hill became the bank of the river, a little upstream from his home. If he could reach that he would be safe. His toes felt numb and swollen. The sledge, still gripped in his left hand, slipped down the slope ahead of him, pulling him forwards.

He heard a vast *crack* then, as loud as someone firing an enormous gun nearby. It echoed off the trees. Finn looked round in shock, thinking he had been shot at. Even through his numbed feet he felt the ground shake. The trees around him shivered, shedding snow and ice in great curtains. What was going on?

"Finn!"

His pursuer bounded towards him, a single figure dressed in black, loping over the snow at speed.

"Finn! It's an avalanche! Run!"

It was Connor. The older boy had followed him all this way. Finn tried to get away, bounding down the slope, half falling, stumbling and weaving between the trunks.

He was too slow. Connor caught him and flipped him around by the arm. Finn tried to pull himself loose and they both rolled to the ground. Snow filled Finn's mouth, cold and gritty. He tried to beat the bigger boy off with his fists, but Connor didn't fight back. Instead he was shouting something.

"Finn. It's an avalanche. Come on!"

He hauled Finn up and set off down the slope, towing Finn with him. From behind them, a growing rumble filled the air, like thunder but becoming louder each moment. Finn looked that way. The hillside beyond the last of the trees was gone, as if a white cloud had descended. What did it mean? He had never seen anything like it. Shock staked him to the ground.

"Finn, we need a tree. A big one."

"A tree?" he said, not understanding. "Why?"

"Just take us! We need a big tree to climb. We've only

got a few seconds. We…"

The roaring drowned out the rest of Connor's words. Finn felt drops on his face as if it was snowing again, but there was only blue sky overhead. Then he turned and saw the snow had come alive, turning into a roaring beast, chasing them down the hillside.

Now Finn ran, Connor close behind him. There was a big tree a little down the slope, one he had climbed a few times. They might be able to reach that. It was hard to keep his footing in the deep snow. Twice he tumbled over. Each time Connor picked him up, only to stagger himself a few paces on. Finn felt cold biting at the back of his neck, jaws of snow snapping at him.

He saw the tree, an old oak, its bulky trunk wide and tall, the upturned wrist and hand of a giant. Once you reached the palm it was easy enough to climb. He just hoped the trunk wasn't too slippery with ice.

"This one," shouted Finn. Connor couldn't possibly hear him, but he nodded as Finn pointed. They ran around the tree, downslope from the thundering snow. Connor looked up into the branches then cupped his hands to give Finn a leg up. It struck Finn that Connor was terrified too. He'd thought, somehow, that all of this, the snow coming to life, the avalanche, was Connor's doing. A trap he'd planned all along. But the other boy's eyes were wide with fear.

Finn stepped into the offered hands and Connor boosted him up to the lowest branch. Finn hauled himself into the tree and, lying wedged between the forking branches, reached back down for Connor.

The world was a blizzard now, the ground and the other trees gone, only Connor's hand visible reaching though the whiteness. Finn could feel the whole tree shuddering as a mountainside of snow slammed into it. He reached down and grasped Connor's hand, pulling him up with a huge effort, almost slipping from the tree as he hauled the other boy into the branches.

They sat there together for a moment, both out of breath.

"Come on," shouted Connor. "We have to climb higher!"

"What's happening?" Finn shouted back. But Connor was already scrambling upwards. Finn glanced down. The boiling snow was nearer, as if the whole tree were sinking into the ground. He turned and climbed after Connor.

They stopped when they could go no farther, high, high up in the ancient tree. The trunk was little thicker than Finn's thighs. They clung on as the tree swayed and jolted beneath them: clung onto the tree and to each other. When Finn closed his eyes, it felt as if the oak was lurching to the ground, whipping backwards and forwards. He gulped down helpless, terrified tears, sobs racking his whole body, glad that the snow was too loud for Connor to hear him.

The avalanche ended as abruptly as it had started. The roaring died away and sunlight found them again. Their tree had stayed upright, although many around had not. A broken pine lay with its top caught in a nearby oak, its trunk like a ramp down to the ground.

Finn looked at Connor. They had both been crying. They let go of each other. It was suddenly very quiet. No birds sang, as if they had all been swept away by the snow. What would happen now? He was conscious of being up there alone with the older boy. He was too weary to fight. He wanted his father to come and carry him home.

The older boy began to laugh, then, full of glee. Finn stared at him, amazed. What was he laughing at? Connor whooped with delight, shouting at the stunned forest all around them.

"Hah! Didn't get us, did you? Can't catch us! Hah!"

He looked ridiculous, bawling out to nobody at all. Finn found himself grinning at the sight of him, then chuckling as well. Soon they were both roaring with laughter, until Finn's cheeks hurt and sharp pain stabbed him in the side. If either of them stopped, the sight of the other trying not to laugh started them off again.

"Hey, avalanche! You missed us!" Finn shouted.

For five minutes or more, neither could stop laughing. Finally, still grinning and giggling, they sat down next to each other in a crook of the branches.

"Why … why were you following me?" Finn managed to ask.

"I wasn't," said Connor. "Not at first. I was looking for somewhere to ice fish and found your tracks. I followed, then I heard the snow breaking. My dad warned me of the dangers, but I didn't believe him. He said there were lots of avalanches when he was young."

"You saved my life."

Connor shrugged, as if near-death adventures happened to him every day. "You saved mine. I couldn't have found this tree without you."

Finn grinned and looked at Connor. The older boy wasn't, in truth, very much taller than he was. He looked much stronger, though, his arms thick with muscles where Finn's were just straight lines.

"You're a good climber," said Connor. "Just like a squirrel." His eyes glinted with amusement beneath his shock of black hair.

"Good job no one has a catapult down there," said Finn.

Connor laughed. He flipped off the backpack he carried and pulled out his catapult. It was a Y-shaped piece of wood with red twine bound around it for a handle. It was strung with a length of strong elastic upon which was threaded a small leather pouch.

"Fancy a go?" asked Connor. "I've got a few stones. I

collect the good ones."

They took turns firing the catapult, making the pebbles rebound off the surrounding trees, seeing who could hit a certain branch, seeing who could fire a stone the farthest. Connor's went so far you lost sight of them, but Finn was at least as accurate as the older boy. Twice he beat Connor to hit a knot on a nearby oak.

"Here's your prize," said Connor. He pulled two apples out of his backpack and handed one to Finn. They both ate hungrily.

"How deep do you think the snow is?" asked Finn. The ground looked much nearer than it normally did.

"Pretty deep. Don't think we could walk through it."

"When do you think they'll find us?"

"Oh, soon enough," said Connor, leaning backwards against the trunk of the tree and closing his eyes. "Our tracks will have been obliterated, but they'll find us. Wait, I know!"

He was alert again and rummaging around in his backpack. This time he pulled out a small, wooden whistle.

"My mother carved it for me. There's a dried pea inside, see."

He put it to his lips and blew, sending out a shrill sound that cut easily through the muffled air.

"We'll blow this every few minutes so they'll know where we are. I've got this, too."

He fished out a small, brass tube. A telescope. Connor stretched it open and held it up to his eye, surveying the woods around them.

"It's our old line-of-sight. There's a crack in one of the lenses but it still works."

"Let me see."

It took a few moments for Finn to get his eye in the right place, and to work out how to focus it. He wasn't allowed to touch theirs at home. The distant trees down the slope sprang into sharp detail. He swept the telescope backwards and forwards, looking for signs of life, for someone coming to rescue them.

"See anyone?" asked Connor.

"Nothing."

"Ah, well. They'll find us."

Connor didn't seem in the least frightened now. It was all like some game for him. If Finn had been on his own, he'd probably have tried to climb down and make his way home. Connor seemed quite comfortable where he was.

"Here, watch this," said Connor.

The older boy stood again and, after a moment's fumbling, sent out a jet of piss into the air. He took great delight in making swirling patterns in the snow beneath them.

"I can write my name!" he called.

Laughing again, Finn stood to join him.

When the daylight started to fade, darkness creeping through the trees to surround them, they huddled back together for warmth, locking arms. Finn shivered with the cold. His eyes drifted shut again and again, but he was terrified of falling asleep and pitching out of the tree. He blew the whistle one more time.

"I heard about your sister," said Connor.

"Yeah."

"Did she want to go?"

Finn shrugged but said nothing. He blew the whistle again, as loud as he could.

This time he heard an answering call, someone shouting in the distance. The two boys scrambled to their feet. Connor snatched the whistle and blew it again and again. Through the gloom they heard more calls, voices growing louder.

It was fully dark by the time their rescuers arrived.

Finn's parents and several workers from the farm, including Connor's own father and two uncles. Not Connor's mother, of course, as she was bedridden and never left her room. Matt was with them, lengthsman's tools slung over his shoulder. Some of the men drove a team of eight heavy horses, pushing a great wooden plough up through the drifts. The horses strained against the hill and the weight of the snow, steam rising off them as they stamped forwards. Men shovelled mounds of snow aside with diamond-shaped spades. Others held up hissing torches that burned with a shifting light and gave off threads of smoke that lay horizontal in the cold air.

At the tree, his father sat on one of the horses and reached up to pluck Finn from the lowest branch. He held Finn tight for long moments, muffling him into his furs, his grip like iron. Finn had to turn his head to one side to breathe but he didn't mind. Then his father held him out at arms' length, dangling him in the air to look into his eyes.

"What were you thinking of? I've told you a hundred times to stay away from the snow fields."

"I..."

"It wasn't his fault," called out Connor from another horse. "It was mine. I was chasing him."

Finn looked across at Connor, who winked. He sat in front of his own father. The Baron was a short, powerful man with a scowling, red face. Finn avoided him at all times. The King of the Valley, they sometimes called him, only half joking. The Baron's family had once been powerful figures in the Guild of Stonecarvers, but he had no authority other than his old title, which some respected and some laughed at. Finn's parents treated the Baron with politeness, but only, Finn thought, because they liked him as an individual. Finn could see the similarity of Connor to his father. Finn, on the other hand, was nothing like *his* father. He was tall for his age but stick-thin.

"No," said Finn. "It wasn't like that. Connor saved *me*.

I didn't know what was happening. I forgot about what you said. I'm sorry."

"Just so long as you're both safe," the Baron said.

"Aye, well," said Finn's father. "No harm done. But listen to what we tell you next time, eh? Avalanches and earthquakes aren't nearly as common as they used to be, but they can still happen."

"I will."

"Come on," said Finn's mother. "Let's get you both home."

The two boys were wrapped in blankets and given soup that had been kept warm in a silver flask. They sat side-by-side on a plank of wood stretched across the horses' traces, facing backwards, rocking together as they made their way back down the slope. Everyone moved slowly, men and horses exhausted by their efforts. They followed the path that had been forced through the avalanche on the way up. Finn, very sleepy, watched the trees drift by over the high walls of ploughed snow.

Back near the waterwheel they went their separate ways, Connor and the horses to the farm, Finn walking with his mother and father to their own house. The snow was thinner there; the avalanche had hit the river some way upstream. Countless lines of footprints punctuated the snow, as if a crowd of people had been darting backwards and forwards looking for something.

His father picked him up, swung him round and placed him onto his shoulders. They headed for home, the electric lights from their windows twinkling to them through the gathering gloom.

"I lost my sledge," said Finn.

"We can make a new sledge," said his father.

"Hey, Finn!" Connor called out. "Let's play together tomorrow!"

Finn twisted to see Connor disappearing into the darkness astride one of his father's horses. Too weary to shout, Finn waved a thumbs-up sign at his new friend.

III

A shower of rain thrummed on the metal roof of the moving engine, heavier and heavier, the sound swelling from drumbeat to roar. Finn clasped his hands over his ears. It was the roar of the avalanche once again. Despite the darkness he screwed his eyes tight shut. He rocked himself backwards and forwards. Water seeped in from somewhere, dripping onto him in slow, fat drops, sloshing around on the floor to soak his feet.

Drainage holes in the floor of the machine squirted plumes of muddy water, flung up by the iron wheels. He imagined the engine sinking into the mud, stuck so that even the horses couldn't haul it out. He imagined mud oozing in through the holes in the floor, drowning him inside his metal cage. He put his eye to the nearest ventilation hole and peered out. They were still grinding forwards. All he could see was sodden woodland slipping by, the black bulk of an ironclad horse, splashes of mud kicked up by dinner-plate hooves.

He glimpsed a row of trees and the wall of a house, the stone red, unlike the yellows and browns of home. His forehead banged against the metal wall as they lurched along. There was a figure, a woman, standing by the side of the road, watching them pass. She held a shawl bunched at her throat with her fist. Finn could only see the lower half of her face, the straight line of her mouth, rain dripping from her chin.

When they passed through villages the whole population would often be there, watching them, not speaking, as if witnessing a funeral procession. Children hid behind the legs of adults. They reminded Finn of the day he and Connor had watched their own village coming out, the day they'd first glimpsed a moving engine and Finn hadn't known what it was.

Occasionally he spotted a Switch House, unmistakable with its telescopes bristling at all angles. He would imagine messages flashing to his own house, to Mrs. Megrim and then on to his parents. *Finn is here. Finn is passing through here.* He would think about shouting to the people, telling them to send a message, say he was still alive, that they hadn't beaten him. But he knew the people wouldn't dare.

It became more and more humid inside the engine, the heat from the machine turning the air to steam. He panted as if he'd been running. He scooped up some of the water sloshing around by his feet and sipped at it. It tasted of mud and rust, making his mouth gritty. He spat the water back out.

They had thrown his backpack inside with him, and he lifted it onto his lap to try and keep it dry. He buried his head in the patchwork blanket his mother had strapped to it, breathing in the familiar, soft smell, wiping his eyes. Then he rummaged inside the bag for one of the honey sweets. He'd planned to ration himself to one a day, make them last as long as possible, but this was already his third since the morning. Still, sucking them helped. They were his secret. They were the only way, for now, that he could defy the ironclads and the master who gave them their orders.

The sweet tasted of sunlight and flowers. Finn closed his eyes and let the memories it brought with it fill his mind.

"Finn!" hissed Connor. Finn knew, immediately, this wasn't part of their game.

They each had bows and arrows, the bows broken-off sycamore branches stretched with string, the arrows lengths of dowel from his father's workshop. They hid among the trees. The winner was the first to shoot the other without being shot himself. The arrows were blunt but you had to be careful not to hit each other in the eye. The problem with the game, always, was in agreeing what was a fatal blow. Arguments were common.

You're dead, Con. I just shot you!

No, you didn't. It glanced off. Anyway, you were already dead because I'd already got you.

Now, at Connor's call, Finn stepped out from behind his tree and picked his way over to his friend. He kept his bow ready, an arrow poised, just in case it was a trick after all. He found Connor lying on the ground, looking out over the steep slope to the valley floor below.

Finn threw himself down beside Connor.

"What is it?"

"Shh!"

It was hot. The air swirled and shifted as Finn gazed down at the distant buildings, the patchwork of yellow fields, the thin line of the river and the lane running down the middle of the valley. The whole valley was laid out like a play set, the houses wooden toys. He amused himself by closing one eye and pretending to pick up a house in his outstretched, pinched fingers. It was the one where Old Mrs. Hampton had lived. He pretended to drop it back down again some way away, on the other side of the river.

Connor had the telescope out and was looking at something down there, but Finn couldn't see anything unusual. The light was too bright. He studied a rock on the ground in front of his eyes, a jagged ball that sparkled with thousands of tiny flecks of light. A good catapult stone. Finn picked it up, clutching it tight in his hand. It was warm and rough. He shut his eyes, enjoying the glow of heat on top of his head.

Days like this always made him think of Shireen. It had been like this, hotter even, when she'd been taken. She was fading in his memory now, her face indistinct. He tried to imagine her as she'd been on that day. He had to make the effort. If he couldn't, she no longer existed. She was there, but her features were a blur. He wondered what she was doing in Engn at that moment. What did any of them do there? His mother's brother, Joe, and his father's uncle and everyone else. He supposed it took a lot of people to keep the wheels turning and the furnaces roaring.

He had seen the machine in his dreams. Steam hammers the size of houses shaking the ground as they struck. Vast banks of clicking, whirring cogs. Pistons pumping and axles spinning. One day, he had decided, he would sneak closer and gaze upon the great machine just as his father had done.

"There! Look, by the Moot Hall."

In the bright light and the hazy air, the old wooden building looked impossibly distant. Finn could see figures on horseback emerging from behind it. They could have been toys.

Connor handed Finn the old telescope. When Finn put it to his eye the distant scene snapped into clarity. Ironclads. There could be no doubt. Two, three, five of them. They had metal-clad hounds with them too, snuffling at the ground just ahead of the horses. The shining metal figures on their barrel-bodied horses were suddenly alarmingly near. Finn felt exposed. He expected one of the human machines to turn in their saddle and look him in the eye, beckon to him. He searched for the robed figure, the leader without the armour, but couldn't see him.

"You think they've come for someone?" asked Finn. Ironclads hadn't been seen in the valley for years, since the day they'd come for Shireen.

"Could be." They were both whispering, although the ironclads were a long way away and wouldn't have heard if they'd shouted. "They're looking for something."

"Wait. What's that?" said Finn. Farther down the track, something like a small, squat house or water-tank lumbered up the valley. It was cylindrical, made of a dull black metal. It had four spindly wheels, like a cart's, but iron rather than wood. It moved without anything pulling it or pushing it. Balls of black smoke *huffed* out of its funnel as it rolled forwards. Finn could hear it even at that distance, the sound of each exhalation strangely delayed, heard a clear moment after the corresponding puff of smoke. An ironclad rode on a footplate at the back of the machine, hands on its levers.

"Let me see," said Connor, pulling the telescope from Finn. "It's an engine!" he said after a moment. "They've brought a moving engine with them."

"What is it? What's it for?"

"There'll be something kept inside it. They use them sometimes. If there's a battle or something. They can go anywhere and nothing can stop them."

"But why? Where are they going with it?"

"Dunno."

There was a fork in the road ahead of the ironclads. One branch led off to Connor's farm. The other went on up through the valley, past Three Tree Hill and Finn's own house. Finn could feel the tension in his friend as they watched the distant horsemen creep up to the fork, and then past it, heading up the valley rather than to the farm.

Connor let out his breath while relief washed through

Finn. He would be lost without Connor. They spent their days playing together. At the same time alarm began to gnaw at Finn's insides. The ironclads worked their way up towards his own house now. But they *couldn't* be coming for him. He was two years younger than his friend. And they already had Shireen. His father had promised him he was safe.

Finn's gaze swept up the valley, following the line of the lane. People emerged from each house, watching the ironclads approach. There was Matt, working at the crossroads, pickaxe over his shoulder. Farther up was Mrs. Megrim, standing at the door to the Switch House on the hill. Two of the riders peeled away and rode up the steep path towards her. Mrs. Megrim strode to meet them and they conversed for some time, the old woman occasionally pointing up or down the valley.

"That old witch," said Connor.

The two of them lived in terror of Mrs. Megrim. For two hours on most mornings she instructed them in their letters and numbers, explaining in tedious detail how the line-of-sight network functioned, or droning on about the history of conflicts between the Guild city-states and the ancient disasters of the Clockwork War. Mrs. Megrim knew instantly if Finn's or Connor's attention wandered, and she would snap them back into the present with a sharp crack of a stick on the desk. Or even across the back of their heads. They weren't even free of her when they were released; she knew *everything* they got up to outside. She would flash messages to their houses and Finn and Connor would arrive home, thinking no one knew about the apples they'd stolen or the fish they'd poached, only to discover their parents knew all about it. Finn wondered what she was telling the ironclads now. He tried to work it out from the movements of her mouth but couldn't.

Sweeping farther up the valley with the telescope, he picked out his father, coming from his workshop to stand with his mother. He wore the thick leather apron he always wore when working at the forge. He carried one of his big club hammers over his shoulder. The ironclads' dogs approached, sniffing around the garden gate. His own garden gate. The main body of riders came up behind them and stopped. For a moment, his heart leaping inside him, Finn thought they were dismounting. But they were only leaning down to speak to his parents. The sunlight glinting off their metal armour made it hard to see what was happening. The conversation continued for some time. Finn found he was gripping the smooth metal of the telescope tightly.

Finally, the ironclads kicked their horses back into motion and cantered on up the lane, dogs bounding on ahead, noses to the ground. Clouds of dust rose into the air as they worked their way farther up the valley. Some way behind, the engine ground after them, never stopping or slowing.

Finn put the telescope down and turned away. He looked at Connor.

"Come on. Let's go."

"Where to?"

Finn shrugged. "Back into the woods. Let's play a different game." He was in no hurry to go home.

"We could play ironclads," said Connor as they walked. It was an old game. The one being the ironclad couldn't be killed. The other had to run and hide. They couldn't fight back. If they were touched, they lost.

"Okay," said Finn.

"I'll be the ironclad," said Connor.

"Okay."

"But this time, don't just run off and leave me, all right?"

They'd played a couple of weeks previously. When night started to fall, Finn had crept back home without saying anything to Connor, suddenly alarmed by the darkening woods and the thought of an ironclad, even if it was only Connor, coming for him. The following morning, when they met again to play, Finn had been wary, knowing he had left Connor alone in the woods, not completely sure if he would be his friend once more.

"Tell you what," said Finn. "Let's say I'm not allowed to lose sight of you. I can hide but I have to be able to see you."

"All right. I'll count to ten."

"Twenty!"

Flinging aside his bow, Finn hared off, leaping over low scrubby bushes into the shadows between the trees. When he was out of sight he stopped, hid behind a bough and looked back. Connor had just started to walk forwards, moving with the stiff legs they both used when pretending to be an ironclad.

Finn ran on, weaving between the trees. He worked his way uphill, thinking to circle around behind Connor. He dashed through pools of golden light where the sun slipped through gaps in the canopy overhead. A brook babbled its way down the slope off to his right. Finn followed its line, intending to leap across farther uphill. The air was pungent with the smell of wild garlic.

Three times he caught a glimpse of Connor. The older boy had stopped pretending to be a machine now and was loping after Finn, following the trail of crushed plants.

Finn ran faster so that he could hear Connor pushing his way through the undergrowth some way behind him but not see him. It was more or less within the rules. With a mad dash, he veered off to his right, leapt into the brook and began to wade upstream. The water was icy on his feet even in the summer. Thirty yards up, the brook turned and there was a small patch of gravel and stone where the two of them sometimes – uselessly – tried to dam the flow. Finn sprang out of the water there, ran along the slope, then angled back down towards Connor. He hadn't heard his friend for some time but knew where he must be. Finally, he flung his back against the bough of a great tree for a moment while his breathing calmed.

Finn peered around the trunk of the tree. Connor was there, just a distant shape between the trunks. It was impossible to see which way he was looking, but he must be walking away, following Finn's trail. He wouldn't be far, now, from the place where Finn had run to the brook. When he saw that, Connor might guess what Finn was up to.

Finn stepped out, tense, ready to run if he saw Connor coming for him. But Connor continued to move away, disappearing again and again behind distant trees. Finn smiled. If he could touch his friend without being seen first, he would be the winner. He set off to hunt Connor.

A heavy hand grabbed his shoulder, jerking him backwards.

"You are to be taken to Engn, boy!"

Finn stumbled backwards and fell to the ground. He looked up, expecting to see the ironclads from down in the valley. But instead, there was Connor, his face beaming. "The ironclads will take you!"

Finn, disoriented, struggled up to his feet. He looked at Connor, then into the woods all around them. Now nothing moved out there except for the birds, oblivious to their games, twittering among the high branches.

"Connor. But you were way over there."

His friend sat back against a trunk and smiled. "I figured you'd try and get around behind me, Finn. So, I just climbed a tree and watched you."

"But ... I saw you. Over there."

"Can't have."

Finn looked around again, confused.

"Come on," said Connor. "Your turn to be the ironclad."

"No! It's not fair. You must have cheated," said Finn. He still buzzed with terror, thinking the real ironclads had caught him.

"Me?" said Connor. "I didn't cheat, you did! I saw you running away. You were supposed to keep me in sight!"

"I did keep you in sight!"

"Didn't!"

"And who says ironclads can climb trees anyway?"

"Who says they can't?"

They were suddenly both shouting at each other, standing face to face. Finn saw Connor's hand flinch, like he was going to hit him. Finn balled his own fist, ready to fight back. They fought, sometimes, Finn's speed more or less a match for Connor's strength. Neither spoke for a moment.

"I'm going home," said Finn, turning away from Connor and striding off through the trees.

"Yeah, that's right," Connor shouted after him. "Run off to mummy and daddy again!"

Finn refused to look back as he strode down the slope away from Connor.

"Watch out for ironclads!" Connor shouted. Finn began to run through the trees, not stopping until he could see the waterwheel and his house beyond it.

He began to walk. Anger hammered through him. He wiped his eyes; he didn't want his parents to know he'd been crying. It was evening by now, but still warm. The air was thick with the buttery tang of fresh-cut grass. He stopped on the bridge, pretending to look at the chortling water, sucking in deep breaths of air.

After long minutes, he turned and made his way along the cable markers to their house. In the twilight he could just see that the dust in the lane still bore hoof marks from the ironclads' horses, along with two wide strips worn by the wheels of the engine. They reminded Finn of his sledge, the day of the avalanche.

Inside the house, his parents were preparing supper, his father peeling potatoes, his mother pushing a pie into the roaring oven, her face lit up red in the fire's glow. The delicious smell of bread filled the air.

"Hello, little one. Are you hungry?"

Finn nodded, not trusting his own voice. He filled a

beaker with cold water from the tap and gulped down the whole thing in one go. He poured himself another.

"How is Connor?" asked his father.

"Fine."

A long roll of paper had billowed out of the line-of-sight. Finn crossed to look at it, picking up the paper with the lines of tiny black dots singed onto it by the lenses of the 'scope. The messages were from people all over the valley. Each said the same word over and over.

"What did they want?" Finn called out. His parents didn't answer for a moment. "The ironclads?"

His mother came out of the kitchen, pushing a stray lock of hair back into place. She had patches of flour on her cheeks. She crossed to stand with Finn.

"They just rode through on their way somewhere, love."

"Who were they looking for?"

"I don't know."

She wasn't telling him the truth. Or wasn't telling him everything.

"Were they looking for me?"

"Of course not, Finn. It was no one we know."

"Why did they come here then?"

"They were just passing through the valley. Up on to Ironoaks and Bears."

"Did they say anything about Shireen?"

"No, love, of course not. Now wash your hands and come to the table."

Finn looked at the scroll of paper from the line-of-sight once more, then dropped it and crossed to sit at the table.

No one spoke as they ate. Finn wanted to ask his parents more questions, but he could see from their frowns that he shouldn't. At least they didn't ask him anything else about Connor.

After they had eaten, he cleared the table in silence and went outside. There was no sign of Connor or the ironclads. He played alone in the garden until it grew too dark to see.

IIII

Finn started awake with a gasp. Metal fingers scrabbled at his bedroom window. He expected to see the mask of an ironclad peering in at him, but there was no one. How could there be when he slept upstairs?

Another tap on the window. Someone was throwing stones to wake him up. There was light outside, but he couldn't hear any of the familiar sounds from down inside the house: the silvery fanfare of the kettle being filled at the tap, the clatter of pans on the stove. Outside, birds were starting to chatter questioningly, but the sun wasn't yet up over the mountain-tops.

Finn clambered over his bed and pushed open his window. Cool, damp air breathed in at him. Connor stood among the cabbages, another pebble ready in his hand.

"Finn! Come on!" He spoke in a whispered shout that sounded very loud in the dawn hush.

"What? Come where?"

"I have to show you something. You have to come now."

"But…"

"Come on!"

"I can't. I have to help my father in the workshop this morning. He'll be awake soon."

"Don't be such a baby, Finn."

"What is it?"

"Just jump down. It won't take long."

Finn looked back into his room, unsure what to do. Everyone was still asleep. He pulled on the clothes that lay scattered around on the floor from the evening before and turned to climb backwards through the window. If he held onto the sill with his fingers the drop wasn't so great. He landed with a *clump* on the soil next to Connor. In the early-morning chill he could feel goose bumps all across his stomach.

"What is it?" asked Finn.

"Come on. I'll show you."

They ran out of the garden, along the lane and up the slope into the woods. It was colder still under the trees, the black only beginning to shade into dark green. Connor led the way to one of the paths that threaded between the boughs. They ran quickly. Their feet knew the way. Neither spoke. They didn't need to speak. Finally, Connor held up an arm and stopped. He began to pick his way through the undergrowth next to the path, as if stalking some flighty woodland animal. He stopped in front of a dense clump of bushes that sat against a steep cliff of mud and stone.

"I found it last night," Connor whispered. "Saw it from the swing when you'd gone."

They'd built the swing a little farther down the bank, Finn edging his way along an overhanging bough to secure a thick rope. When you pushed off from the bank the ground fell away, leaving you spinning through the treetops. The trick was to make sure you had enough speed to reach the bank again. Otherwise it was a long drop to the ground.

Finn peered into the thickets ahead of them. It was

lighter now, but he could make out nothing unusual. Connor bent to push his way through and Finn, shrugging, followed his friend in, eyes closed as the branches slapped into his face.

A flattened patch of grass lay within the circle of bushes. Something large had lain there, crushing the grass into a nest. A bear? Then he noticed some old scraps of clothing and a blackened circle where there'd been a fire. The faintest smell of smoke and damp ash lay in the air.

"Someone was here?"

Connor nodded. "The person the ironclads were hunting. They must be on the run and hiding in the woods."

Finn didn't like the thought of someone else in their woods. With the bank behind them and the bushes all around it was impossible to know if the intruder was nearby. And the ironclads could still be around. His parents didn't even know he was out of the house.

"Come on," he said. "Let's go back."

"But there's another trail," said Connor. "Leading on. Let's follow it, Finn."

"Think how many ironclads were hunting them, Conn. The engine they had with them. It's not safe."

"I'll bet it's a wrecker," said Connor, his eyes wide with excitement. "The ironclads must have uncovered some plot to blow up one of the great wheels, or, I don't know, bring down one of the chimneys. It *must* be a wrecker on the run and the ironclads have chased them here. You know what they do to wreckers if they catch them."

It was another game they often played. One of them, the ironclad, would defend an Engn built from planks or branches. The other, the wrecker, would try his best to destroy it, kicking it to pieces or lobbing stones at it from a safe distance. People whispered many stories about the wreckers and how they worked in secret to destroy Engn. How the masters could never tell who was secretly working for them.

Finn looked back down at the crushed circle of grass. He wondered what it was really like to have the ironclads hunting you. He shivered. He certainly had heard stories of what they did to the wreckers they caught. He didn't like to think about it.

"I'm going home."

"Finn!"

"I told you, I have to help my father this morning."

"But the trail! Look, I'm not going to follow it on my own."

Finn turned back from the edge of the little clearing to look at Connor. There had been so many adventures over the years. They couldn't ignore this one.

"Okay. This afternoon, we'll follow the trail then. When it's properly light." He didn't say it, but that would give the wrecker more time to get away, too.

"Promise?" said Connor.

"Of course."

Connor grinned and slapped him on the back.

"Come on then, let's go home. I'm starving anyway."

"Yeah. Me too."

They raced back along the path, roaring with laughter as each attempted to barge the other into the undergrowth. Their fight from the previous evening was forgotten, their easy friendship resuming as it always did.

They parted back where the path ran nearest to Finn's house. It was later than he'd thought. The sun was rising over the mountaintops in front of him, casting impossibly long tree shadows across the valley floor. He had to hurry. If he was lucky, he might be able to climb back into his room before his father and mother noticed he was gone.

He began to run again on the lane towards home. He was sprinting so quickly he ran straight into Mrs. Megrim striding around a corner on her way up to the Switch House, black walking-stick thrust out before her. She always started work before even the farmers, priding herself on being ready for the earliest messages of the day.

She was ancient, as thin as a stick and slightly bent in the middle. Still, it was Finn that was sent sprawling to the floor. Mrs. Megrim stood over him, unmoved. Her grey hair was locked into place with long, sharp pins. Her eyes were black dots.

"What do you think you're doing? You nearly knocked me over, you young idiot."

"I'm, I'm sorry, Mrs. Megrim. I didn't see you."

"Don't you have eyes?"

"No. I mean, yes. Of course."

"What are you doing running around knocking people over at such an hour anyway? Up to no good again! Ida and Dan have no control over you. I'll have words with them!" She held up her stick, ready to strike Finn.

"I'm fetching something for my dad. I've got to hurry," said Finn. He scrambled to his feet.

"I'll have words!" she shouted again as Finn hurried away from her. "And don't be late for your lessons!"

His bedroom window was shut when he got home. He'd left it open, hadn't he? He'd have to use the door. He lifted the latch as quietly as he could and slipped inside. He thought he was alone at first, but his father was sitting at the table in the shadows, sipping a mug of tea.

"There you are. Been up to no good, have you?"

His father sounded amused rather than angry. Finn's eyes adjusted to the gloom. His father grinned the grin he used when he remembered being a boy himself.

"No. Just playing in the garden. I woke up."

"Just as well your mum's not up, eh? Come and eat."

The morning passed quickly for Finn. The acrid smell of solder filled the workshop as his father repaired a pump used to suck water up from the river for the fields. The tip of the soldering iron glowed bright red as his father pulled it from the smouldering coals of the forge. Diamonds of bright sunlight from the high windows in the roof suffused the room in golden light. It was another hot day. They had the great double-doors flung open, but it was still airless. Finn was glad his father wasn't smelting iron or blowing glass.

A great bank of wooden drawers took up one wall of the workshop. Some were tiny, filled with pins and washers, screws and cogs. The largest could hold whole engine-casings or axle-boxes. The workshop was always a clutter of broken machinery, wiring, tools, wood being turned on the lathe, disassembled devices that Finn didn't recognize. All the parts and pieces of the machines used by people up and down the valley, all of them built or repaired by his father. His father was always busy. Today, it was Finn's task to put as much back into the drawers as possible.

He was supposed to be learning all the crafts his father was expert at. It was the same in most families, the children learning the skills of their parents. Sometimes, however, it didn't work that way. Perhaps a couple had no children, or else their offspring didn't have the aptitudes required to pick up the skills of their parents. No one had said as much, but Finn strongly suspected that was the case with him. His father's endless tinkering and hammering bored him. He wandered around the workshop, his thoughts elsewhere, picking up handfuls of items and dropping them with a clatter into drawers that contained similar-looking objects. A set of stained, wooden step-ladders allowed him access to the higher drawers. He stopped at the top and looked down on the workshop, enjoying the unusual perspective. His father ground a piece of metal into shape, sending showers of white-hot sparks all across his arms and the workshop floor.

"Stay away while I'm shaping this bracket," his father

called without looking up. "I don't want you to get burned."

"Okay."

Finn found a drawer for the metal springs he held and dropped them inside. It was boring working there with his father, but he liked it too, somehow. He felt safe, surrounded by the familiar clutter. He liked the smell of wood and metal. He thought about Connor, and the wrecker being chased through the woods just near his own house. Today, for once, he was in no hurry to escape outside.

When the afternoon came, he was allowed to run off and play. His mother gave him a pasty, some apples, and a flask of water.

"Are you playing with Connor?"

"Yes."

"Enjoy yourself."

"I will," he replied. But he walked, rather than ran, back towards the woods.

Connor was waiting for him on the iron gate. It had once separated two fields up near the edge of the trees. Now the stone gateposts were crumbling and the rusty gate, although it still swung on its hinges, was never used. It would be useless anyway: the walls that once kept the two fields separate had long since crumbled into a low line of rubble. But you could still climb onto the bars of the gate and, kicking off from the ground, swing around, the iron hinges squealing unmusically. If you kicked off hard enough, there was a great jarring jerk as the gate clashed into the stop on the gatepost and rebounded. The usual game was to hold on while trying to shake the other off. But today, Connor jumped off the gate as Finn approached.

"You're here at last."

"Been busy."

"So was I, but I managed to get away ages ago. I brought these."

In his hands Connor held his catapult and also a knife, the sort his father's men used to trim and weave the hedges around his fields. He reached into his pocket and pulled out a smaller fishing knife and handed it to Finn.

"We'd better be armed. Ready?"

Finn looked at the stubby blade of the knife Connor held out for him, then grabbed it.

"Ready."

They ran into the trees and back to the bushes where they had found the wrecker's nest. Finn's heart thumped as they approached. But no one was there and there were no new tracks. But, just as Connor had said, quite clear now, a trail led off into the deeper woods higher up the slope.

"We'd better be quiet. In case the ironclads are nearby," said Finn.

Connor looked at him, his usual grin absent, and nodded.

The pathways in the woods there were twisty and difficult to follow, moving around as the animals trod out new ones. Finn soon lost track of where they were, although he could tell from the sloping ground which way they must be traveling. They crept through a forest of ferns, great curving stalks as high as their shoulders. They took turns to pick one, strip off most of the fronds, and spear it through the air to see who could get one the farthest. They stopped repeatedly to examine the ground, looking for footprints or snapped grass stalks. The trail was clear enough. Someone had definitely come that way.

The trees soared into the sky, unclimbable, their lowest branches far, far off the ground. Green avenues opened between them as they walked. Finn wanted to stop and walk down one, to see what magical place it led to, but

Connor hurried on and he couldn't stop.

They came to a place where the path dipped through a massed tangle of dense bushes: bramble and gorse and some plant with shiny, squeaky leaves and big purple flowers. At the bottom of the dip Connor stopped.

"I don't understand. The tracks just end here."

It was gloomy in the little dip, colder, the sky farther away. The two of them searched around on the floor looking for some explanation.

"Look," said Finn after several minutes searching through the vegetation at the side of the path. "Someone's been this way."

He stepped forwards and pushed aside thick, overhanging branches, expecting to see into the denser greenery of the bushes. To his surprise, another path led up a cleft in the ground, completely obscured by the dense growth around it.

He stepped through and held the branches back for Connor to follow. They climbed for a while, then emerged onto a bank with steep sides that wound its way along the side of the slope. The ground was carpeted with a spongy layer of pine needles. They picked their way forwards, neither of them speaking, glancing at each other from time to time.

Up ahead, the path led into an open space. Beams of sunlight, solid-looking, shone down through high gaps in the canopy. That must be where the person had gone. He wasn't as good as Connor at following tracks, but even he could see the trail was fresh. There was a good chance the wrecker was still here, just up ahead.

They drew their knives and stood side by side on the path. Finn's stomach fizzed with anxiety. He wanted to run away. But they had faced many enemies over the years, real and imaginary. And Finn knew – they both knew – that if it came to a fight, each would defend the other to the end.

They stepped forwards, expecting to be attacked at any

moment.

One of Finn's memories snapped into place. Sunlight and brown hair. He knew this place. He had never, in all the years since, been able to find it again. Now they were there. And he knew exactly who the person must be. She had come back, after all this time, come back to their secret place.

He pushed forwards ahead of Connor and bolted into the clearing.

"Shireen! It's me!"

But it wasn't his sister. A girl he had never seen before peered at him around a bundle of filthy blankets, her face full of panic. She backpedalled on the ground, scrambling to her feet. In her hand she held a knife of her own, long and sharp, its edge serrated. She waved it at them, ready to fight.

V

Finn started awake with a gasp. The engine had shuddered to a halt with a great sigh of steam, hurling him forwards. He waddled on skinned, stinging knees to press his eye to one of the square holes in the side of the machine.

He could see a square of hedgerow atop a stone wall. There were voices, muffled by the iron walls and the roar of the furnace. Somewhere up ahead, out of sight, the master was arguing with someone. It couldn't be one of the ironclads; they never disagreed. Someone they had met in the lane.

Finn turned his ear to the hole. The master shouted, dismissive, angered. Another voice, a man's, wheedled and complained in response. Finn tried another of the tiny holes, nearer the front of the engine. Glimpsed between the jostling bulk of the horses, he could see a beggar standing in the road, a gaunt face peering from a bundle of tattered rags. The beggar held his hand out, palm upwards, pleading. The master put something into his hand and turned away, shouting to the ironclads to move on.

The jolt sent Finn sprawling onto the floor again. He turned to look out to the side as they jerked forwards. The beggar sat by the road, cradling the coins as if they were something delicate. He looked up as the engine ground past. The grimy face was immediately familiar. Matt: thinner and dirtier, but unmistakable. The lengthsman waved as they trundled past, even though he certainly couldn't see Finn. A look of delight lit up his filthy face.

Finn scrambled to the back of the engine to watch Matt as he disappeared from view.

They stopped when it was nearly dark. They had ridden through more rain, hours of it. The master, when he hauled open the engine door, stood dripping and bedraggled. The rain plastered his hair to his head. His sodden purple robes weighed him down.

"All right for you in there, isn't it, boy, all dry and warm. Any more of this and I'll be swapping places." He gazed up into the leaden sky, water running off his cheeks, as Finn clambered out, still chained to the machine. The ironclads stood some distance away, removing the saddles from their horses. They were too far away to overhear.

"Ah, how I hate the outdoors," said the master in a quieter voice. "Give me the comforts of Engn any day. If I could spend the rest of my time there rather than wasting my life rounding up strays like you, I'd be happy."

"Then why don't you?" asked Finn. "You're a master. You can do what you want."

The master looked at him. His name, Finn knew from the ironclads, was Whelm.

"You don't know a thing, do you?" Master Whelm said. "The Iron Wheel doesn't work like that."

"The Iron Wheel?"

"The masters that control Engn. Don't you know anything? I'm Seventh Wheel and that means I have to do whatever the Sixth tells me." He held up his hand to indicate a single iron ring adorning his index finger.

"Sixth Wheel masters wear two rings. They in turn

obey the Fifth, who have three rings. That's the way it works. Masters of the First Wheel have seven rings and they obey only those in the Inner Wheel."

Finn knew none of this. But he needed to find out all he could about the workings of Engn. If he couldn't manage to escape before they got there, any piece of information could prove to be useful.

"So, the eight wheels together are called The Iron Wheel?"

"That's what I just said, isn't it?"

"And the Inner Wheel wear eight rings?"

"Of course they don't, idiot! They don't need rings. They do as they please."

"So how do you become one of them?"

The master shook his head, staring out through the drizzle as if he could see something out there.

He shrugged. "It takes years. Most people are old by the time they make it. If they ever do."

"But the ironclads, all of us, we do as you say."

"It's all different in Engn."

The master looked young then, little more than a sullen, dishevelled boy. His sopping cloak hung off his shoulders.

"Then why do you want to get there so much?" asked Finn.

"Because I just do!" The master was angry now. "Enough of this, boy. Leave me in peace."

He stamped off to shout at the ironclads. Finn sat down, his back to one of the wheels of the engine. He studied the iron ring around his ankle one again, but it was no use. He could never hope to crack or bend the metal, or to slip his foot free. An ironclad came over and handed him a bowl of lukewarm stew and a flask of water. Finn ate and drank, watching Master Whelm, who sat alone, gazing at the road ahead. When he'd finished, another of the ironclads – Finn could easily tell them apart now – came over, unshackled the chain from the engine, and led Finn into the woods so he could relieve himself.

Back at the engine, the chain once more secured, Finn lay down and tried to sleep, slipping in and out of dreams as he tried to get comfortable on the hard ground.

"Are you working for them?" asked the girl, keeping the knife pointed at their faces. "Did they send you after me?" Her gaze darted between them.

"You mean the ironclads?" asked Connor. "Of course not. Are you a wrecker?"

The girl looked confused. "Me? No. I've never been anywhere near Engn."

Finn lowered his knife. She didn't look dangerous. She looked *starving* if anything. Starving and exhausted. Green and black smudges covered her face, as if she had attempted to camouflage herself. Her eyes were wary, like those of a panicky horse. A bush of tangled hair straggled out from her head. Dried blood from an old cut stained her cheek. She was maybe a year older than Connor.

Finn and Connor lowered their knives.

"Why are they chasing you?" asked Finn.

The girl shrugged.

"How long have you been out here?" asked Connor.

"Eighteen days now. Maybe nineteen. I've lost count."

"Here." Finn fished the pasty out of his backpack and broke off a lump. The girl looked wary but her hunger was too great. She grabbed the food and began to stuff it into her mouth. She sat down on the log, no longer watching them. It was the same log, Finn was sure, that he and Shireen had shared all that time ago.

Finn and Connor perched next to her, one on each side. Finn broke the rest of the pasty into three and handed it round. Connor had bread and a hunk of beef that he hacked into three with his knife. Finn passed around the water.

"So, what did you do to them?" asked Connor. "It must have been something incredible."

"Didn't do anything," the girl mumbled through a mouthful of food.

"But there were loads of them hunting you," said Finn. "Dogs too. And they had an engine with them. We saw it. A machine on wheels that moved by itself."

"What? You've seen the ironclads?" The girl stopped chewing. His eyes were wide with shock again. "They're here?" She glanced past them at the wall of trees, expecting her pursuers to burst out at any moment.

"They passed by yesterday, heading up the valley," said Finn. "But they must have lost your trail."

"They know I'm here somewhere," the girl said. "There are only two ways out of the valley." She looked down at the ground. "I don't know what I'm going to do. They'll find me sooner or later. They never give up, never."

There were tears in her eyes. She had already been crying, Finn could see, smudges running down the grime on her cheeks.

"We'll help you," said Connor. "We can bring you food. And keep an eye out for the ironclads. We know these woods better than anyone. We can watch the tracks and not be seen." He looked thoughtful for a moment. "Hey, I know, there's an old barn in the high meadow on our farm. The cows shelter in it but there's an upper floor no one uses."

"I could stay there?"

"Sure. No one else would know."

"We play there sometimes," said Finn. "There's these little slit windows you can see out of. No one could sneak up on you."

"Is it far?"

"Back down the valley a bit," said Connor. "We can go through the woods and cut across the field if there's no one around."

"We'd have to make sure Mrs. Megrim didn't see us," said Finn.

"We'll keep the hill between us and the Switch House," said Connor. "It'll be easy."

The girl looked reluctant, not able to bring herself to trust them.

"How did you escape the dogs?" asked Finn. "They must have had your trail."

"I waded up the river," she said. "At night, so no one would see."

"Smart," said Finn. "When they came for my sister there was nothing we could do."

"They took your sister?"

"Years ago. I was only young."

Sitting there, the memories of that day were vivid now. Thinking Shireen had returned had brought her surging back. It was a strange coincidence that he had found the glade again just as the ironclads had returned to the valley.

"What's inside the engine?" asked Connor.

"Wasn't anything inside it. It's just a cage. It's what they put you in when they catch you. To make sure you don't get away when they take you to Engn."

Finn looked to see if the girl meant it. He and Connor spent their lives roaring through the woods, running where they wanted, going miles and miles. They could walk all day together and not feel tired. The thought of being caged inside that smoking, iron box was too much.

"We'll take you to the barn," said Finn, standing up. "You'll be safe. We'll make sure no one sees you. I promise."

The girl hesitated for a moment more then stood. She stooped to pick up her bundle of blankets and looked back at Finn.

"Thanks."

"What's your name?" asked Connor, also standing up.

"Diane."

"I'm Connor. This is Finn. We'll go first to make sure no one's watching."

They stood together in the shadows of the trees, looking out onto open fields. The stone barn sat a little way away. Nothing moved apart from two buzzards wheeling high in the sky, calling out in distant, mewing cries.

"The lane's empty," said Connor. "Let's run across before anyone comes."

"What about this Mrs. Megrim?" asked Diane.

"She can't see us here," said Finn.

"I'll go first and make sure no one's around," said Connor. He loped off down the slope and into the wide, mouth-like opening of the barn. A few moments later they saw his arm thrust out through one of the slit windows on the upper floor, waving to them to follow.

Diane looked at Finn. Finn smiled at her.

"Come on," he said, and the two of them ran to the barn wall. The yellow stones were warm to the touch from the sun that had been on them all day. No one called or shouted. They stepped into the darkness.

They scrambled up a rough staircase of straw bales that led to the upper floor. Large cracks between the wooden boards let him see down to the ground underneath. The boards creaked but seemed solid enough to stand on.

"We can cover the floor with straw for you to sleep on," said Connor. He held a rusting sickle blade, using it to hack open one of the bales. They soon had a thick layer of it in one corner. Diane pushed more of the bales together to form a low wall between the hatchway and her bed.

"In case anyone looks in," she said.

Finally, they sat together on the carpet of straw. Finn and Connor threw handfuls of it at each other, laughing, and soon Diane, smiling at least, joined in. They ate the last of the food together.

"We'll bring you more tomorrow," said Finn. "And some water from the river."

"Thanks," she said. "Thanks for everything." She lay down and closed her eyes. She looked exhausted.

"We'd better go," said Finn. "We'll cut back through the woods so no one knows we've been."

"And don't worry," said Connor. "No one ever comes here."

She nodded but said nothing else. Finn and Connor exchanged glances, then jumped back down to the ground floor to run back into the woods.

Ambling down the lane on his way home that evening, Finn met Matt. The lengthsman whistled as he walked. He had a mattock and a shovel slung over his shoulder. The skin of his arms and face was grey with a coating of dust from the lane he'd been working on. He smiled cracks in it as he spotted Finn.

"Hello, young man. What mischief have you been up to today, then?"

"Playing with Connor."

"Ah!" said Matt, as if this were a great secret. "Any more sign of them ironclads?"

Finn shrugged.

"Well, let's hope we've seen the last of them, eh?" said Matt. "Those contraptions of theirs make a real mess of my lanes."

"Yes."

"Mind you, they're mighty powerful and no mistake. They say if you teamed ten horses together and put them in a tug-of-war with the engine, the machine would win.

Imagine that! That would be some sight to see, eh?"

Finn nodded.

"Well, tell your dad I'll be round first thing tomorrow."

"I will."

The lengthsman turned and, still whistling his tuneless tune, strode off.

That night, Finn's mother tucked him into bed. Finn thought about Diane, out there alone in the barn with the darkness and the owls. Was she asleep yet? He thought about the ironclads. His mother sat with her arm around him, stroking his hair. The hard stone walls of his room faded away into the shadows, leaving them alone in the bubble of light from the bulb. Occasionally the glow dimmed as the current from the waterwheel fluctuated, then snapped back to full brightness. His mother spoke quietly to him, whispering to the top of his head.

"Is there anything wrong, Finn? You were very quiet at tea."

"I'm fine."

"Are you having the nightmares again?"

"Sometimes."

"They're just dreams, you know. They can't harm you."

"I know."

They sat in silence for a time. Finn traced the patterns on his blanket with his finger.

"Mum, why don't people destroy Engn?"

"Now Finn, you mustn't say things like that."

"I mean it. Why doesn't everyone get together and go there and tear it all down?"

His mother sat up and turned to look at him, grasping his shoulders.

"Now listen to me, Finn. You mustn't say things like

that. Not ever. Do you understand? If people hear you, you could get into trouble. Real trouble. You can't trust everyone in the valley." Her voice was louder, urgent.

"I know."

"You must promise me."

"I promise."

"Good."

She sighed and turned to sit next to him again. They sat together in silence.

"It just isn't that simple," she said after a while. "Some people tried to do what you said, many years ago. It didn't go well. Lots of people died at the walls. There were attacks on the masters, too, and that was why Engn started sending out ironclad guards to protect them. The villages and towns of those responsible were destroyed as an example, burned to the ground. It was terrible."

Finn nodded. Mrs. Megrim had mentioned such things in her history lessons. "But why do people put up with it? Why do they allow the masters to come and take people away?"

"I know it's hard to understand, but I think over time folk simply learned to accept the occasional loss in exchange for a peaceful life. People who tried to fight back suffered the consequences: an army of ironclads burning their houses to the ground, salting their fields, poisoning their water supplies. Most people aren't directly affected – it's somebody *else's* child that gets taken – so they look the other way and refuse to get involved. It's surprising how people can become accustomed to an evil and accept it as simply the way the world works."

It was like Engn and the ironclads and everything else were now so big and ever present that people had stopped seeing them, stopped thinking things could be any different. It was like not being aware of the ground because it was always simply *there*.

"Why do they even need children?"

"They need laborers and makers and all sorts, things I

couldn't begin to understand. Engn is a special place; it's vast and miraculous, a place of wonders. Generations of people have laboured to build it. Some have gone there willingly; a master of Engn lives a privileged life of unimaginable luxury. But there are never enough hands to do all the work required. There are tasks that have to be carried out that no one wants to do, dangerous and dirty tasks, and so they started taking people. One or two, very occasionally, from all around the valley – that was the arrangement."

"So, they'll be forcing Shireen to do these terrible things?"

"I'm sure half the stories you hear about what goes on can't be true. Shireen's smart; she'll be okay."

"I hate Engn."

"Oh, Finn." She hugged him close. "I know it all seems frightening. You'll think differently when you're older. Sometimes people go there to do things, become things, that they never could out here. Like an adventure."

"Did you ever want to go?"

"Well, once, I suppose. But then I wouldn't have been able to have you, would I?"

"Or Shireen."

"Or Shireen, of course."

"I'm glad you didn't go."

She squeezed him tighter for a moment. "Come on. It's time you were asleep."

They sat like that for a long time, neither speaking, until Finn's eyes drifted shut.

VI

Three days later, Finn, Connor, and Diane lay in the barn. The sweet, dozy smell of hay and cows filled the air. Bars of sunlight streamed in through the narrow windows, thick with drifting specks of light. Birds called from the nearby trees, but otherwise there wasn't a sound in the whole of the world.

The three of them snoozed next to each other in the airless warmth. The hay prickled Finn's back. He and Connor planned to spend the night there themselves, when they could think of a suitable story for their parents.

"How did you know they were coming for you?" asked Connor.

Finn opened his eyes to squint at Diane through the flickering haze of his own eyelashes, but the light was too bright and he closed them again.

"My village isn't like here, with mountains all around," said Diane. "We're on the edge of the plain. We saw them approaching."

"But how did you know they were coming for *you?*

asked Finn.

"There was no one else. They took my cousin five years ago and a friend a few years later. They must have been coming for me. Once it was rare for people to be taken; now they're coming for everyone."

"So, you just ran? Without telling anyone?"

"Yep."

"I'd do the same," said Connor. "Definitely."

Finn wasn't at all sure he'd be brave enough, but he had another question. "You knew all about Engn? I mean, about what they do to you there?"

"Hadn't just heard. My cousin was with them when they came back for my friend. Only he'd become an ironclad. He wasn't the same person anymore."

"Wait, they aren't machines then?" asked Finn. "They're just people?"

"I suppose," Diane replied. "Mostly, anyway. He took his mask and helmet off and it was definitely him."

"What do you mean he wasn't the same person?" asked Finn.

"My cousin wouldn't harm a fly. We'd go fishing and he couldn't even bring himself to kill the trout and the salmon we caught. Didn't even like putting the worm onto the hook. But not when he came back from Engn. My friend's mother tried to stop him entering her house and my cousin just struck her, knocked her over. Broke her nose. And he didn't speak the whole time. He didn't say a single word."

Finn opened his eyes again and looked at Diane. She seemed so much older and wiser than even Connor was. He could tell Connor thought so, too. Since Diane had arrived Connor had changed. He'd become quieter, more thoughtful. Finn often caught him staring at her. He found himself staring at her sometimes too.

"They'll stop looking for you sooner or later," said Connor. "They'll have to."

"Maybe. Sets a bad example though, doesn't it? If I get

away, others will try as well."

"But you have got away."

"For now."

They were silent for a time. Finn had smuggled out half a loaf of bread that morning. Connor had a rainbow trout, freshly tickled from the river. He also had a whole cabbage, as large as a cow's brain, pulled from his father's fields. Finn peeled a leaf off and crunched into its sweet, squeaky flesh.

"Why do they even *need* so many people?" asked Connor.

"When the wind is in the right direction in my village, you can hear the booming and crashing from across the plain," said Diane. "It gets louder each year."

Finn tried to imagine a machine that vast, something like his father's furnace, but filling the whole valley. He couldn't do it.

He sat up. "Come on, let's play the Engn game again," he said.

"Okay," said Connor. Diane opened her eyes but didn't reply.

"It's your turn to be the ironclad, Conn," said Finn. "We'll be the wreckers."

"Okay."

They peered out through the slits in the walls of the barn to check no one was around, then jumped down to the ground floor. They raced out of the back of the barn for the safety of the tree line.

The game had changed in nature now. One of them still had to be the ironclad, defending Engn from the other two, but secretly they were working *for* the wreckers. They had to maintain the pretence until the vital moment, otherwise the other, imaginary ironclads would find out. But if you could sneak up and touch the ironclad without being seen, you had won. The one defending Engn could stop being an ironclad and become a wrecker, their true identity revealed.

They built the city between them, leaning branches together in a line between two trees. Connor scrambled inside to guard it. In his hand he held his stick, a whippy sycamore branch stripped of its twigs, that he would lash them with if he caught them. He had the sickle blades with him, too. By common agreement, whoever was playing the ironclad clashed these together when pursuing the others.

Finn and Diane raced off into the surrounding woods, whooping and shouting. When they were far enough away, they stopped to whisper their plans. They ran in opposite directions, Finn circling around, Diane creeping a little nearer to hide in the undergrowth. As Finn ran, trying to make as little noise as possible, he counted to himself. They would start sneaking up on Connor when they reached one hundred.

It was impossible to see Connor hiding in the shadows, impossible to know which way he was looking. When he had counted, Finn began to creep forwards. He kept one of the two trees between himself and Connor as much as possible. Diane would be doing the same from the opposite direction. If they had successfully counted at the same speed they would arrive at the same moment. Then, if one of them could touch Connor, the game would be won.

The woods were very still. Finn could hear nothing but the rush of his own breathing and the occasional *tick* as he stepped on a twig. At any moment he expected Connor to come roaring out, waving his stick. But he reached the trunk of the tree without being seen.

He took a breath, preparing to dash out into the open. But Diane was there ahead of him. She must have counted more quickly. She ran into the clearing in front of the wooden hut. Connor emerged, his voice booming, scything his stick backwards and forwards with a *whoosh*. Diane backed off but didn't run, trying to dodge past the stick to touch Connor.

Finn crept forwards. Diane had noticed him but

Connor's back was to him. If Connor turned, Finn knew he would have no chance.

He was very close when Diane, with a shout, leapt at Connor. For a moment Finn thought she might make it but the whirring stick caught her in the side. Her back arched as she shouted in pain and crumpled to the ground. Connor, satisfied that Diane was beaten, turned to see if Finn was nearby.

Finn lunged at Connor even as he turned. Connor's branch whipped into Finn's legs, a sharp, painful blow on his left thigh. But Finn had already touched Connor's side as he turned. Finn had won.

There was silence for a moment. Finn and Connor stood looking at each other. Connor still wore his stern, ironclad face.

"I got you first, Connor!" said Finn. "Come on, you're a wrecker now." Diane, watching them from the ground where she was rubbing her side, said nothing.

Connor held the stick up behind his head again, ready to swing it at Finn. "You are an enemy of Engn and you will die!"

"Connor! I got you first."

"No one can defeat the ironclads!"

"Connor!"

Connor's arm flinched. Finn stepped backwards.

"You're not an ironclad anymore! Those are the rules."

With a roar, Connor leapt, but at the wooden building rather than Finn. He began to kick and trample the walls. Finn joined in with him, and, after a moment, Diane too. Soon they had reduced Engn to a tangle of branches on the forest floor.

Afterwards they sat among the ruins, Finn and Diane examining the wounds they'd received from Connor's stick. Finn had picked up a splinter during the fight, too. He tried repeatedly to pluck it from his palm with his fingertips but couldn't get it.

"Here," said Diane to him. "Let me try. You have to

get it out or it'll get infected."

She held his hand in hers, turning it into the light, then lifted it to her mouth to try and pull the splinter out with her teeth. Finn could feel her warm breath on his skin, the moist tip of her tongue tickling him. Then she got it. She spat the splinter, a long, curving thorn, to the ground.

"Better?" she asked.

"Better, thanks."

He grinned at her. She let go of his hand and nodded over towards the ruins of Engn.

"You know something?" she said. "If they ever do catch me and cart me off there, I *will* join the wreckers. I'll do whatever it takes to destroy it for real. So no one else has to be taken."

She looked suddenly very serious, very grown up. She looked scared.

"Hey, I know, we should swear an oath," said Connor. "In blood, to make it unbreakable. We could swear that if any of us ever *does* get taken, that's what we'll do."

"You mean join the wreckers?" asked Finn. A game in the woods was one thing. To do it for real was another.

"Of course," said Connor. "Diane? What about you?"

She nodded.

"Finn?"

He wasn't going to be taken to Engn anyway; it didn't really matter. And it was what he'd want to do, if he were brave enough. "Okay."

They bunched into a circle, legs crossed, knees touching. Finn drew his knife from its leather sheath and examined the blade.

"Use your hand," said Diane. "Not your wrist. If you cut your wrist you'll bleed to death."

Connor held his knife over his palm, then glanced around at them.

"This is our greatest secret," he said. "No one else must ever know."

"Agreed."

"Agreed."

"We vow to destroy Engn, by whatever means it takes."

"Agreed."

"Agreed."

Connor drew the knife across his hand, scratching a red line that pooled blood into his palm. He passed the knife to Diane, who did the same. Finn, refusing to look afraid, refusing to cry out, opened the skin of his own hand, too.

The three of them placed their hands together, grasping one another, their blood mingling as it dripped to the woodland floor. The flap of skin on Finn's palm, rubbed by the others' grips, made him feel sick.

"This oath is unbreakable," said Connor. "On pain of death." Diane and Finn repeated his words. They sat for a few moments, hands still touching, then let go.

"I like your rings," said Finn.

Diane wore intricate, knotted spirals of silver on several of her fingers, winding from her knuckle to the middle joint.

"Everyone has them back home," she said. She slipped one off and handed it to Finn. It was smeared with her blood. "Have it."

"Really?"

"Of course. Here's one for you, too." She handed another ring to Connor.

"Thanks."

They put the rings on. Finn's was tight and it made his finger throb as he screwed it up over his joint. He held it up to admire. Connor grinned as he studied the ring on his own finger.

"Come on," said Diane. "We should wash our cuts."

They stood and raced off through the trees together, towards the bright waters of the river. There, Finn lay down on the bank, and dipped his hand in the flowing water. He watched as wisps of blood from his cut floated off before dissolving away. The cold stopped his palm stinging. He lifted his hand out and watched as beads of blood started to seep out again.

Connor held out a rag for him. "Wrap it around your hand."

Diane sat on the bank, dipping her feet in the river as she bandaged her own hand.

"This water is lovely," she said. "It's a shame it isn't deep enough to swim in."

"We could go up to the millpond," said Finn.

"Would we be seen?"

Finn thought about it, running through the journey in his mind, working out whether the lane was visible from anywhere.

"No. We'll be okay if we stay near the river."

Diane stood up and laughed. "Come on then, let's go."

They ran along the bank, occasionally leaping over tiny creaks feeding into the main river. But they paused when they reached the millpond, each suddenly awkward. Finn and Connor had often swum naked in the pond. With Diane there, it was different. She glanced at the two of them, seeing their awkwardness, embarrassed at her own.

She shrugged. "Come on. Last one in's a tadpole."

She wriggled out of her skirt and shirt and, with a salmon leap, dove off the bank. Finn watched her white legs passing into the glass of the pond. A moment later she emerged in the middle, wet hair plastered to her face, laughing with exhilaration. She swam around in circles, clearly at home in the water, then dove back down again with a splash and a kick of her feet. Finn and Connor, grinning at each other, shed their own clothes and jumped in after her.

The next morning, after breakfast, Finn scoured the

kitchen for food he could smuggle out. He had three pears in his pockets and was just cutting the crust off a loaf of bread when his mother came into the kitchen. He tried hard not to look as if he was doing anything wrong.

"Still hungry?" his mother asked. "It seems we never feed you enough these days."

Finn shrugged. His mother didn't look suspicious or angry. Still, it was hard to tell what adults were really thinking. If his parents knew they were hiding Diane from the ironclads they would be furious. Worse than furious. He wanted to tell them, and nearly had on several occasions, but then Diane might be put in danger.

"I'm playing with Connor. We said we'd bring food to eat. So we can stay out all day."

"Off you go then. And be careful not to cut yourself again. Come straight back if you do."

He'd tried to hide the wound on his palm but his mother had noticed it when they were eating and had made him wash it again under the tap. He'd invented a story about cutting it while clambering over an old gate. He just hoped his parents didn't talk to Connor's and realize they had identical scars.

"I will. Bye!" He sprinted past his mother, bread tucked under his arm.

"Hey, not so quick, Finn!" she called after him.

"What is it?"

His mother caught up with him and kissed him on top of the head. She didn't have to bend down much anymore.

Finn sighed and turned to run off.

"And make sure you're home before dark," his mother called after him.

"I promise."

Outside, Finn fished the ring out of his pocket and wound it onto his finger. A groove spiralled up his skin, now, that it fitted into. It didn't throb any more. He grabbed his stick from where he'd left it last night, leaning on the hedge next to the garden gate. Now he was ready to meet Connor and Diane.

His stick was gently curved. He'd carved a series of notches along it, one for each kill. He had twenty-two now. Diane only had eight or nine but Connor had over thirty. Their latest game was one of mass murder. Connor had started it a few days earlier, after explaining that butterflies were destroying his father's cabbage crop.

"It's the white ones that do the damage. My father said he'd pay me for each one I kill."

At first Connor had prowled his farm, creeping up on butterflies and attempting to smash them to death with his stick before they skipped away. Soon all three of them were playing the game. They ranged across the valley in search of white butterflies to bludgeon. Every time you got one you carved another notch onto your stick.

Today they made their way along narrow woodland paths through patches of nettles and vast banks of brambles. A light drizzle was falling outside the woods, but the trees kept if off them, except for the occasional fat *blip* of water falling from the high branches to hit one of them on the head.

They peered around for the glorious sight of a shimmering, white butterfly. Whoever spotted it first was allowed the kill – that was the rule. You had to run after it, keeping it in sight but not getting too close, waiting for it to settle. There was an art to it. Sometimes the butterflies escaped, flitting across uncrossable oceans of undergrowth. Sometimes you thought you had them but they fluttered away even as you swung your stick down at them. But sometimes, gloriously, you got one, striking it before it could move, reducing it to twitching tatters of paper embedded in the ground.

"There's one!"

Connor sprinted down the path, attention focused on a white butterfly circling in front of him. Finn ran after him with Diane walking along behind. The butterfly appeared to know it was being hunted. It stopped occasionally, as if for a rest, but skittered on whenever Connor drew close. It veered off the path, flying high up over mountain ranges of fern and bramble. Connor, not stopping, lunged into the thick undergrowth, beating a new path through the bushes with his stick. Finn soon lost sight of him.

"You'll never catch it!" Finn shouted. "Let's find another, Conn."

"No! It'll have to stop soon." Connor already sounded distant, his voice muffled. "Come on!"

Diane came to stand next to him.

"He doesn't give up, does he?"

Finn shrugged. "Come on. Let's follow him."

Finn and Diane took the path Connor had trampled through the undergrowth. They soon caught up, felling the ferns in front of him with wide sweeps of his stick.

"It's gone, Connor. Let's find another."

"A bit farther," said Connor. "I just saw it, not far ahead."

They cut their way on through the undergrowth. Finn was hot from all the running but at the same time his arms were icy cold from the wet ferns. It was impossible to know where they were or which way they were going; the walls of green around them were too high to see over. Finn was just about to shout that he was turning back when Connor called from up ahead.

"Hey, look where we are!"

Finn caught him up. They had come to the edge of the bushes at last. A clearing stood before them. The sight was immediately familiar. The walls of trees. The log. It made sense; they weren't that far from the secret path he and Connor had found when they'd tracked down Diane. Still, it felt suddenly like a bad omen. The place was forever associated with the appearance of ironclads in Finn's mind.

"Any sign of the butterfly?" asked Diane, catching them up.

"No. It's gone," said Finn. He stepped past Connor into the glade.

"Finn! Look!" said Connor.

Over on the old log there was a butterfly. But not the small, white one they had pursued. This one was much larger, the size of one of Finn's hands. Its wings, spread wide to the sun, were bright red with purple spots for eyes. Finn had never seen such a large, dazzling creature in his whole life.

"Quiet," said Connor. "I'm going to get it. This one's worth two notches at least."

"Connor, you can't," said Finn. "It's not one of the whites. It isn't harming anyone. I mean it's … it's beautiful."

But Connor crept towards the butterfly, stick held up high in the air ready to swing. The butterfly's wings twitched closed and open once or twice but it didn't move. It was basking, Finn could see, in a patch of warm sunlight.

"Connor, let's leave it."

Connor ignored him. Finn glanced at Diane, who frowned and looked puzzled but didn't move.

With a whoop, clapping his hands, Finn darted forwards towards Connor, hoping to scare the butterfly into flight. At the same moment, Connor brought his stick down with a *thwack* onto the log. The butterfly was already moving but Connor caught its wing, knocking it back to the ground. He scrambled after it, bashing at it again and again. Finn tried to stop him but Connor struck the butterfly properly, pinning it down, its wings flapping uselessly. A few more blows and the flapping stopped.

"You shouldn't have done that, Connor. That wasn't part of the game."

Connor turned to look at them, his eyes wide with triumph. Finn was about to reply when a sound blared out through the trees around them. The sound of a horn being blown. Connor's words died in his mouth.

"What's that?" asked Finn. It was familiar. It sounded like some wounded, angry animal, but there was a metallic edge to it too. It made his spine shimmy to hear it.

"Don't know," said Connor.

"It's the ironclads," said Diane, looking at the two of them in open alarm. "They've found me."

VII

"What's this, boy? Give it to me."

He'd been twisting Diane's ring around and around on his finger, lost in his memories. The master let him out of the engine twice a day, morning and evening. He liked to sit where he couldn't see the engine or the ironclads and pretend, for a few moments, he was free, even though his ankle was still shackled to the machine.

"It's nothing," said Finn. "It's worthless, it's just wire." He unscrewed the silver spiral over the joint in his finger, to hide back in his pocket. It came off much more easily now.

Master Whelm stood over him, his mouth twisting as if he was trying to smile but didn't know how. The ironclads sat nearby around a fire, watching what was about to happen. They had taken their helmets and masks off and the skin of their unfamiliar faces was baby pink. With a kick, the master sent Finn's food, a bowl of potatoes and greasy stew, spilling over the grass. Finn hadn't eaten any of it, but he wasn't hungry anyway.

"Give it to me," said the master, holding out his hand.

"It's nothing. It just reminds me of home."

"Give it to me. Or I'll cut your fingers off so you can't wear it again."

Finn studied the master, trying to decide if he was serious in his threat. He might be. But what use would a fingerless boy be in Engn? Finn thought about pretending to hand over the ring but punching the master in the face instead. If he caught him hard enough, like Connor had taught him to do, he might be able to knock him out for a moment. Grab the keys, unlock himself and be free. But, of course, there were the ironclads, watching everything. They would never allow such a thing to happen. This idea was like the thousand other plans for his escape he'd come up with on their journey. It would never work.

Reluctantly, Finn handed the ring to the master.

"Made it yourself, did you, boy? Think you're an artificer, do you?"

"Yes. No."

The master shook his head. "What are they going to do with you in Engn?" He spoke loud enough for the ironclads to overhear, enjoying his little scene. "Throw you into the furnaces within a week I'll bet."

The master stood very close. He looked angry and bored at the same time.

"The furnaces?" asked Finn.

"The furnaces?" The master mimicked Finn's voice. "Don't you know what furnaces are?"

"Yes. Of course."

"The furnaces are where they throw you when you're no use to them anymore. Or when they just want to get rid of you."

The master held the silver ring to his eyes, examining it. Could he identify it? Did he know it had come from Diane's village?

"Means a lot to you, does it?" he asked. "Did your mummy gave it you so you wouldn't forget her?"

"No. Please, it's just wire. It's nothing."

The master smiled and dropped the ring to the floor. With his boot he ground it into the grit of the lane. His boots were studded black leather. Every day, one of the ironclads polished them to a shine. When he moved his foot, the ring was a flattened lozenge of wire on the ground.

"Must have been a pretty piece, your mother, once," said the master. "Starve some weight off her and she'd just about do. I wonder how *grateful* she'd be if I went back and promised to look after you in Engn?"

Finn's fist clenched. The master was certainly close enough for him to strike. But that was what he wanted, wasn't it? He was goading Finn, trying to make him attack. Perhaps he wanted an excuse to punish Finn. Perhaps he was just bored. Whichever it was, Finn restrained himself. Not now. He would pick his own time to fight back.

"I don't know."

The master considered Finn for a moment, then seemed to give up in his attempts. He laughed and strode away, shaking his head, saying something to the ironclads that made them laugh.

Finn stooped to prize the ring out of the ground with his fingernails. It was ruined, squashed flat. He tried for a time to work it back into shape but it was useless. He slipped it into his pocket, looking around. The mountains were just hills, now, much farther apart as the valley opened out. The river, fed by all its side streams, was a wide sheet of water, glass-still, barely moving, far too wide to bridge.

They had passed a village earlier that day. The master had demanded food and drink from the silent villagers, who had supplied it without arguing. Finn wondered if it was Diane's village. If, even, Diane was somewhere there, hiding behind a building or a tree, peering out to grin at Finn. He'd seen no sign of her.

He lay back on the ground and closed his eyes. Where

was she now? He thought about her often. Was she still alive? Had the ironclads ever caught her, or was she still living wild somewhere, still running?

The moving engine snorted and sighed, heat blasting from the fires within it. The shackle tethering Finn's ankle pulled at his skin, cutting into him where his flesh was red and swollen. His lips were dry and cracked. At home, his mother would have given him beeswax to soothe them.

Finn put it all out of his mind and lost himself in a fantasy of finding Diane in the wilds somewhere, the two of them running through the woods and fields together, laughing and shouting. They plotted ways to bring down the walls and towers of Engn as they had promised. The people inside stumbling from the ruins, blinking into the light…

"Get up, boy."

It was the master again. He kicked Finn in the side to stir him from his doze.

"Your carriage awaits. We'll travel until it's dark."

Not looking up, Finn made his way on hands and knees back into the moving engine.

No one moved for a moment. On the ground, forgotten, the ruined butterfly's wings lifted in the breeze.

"I have to get away," said Diane. "I have to leave here now."

"But all your stuff," said Finn. "Your knife and blankets. It's all still in the barn."

"I'll manage without them. I'll go up into the mountains. They might not follow me up there."

"No," said Finn. "You're safe for a bit. They won't find you here. We'll go and fetch your things."

"It's not safe," said Diane.

"Give us half an hour. You'll have no chance without your knife."

She said nothing. She looked terrified.

"Come on, Conn. We'll have to hurry," said Finn.

"Make sure you're not followed!" she called after them as they ran out of the glade.

They raced through the woods to peer out over the valley. No ironclads in sight. The water of the river sparkled as if nothing had changed. The breeze sent waves rippling through the golden fields of wheat in front of them.

"We should split up," said Finn. "I'll go through the woods. You cut across the farm. One of us will make it."

"Right," said Connor. "Bet I get there before you do!" He scrambled down the slope, half-revealed tree roots forming a series of rough steps. Finn turned and fled along the path, leaping over fallen logs and ducking under low branches.

He didn't stop until he reached the point where the finger of woodland reached out towards the barn. Once again, he paused and peered out. His heart pounded away and his lungs burned as he breathed ragged breaths. Still no one to be seen. Perhaps Connor had already made it and was inside, or was on his way back to Diane.

Finn trotted out across the field, across the muddy triangle of bare soil trodden out by the doorway, and on into the warm darkness of the barn. He stood while his eyes adjusted a little, then gave the low whistle they used to call to each other in the woods. No one whistled back.

He clambered up the haystack staircase to the upper floor. The slit windows let in little oblongs of daylight and by them Finn could see Diane's stuff was all as she had left it. He had beaten Connor. As quickly as he could he bundled everything into a blanket, tied up its corners, slung it over his shoulder and leaped back down to the ground.

Standing outside he tried to decide what he should do.

It had taken him longer to get there than he thought it would. What if Diane gave up and left? The quickest way back to her was up the lane, but that meant he might be seen. He might even meet the ironclads. If he took the path through the woods again it would be safer, but then he might be too late. He stood for a moment, fighting back the urge to just start running. He had to think.

The lane. He half walked, half ran along the field track, moving as quickly as he could without looking like he was in a desperate hurry. If anyone asked him, he could just say he was on his way home. The blanket was just an old blanket, there was nothing suspicious about it. He kept expecting to meet Connor but saw no sign of him. Where had he got to?

Lines of hoof prints lettered the dust of the lane. Heavy horses, lots of them, had passed up the valley recently. There were no wheel-ruts this time. No paw marks either. Perhaps the dogs were ranging through the woods. He'd made the right choice. It was much safer on the road.

He began to run again, holding his side to try to ease the stitch tugging at him. No one would think it odd he was in such a hurry, would they? He was just racing home because there were ironclads in the valley.

He reached the crossroads and stopped for a moment. It was still very quiet. The hedgerows hissed in the breeze. He began to think everyone else had been taken, everyone in the whole valley carted off to slave in Engn. He wanted to rest but dared not. Diane had to get away.

He set off again, running as fast as he could now, up the sloping lane towards home, past the path to the Switch House and on. He was running so fast he careered round a bend and nearly ran into the ironclads. Two of them rode abreast, their horses' great hooves stamping forwards, their metal armour glinting in the sun. Finn stumbled to a halt in front of them. The ironclads kept on coming, saying nothing. He should stand aside and let them past. Anything else would look suspicious. He had to pretend he had nothing to hide. He was just a boy on his way home. They weren't coming for him.

The ironclads trod nearer, a great wall of snorting horse and shining metal. Finn turned and hared back towards the crossroads, anywhere to get away from them. He ran and ran, Diane's bundle dangling around his legs, threatening to trip him up. He expected to hear the horses stir into a thundering gallop after him, the metallic call of their horn. He was nearly back at the crossroads when he half stopped and glanced over his shoulder to see if they were pursuing him.

A hand grasped his shoulder.

"Finn! Come here this moment!"

It was Mrs. Megrim, standing at the foot of the Switch House path, grabbing his arm with iron fingers.

"Let go of me! Let go!" He squirmed and pulled but couldn't get away from the old woman.

"Listen to me, you young fool," she said. She shook him hard and spoke in a low, jabbing whisper. "You can't just run around with the ironclads here! They're not stupid. They'll see you've been helping Diane, and what then? Listen to me!"

In an instant, everything made sense to Finn. *She* had seen them, spying on them with a line-of-sight. She must have sent trunk messages through to Engn, telling the ironclads where they were.

"They know because you told them! I hope you're happy now."

She let go of him at that and stepped back as if she'd been struck.

"Me? You think it was me? Haven't you been listening all this time I've been teaching you?"

"Of course. But who else would have told them?"

"Oh, it wasn't me, little boy."

"Of course, it was! Now let me go!"

She glanced up and down the lane for a moment. Finn could hear the clank and thud of the ironclads approaching around the last curve of the lane.

"Finn, listen to me," said Mrs. Megrim, shaking him once more. "It's not safe out here. Come up to the Switch House. You'll be safe there. Please."

He tried to squirm his way free. "You just want to hand me over so I can tell them where she is!"

"No, no! There's no helping Diane now. They'll take her away to Engn and there's nothing you can do. Did you think you could beat them, boy? Come on. It's you we need to save."

"No!"

"Yes!"

She dragged him from the lane, making him stumble to his knees. She was surprisingly strong. Behind him, Finn saw a flash of silver as the ironclads appeared round the bend. If he got free now, they would see him anyway. Perhaps if he hid in the Switch House, he could let them pass by and then carry on up to the woods. He stopped struggling, rose to his feet and pushed past Mrs. Megrim, up the spiral path that wound around the low hill. The old woman followed, keeping a tight grip on the wool of his jerkin in case he tried to make a dash for it.

It was dark inside the Switch House, as it had to be. It smelled of paper and dust and, for some reason, lavender. He had never been allowed in before. Three of the walls, those facing up, down, and across the valley, were peppered with small, round windows, bright circles of daylight. Most had line-of-sight telescopes peering out of them.

Stepping awkwardly in case he walked into something, Finn crossed to peer through one opening at the front of the house, overlooking the lane. He could see four ironclads, two lines of two, trotting past towards the crossroads. One of the two at the back turned his head to look up as he went by, as if well aware Finn was up there watching. Finn held his breath. The horses didn't stop. He was safe. They really weren't coming for him.

He turned and sank to the ground, shoulders heaving. He dropped Diane's bundle to the floor, where it spilled open. He would leave it for a few minutes then go and find her.

His eyes were adjusting now. He looked around. He knew well what happened at the Switch House thanks to Mrs. Megrim's lessons. Still, it wasn't what he'd expected. He'd always imagined a room where beams of light crisscrossed, a great nest of them, each flickering as the coded words flashed through from up or down the valley. He'd imagined banks of brass machinery, mirrors and lenses on mechanical arms that snapped into place as you turned knobs or pressed buttons, connecting two telescopes with mechanical precision so that two households, perhaps miles apart, could communicate.

Instead, three walls were dominated by a higgledy-piggledy assortment of line-of-sight telescopes, each poised at a different angle, positioned to line up with the 'scopes set up in each building. Some buildings, of course, weren't even directly visible. There were mirrors rigged all along the valley so that signals from distant houses could bounce their way up. Just behind each 'scope, a mirror on a spindly metal stand directed light onto the fourth, black-painted wall. Covering this wall – the bank wall – small squares drawn with chalk were labelled with names stamped onto metal plaques: the name of the house or the title of the inhabitant. Here, all incoming messages flashed until they were routed through to their recipient. Finn found his square in the top row. *Blacksmith* was shortened to *Smith*. It was flashing a pattern of longs and shorts now, the address of the house his mother or father wished to connect to. He didn't recognize the pattern.

Most of the telescopes were banked like this, but two pairs were connected, their mirrors moved aside and lenses placed between them at precise angles so that they lined up. Finn could just see the rapid glimmering of light in the eyepiece of one of the 'scopes. He wondered what was being said.

Mrs. Megrim sat nearby, peering through a line-of-sight down the valley. Four or five connection requests flashed on the wall behind her, but she ignored them all. Which she prided herself on never doing.

"What are they up to?" he heard her say to herself.

"They're going the wrong way," she said in reply. "I don't understand."

"I have to go," said Finn.

"No!" She turned to look at him. Her features were indistinct in the low light, but Finn could feel her eyes on him, pinning him to the spot. "You can't. It isn't safe."

"Only because you brought them here."

"You young idiot. You know nothing."

"I know enough."

Mrs. Megrim turned to her wooden desk, filling a corner of the room where no line-of-sight holes perforated the walls. A dim red lamp gave off just enough illumination to see by. An open book lay upon the desk, next to a sheaf of papers. Line-of-sight printouts. She picked these up and thrust them into Finn's hands.

"Here. Here's your betrayal." She turned back to peer into her telescope.

Finn held up the sheets of paper to one of the holes in the wall and began to read. They were all trunk messages, destined for outside of the valley. He didn't recognize the destination address.

"Where is 1A11?"

"Isn't it obvious?"

"Engn?"

"Of course."

The messages were all encrypted, the sequences of lines and dots gibberish. A child could read a normal line-of-sight message, but not these. The sender's address was perfectly clear, though. Each message, all ten or twenty of them, had been sent by Matt.

"What do they say?" asked Finn.

"I've no idea. I can't read encrypted messages, despite what people say."

"How long has he been sending them?"

"Him? Oh, off and on for years. Some of them I deliberately don't route properly. Sometimes I just blur the imaging. Occasionally I let one through so they don't get too suspicious. But all *those* are from the past week."

"Since Diane came."

"Since Diane came."

"Did you let any through?"

"It's against all the rules to interfere with a line-of-sight communication, you know. It's more than my job's worth."

"Yes, but did you let them through?"

She turned from her telescope to look at him again. Her wooden chair creaked as she moved. She spoke in a whisper.

"No. I blocked every single one of them."

"Why?"

"Because I don't like him and I don't like *them*," she said.

"And you think he saw us playing together somewhere when he was out mending the roads?"

"Of course, he did. I'm surprised the whole valley didn't see the three of you running around and making trouble. They must have heard you *shouting* at least. What did you think you were doing? None of you have the sense you were born with."

"He sent a message through you didn't intercept?"

"Must have. The well-used 'scopes often get left set up so we don't have to keep switching them in and out, and I can't be here all the time. I have to teach you, for one thing. Try and drum some common sense into you."

"But why? Why would he tell the ironclads about Diane?"

"Matt was a nasty, scheming bully when he was a boy and he's no better now. He thought there would be something in it for him. Why else?"

"You're saying somebody at Engn knows his private key?"

"So Matt seems to believe."

"How is that possible?" People only shared their private keys with people they trusted completely.

Mrs. Megrim paused before replying, perhaps deciding how much she should tell him. "Matt's family weren't from here originally. His father came as a young man, said he was from somewhere up north. The whisper on the wires is Matt is an informer like his father before him. There are people like him all over, sent from Engn to keep an eye on folks and report back anything interesting. Being a lengthsman – even such a poor one – allows him to travel around, keep an eye on things going on all up and down the valley."

Finn thought about that for a moment.

"Then do you think he would have mentioned me and Connor? Helping Diane, I mean?"

She sighed. "I can't say for sure. But possibly not. He needs your dad because he's such a useless lengthsman. And he's afraid of the Baron. He's not stupid. Perhaps he only mentioned her."

"We just didn't think," said Finn. "We thought *you* were spying on us. Matt is just so … harmless."

"That's because you're children, and all children are stupid. And I was spying on you. I just don't report to Engn."

Finn hauled himself to his feet.

"I have to go," he said again. "Diane is waiting for me. They might not have found her yet."

There was silence from Mrs. Megrim. The darkness gathered deeper around her as she concentrated on the vision in the telescope. More connect lights flickered on the bank wall now. Finn counted fifteen of them.

"Mrs. Megrim?"

She turned away from the line-of-sight and slumped

into her creaking wooden chair, just a huddled shadow in the gloom of the room.

"Oh, no," she said.

"What is it?" asked Finn. "What have you seen?"

"Well," she said. "It seems not just children are stupid." All the iron had gone from her voice.

"What do you mean?"

"Finn, I'm sorry. You'd better look."

He crossed to stand next to her, sending one of the lens stands clattering to the floor. He bent to peer through the telescope.

The scene was a blur of greens and blacks and sparkles of sunlight. He turned the little knurled wheel below the eyepiece and the image sharpened into crisp detail.

A phalanx of ironclads rode in close formation down the lane from the farm. At their head rode one of the masters: unarmoured, purple robed. There was also a smaller figure within the cluster of riders. He couldn't see who it was at first but then, between the joggling heads of the ironclads, he caught a clear glimpse. It was Connor. They were taking Connor away to Engn.

"No!"

Finn burst towards the door, scattering stands and telescopes to the ground. Outside, in the blinding light of day, he stumbled down a step, rolling to the ground. Squinting, he stood and raced on, around the spiral path to the lane, then on to the crossroads. He arrived just as the ironclads arrived.

"Connor!"

He could see his friend clearly now. Connor's face was open-eyed disbelief. He sat astride one of the vast horses the ironclads rode, swaying gently in time to its leaden, unstoppable stride, hands behind his back.

"Connor!"

Now Connor saw him. He looked defeated as he stared at Finn. Something else too: apologetic, perhaps. He didn't speak.

"Connor," said Finn one more time, but quietly, to himself. The ironclads stamped by, the sweet smell of the horses mixed with oil and metal. They turned the corner at the crossroads, heading down and out of the valley. Finn could see that Connor's hands were shackled to his saddle behind his back. On his finger, clearly visible, was Diane's ring. The finger waggled. *Goodbye*, he was waving. Goodbye and also, don't forget our vow. Don't ever forget.

Finn stood and watched, powerless. The clear understanding that his childhood was over, as utterly as Connor's was over, came to him. They were boys no longer, just as Diane was no longer a girl. Soon enough, Finn knew, he would be a man and then, sometime after that, he would die. And he would never see Connor again.

The dust kicked up by the horses tasted gritty and bitter in his mouth. He wormed his own finger into the ring hidden in his pocket. He stood and watched as Connor grew smaller, his head slumped forwards as he rode away.

"I'm sorry," said Mrs. Megrim, standing behind him. "If I could have done anything I would. I thought they'd come for Diane. I didn't think…"

"Diane," said Finn. "I have to help her."

He was running again, back to the Switch House. He crashed in, bundled Diane's gear back into the blanket, then tore down to the lane towards the woods. He didn't care if he met his parents or the ironclads or anyone. He didn't care about the tearing pain in his side. He ran and ran, past his house, dashing headlong through the woods, leaping branches and ditches in his way, pushing through nettles as if they weren't there.

He arrived, panting, wide-eyed, in the clearing.

She was gone. He was alone in the clearing. He slumped to the log, his breathing still wild, looking around at the trees, wondering what he was going to do.

He stayed there for a long time, but no one came to take him away. No one knew where he was. Eventually the darkness thickened between the boughs of the trees. He stood and wiped his eyes with the palms of his hands. He left Diane's stuff on the ground, in case she came back, and walked away.

VIII

Three years passed in the valley. Three summers of wilting heat, three winters of snow. Finn ranged farther and farther from home, up beyond the mountain slopes where the avalanche had caught them. Down past Three Tree Hill and the farm. His mother and father, watching him set out alone each time, sighed and held each other but said nothing.

He spent more and more of his time at the Switch House, helping Mrs. Megrim. When the old woman was ill, he ran the junction on his own. He no longer attended her lessons as she claimed she had taught him everything she knew. He grew to love the dark seclusion of the little room. No one else was allowed inside. The quietness of it wrapped around him like a warm blanket. He loved the patient gaze of the telescopes and the smooth paper of the ledger in which they recorded every communication they switched. He loved the clear mechanisms and rules. They represented the whole world ordered, categorized, explained. Everything had its address and every message could be routed to its proper place by following the rules. Life and all its complexities and anxieties were reduced to a simple code of flashes, each flash understandable and rational. The world seen from the Switch House made sense.

He loved also the thought of having the whole valley, the wider world beyond, there in front of him, brought flickering down the lines of light. He could peer through any one of fifty telescopes and see almost anywhere he could think of. The slightest turn of the focus wheel was all that was needed to turn blurred confusion into crisp detail. Sometimes he panned a spare telescope across the fields and hillsides, picking out the barns and the trees where he'd once played with Connor and, briefly, Diane.

More and more he preferred to sit in the darkness and wander the valley with his eye. He was a spider at the centre of a web, all-seeing. Like Mrs. Megrim, he knew everything that took place in the valley, learning to read the faint flickers of light as they passed between line-of-sight eyepieces in the darkness. He knew who loved whom and who hated whom. He felt closer to all the people he shared the valley with even though there were many he had never seen or met.

Of course, he didn't have access to messages from all across the world. Mrs. Megrim had explained it all in tedious detail often enough. Their line went through numerous hamlets and villages down their valley before heading across the plain to Engn, the centre of the web. Other lines worked their way from Engn out to other areas: valleys, lakesides, forests, and the great cities that ringed the plain.

He didn't even know everything that was communicated upon their line. They still switched through encrypted message occasionally. Then all he could tell was who had sent them and where they were going. Almost always they were for 1A11, and almost always they were sent by Matt Dobey. Engn, for its part, never replied.

There was one such message now. Finn was alone, Mrs. Megrim at home in bed with some unspecified problem with her insides. Matt's message had come through mid-afternoon. As he routed it through to the trunk line, Finn had set up a splitter lens to take a copy of it for himself.

He sighed as he studied it. He sat at Mrs. Megrim's desk, her red lamp giving him just enough light to see by, the bank wall to his right so that he would notice any connection requests flickering.

He had four of the encrypted messages now, kept rolled up in a length of steel pipe borrowed from his father's workshop. Everyone knew the operators intercepted messages. They were supposed to, to check they weren't garbled. But to keep a *copy* of one was a serious offence. He only ever dared do so when he was alone.

He frowned as he studied the jumbled streams of letters and numbers. As ever, he could make nothing of them. Each message started with the same few lines, and certain combinations of characters repeated themselves in the messages. That had to be significant. Could he use that to somehow work out the original messages? He couldn't see how.

Of course, he knew how to send and receive encrypted messages. At the base of each line-of-sight was a set of ten tiny brass dials, each marked with the digits zero to nine. Every house had their own combination they dialled if they wanted to send an encrypted message. People rarely bothered as it was all so fiddly. The sender first had to send a plain text message warning the recipient to set the key at their end. The encryption was reliable, unbreakable, but it depended on people remembering each other's keys, and the fact was most people couldn't even remember their own.

In the half-light of the hushed room, Finn set up two 'scopes now, pointing at each other, going nowhere else. Perhaps it was possible to work out what the messages were by replaying them. He punched in the encrypted text at one end and then walked around to see what came out of the other. It was just more gibberish, even more random-looking than the original. Of course, he had the wrong key. The dials at both ends were at all zeroes. He tried setting the dials at the receiving end to all ones, then to all twos, then to a random ten-digit number, but each time it was just the same: different patterns of letters and numbers, just noise and interference rather than message.

He toyed with the idea of going through every combination on the dials but soon gave up on the idea. A whole lifetime wouldn't be enough. He just didn't understand how the line-of-sights worked. Somehow, they decrypted the messages without trouble. Some clever machinery. He had taken one apart, once, an old one they didn't need any more, but he had learned nothing from the tiny wheels and cogs that had sprung into a useless jumble even as he opened the case.

There was only one answer. If he wanted to find out what Matt was saying to Engn, he needed to know Matt's key. But the thought of breaking into his house, perhaps when Matt was away working down the valley, repulsed him. He had never been inside Matt's house. He and Connor had crept close once but movement inside had startled them into flight. Besides, Matt was sure to reset his dials after use, not leave the combination visible for all to see.

There was a knock on the door, three sharp raps. He gasped as he looked up. It was Mrs. Megrim, warning him to cover his eyes before she came in. Finn stuffed all the printouts into his shirt and rotated the two line-of-sights so that they faced in random directions. The door opened.

"Mrs. Megrim! I thought you weren't well."

"I'm well enough to hobble up here. And what are you up to? There's a waiting connection on the bank wall."

Finn glanced up. He'd missed the flickering pattern while concentrating on Matt's messages. He needed to be more careful.

"It's just Mrs. Griffin calling her daughter for her daily moan," he said, while hurriedly lining up the two telescopes. "The same as every day."

"That's not the point. Our job is to switch through all messages. If you can't be trusted with it, I'll have to find someone else."

"Sorry."

Mrs. Megrim sat down, awkwardly, stiffly as if the bones in her hips had fused together. "Very well. And what else have I missed?"

"Nothing unusual. A lot of chatter about the harvest. Oh, and another encrypted message from Turnpike Cottage."

"Was there indeed? What's he saying to them now, I wonder?"

Finn shrugged his shoulders. He had thought, once, that Mrs. Megrim had a way of reading encrypted messages, some secret machine she could use, but months of gentle questioning had convinced him she didn't.

"I wish I knew," he said.

"Stirring up trouble again, reporting back to his paymasters. If we're not careful we'll have more of his bloody ironclads running around the valley." Finn glanced up at her, surprised. Mrs. Megrim never swore. Her voice was thin and angry today, scraped away by exhaustion or pain.

"I don't think you should be here, Mrs. Megrim. You don't look well."

"Thank you, Finn. I'm perfectly well, for your information."

"Of course, Mrs. Megrim."

"Now off you go home. You've been stuck in here all day. I'm sure you must be starving."

"Are you sure?"

"Yes, yes of course. I'll let your mother know you're coming."

Back home, his parents were waiting for him with Matt, the three of them sitting together at the table. Their faces turned towards him as he entered. For a moment alarm thumped through Finn. They knew what he'd been up to. Somehow Matt had found out. But then the lengthsman drained his tankard, yawned and stood, his usual grin on his face.

"Many thanks for the drink. I'll leave you to your domestic bliss."

His father had been helping Matt re-lay some drystone walls up the valley. He must have just dropped in on his way home. He brushed past Finn at the doorway and winked, as if they shared wonderful secrets. Finn said nothing. He stood watching as the lengthsman pushed open the garden gate and disappeared down the lane. Somehow, he had to discover Matt's line-of-sight number. But how?

Later, after they had eaten a tea of lamb stew and dumplings, Finn and his mother went up to the woods to pick blackberries. Mountainous brambles massed under the eaves of the oak trees up the lane. As he plucked plump fruit from the spiky bushes, the problem of Matt's number turned over and over in his mind.

"Mrs. Megrim doesn't like Matt much, does she?" he said as he tried to pull tiny thorns from his purple fingers.

"She didn't tell you about it all?"

"Tell me what?"

"About what happened."

"No, never."

"Well, it was all a long time ago. I was just a girl myself, long before I married your father. She had twins, two boys. Tom and Rory. Both full of mischief, but you could never get cross with them. They had such lovely smiles. A bit like you and Connor when you'd been up to no good."

She glanced a smile at him through the tangled brambles.

"What happened to them?" he asked, although he

knew what the answer must be.

"The ironclads took them. Both on the same day."

Finn frowned. "I thought you said they never took two from the same family?"

"Yes, well, that was unusual. The master said it was because it would be cruel to separate twins but, I suspect they had doubts about Mrs. Megrim. She's never been the same since that day. You might find it hard to believe, but she used to be good fun, always laughing."

"I didn't know."

"No, well, she doesn't talk about it much."

Finn worked away without saying anything for a time, harvesting the berries and dropping them into his pot. Some, the biggest and juiciest, he ate.

"What does that have to do with Matt?"

His mother cast a calculating glance his way. "Well, Matt was great friends with her boys. Inseparable they were. But Matt stayed here and *they* were both taken. It's ridiculous, of course, but I think she blames him."

"Perhaps she's right. Perhaps he told the ironclads about them."

"None of us have any say in the workings of Engn, Finn. The ironclads decided to come for her boys and that was that. Matt was just lucky."

"So, what do you think of him?"

She was in two minds as to what to say, he could see, caught between treating him as a child and an adult. She didn't speak for a moment as she reached high up for the large, jewel-like blackberries massed on top of the bush.

"Well, your father says he wouldn't trust him to put a spade into the ground without missing. Me, well, I don't have much to do with him. I don't really know him very well, not now. I feel sorry for him, I suppose."

"Why?"

"He's all on his own, isn't he? No family, no children. It must be a lonely life."

"He never married?"

"No. Not for want of trying, though. In fact, he asked me to walk out with him once, a long time back. He was very persistent, you know? But I was already seeing your father."

"Dad gets on with him, though," said Finn. "They're always laughing together."

"Your dad likes to get on with everyone. It's a good way to be. He tries to help even when he should be doing his own work."

"Matt never helps him out."

"No."

Finn scowled. Plans buzzed around in his mind. So far as he could see, there was only one way to read Matt's messages. It was a dangerous plan and probably wouldn't work, but he had to try. His mother's words had helped him. He had always thought his parents and Matt were good friends. It didn't feel so bad doing what he planned now.

"Come on, young man," his mother said. "I think we've enough for three blackberry pies. Let's go home."

Finn hooked his arm through hers as they made their way back down the lane, swinging their pots of fruit. As they walked, Finn began to work through all the details of his plan, along with all the ways it could go wrong. He tried not to think about what would happen to him if it did.

It was three months before he had chance to put his plan into action. Mrs. Megrim, thinner and more stick-like each day, still insisted on working at the Switch House. But then she slipped on a patch of ice at her front door and broke her wrist as she tried to save herself. Finn was entrusted to run the network alone for a week. Not that Mrs. Megrim left him alone. She sent messages through nearly every hour, reminding him to complete some task or other, nagging him to keep an eye on the bank wall. Finn grinned as he read each one and replied dutifully that he would do as she said.

Meanwhile he prepared. He had the message he would send clear in his mind. He just needed Matt to start transmitting. But Matt's line was silent for the first day, and the second, and the third. Sometimes he went weeks without communicating. Finn was just beginning to think he would miss his chance when, late on a dull, grey day, a light began to flicker in Matt's bank square. The address was clear. 1A11.

With a practiced hand, Finn aligned Matt's 'scope with its receiver. But not the trunk line. The message wasn't going to leave the valley. He would capture it and put it with all the others, in case he was able to decipher it.

Once the complete message had been sent, Finn paused, heart hammering, his finger hovering over the line-of-sight connected to Matt's. He had to get the timing just right. If he was too quick, Matt would be suspicious. But if he left it too long Matt might not be there anymore.

He'd resolved to count slowly to thirty. He got as far as twenty before giving in and sending his message back down the line to Turnpike Cottage. He punched in each character of his message slowly, one at a time, as, he thought, a machine might. It was probably unnecessary, but he was taking no chances. Mrs. Megrim could spot his line-of-sight style but he doubted anyone else could.

Sent in plain text, the message flickered off through the night to Matt.

Send key to confirm identity immediately. Masters of Engn.

He made the message as terse as possible, hoping to alarm Matt into cooperating, hoping he would comply from fear of displeasing the masters. He also overwrote 3C87, the sender address of the Switch House, with 1A11. This was, in fact, very easy to do, although not many people knew it. Then he sat back and waited, not moving, only half believing he'd actually carried out his plan. He regretted it almost immediately. What would Matt do? He imagined him sitting down there at Turnpike Cottage, reading the message, frowning. There was no way he would fall for it. If another encrypted message came through, Finn knew he was in big trouble. His only defence would be to deny all knowledge. Messages could be intercepted anywhere; the journey to Engn must hop through ten or twenty Switch Houses. He waited and waited. He was about to turn Matt's 'scope back to bank and hide all the evidence of what he'd done when the second message came through. It was very short. Unencrypted. Ten digits with no explanation. Finn scribbled them onto one of the printouts as they came through. Then he waited, counting to twenty once again. Finally, he sent a second message of his own.

Confirmed. Resume encrypted communication. Masters of Engn.

He had done it. It was incredible. Shaky with panic, Finn returned Matt's 'scope to bank. He imagined Mrs. Megrim bursting in at any moment, demanding to know what he'd been doing. No one came. The only sound was the winter wind moaning through the trees outside. Finn sat and gave his full attention to the bank wall for the rest of the evening, the perfect Switch House operator.

The following day, Mrs. Megrim was still house-bound. A line-of-sight from her gave Finn a list of additional duties to perform. The lenses of all the 'scopes were to be polished, but only after each was substituted for a temporary device so no communications were lost. Each 'scope was to be re-collimated and checked by sending down a test message to each house. The floor was to be swept clean and the bank wall given a fresh coat of black paint.

Finn worked hard for three hours, completing all his labours as well as routing through seven messages. Finally, he could wait no longer. He peered out through the 'scope ports, up and down the lane, checking no one was coming. Then he set up two unused devices in the middle of the room, pointing only at each other.

On one, the receiver, he dialled in Matt's ten-digit code with his thumb. Then he sat at the sender and began to punch out the most recent of the encrypted messages. It was slow work. In the dim light he had to be very careful each character was correct. There were no words, no meaning to the message, to guide him. Finally, when it was done, his stomach fizzing with anticipation, he stepped around to the receiver to see what message had been printed out.

He expected more gibberish. It would mean not only that he couldn't decipher the messages, but also that Matt had suspected something and sent a false key. But there, in perfectly-formed words, was a message, an actual message. The first line read *To the Lords and Masters of Engn*.

Within an hour he had all the intercepted messages unscrambled. He disassembled the line-of-sight rig, then stepped outside to burn the dog-eared encrypted print-outs he'd been carrying around for so long. The small iron brazier they used to destroy all paper copies soon consumed the messages. To be doubly sure, he stirred the embers around with a stick, encrypting them irrevocably and permanently. The smell of the smouldering paper was sweet.

Back inside, he checked again that no one approached. Only then did he sit down in the circle of red light at the desk to properly read what Matt had been saying to Engn.

Half an hour later, he rolled the decrypted messages up into a thin scroll and slid them into his sleeve. It felt like he'd been holding his breath since he started reading. He shook his head. Were there really people like Matt all over the land? Spying on friends and neighbours, reporting everything back to Engn, picking out children for the ironclads to come and take? Or was Matt the only one, playing some game for his own gain? He would probably never know. He did know that Matt couldn't be allowed to get away with it. And while they could stop the messages being routed through, that wasn't enough. Matt had to pay for what he'd done. The conviction burned bright in Finn's mind.

He walked home slowly through the darkness that evening, ignoring the cold, letting his feet find their own way, while he pondered how he would go about it.

IX

They were two days into the crossing of the great grass plain. Finn, squinting out through the back of the moving engine, could see the mountains of his home shrinking away, melting into the horizon. Up ahead, the track led straight west, directly towards Engn. He'd seen no villages out there, no people at all apart from another troop of ironclads on the road yesterday, heading out to the mountains. Only an occasional Switch House, relaying messages to and from Engn, broke the monotony.

He closed his eyes again. The hours and days passed in a daze. He lost track of time and of where he was. Sometimes he thought he was back in the Switch House, the engine's air holes the line-of-sight ports. He would jerk awake thinking there was a message to route, or that Mrs. Megrim had shouted something to him. At other times he was trapped inside a giant cylinder, the piston hurtling towards him to stamp him flat. Or he was drowning in coal, the ironclads lifting him up to hurl him into the engine's roaring furnace.

He no longer heard the rumbling noise of the moving engine except when its note changed. It slowed now, something different in the sound of its usual huffing rush, a rattling grate that sounded like bare metal rubbing against metal. He peered outside. Mid-morning. The sun beat down, the metal roof of his prison nearly as hot as the floor. They weren't due to stop to give him food and drink for hours yet.

Someone, an ironclad by his shape, heaved the door open. Finn shielded his eyes with his hands and squinted to see what was happening. An armoured gauntlet grabbed him and dragged him from inside the engine, sending him sprawling to the grass.

"Something for you to see, boy," said the master from somewhere in the light.

Finn's eyes began to adjust to the glaring white. They had come to a halt upon a low rise in the ground. The ironclads had climbed down from their snorting, stamping horses and were gathered around the moving engine, peering into its workings. They shook their heads as if they couldn't agree was wrong with the machinery.

Finn turned to look the other way, ahead across the plain. The track ran off in an unbroken line from Finn's feet to the horizon. He could see grey clouds massing there, like the bulk and peaks of another mountain range. At one point the clouds formed a sharp funnel down to the ground, as if they were being sucked out of the sky. He had never seen anything like it. He wiped his eyes and looked again. Now he could make out buildings beneath the funnel, a great clutter of misshapen blocks with chimneys of different heights reaching up. A plume of grey smoke poured from the tallest chimney, widening into the delta that merged with the clouds. The whole sky was being made there – a sky of smoke from the chimneys of Engn.

"A wonderful sight, eh?" The master sounded happy for once, as if he and Finn were just old friends out for a walk. "Your new home, boy."

Here and there, bars of sun through the clouds picked out the distant scene with white spotlights, glistening off metal towers and wheels nearly as high as the chimneys. It stretched all across the horizon: an entire, artificial mountain-range of machinery.

"That's Engn?"

"We'll be there tomorrow. Assuming these fools can fix the machine."

The master turned and left to shout at the ironclads. Finn continued to gaze at the scene, trying to grasp the scale of what he was seeing. He stood there until a tug on the chain shackled to his leg nearly pulled him over backwards. The ironclads were attempting to jolt the engine back into motion. It spluttered and squealed but refused to fire. One of the ironclads lay on the ground, removed his helmet and wormed his way underneath the machine. Soon, only his legs and boots were visible. After several minutes of banging and clunking he began to squirm back out. Oily grime smeared his arms. In his hands he clutched a thick iron chain that had coiled around his wrist as if it were a living snake.

"Timing chain's broken," the ironclad said. "We need to vent the steam, otherwise the engine will overheat. It could explode."

"But you can fix it," said the master.

"If we work through the night."

"Then get to work."

The ironclad nodded and prepared to work his way back beneath the machine. The master scowled, angered by the delay. He kicked the ground with his boot.

"Do we camp here?" asked Finn.

"Got no choice, have we? I suppose we'd better unshackle you in case the thing does blow up. You wouldn't be much use in pieces."

The master took the key to Finn's chain and reached inside the engine to free him. Finn looked around. For the moment, no one was watching him. It would be a good time to escape. The engine was broken and the ironclads were all off their horses, huddled around the machine. His stomach fluttered as he prepared to run. But the grass plain stretched unbroken around him, vast and empty. Where would he run to? Sooner or later they'd catch up with him. He'd bide his time. Perhaps the engine would explode and kill all the ironclads. Maybe then he'd have a chance. If he could steal one of the horses, he could perhaps evade the master at least. He'd watched how the ironclads rode, the way they controlled their mounts. He could manage it, he knew.

"What's this, boy?" The master had turned to face him. He held the end of Finn's chain in one hand but in the other was a folded square of paper. Finn's heart hammered. It must have fallen from his pocket inside the engine.

"It's nothing."

The master dropped the chain and stamped one of his feet down onto it to stop Finn running. He unfolded the paper.

"Well, well, secret messages. We were told you were a tricky one. A trouble-maker. Going to join the wreckers, are you? Going to overthrow us all?"

The master showed the scrap of paper to the standing ironclads, his grin broad. A murmur of amusement came from them. Standing there, the idea of being able to defeat any of them, even one of them, seemed utterly ridiculous.

"Wreckers? What are wreckers?" he asked.

"Oh, very clever," said the master. "Do you think we don't know all about your secret plans?"

Finn's insides fizzed with alarm, clenching his stomach like a fist. They knew. They knew everything. How did they know? The pact with Connor and Diane was his only hope, his only light in the darkness. Without that he had nothing.

"What plans?" he asked. It sounded unconvincing even

to him.

The master shook his head. "Everyone we take has secret plans to wreck the workings, boy. Save the world. You're no different, I'm sure."

They didn't know everything, then. Maybe, somehow, he still had a chance.

"So, you once wanted to destroy Engn, too?"

The master stepped forwards, looking like he intended to strike him. Finn cowered back from the blow, eyes closed. But it didn't come. When he opened his eyes again the master stood before him, shaking his head.

"Perhaps I did. Childish fantasies. They don't last once you grow up a bit and find out how the world really works. Don't worry. We'll soon have that defiance beaten out of you."

Watching Finn's eyes, he tore the square of paper into half, and then into halves again, and again, until he held only scraps.

"Open your mouth, boy."

"Why?"

The master did strike Finn, then, a blow to the side of his head. Finn seemed to feel his brain bang into the side of his skull.

"Do as you're told," said the master. "Open your mouth and keep it open."

Finn opened his mouth. The master began to stuff the squares of paper inside. "Now chew them up and swallow them like a good boy."

Finn's mouth was already parched but he did as the master told him. The taste of the ink made him retch.

"Swallow!"

The side of his head where he'd been struck thudded with pain. With an effort he swallowed the paper down. It felt like sandpaper on the back of his throat.

"Show me!" said the master.

Finn opened his mouth again to show him the paper was all gone.

"Very good," said the master. "Now, follow me."

The master strode away from the broken machine, yanking Finn along after him with the chain. He stopped some distance away from the machine and sat down. He hooked the end of the chain through his own belt and locked it in place, ensuring Finn couldn't escape. Then he lay down and closed his eyes.

"Sleep if you want. Just make sure you don't disturb me, boy."

Finn sat down. There was a rock embedded in the ground near his hand. Could he prize it out? Bash the master over the head and escape? When he was sure the master was asleep, he set about working the stone free. But it was too large, buried too deep. After an hour of scraping away the skin of his fingers he gave up. It was no good. He would never be able to escape the ironclads. At least he still had his secret. Still had that hope. He lay down, losing himself to fantasies of seeing Engn, that vast mountain range of machinery, explode in a fireball. Later, he slept and dreamed dreams of his old life back home.

"I wanted to talk to you about Matt," said Finn.

His father was stripped to the waist, fixing one of the Baron's threshing machines. To Finn they always resembled giant beasts, the raised chutes their heads. They were the largest machines they had in the valley. This one stood near a field cable point from which his father powered a light so he could inspect the interior workings of the machine. The cables under the fields were buried especially deep so that ploughs didn't cut through them, and there was no line of lightning-stakes, only marker posts embedded in the hedgerows to indicate the line. In the summer, they used the cable points to power pumps to water the crops. His father had to dig down deep to find the outlet, sealed in a waterproof metal case.

Finn peered at the blackened, oily mechanism of the thresher, trying to make sense of its workings. His father, not looking round, snorted with amusement at Finn's words. "What about him?"

"Well, the thing is, when you work at the Switch House, you see all the communications passing through. I mean, you're *supposed* to, to check everything is functioning."

"Aye, and so Mrs. Megrim gets to know everybody's business. She knows our secrets before we do."

"Well, she's not the only one."

His father turned to look at him. His hands and wrists were black with oil. The spanner in his hand was black, too, so that hand and spanner looked like they were joined. Like he had a spanner for a hand. "If it's something about Matt then you shouldn't be telling me. You shouldn't be telling anyone, should you?"

Finn sighed and looked around at the field, an expanse of mud and spiky stubble from the previous year's harvest. "I think I should. There are things people need to know."

His father looked at him, eyes narrowed beneath bushy black eyebrows. "Oh?"

Finn stooped down to pick up the bottle of cider his mother had given them and unscrewed the top. He handed it across to his father.

"The thing is, he's been sending messages to Engn."

There was a pause while his father drank. He handed the bottle back to Finn. It was smeared with black oil.

"Messages about what?"

Finn sipped at the sweet, sharp drink. "About us. He tells them everything about us."

"Such as what?"

"He said I was clever, quick-witted." He didn't mention everything Matt had said. *Still physically weak. Might make a good master one day if he could be tamed.*

"He told them about you?" asked his father.

Finn nodded. "He must have told them about Connor, too. And Shireen, and everybody. I mean, how else could the ironclads know about us all? Someone must let them know."

"Surely he would encrypt messages like that."

Finn set down the bottle and pulled the rolled-up tube of papers from an inside pocket. He handed them over. "There are still ways to read them if you know how." He hoped his father wouldn't ask for details.

His father unfurled the sheets and began to read, brow creased, lips moving with each word. Finally, he looked back at Finn, his face flushed red beneath the grime and the black of his beard.

"I'll kill him. If I thought he was responsible for anyone being taken…" He raised his spanner like an axe, ready to charge off and bludgeon Matt to death there and then. "Finn, you wait here."

His father strode off across the fields, heading for the gate and the lane beyond it, the thresher forgotten. Turnpike Cottage wasn't far away.

Finn raced after him. Not quite believing what he was doing, he ran around to block his father's way.

"No. We have to be careful."

"To hell with being careful! I'll kill him."

"But if anything happens to him the ironclads will suspect. They'll come here."

"He's not going to get away with this."

Finn was nearly as tall as his father now, although still stick-thin in comparison. Their faces were close together. Finn spoke quietly, almost whispering, although there was no one around to hear.

"No, but I've been thinking. There's a way to stop him without attracting any attention."

His father was breathing deeply, trying to control his anger. Finn marvelled at the way his father, his own father, was listening to his advice.

"If anything were to happen to you, Finn, I couldn't live with it."

"That's why we have to be careful."

His father sighed. "You are the clever one, Finn. He got that right at least. You're your mother's son. Tell me."

"Let's have some more cider."

His father nodded, his chest still heaving. They returned to the threshing machine and sat with their backs against it. The metal was warm in the glow of the spring sun. They passed the drink between them. The cider soon made Finn feel lightheaded and detached, as if he wasn't really there in the field with his father, planning Matt's fate.

"The thing is," began Finn, "Matt's a useless lengthsman." The words were slippery. He tried to concentrate. "You know it. Everyone knows it. Without help he couldn't do his job properly. Without *your* help. The lanes would become rutted, the cattle would escape, the drainage channels would silt up, and the electricity supply would fail."

"You're suggesting I stop helping him."

"Exactly! You can just say you're busy. I mean, you *are* busy. Sooner or later everything will fall apart and the village won't put up with it. They'll have to find a new lengthsman. Matt will be turned out of Turnpike Cottage and then he can't send any more messages to Engn."

His father was quiet for a while. Finn began to worry he'd spoken out of turn, that his father was angry. The implication of his words was clear. By helping Matt all these years, his father had allowed the lengthsman to keep his position and carry on making all his reports to Engn.

When his father finally spoke, his voice was quiet.

"I can see the sense of it. I'll have to be canny, cut down slowly the help I give him. It'll take time to work, Finn, and I won't wait forever."

"I'll intercept any messages he sends from now on."

His father nodded, frowning. "Okay."

They sat together there for some time, finishing the

cider. *Another secret pact,* thought Finn. He wondered how many more there would be.

For two or three weeks, nothing happened. Finn began to think his father had changed his mind. Twice he caught his parents in hushed, earnest conversation when he came into the room. Perhaps they'd decided to do nothing after all.

But, one morning, late for the Switch House, Finn dashed out into the garden and bundled straight into Matt coming up the path, axe and shovel over his shoulder.

"Whoa, young man. Late again? Don't want to get into trouble with Mrs. Megrim, eh?"

"No."

Finn dashed past, but when he was out of the garden he stopped and peered around the stone wall to see what happened.

His father was at the door now, talking to Matt. Finn couldn't hear their words. His father nodded once or twice with his head, pointing up the valley. They conversed for perhaps a minute. Finally, Matt walked back down the garden path, alone.

Finn took off a boot, pretending to knock stones from it on the wall. Matt swept past him. For once, the lengthsman didn't smile, didn't say anything. Staring at his boot as he tied it, Finn grinned to himself.

Four months later, Finn stood outside the Moot Hall, leaning against the weathered, stone-like wood of one of the pillars. Muffled murmurs and the occasional raised shout came from inside. He could make out nothing of what was being said. They'd been arguing for nearly an hour.

He looked up at the wooded slopes of the valley, the trees like frozen explosions of leaves. He remembered the day he and Connor had watched the ironclads through the telescope. They'd never seen the moving engine again. He wondered what had happened to it.

Connor's father, the Baron, burst suddenly out of the hall, a babble of noise escaping with him. He looked furious. He saw Finn, thought about ignoring him, then stopped. They hadn't spoken since the day Connor had been taken.

"Says it's all our fault if the power fails and the carts get stuck. Our fault!"

Finn didn't know what to say. He wanted very much to tell the Baron all about the messages, about what Matt had really done. But, of course, he couldn't.

He wanted to explain about his own guilt, too. Because the truth, the terrible truth he had admitted to no one, was that Finn was secretly pleased Connor had been taken. Not that he didn't miss his friend every day. But Connor being taken made it even less likely *he* would be. Engn had to leave some behind and there was really only him left now. And the truth was, Connor would be able to survive in Engn much better than Finn could. Connor was strong; he could fight; he could look after himself. People naturally did what he said; he was his father's son. Finn wasn't any of those things. Connor just might be able to destroy Engn as they'd vowed, but Finn knew he would never be able to. He'd always known it, even that day by the river with Diane. He would never be brave or clever or strong enough. It was better that Connor had been taken.

He wanted to say all this but could not.

"What do you think they'll decide about Matt?" he asked.

"Oh, they'll kick him out. They just want to argue

about it some more rather than getting on with it. But I'm not staying to be told I don't know how to run an estate."

With a scowl and a shake of his head, he turned to walk away from the Moot Hall.

"I'm sorry about Connor," Finn shouted after him. "He was my friend," he added uselessly.

The Baron stopped and half turned. He nodded his head, then strode off towards his farm.

It was another half hour before the moot ended. Matt was the first to leave. Once again, he didn't speak to Finn as he brushed past.

It was a glorious summer that year, warm without being too hot, rain falling at night to keep the fields green and lush. Once, the sky beyond the mountains blazed vivid scarlet, the glow remaining visible long after the sun had set. People said they'd heard muffled booms in the night, felt their walls shake and skip. Some whispered it was Engn, burning. People looked nervous, afraid of what it might mean. Finn, secretly, was delighted. He wondered about Connor. The glow was there the following night, too, but by the third evening it had gone. Some were convinced Engn had been destroyed. They got on with their lives. No more ironclads came to the valley.

Now that the encrypted messages from Turnpike Cottage had ceased, Finn enjoyed working at the Switch House more and more. He began to take interest in the mundane communications that flashed up and down the valley, the petty gossip that had once so bored him. He and Mrs. Megrim shared many jokes, a raised eyebrow in the gloom enough to make them both snigger with laughter.

Best of all was Badger. His parents had given her to

him a few months back.

"Finn, we've got a surprise for you," his mother said one evening. "She's still just a puppy but she'll need lots of walks. You can take her up into the woods with you." She was a bouncy, black-and-white dog, all tongue and paws, her fur as soft as an owl's feathers.

Badger ran everywhere at full tilt. Sometimes, when they were out in the woods, he didn't see her for minutes at a time. She was just a rustle of undergrowth off in the distance, a twitch of ferns. But she always came back to him, tongue lolling. Together they visited all the paths and clearings he and Connor had once known so well. It felt as though he was discovering them all afresh, as if they were different woods to those he had played in as a boy. They would walk past the place by the swing where Diane had slept, or the tree he and Connor had hidden in from the avalanche, and Finn would tell Badger all about it, about what had happened there. His words sounded like stories he was making up. It was all so long ago.

Matt was long gone and the new lengthsman, Flane from down the valley, did his job without help from Finn's father. The harvest, when the time came around, was a good one, and the barns and storehouses were full for the winter. Badger grew bigger each day but still raced everywhere, full of enthusiasm for everything. She made Finn laugh just to look at her.

They often went to the glade, Shireen's glade. It was one of Badger's favourite walks. The path through the bushes that had once been so hard to find was now well-worn.

They went that way now, Badger dashing ahead of him, knowing the way. Finn followed. She'd come back to him sooner or later. He sat down in the glade to wait. The log was old now, crumbling to the touch, orange and soft like a sponge. Diane's blanket and the stuff wrapped in it, left there years before, had disappeared soon after she'd gone. Finn sometimes wondered who or what had taken them.

Badger came bursting through the wall of trees to stand in front of him, panting and wide-eyed. She flopped to the ground. Finn knelt down and stroked her feathery fur.

"I told you about this place, didn't I, girl? What happened here." He'd told her the stories often. She looked up at him, head cocked on one side as she tried to understand his words. "Shireen and Connor and Diane. I told you all about them, eh?"

He stopped and looked up, suddenly cold, like a shadow had passed over him, although the circle of blue through the treetops was as bright as ever. He was only troubled because of the rumours that had been flashing up and down the line-of-sight for the past few days. Ironclads. Ironclads in the valley again. He paid them no attention. It happened. Someone misunderstood someone else and everyone started panicking.

He stood up. His cheekbones ached as he clenched his jaws tight. He forced himself to breathe deeply. He was being ridiculous. He needed to relax. It was okay.

The trumpet-call cut through the warm air, sending birds racketing off through the branches.

When it had faded away, he looked back down at the dog, waiting to continue their walk. Of course, she had no experience of the ironclads, had no idea what their arrival meant. And what did it mean? Perhaps they were still tracking Diane, even after all that time. The thought filled him with dread. He had to find out why the ironclads were there.

"Come on, Badger," he said. "I think we have to go."

They were waiting for him at home. He saw the horses as he came around the turn in the lane. He thought about running there and then. But they couldn't have come for him. His father had promised him he was safe. His father and mother would explain everything, sort everything out when he got home. Badger kept glancing up at him as they approached, unsure what it all meant. The horses were tethered to the fence, just as they had been for Shireen. They were smaller than he remembered, but still massive in their black and silver armour.

There was silence as he opened the door and walked inside. His father sat at the table, his head in his hands, face invisible. Two ironclads stood behind him. His mother was filling a canvas backpack and wiping tears from her eyes as she did so. She strapped the patchwork blanket from his bed to the top. The master stood behind her, with two more ironclads beside him. The master was young and handsome with straight, blond hair. Only the mocking look in his eyes spoiled things. He smiled.

"Finn," his mother said and rushed towards him to squeeze him tight. "Finn, Finn. I'm sorry. I'm so sorry."

Looking over his mother's shoulder at his father he could see now that there was blood on his father's hands. He was covering a wound on his forehead. What had happened? Had he tried to fight the ironclads?

"Father? Are you all right?"

His father looked up, squinting through the pain. He held a rag to his forehead, soaked through with blood.

"I'm fine, Finn."

"You said they wouldn't take me. I don't understand. Tell them they can't take me."

He had never seen his father crying before, but there were tears on his cheeks now, rolling down to lose themselves in his great, bushy beard. He didn't speak again. All he could do was shake his head, clutching the rag to him.

His mother released Finn enough to look into his face.

"We'll put together everything you'll need," she said.

Within an hour they were lumbering down the lane. Finn could hear only the clanking and tinkling of the ironclads' armour and the occasional snort of a horse. His mount was already uncomfortable, her great flat back too wide for his legs. The shackles on his wrists prevented him riding properly. He already felt bruised, and each step of the horse sent another bang of pain through him.

His mother and father, his house, his garden – it all shrank away behind him. He would never see them again. But that was a nonsensical statement, too big to take in. It wasn't possible. He twisted his head back to watch them, his mother and father standing together, not moving, arms around each other. Badger was tied to the gatepost behind them, straining at the rope to follow Finn down the lane. It looked as if his father was holding his mother up, stopping her from sagging to the ground. They'd been allowed a few minutes only, a few words, before he was lifted onto the horse.

"Keep your head up, son," his father said. "Don't take any messing from anyone." He'd wanted to say more but couldn't. His wound still bled, a line of fresh blood running down the side of his face.

His mother had held onto Finn's hand as they started moving, walking with them. "I've packed your hat, and your warm jumpers, and everything you might need. Will you be all right, Finn?"

He didn't have a voice just then. He nodded, looking down on his mother's upturned face. Her eyes were raw.

"Here." His mother gave him a boiled sweet to suck; a taste of honey that would always remind him of her. "I've slipped a bag of them in. Take them with you. Perhaps they'll last you all the way there."

Finn nodded again, not able to understand what was happening.

They picked up speed and his mother had to trot to keep up, still clutching Finn's shackled hand.

"Finn, I…"

An ironclad, riding alongside, reached out to knock his mother's arm free. With a jerk of his helmet he told her to stop, go back. Obeying, disbelief on her face, she walked to a halt and then stood, the rest of the ironclads passing around her. It looked to Finn as if she was moving away from him, receding backwards into the past, into his former life, with each jolt from the horse.

He watched as she disappeared around a bend. He looked at the ground, at the hedges. Everything he could see was utterly familiar. He knew each boulder in the ground, the twist of each trunk in the hedge. They were his world, seen and not seen thousands and thousands of times. He told himself once more he would never see any of them again. He still could not grasp it. He watched a stump in the hedge slide by, a stump that always looked to him like an old woman's face, creased and wrinkled. Old Mrs. Hampton, he thought. He had never pointed it out to anyone. He never would, now. He wanted to cry but he felt too stunned, the feelings too vast to squeeze through his eyes.

Up ahead, Mrs. Megrim stood at the side of the line at the foot of the Switch House path. He thought she was going to shout something to him, but when they were near, she stepped out in front of the master on the lead horse. She looked tiny and frail standing there, as if the gentlest wind would blow her away. Wisps of grey hair swirled around her head. She would surely be crushed by the horses' armoured hooves. But she refused to yield. Her eyes were black pebbles. The master and the ironclads reined in.

Saying nothing, she picked her way between the horses. She stopped in front of Finn, put her hand on his leg. Making sure no one else could see, she showed him the folded square of paper she held in her hand. He couldn't take it with his hands tied behind his back, so she slipped it into the pocket of his trousers. The look in her eyes made clear what he already knew. This was important. He mustn't forget. It was a look he was well used to. He tried to smile at her.

The master at the head of the column goaded his horse into action with a jab of his heels then, reasserting his authority over the troublesome old crone. The spell broken, the others lurched forwards to follow. Mrs. Megrim had to scurry to the side of the lane between the flanks of the horses. Finn's last sight of her, turning his head backwards, was of a crumpled huddle of black in the dust at the side of the road where she had fallen.

They walked on, past the crossroads and Three Tree Hill. On and on, down and out of the valley.

X

They rode like that for three days, Finn shackled to his horse or, at night, either to one of the ironclads or to a post hammered into the ground. They took turns to watch him. He saw no chance to escape.

They were soon farther from home than he'd ever ventured before. The buildings and trees looked more and more strange. They resembled those he knew but had different shapes and formations, as if someone had taken his familiar world and jumbled it up.

Whenever they passed through a village, the people stopped to watch them go by, saying nothing, sullen eyes staring. Finn knew from their faces what they were thinking. *Don't stop here, don't stop here.* Or perhaps, *Thank the stars, they've already taken someone. They haven't come for one of ours.*

He slept little. Again and again, he slipped into memories of his old life, awaking with a sickening shock to his surroundings each time. Sometimes it seemed his memories were real and solid, and the relentless plodding of his horse was a nightmare he repeatedly slipped into. He would fall sleep, only to jerk awake again as he slumped forwards. Occasionally an ironclad leaned over to prod him with a gauntleted finger. No one spoke to him. He was an object, a package, a sack, to be delivered to Engn.

They were passing through a stand of trees early one evening when he finally succumbed to sleep. He found himself falling sideways off his horse. He was still attached by the shackles behind the saddle so that he was left dangling by his arms, face near the ground and the great stamping legs of the horse, his shoulders pulled at a painful angle.

The master called a halt and came over. He dismounted and looked at Finn for a time, amused at the sight of him. The sharp pain in Finn's arms grew with each second.

"Is that how you ride where you come from?" the master asked. There were snorts of laughter from the ironclads, a rare sound from them. "It's an interesting technique."

"I fell off," said Finn.

"Ah, did you? You're supposed to hold on, you see. With your knees. A shame no one explained to you."

"I fell asleep."

The master sighed. "Oh dear. I didn't realize it was past your bed time." He took a key from his robe and, reaching up, unshackled Finn from the horse. Finn crashed to the ground face-first, unable to get his numb arms down to save himself in time. There was the immediate taste of blood in his mouth and a sharp pain in his nose. He spat out soil and turned over.

The master stood over him, shaking his head.

"We're going to get nowhere at this rate. We'll stay here tonight. Tomorrow we'll meet up with the Eagle column down at Fiveways. They should have room in their engine for you."

"Their engine?"

"They have a moving engine. I believe you've seen one

before?"

"Please, no. I can ride properly. I can stay awake; I promise I can."

The master shook his head. "You can sleep all you like in the engine. Right now, you should stop your nose bleeding. You're making a mess of the woods."

He turned away to instruct the ironclads to begin setting up camp.

They rode a short way the following day, to a point where five lanes met. A spur of the woods came close to the road there, but there were no buildings, only a wooden signpost indicating where each road led. The other ironclads were already there: three of them with a master and, steaming and hissing, one of the wheeled engines. It might have been the same one he'd seen all those years ago.

The two masters conversed for a while. Then Finn's master returned. He nodded to the ironclads. "Put him inside."

Finns struggled, trying once again to rip his hands free of the shackles that held him. "No!" he shouted. "Please, no!"

He was still struggling as the ironclads grasped his limbs and carried him to the waiting engine to hurl him inside.

The jumble of white buildings sat alone in the middle of the wide green plain at the junction of their track and numerous others than ran crossways. A single yew, the only tree Finn had seen since they left the mountains, towered over the walls, as if carrying them under its great wide arms.

Beyond, towards Engn, the country changed. Earth and stone had been heaved up into great mounds, as if someone was trying to construct a new mountain range. Here and there he could see piles of broken, rusting machinery. Pools of oily water reflected the mounds like mirrors. The air smelled of oil.

"What is this place?"

"The Halfway House," said the master. "We'll stay here the night."

Behind them, the moving engine ticked and clanged as it cooled. The ironclads had left them, leading the steaming horses to a stable block that adjoined the Halfway House. Finn and Master Whelm stood alone in the courtyard. The master seemed subdued, reluctant to follow the soldiers inside.

"Why is it called that?" asked Finn. "We're nearly at Engn now." The great machine loomed behind the Halfway House, looking close enough to touch. He'd felt the thrumming of it through his feet as he climbed out of the moving engine and stretched life back into his limbs.

"When the foundations were laid five hundred years ago and the first wheel was put into the En, this place was halfway to the mountains," said the master. "Engn has grown since then."

"And when we get there tomorrow ... what will happen to me?" asked Finn.

The master turned to look at him. With the wind hugging his purple cloak to his body he looked smaller and thinner than usual.

"Your father was a blacksmith?"

"Yes. Why?"

"Who you are counts for a lot. I mean, who your people are, whether they have guild connections. Shouldn't but it does."

For once, the master seemed willing to talk. It occurred to Finn that no one talked much to Master Whelm, either. The ironclads kept to themselves and the master rode in silence. He was free, of course, and people did what he told them to. But still, it had to be lonely.

"What did your family do?" Finn asked.

The master shook his head, dismissing the question. He spoke quietly. "Nothing grand anyway."

"My friend Connor was the Baron's son. He was taken to Engn a few years ago. Do you know him?"

"Engn isn't like that little hamlet of yours, boy. There are thousands and thousands of people there. But the son of a Baron won't be stuck on the Seventh Wheel for the rest of his life, you can be sure of that. That's the way it works in Engn, lad. Maybe he wasn't just another pair of hands for the factories or the mines; maybe they took him for a reason."

Finn thought about the master's words. That was good news. If Connor could work his way into a position of influence, perhaps into this Inner Wheel, then surely he would be able to find some way to sabotage Engn. He would be there even now, working on his secret plans. There was hope.

"Why do they even need so many of us? My father said I was safe because my sister had been taken."

Whelm shrugged. "Once that might have been true. I told you, Engn has grown. It needs more and more people to build it and maintain it. A generation ago you and your friend might have been left alone, but not these days. That's why we're sent out. Although pickings are scarce — we hardly need all these ironclads to harvest a few scraps like you. There's been some talk of reducing the number of patrols, or of sending us further afield."

"So, what about you?" asked Finn. "What happens to you when we get back to Engn?"

The master stared at the Halfway House or, possibly, at the smoke and stone, the glinting metal of Engn beyond it.

He still looked unhappy.

"Enough talk, boy," he said, his old sneer returning. "I'll shackle you in the stables with the animals. We'll leave at dawn."

The following day, Finn was at least allowed to walk again, tethered to the horse by his wrists. This close to Engn there was little or no chance of escaping. The moving engine had been handed over to another master staying at the Halfway House that morning. They trotted slowly towards Engn, the master apparently in no hurry to reach their destination.

They passed through clusters of ramshackle huts: five, ten, twenty of them grouped around the scorched circle of a fire or the stone lip of a well. Men and women, thin and pinched and dressed in rags, flitted around drawing water, repairing their hovels, or just sitting and watching them vacantly as they passed.

"Who are they?" asked Finn. "What are they doing out here?"

"These?" replied the master. "They're nothing. Parasites. They huddle around the walls of Engn, begging for handouts."

"But who are they?"

"Who knows? Perhaps they have someone inside and they've come to be as close as possible." Master Whelm snorted. "It's pathetic. We should clear them all out, send them home. Cockroaches." He shouted his last word so it would be heard by everyone around. No one reacted.

"Some of these houses look like they've been here ages," said Finn. "One or two have the remains of stone walls."

"Oh, they didn't build all this, the wells and the walls.

These were the villages of the original builders of Engn, the first builders. Hundreds of years ago. All these scum have moved in since, spread over everything like a fungus. They squabble over their rotting planks while slowly starving to death."

An old woman – short, slight, frail – watched them as they trotted by. She held a sloshing pale of water in her hand. Her face was expressionless but she studied Finn intently, as if hoping to see someone she knew. Finn nodded at her. The woman frowned, turned and walked away, clearly concluding Finn was of no interest.

By the early afternoon, Finn stood at the base of the great cliff face walls of Engn. Except the walls weren't walls; they were a series of constructions and edifices joined together. Stone ramparts and the curving metal sides of vast tanks or furnaces. The sun blazed overhead but he could feel a greater heat from the metal on his back. The ground thrummed, dancing with regular *whumps*. He peered upwards. Fast-moving white clouds scudded through the air from over the city, giving him the clear impression that the walls were falling and falling forwards, threatening to crush him. The heat, the walls' height, the illusion of movement – all contributed to a dizzying feeling of nausea. He longed for cool water. The air smelled of ash and burned oil. Smoke billowing from the chimney above him formed a solid mountainside of black and grey, thick enough to walk up.

All the way across the great plain, part of him had wanted to reach Engn, to see up close the towers and turning wheels, to understand what they did, what they *were*. Was the city one great machine or a collection of many? Now that he stood at the walls, he found he wanted to step back again, to see the place from a greater distance, to try and take it all in. Up close he was no nearer making sense of it. The black iron pipes running horizontally around the walls above him were vast, surely big enough for him to walk through. But he could no longer see where they led, how they connected. He couldn't begin to guess their purpose.

In one of the stone sections of the walls, hundreds of small square windows ran in lines twenty or thirty feet up. Some blazed with light, some were dark, like blind eyes. What went on in all those rooms? Who moved around in there and what did they do? It seemed impossible, staring upwards, to understand it all.

He looked back down at his feet. The road from the Halfway House, paved with red bricks now, had taken them directly to a vast arched doorway in the walls. It would have been tall enough for a cart stacked high with hayricks to pass through. But the doors, wooden and banded with a crisscross pattern of iron strips, were locked shut. Twenty-four ironclads stood in front of them, muskets in their arms, unmoving.

Beside the barred door, leaning against the wall, stood a ramshackle wooden hut with a single window in it. Master Whelm awaited his turn to speak to someone in there, Finn's chain in his hand. Finn could see a bushy grey beard wagging inside the darkness of the hut, a hand writing something in a book as other masters reported in. Next to the hut stood a line of boys, six of them, all watching Finn. They were, he could see now, chained together by their ankles, the chain secured to an iron ring cemented into the wall.

"Who are they?" asked Finn.

"Today's newcomers. You'll be joining them soon."

Red-brick tracks fanned out in all directions from the gates of Engn. Just that morning he'd seen five or six groups of ironclads converging on the city, two of them with moving engines of their own. A clutch of boys or girls shuffled or rode along with each. How many people were brought there each day? And what happened to them all inside?

The boys by the wall watched Finn with a mixture of suspicion and outright hostility. Their clothes were all odd: unusual cuts and colours. Where were they all from? Two of them whispered to each other, something inaudible but clearly amusing. They laughed together as they looked at him.

Whelm's turn at the hut came, and he stooped to speak to the old man sitting inside, just a beard and a nose sticking out of the darkness.

"Another for you, Master Gatekeeper."

"Just the one, Whelm?"

"Just the one."

The gatekeeper peered out at Finn. He caught a glimpse of bright beady eyes, a frown.

"You needed a moving engine to capture that? Doesn't look like he could put up much of a fight."

"Kept falling off his horse, didn't he?"

There were sniggers from the gaggle of boys. Wherever they were from, they clearly understood what was being said. Master Whelm handed something in to the gatekeeper, a small strip of metal with numbers on it.

"Fine, fine, I'll book him in," said the gatekeeper. "Not going to be one for the ironclads, though, is he?"

"No," said Master Whelm.

"Name?" said the gatekeeper.

Master Whelm elbowed Finn in the side to make him answer.

"Oh. My name is Finn."

"Finn what?"

"I, I don't know. Just Finn."

There were snorts of laughter from the other boys now. Finn heard them whispering to each other. *Doesn't even know his own name.*

"You must have a family name too?"

"No. I'm just Finn."

"What does your father do?"

"He's the blacksmith."

"Very well. Finn Smithson it will be."

"What will he do inside?" asked Master Whelm.

The gatekeeper examined the strip of metal, then began turning the pages of his book. "Ah, yes, here he is. Interesting, interesting. He has potential, I see."

"Potential for what?" asked Finn.

"Of course, it all depends on whether he passes the tests," said the gatekeeper, ignoring Finn. "And hardly any do, of course. So many try and so many fail. But he's a possibility."

"What do you mean?" said Finn. "What are these *tests*?"

The gatekeeper began to scratch away in his book with a metal pen. Without looking up again, he waved Finn over towards the group of boys. The master pulled Finn away from the hut and set about shackling him to the chain alongside all the others.

"What did he mean about the tests?" asked Finn.

Master Whelm shrugged but didn't reply. When he'd finished with the ankle-lock he stood back and looked at Finn.

"Goodbye, then, boy. Good luck with … everything." He looked like he was going to say something else, but instead he turned and walked to his ironclads, not looking back.

Finn smiled at the lad beside him: a tall, gangling, black-haired boy in green clothes. He had an intelligent face. But he scowled in response. None of the boys spoke to him. Some eyed him suspiciously, as if he was to blame for them being there. The others ignored him completely.

The sun blazed hotter and hotter. A narrow line of shadow ran along the foot of the walls and the boys huddled there, despite the heat radiating from the metal. Finn sat on the ground and leaned against the wall. His back was soon sticky with sweat. He longed even more for cold water. He longed for a honey sweet, but he had eaten the last of them days ago.

Far across the grass plain, the mountains of his home were a faint, pencil-sketch line on the horizon, no longer solid. Somewhere partway across, between the mounds of earth, he could just see a group of figures, black sticks shimmering in the haze. Perhaps it was Master Whelm heading back to the mountains, or another group being brought to Engn. He wondered, again, what it was all for. What exactly they had been brought here to *do*. He wondered if Connor had once sat in this same spot, asking himself the same questions.

They stayed at the foot of the wall for several hours. Two more boys joined them in that time, brought in by a pair of ironclads. They were both stocky, strong-looking boys, farm laborers maybe, who clearly knew each other well. They talked in low tones to each other as they were led to the wall. They resembled each other a little, Finn thought. Cousins maybe.

Finally, without warning, the great doors began to creak open. Glimpsed through the widening crack, Finn could see they were hauled by thick chains that ran to two floor-standing steam engines inside. Walls reached up beyond the engines: more sheer walls of stone and metal. Here and there he could see windows and doorways. Winding around and through everything ran a confusion of pipes and ducts, wires and walkways. Distantly, he could see people up on the walkways, appearing and disappearing in and out of the entrances. He was reminded of ants he'd once found within a broken machine in his father's workshop. Tiny insects crawling around in a vast machine they could never hope to understand.

A large open square lay between the gate and these inner workings. People stood there, hundreds of them, all in regimented lines a fixed distance apart, none of them moving, like pieces in some vast chess game. He could make no sense of what they were doing. He glanced at the other boys, but each looked just as puzzled as he was. Puzzled or alarmed.

The ironclads standing in front of the gates moved aside, then, to let someone through. A new master strode out. He was older than Master Whelm. His purple robes were trimmed with gold. Three rings adorned his left index finger where Master Whelm had worn only one. Fifth Wheel.

Finn and the others scrambled to their feet. The new master strode up to them and stopped to inspect them. He was a squat, ugly toad of a man, but his head was that of a pig, his eyes black specks. He held his mouth open as he gazed at them, as if in dumb bemusement at what he was seeing. But his voice, when he spoke, was hard and clear.

"My name is Master Owyn," the new master said. "From now on I am your father and your mother and your sister and your brother. You will do what I say. Do you understand me?"

Without waiting for a reply, he turned to the ironclads standing by the great gates.

"Unshackle these boys," he said. "And bring them inside Engn."

XI

Master Owyn stepped towards the tall, dark-haired boy standing next to Finn. He pinched the fine hair at the boy's ear between thumb and finger and lifted. The boy's delicate skin stretched painfully. He cried out and tried to balance on tip-toes to reduce the tugging.

"I said, do you understand, boy?"

"Yes, master. Yes."

"Better. From now on do as I say, yes?"

"Yes, master."

Master Owyn released his grip on the boy. They stood in an eight-sided open space, the Octagon the master had called it, deep inside Engn. They'd marched for hours from the gates to get there. Finn's head throbbed from the terrible rush and noise of it all.

He'd have no chance of reaching the gates if he tried to retrace his steps. He could recall only an endless maze of clanging metal walkways, around and between and *through* the machinery. They'd walked beneath shining steel pistons the size of tree trunks, pumping in and out; over vast tanks of seething molten metal; through booming, echoing pipes that Finn expected to flood with roaring water at any moment. They'd walked in silence through immense halls of racketing machines moving at impossible speeds, snapping so fast Finn couldn't even blink quickly enough at each *clack*. Past vast wheels that drove metal axles revolving at alarming speeds, or else clattering metal chains, the links of which were as big as his whole body. Walking close to the wheels was a dizzying experience; their constant motion made him feel it was the solid ground that lurched and spun. Either that or the wheels had shaken themselves free of their frames and were cartwheeling forwards to crush everything in their path.

They'd ducked underneath or squeezed between ducts and pipes of all sizes, from the tiny to the vast, some freezing and some burning to the touch. All of them numbered. Somebody, somewhere, knew them all and where they went. At one point they'd worked their way around a circular construction with countless metal rods protruding from it, like a giant's crown. Sparks of blue electricity leapt between the rods, zig-zagging their way upwards into the sky. A spider's web of cables spread out from the tower, hundreds of them leading off in all directions, towards other parts of the machinery. Finn had tried to follow some of the wires with his gaze but there were too many, crisscrossing, splitting, joining. The cables, too, were all tagged with a number. How could anyone understand it all? Some of the cables led to silvery glass orbs, like large incandescent bulbs, that were embedded in the walls or sitting atop iron tripods. The lights didn't appear to function, however, as none were ever lit.

They'd walked in line through the machinery: around and over and under countless buildings whose purpose he couldn't begin to guess. Except they weren't buildings. They were housings, tanks, cylinders, casings. People lived and worked there, threading their way past spinning wheels, ducking beneath chains and belts, but these weren't buildings built for people. They were merely components. Parts of the machine.

The air was solid with crashings and roarings, the ringing of bells and the clashing of metal, the taste of smoke and burning metal. Lights blazed and fires roared. A growing pain in Finn's head banged along with all of it. Three times a nearby explosion made Finn jump in alarm. Once, deafened by some roaring flame, he didn't hear a shouted warning and was nearly struck by a swinging weight that swooped to and fro across the walkway like a giant pendulum.

Finally, much to Finn's relief, they'd stopped in the Octagon. He was utterly lost, utterly spent, but he didn't care. All he wanted to do was rest his aching body.

Grey stone walls stretched up all around them. Halfway to the top, the walls blazed gold in the bright sunlight, but the ground was deep in shadows. Windows dotted the walls, without any apparent pattern. Occasionally there was a flash of blue light from them, as if something inside had exploded in silence. Here and there he could see doorways that opened onto the yawning drop to the ground without a railing to stop anyone falling out. Above each doorway a black iron bracket protruded, holding a pulley for hauling up heavy loads. One of the walls was clearly part of the housing for one of the great wheels. *The Titan Wheel*, according to an embossed iron plaque. The square, iron end of its axle protruded through the wall, rotating in its bracket.

The floor on which the boys stood was fashioned from flints: hard, sharp shards of stone set edgeways into the ground like knives. It was a field of knives, waiting to cut anyone who stumbled or tripped while crossing. Finn could feel the edges of them through the leather soles of his boots.

"What is your name?" the master said to the tall, dark-haired boy, who stood rubbing the side of his head. The master's voice echoed off the high stone walls.

"Graves, master."

"Graves. Very well. You look like the oldest. Hopefully you've learned your lesson. I'm making you Warden. You're to keep order when I'm not around. Do you understand? You other boys must do as Graves says, yes?"

"Yes, master," they chorused with little enthusiasm.

Finn glanced up at Graves. The taller boy was grinning now, his eyes narrowed. The two stocky cousins, the farm laborers, standing on the other side of Graves, whispered something to him. The tall boy nodded his head and muttered something in return.

"Tomorrow you join in the great work of building Engn," said Master Owyn. "At sixth bell you are to gather here to begin your apprenticeships. Do you understand?"

Master Owyn nodded at the chorus of yesses.

One of the doors in the walls opened, some mechanism of black iron rods moving it from within. Two figures emerged to march across the flints towards Master Owyn. They wore scarlet robes, their features invisible inside their hoods. They stopped to speak to the master. They conversed for some time, Owyn occasionally glancing at the boys. At, Finn felt, *him*. He had the distinct impression the master was being given orders. Which wheel were these others from? He couldn't see their fingers to count their rings.

They finished their conversation and the two newcomers strode away. Finn watched them go. As they were leaving the shorter of the two turned his head to glance backwards, revealing the line of his chin and nose for a moment. He appeared to look directly at Finn. There was something familiar in the way the man walked, something about the outline of his face that Finn recognized. With a skip of his heart he saw that it was — it had to be — Connor.

His friend had been at Engn for four years now. If this really was him, he'd clearly already managed to work his way into a position of authority. He must have heard of

Finn's arrival and come out to give instructions to Master Owyn, putting some scheme into action. Only, it was the other hooded figure, the taller, who appeared to be giving the orders. Connor had barely spoken during the conversation, merely nodding his head from time to time. He also, Finn noticed, walked slightly behind the other as they strode away. Perhaps he was only an acolyte to the other man. In which case, would he be able to control Finn's fate? He didn't know. He didn't understand enough about Engn to make sense of anything.

"This way," said Master Owyn. He indicated a smaller, more ornate doorway in the wall to his right. Inside, they gathered in a cramped, cylindrical room. A flight of narrow steps wound up and up around the wall, the top of the stairs invisible in the gloom. A longcase clock stood against the far wall beneath the curve of the stairwell, its wooden case taller than Finn. A pendulum scythed backwards and forwards within it, picking through the seconds. In the very centre of the room hung a rope ending a short way off the ground. Its end was blackened and worn smooth. Like the stairs, the top of the rope faded away far above them.

Without pausing, the master bound up the stairs two at a time, putting Finn more in mind of a bullfrog than ever. Walking in line, the boys followed. As he climbed, Finn tried to understand how the spiral stairs stayed up without a central pillar of stone to support them. The edges of the steps were worn smooth and must have been there for years, but still he walked as close to the outer wall as possible as he climbed.

Master Owyn stopped at the top. He wasn't at all out of breath. He stood and waited on a narrow landing, a balcony with an iron railing around it and three wooden doors leading off.

"Come on, come on, hurry up. Do you good, toughen you up."

Finn peered over the balcony. The circle of floor was a

long, long way below. The rope dropped from a hole in the ceiling just above their heads down to the ground, just far enough away to be out of reach.

The master pushed open one of the doors and led the boys into a large, high room, its walls faded whitewash. There was a single window that rattled and rumbled in the wind. At Finn's first glance he saw rows of iron bars spaced out all around the room. But no, they were the black, metal railings of beds, twenty or thirty of them laid out with precise regularity all around the walls of the room. More beds, four of them, had been placed end to end down the middle of the room. On each bed was a small ziggurat of folded linen: blankets, sheets, a pillow. Next to each bed was set a square wooden cupboard, little doors open in readiness.

"Make yourselves at home, boys." The master smiled his unconvincing smile. "Take a bed each. You will be inspected each day to make sure they are made and everything is tidy. When you hear the sixth bell tomorrow, descend the stairs to the Octagon and I will show you what you must do."

Each boy ran for a bed, most of them already seeming to know which the better ones were. Graves ran for the far corner. The two stocky cousins took the beds next to him. Finn scurried off in the opposite direction to claim one of the beds at the opposite end of the room.

"Smithson! Not you."

Finn, not recognizing his new name, paid no attention. He headed towards an unclaimed bed, determined to reach it first.

"Smithson! Don't you know your own name, boy?"

Finn turned in alarm to see the master staring at him from the doorway, his face flushing red with anger. The other boys sniggered or tutted.

"Yes, master."

"Come with me. You're to ring the sixth bell to wake the others. You can pick a bed later."

Finn could feel the other boys' gaze upon him. Why was he being singled out? Graves and his lieutenants already seemed to resent him. This could only make it worse.

"Yes, master."

That night, when he returned to the dormitory, the only bed left was one of the four in the middle of the room, exposed on all sides. The others smirked when Finn dropped his bag onto it. Saying nothing, he unpacked and placed everything he owned inside the wooden cupboard. He unrolled his patchwork blanket and spread it over his bed. It was spattered with mud from his journey in the moving engine. But it made his bed seem like his own: a small, rectangular piece of home.

From somewhere outside, up above them, a cracked bell began to ring out. Finn counted twenty-eight. The other boys dashed for the door to clatter off down the stairs. Clearly someone had told them what to do. He ran after them, jumping two steps at a time to catch up. Outside into the darkness, across the flints and then back in through another door. The warm smell of food, stewed meat, enveloped him. He couldn't recall when he had last eaten, but he didn't feel hungry. The other boys sat down on long, wooden benches and began to eat voraciously. Finn, not wanting to be singled out again, sat and joined in.

That night, past the thirty-second hour, he lay in bed, listening and thinking. He was exhausted but couldn't sleep. He had his eyes open even though it was too dark to see anything. The slim brass case Master Owyn had given him while explaining his additional duties was clutched in his hand. He would be in terrible trouble if he missed the alarm and didn't wake at the right time. Perhaps anxiety about that was keeping him awake. The machinery of Engn still hummed in the walls. Some of the boys whispered to each other, although they were supposed to be quiet. He could also hear a boy he didn't know sobbing under his covers. A part of him felt pleased about that. It might distract Graves and the bigger boys from him. He lay and thought about everything that had happened. He tried to imagine the darkness was that of his own room, back home in the valley.

The attack when it came was sudden and unexpected. His covers were yanked from his bed and Finn was sent sprawling onto the floor. Three or four boys, laughing and whooping, kicked him and kicked him on the ground. One foot caught him on the nose, sending sharp pain through him. He cried out. He heard his wooden cupboard being tipped over.

"Give me his blanket! Give me his blanket!"

It was one of the two cousins. Croft and Bellow they were called, but he couldn't tell which it was who spoke.

"Out the window!"

Graves too was with them; Graves who was supposed to keep order when the masters weren't there.

The kicking and kneeing had stopped now as the scrum of boys moved away to the window. He heard it being pulled open and a roar of delight as something, presumably his blanket, was hurled out into the night. Finn tried to stand up, holding his nose with one hand.

The electric lights snapped on. Master Owyn stood in the doorway, open-mouthed shock on his face. The other boys jumped back into their beds. Some pretended, unconvincingly, to be asleep. Finn stood alone in the middle of the room, the sheets of his wrecked bed strewn about him, his possessions scattered on the floor.

"What do you think you're doing, Smithson?"

Finn swallowed, unable to find his voice for a moment. He tasted blood from his bleeding nose. He knew instinctively he couldn't say what had really happened. It would only mean more trouble from Graves and the others. He didn't understand why they hated him so much. He hadn't done anything.

"I fell out of bed, master."

Snorts of laughter sounded from all around the room. Master Owyn scowled.

"Make your bed and get to sleep immediately, boy. I'll talk to you about this tomorrow."

"Yes, master."

In the darkness, Finn made his bed as best he could. But when he climbed back in, it was clear he hadn't made it properly. The sheets were twisted and knotted around him. He shivered without his blanket. He lay curled up in a ball, his stomach churning with anxiety, listening out for the sounds of further attack from the other boys.

He suddenly remembered the brass case. He had been holding it but must have dropped it at some point. He couldn't feel it anywhere in the bed. He slipped out and, shivering in the cold, began to crawl around, feeling for it with his fingers. He was just beginning to think Graves and the others must have thrown it out of the window when he felt it, hidden beneath his little wooden cupboard. He scrabbled it out and climbed back into bed, still shivering, heart still pounding away.

Eventually, he fell into a troubled sleep, his first day in Engn over. Tomorrow would be another day he had to somehow get through. Tomorrow and all the remaining days of his life.

XII

The following morning, Master Owyn led them through another doorway off the Octagon. The bright light inside made Finn squint for a moment. Naphtha lamps, set in circles the size of cartwheels, hissed in the air just above his head, their acrid smell sharp as nails in his nose. He could see the metal chains holding them in the air stretching up into the shadows above him. The hall soared above him, its ceiling completely invisible. The stretching walls were windowless and grey, cut from large, regular blocks of bare stone.

The chinking and clanking of metal was clearer in there, the stifled roaring of machines a monotone hum in his ears. He breathed hot, muggy air that seemed to immediately sap him of his energy. He wanted to sleep but, of course, could not.

Most of the room was taken up by a vast, square, iron table. It was open in its centre, as if four rectangular tables had been placed together, but Finn could see it was a single item, each side perhaps fifty paces long. The legs were intricately cast with a design of interconnecting cogs. Stains marked its wooden top. It was clearly old, the sharp corners of the wood worn to smooth curves. A great many men and women sat at it, each working on a small metal object set on the table before them.

The artificers glanced up as Finn and the other apprentices arrived. They laboured in silence but Finn could see whole conversations passing between them in the looks they shot one another, the way they nodded their heads towards the new arrivals. Most wore joyless, blank expressions. Some smiled and others frowned.

The master turned and waited for them all to come into the room. Something approaching a smile had replaced his usual brute scowl, too. They stood in a semicircle before him, saying nothing. The master brushed something off the cuff of his gold and purple gown, then stared into the face of each apprentice until they were cowed and still.

He turned and picked one of the metal objects from a brass trolley behind him. He unwrapped it and held it up for them all to see, admiring it as if it was a wonderful fruit he had plucked from a tree. It was about the size and shape, thought Finn, of a sheep's heart. He had often watched one of the Baron's men butcher one of the creatures, fascinated at how it could flower into so much meat and offal and bone, at how much blood puddled the earth.

"You, Boyle. What do you think this is?"

"I don't know, master. A weapon of some sort?"

"Does it look like a weapon, boy?"

"Not really, master."

"Then why did you say it was?"

The boys sniggered at Boyle's humiliation. Satisfied, Master Owyn continued.

"These are self-governing valves. They are used throughout Engn. They are an essential component of countless mechanisms and devices. Without the miracle of this simple device, the machine would not function. You,

Croft, what did I say it was called?"

"A valve, master," said Croft. "A self-governing valve."

Master Owyn grunted, then held the device up to his eye to indicate there were holes bored through it. He rotated on the spot, looking at each of them as if through a telescope.

"Vapor or liquid flows through these bores. But the flow is moderated by the helical valve mechanisms within. As I turn this knurled wheel you will see a spring-loaded flange inside the tube closing. It is possible, by accurate turning of the various wheels, to control the flow of the liquid or gas down any one of three different channels or even back the way it came. Do you understand?"

He passed the device to Croft, standing at one end of the semi-circle.

"Pass it round. Examine it closely. You must each become adept at constructing these valves."

Croft glanced at it for a moment then handed it on to Finn, smirking as he dropped it unexpectedly into Finn's half-outstretched hand so that it nearly fell to the floor. The valve was heavy, almost solid metal. Its surface was highly polished, gleaming and black at the same time. Finn turned it over and over in his hands, noting the knobs and wheels the master had mentioned. He could make little sense of it. There were, in fact, a total of seven round holes bored through it of varying diameters, each meeting in the centre of the valve. A small plate riveted on one side of the valve presumably allowed access to the inner workings. A single, long number was etched onto the plate.

He could see no way of attaching the valve to any pipes or ducts; there was no thread or seal around any of the holes. But there must be a way. He passed the valve on, marvelling at the complexity of Engn. How were so many valves controlled? There must be hundreds under construction in the room, and a great train of the trolleys already full beside the table waiting to be wheeled away. They were *self-governing*, so presumably, they needed no adjustment once set up. But how were so many thousands and thousands of tiny wheels and screws adjusted so that water and gas flowed in precisely the right amounts to their correct destinations? How were they monitored and checked so that worn out ones were replaced before they failed? It was incredible that it all worked, that the great wheels turned without failing.

"Now, follow me," said the master, turning away from them, his cape billowing out around him.

He strode towards the table and indicated to Graves, Bellow and Croft three empty seats where they were to sit. To Finn's eye, the boys looked suddenly smaller as they sat down, like children at an adult's table. A man pushed another brass trolley around the inside of the table and he stopped in front of Bellow. Before him he set out, in a very precise and careful way, an array of metal objects that he picked from his trolley. They were the individual parts of a completed valve, Finn could see, the outer casing itself along with an assortment of delicate springs, clips, and bearings.

"Touch nothing for now," said the master.

He led the rest of the group around the table, stopping at each empty seat to indicate to one of them where they should sit. Soon there was only Finn left, and no unoccupied places around the great table. What did the master have planned for him now? The thought that it might, again, be some special treatment, something to mark him out from the rest, filled him with a flood of anxiety. He saw Croft nudging Bellow over by the doorway, nodding at Finn. Then Bellow said something and they both laughed, relishing in Finn's discomfort.

Finn carried on walking, following the master. They were on the opposite side of the great room now. Another entrance led off, its high wooden doors covered in scratches and scuff marks. These were barged open as another trolley-load of valve parts was wheeled in, granting Finn a glimpse of what lay beyond: an unlit passageway and, some way beyond it, another brightly lit room. He could also see, silhouetted against the far doorway, four standing figures: more ironclads by their outlines, protecting that far room. What went on through there?

The master stopped behind one of the artificers, an old man with a bald head and a bushy grey beard billowing from his chin. The man's head was slick with sweat from the lamps. Finn watched as he constructed one of the valves with a practiced flick of his fingers, placing clips and springs into the device with the greatest care.

The master tapped the man on the shoulder and he turned around quickly, startled, confusion clear on his face. It took a moment for his eyes to focus, so lost had he been in his work.

"This is the boy's place now," said the master. "Complete the valve you are constructing and go."

The man didn't move. He was clearly having trouble understanding what the master meant. "Go? But ... I've worked here forty years. Never missed a day. I can't just go."

"This boy is taking your place now."

The man looked at each of them in turn. "But where do I go?"

"Where did you come from?"

There was another pause as the man considered the question. "The western edge of the plain. Enloth in the Greendowns."

"The City of the Lensmen? Your people are glassworkers?"

"Once they were. That's all changed now, of course. That was why I came here."

"That is where you should go back to."

The man's lips moved, but no words came out. He looked at Finn as if he might be able to explain what was happening, then turned back to the table and the valve he was working on. *Forty years*, thought Finn. How many valves had the man constructed in that time? Had he sat

here, in this same chair, all that time? And what would
happen to him once he left Engn? The name Enloth was
distantly familiar from Mrs. Megrim's lessons. Hadn't it
been all-but destroyed in the Clockwork War? It had to be
many weeks' travel away. Could this man even make such
a journey?

The man completed the valve he was working on and
laid it gently on the table before him. He sat still for a
moment, staring at the completed valve, then at his hands.
They were rough and calloused, the colour of tanned
leather. The man breathed out, his shoulders sagging. One
of the trolleymen picked up the valve, wrapped it in a sheet
of green cloth, and placed it into his brass cart before
trundling on around the table. The man stood up,
collecting his tools from the tabletop.

"Leave the tools," said the master. "The boy will use
them now."

"Leave them?"

"Leave them."

The man stared at the tools in his hands for a moment,
his brow furrowed as if he were trying to understand some
difficult idea. Then he set the implements down. He
walked away from Finn and the master, back around the
table to the Octagon doorway. Finn expected him to look
around as he went, see the room one last time, say
goodbye to the other artificers, but he went with his eyes
fixed ahead of him, saying nothing. In a few moments he
was gone.

Finn sat down on the wooden chair, still warm from
the old man. The pieces of another valve were being laid
out on the table before him. He tried to see how they
might fit together, how the mechanism operated, but could
not.

"Instruct the boy," said the master, talking to a woman
who sat next to Finn, working on a valve of her own. The
woman nodded. She was younger than the old man,
perhaps the same age as Finn's mother. But her face was

expressionless, no warmth to it, as she glanced up at Finn. She had her brown hair tied back in a rough sheaf, giving her face a taut appearance. Her hands were as calloused as the man's had been. Once she completed the valve she was working on, she turned to Finn.

"Right-handed? Take the valve body in your left hand, and one of the pressure clips in your right. There's a slot right inside you have to hook it into. Twist it around as you push and it will snap into place."

Finn stared at the objects before him, trying to understand what he was being told. The *valve body* was obvious enough but there were any number of metal pieces that might be *pressure clips*.

"Here," said the woman, irritation clear in her voice. She picked up a crescent-moon shaped metal strip with a saw-like edge and gave it to Finn. "Place this end in the trunk tube and twist it into place."

Finn tried to follow the woman's instructions. He managed to work the clip into the hole but couldn't get it to clip into place.

"Press harder," said the woman. "You have a child's fingers."

Finn tried to twist the clip around. It was hard inside the narrow valve tube. He scraped off skin from around his knuckles, exposing delicate pink flesh that pooled with blood.

"Harder. This should only take you a moment," said the woman.

There was a snap as the clip fitted into place and, immediately, a shock of pain in Finn's index finger. He cried and let the valve thump down to the table. His finger was bleeding openly, the pain raw. It looked as if its tip had been sheared off by the serrated edge of the clip.

The woman smiled and held up her own right hand. The curved end of her middle finger was gone too, although it was healed over.

"You'll get the hang of it," she said. "Once the

bleeding has stopped, try the other clip. The trick is to pull your finger out of the way at just the right moment."

Finn wrapped a rag around his bleeding finger, the oil on it making his wound sting. He squeezed hard to stanch the flow of blood.

He looked around the room. No one paid him any attention. It seemed no one had even heard him cry out over the background thrum. Master Owyn had left. Directly opposite him sat Bellow and Croft, each of them lost in concentration, struggling to get their own clips into place. Finn watched them, waiting to see what would happen, whether they too would catch the ends of their fingers. He could probably warn them by shouting across the room. He decided not to. With comic timing, both managed to work their clips into place at precisely the same moment, dropping their valves and yelping in unison. Finn couldn't stop himself smiling at the sight of them.

"The man who sat here," said Finn to the woman. "What was his name?"

"No talking," she said, her attention back on her next valve.

Above the woman's head, on the wall, was a great brass counting frame made up of rows and rows of black metal beads sliding along horizontal runners. He studied it, trying to make sense of it. Each row was numbered. Finn watched as one of the trolleymen picked up a long wooden rod and flicked some of the beads to the right, consulting a piece of paper as he did so. The man glanced across at Finn, then clacked all the beads on another of the rows back to the left.

A tally of how many valves you produced. He could just make out a green, oval plaque next to his row that said *56*. His number. He returned his attention to his valve. The bleeding had stopped now. He lifted another clip and prepared to work it into place.

They worked for six hours, then after a short break another six. Then another six. Half the day, all told. By the end, Finn's head throbbed and he could barely keep his eyes open. Three of his fingertips were bandaged. He followed Graves, Croft, Bellow, and the others out of the room and back into the refectory for more food. This time, at least, he was hungry and very, very thirsty. He ate the lumpy stew without talking to any of the other boys. At least the others also looked exhausted. With any luck they would be too tired to bother him that night.

In the end they came for Boyle in the next bed. Finn lay with his head under his covers, listening as the other boy cried out in pain. Graves, Bellow, Croft and a couple of others took turns punching Boyle through his bedclothes. The contents of his cupboard were thrown out of the window. They threatened to hurl Boyle out, too. The rest of the boys said nothing and did nothing. Finn, relieved they weren't attacking *him*, did nothing either. What could he do?

Plans for escape, for the destruction of Engn, buzzed around in his exhausted mind. He wondered if Connor had ever slept in this room. He shut out the sounds of Boyle's bed being lifted and turned upside with the boy trapped underneath it. Within moments, he fell into exhausted asleep.

The small brass case Master Owyn had given him on the first evening woke him at three quarters to the sixth bell. Finn slept with it under his pillow, now, terrified he wouldn't hear its gentle buzzing. It was a clock of sorts but with no dial or hands, no features at all except for a small square hole on one side. And, embossed in tiny figures on its base, the number *520*. You could hear a gentle ticking and whirring from inside it if you put it to your ear. The little device woke Finn every morning, so that he could ring the sixth bell to wake up all the others.

He rose and dressed as quietly as he could. A thin light slanted in through the window. The other boys were stationary shapes underneath their blankets, breathing peacefully as he crept past. Boyle, next to him, hadn't managed to right his iron bed. He lay asleep on just his mattress, knotted up in a tangle of sheets and blankets.

Finn stepped out of the dormitory, closing the door as gently as he could so that he didn't wake anyone early. He crossed to the door on the far side of the balcony. He ran across as quickly as he could, conscious of the great gulf of space beneath him. The balcony, like the winding steps, had little in the way of support to hold it up. Through the other door was the cramped spiral of wooden steps Master Owyn had shown him. They led up higher and higher before opening into a small dusty room filled with wooden crates, cobwebs, and broken beds. A square skylight above his head gave him a view of the clock tower overhead and, elongated by the oblique angle, the face of the clock he had to time himself by.

The big hand of the clock leapt a whole minute at a time. Finn had been told to wait for the moment it jerked onto one minute before six, then race off immediately. He then had exactly that minute to run down the spiral stairs and start pulling on the bell-rope. If he ran, he would get there just in time.

Engn was a place of bells. A bell was always ringing somewhere, clanging nearby or tolling in the distance. Very often two or three would argue away at the same time, trying to shout over each other. The bells, Master Owyn had said, told everyone what to do, where to go. There was a language to them. A code. Each had its own particular tone or timbre. Some were leaden, booming roars. Others rang out reluctant notes, repeated at long intervals. Some were barely audible. But each was different. The boys would be in the refectory, or milling around in the Octagon, when Master Owyn would stop speaking and cock his head, listening. *The Quarter Bell*, he would say, or *The Change Bell. Hurry now.*

To Finn, there was never any discernible difference to the clamour. It seemed incredible everyone heard *their* bells and went to where they were supposed to be. What happened if bells were missed, or late, or early? Did everything just stop working?

It was his job to sound the Sixth Bell to wake up all the other apprentices in the morning. He'd been told very clearly to make sure he rang it each day at just the right moment. If he didn't, everything would go wrong.

"Why don't I just wait downstairs by the longcase clock and time the bell by that?" he'd asked the master after he'd been given his instructions. Master Owyn had scowled at him. Trapped with him there in the tiny room, Finn had been suddenly afraid.

"Know best, do you, boy? You have to do it this way, by the tower clock. That's the way it's always been done."

"Yes, master."

Today he had a couple of moments to spare. The hand on the clock above him had just swept onto the notch three minutes away from six. There was time to try out his plan. He scraped one of the wooden boxes across the floor and set it underneath the skylight. Standing on top he reached up and tried to push the small window open. It was very heavy, its frame thick lead, but he managed to budge it a little. He looked around for something he could use as a wedge. Using a tube of black iron from a broken bedstead, he managed to lever the skylight upwards so that it stood vertically upwards.

Finn poked his head through the gap.

A wind, cold in the early morning, chilled his face. He

gazed out across a vast new world; a landscape of slate slopes with gutter-rivers running through it, the peaks of the roofline its mountains. Clumps of moss for bushes and woods clung to everything but the vertical cliffs of the grey stone buildings. He could see for miles, across acres and acres of roof. It was a wonderful sight. He felt the urge to climb outside and run across those slopes, just as he had once raced over the hills and valleys at home. Perhaps there was even a way to get back to the outer walls of Engn, to escape by leaping across them.

One of the great wheels turned just off to his left, its relentless churning motion filling him with alarm for a moment, making him think something was flying towards him. Along the ridge of the rooftop, a line of large crows watched him with a suspicious eye. He marvelled that they chose to say in Engn when they could fly away. Beyond them, visible between the ridge and the rampart of the clock tower, he could see a dome. Some green metal covered its curved surfaces and it had windows set all around its base, forty or fifty of them. The dome had to be huge. Finn tried to work out where it was in relation to the rooms and halls he knew. It was then he noticed the silhouette of someone in one of the dome's windows, watching him.

The head and shoulders of a figure, black against the lighted interior. Finn ducked down, knowing it was futile. Who was watching him? Master Owyn, perhaps, checking up on him? Or someone else? Perhaps it was Connor. Finn peeped back over the lip of the skylight. The figure still stood there. Now it moved. It opened the window, catching the rising sun in a blinding flash. Against the light inside Finn still couldn't make out who it was, but now he could see the figure waving. No, not waving, beckoning. Telling Finn to come.

He looked around. What did it mean? And how could he possibly reach the dome? The skylight was big enough to poke his head through, but his shoulders certainly wouldn't fit. He looked down at the frame of the window from the outside, to see if there was some weakness, some way of making the opening larger, but there was nothing. When he looked back up, the figure was gone, the window in the dome closed once more.

A bell began to chime, a deep metallic boom in the cold air. Finn looked up at the clock. It was already the sixth hour. He had missed his cue. With a gasp he hauled the skylight shut, jumped from the wooden box and hurled himself down the stairs.

He reached the rope in record time. The longcase clock still hadn't ticked over to one minute past. Finn began to tug on the thick rope snaking up into the campanile over the dormitory, working the swinging bell up to speed until, finally, it began to clang and clang to wake the other boys. He pulled on the rope for a minute and then strode off for breakfast before any of them came down.

His stomach fizzed with anxiety that someone would have noticed the late bell. He couldn't face eating the bread and butter laid out for them on the long wooden tables. Master Owyn, strolling around the edges of the room with his hands behind his back, glanced at Finn but said nothing. The other boys arrived in a clamour of shouts and laughter.

Finn began to relax. Chewing a mouthful of bread, he thought about what he'd seen. It couldn't have been Master Owyn in the dome because the master was there. Who, then? One of the other boys playing a trick on him? But that wasn't possible either. The others were as trapped as he was. Someone else he hadn't even thought of? Perhaps the stories about the wreckers were true after all, and one of them was trying to reach him?

He sat and thought about all this, and about Connor, and about the tests the gatekeeper had mentioned, until a bell rang to tell them it was time to return to work in the Valve Hall.

XIII

The following day, after their third stretch of valve construction, Finn and the other boys clattered into the Octagon to play scrum. In theory it was a ball game, with two clear sides and a definite set of rules. The ball was a sack of leather, sewn into a rough sphere and filled with some sort of stuffing. A doorway on each side of the Octagon was used as a goal, the aim of the game being to wrestle the ball into the opponent's doorway. In practice the game generally descended into a mass brawl, with a cluster of pushing, shoving, kicking boys lurching around the Octagon, the ball somewhere within.

Finn stood on the edge of the pack, watching as one of the older boys, Tanner, wrestled the ball away and began to pound towards the opponent's goal. Tanner was a magnificent player of the game: strong, fearless, fast. He could keep running with four, five, six other boys hanging off him. Tanner always scored and all the newcomers were in awe of him. Finn grinned at the sight of him. Tanner was on his team today, while Graves, Croft, and Bellow were on the opposing side.

Finn thought, once again, about the beckoning figure in the dome window. He'd looked again that morning but seen no one. And what, exactly, had the figure been telling him to do? Was he somehow meant to find another way onto the roofs, pick his way across to the dome? There were large gutters that could act as walkways, but was there a way to get all the way across? There might be some great drop down to the ground somewhere. Perhaps he was supposed to find some other way to escape the Octagon and the Valve Hall. He couldn't think how. In any case, perhaps that wasn't it at all. Perhaps the test was to discover whether he ignored the invitation, whether he resisted temptation. How could he tell?

The doorway that led out of the Octagon, the one they'd come through the day they arrived, wasn't too far away from where he was standing. The wrestling mass of boys was a long distance away, over in the far corner. He could creep out of the Octagon now without anyone noticing. He backed into the shadows of the wall. His heart thumped. He wondered if he dared do it. He remembered the day, long before, when he stood on the branch of one oak tree and thought about leaping across to the next. He *could* do it, he knew. Was that what the figure in the dome had wanted?

But if he did flee, what would he do then? He'd never be able to find his way to the dome, or even back through Engn to the gates. He'd be crushed in some part of the machinery, or the ironclads would find him and haul him back. He had no chance. But, still, it was tempting to try. Delicious to consider it.

"Smithson!"

A chorus of voices brought him back to the Octagon. He'd stopped paying attention to the game. Bellow was charging towards him over the flint ground, the ball tucked under his arm, a throng of the other boys racing after him. Finn was suddenly the only player standing in Bellow's way.

He could tell Croft and Bellow apart now. They were indeed cousins, and had grown up on the same farm, their mothers, sisters. Croft was the shorter of the two. He had a scar across his upper lip, an old wound that twisted his face into a constant scowl. His cousin was taller, his face unmarred, handsome even. Bellow was, if anything, crueller than Croft. When they attacked one of the other boys it was Bellow who laughed out loud at each cry of pain.

"Smithson! Stop him!" It was Tanner, pounding after Bellow but not close enough to catch him.

Finn trotted forwards into Bellow's path and prepared to try and stop the charging boy. Perhaps if he could hold him up for long enough the others would arrive to help. Bellow roared with delight and flew directly at Finn, one arm outstretched towards Finn's face, hand clenched into a fist.

Finn wanted to turn and run. Bellow, stronger and taller, would send him flying. But he had to try and stop him. Finn hated to be beaten. He *wouldn't* run. Bellow was only feet away now. The taller boy could have simply dodged around Finn, fending him off with his hand to score an easy goal, but instead he charged directly at Finn, intending to knock him flat. That was Bellow's mistake. Finn had learned a thing or two in all the games he'd played with Connor.

He waited until the last moment then, dodging underneath Bellow's outstretched fist, hurled himself into Bellow's legs. A knee caught Finn on the chin, making him bite his tongue hard, but he grabbed hold of the bigger boy's knees and squeezed, preventing Bellow from running.

Bellow, carried forwards by his own momentum, crashed face-first into the hard flints, the ball squirting out to one side. From his position on the ground, Finn saw Tanner pick it up and hurl it back into the throng, away from their goal. Tanner nodded at Finn then charged off to re-join the game. Finn rose to his knees and then to his feet. Nearby, Bellow also sat up, his hands clutched to his nose and forehead. Blood seeped between his fingers.

"You'll pay for that, Smithson. I've broken one of my teeth. I'll break all of yours."

Finn stood and simply grinned. He'd regret it later, but he couldn't help himself. "You should have a nice scar there," he said. "Now we won't be able to tell you apart from your cousin."

He turned and trotted off towards the mêlée.

After the game, they trooped back across the flints to wind their way up to the dormitory. Finn avoided Bellow and the others. Tanner had scored twice and Bellow's team hadn't scored any. Several boys patted Finn on the back for his tackle as they pushed inside the doorway.

At the bottom of the stairs they stopped to watch an old man descending the spiral staircase. He stooped under the load of a heavy weight strapped to his back that looked as if it would topple him forwards at any moment. The man grimaced with the effort of walking, staring at the steps in front of him, clutching the handrail with a mottled hand. He looked a little like the master in the little hut, the gatekeeper on the first day. The same nose, the same bushy beard. Were they brothers? His hair was an explosion of grey, wiry hair. He ignored the crowd of boys gathered at the foot of the stairs and pushed through to reach the longcase clock. The rope that led up to the campanile swayed slightly, as if someone had recently been swinging on it.

The old man squatted so that the weight on his back rested on the ground. He shrugged leather straps off his shoulders. The boys watched in silence, unsure what was happening. The weight, Finn could see now, was a wooden case containing another clock. An arrangement of gimbals cradled the mechanism, presumably so the man's movements didn't interfere with its accuracy.

A large ring of keys jangled on the man's belt: hundreds of them, large and small, silver and gold and dull steel. He picked through them to select one and unlocked the longcase clock. He slipped a pair of tiny, round glasses out of a pocket and perched them on his sharp nose. He began to adjust wheels and knobs within the longcase. Patches of pink scalp were visible through his wild grey hair. He turned to the clock he carried and compared the time, adjusting the longcase several times. Then, with his eyes shut, he adjusted the swing of the pendulum with a gentle hand, stroking it back into its proper path.

Finally, he locked the longcase clock back up, stood and took a small black leather book from another pocket. He wrote something down with a pen. Finn could see pages of text set out in columns, something like the line-of-sight logs from back home.

Only when the notebook was put away did the man appear to notice the boys. He gazed around at his audience. Most of them were much taller than he was. He looked suddenly like a cornered animal. Finn saw Graves nudge the boy standing next to him. Croft.

"Hey, old man," asked Croft. "Have you got the time?"

The boys sniggered. The man said nothing for a moment, simply staring at Croft as if he didn't understand.

"What's the matter? Don't you understand?" said Graves. Finn, watching the old man saw the briefest spark of something unexpected in his eye: a look of amusement. It was there for only the briefest moment. Then it was gone and the old man was a cornered rat once more.

The man turned to the longcase clock and reached up to tap its face, as if explaining to Graves what its function was. "Clock 519, acolyte's stairwell, synchronized to master time," he said.

He dropped to his knees, his back to his burden, and hooked the leather straps over his shoulders once more. With a grunt of effort, he straightened his knees and stood up, his back bent by the weight. He walked towards the boys who blocked his way into the Octagon. It looked to Finn like they weren't going to let him through.

But instead of trying to push through the door, the old man turned and began to ascend the stairs. Each step lugging the great clock was clearly a huge effort.

"Do you need help carrying that?" Finn called after him.

Most of the boys hooted and groaned. The old man glanced backwards. For the briefest moment, once again, Finn saw a different expression flash across his features. An intelligence, an appraising look. Then he shook his head and the look was gone, shaken loose.

"Clock 520," he said, nodding upwards with his head. "The Sixth Bell Tocsin."

Finn watched as, step by step, the great square clock wobbled its way upwards on shaky legs.

The other boys looked at Finn, some grinning, some shaking their heads. Graves stood, inevitably, with Croft and Bellow. They were not laughing. They scowled at Finn. He had spoiled their game. Twice this evening, he had spoiled their game. It meant trouble. Finn grinned at them but they didn't smile back.

Master Owyn heaved open the wooden door from the Octagon, then, to find the boys all standing there. Anger coloured his face.

"What are you all doing? Didn't you hear the Thirtieth Bell? You're supposed to be upstairs. Are you too stupid to understand?" He addressed his question to Graves, who said nothing.

Master Owyn stepped forwards and jabbed Graves hard in the chest with his finger, knocking him backwards. They were of an equal height, Graves and the master. For a moment, Finn thought the boy would retaliate.

"I asked you a question, boy. Why are you all still down here?"

"Waiting for him to go up, master." Graves nodded upwards towards the clock-winder.

"Waiting for whom? There's no one there, boy. Do you think I'm stupid?"

The boys looked up together. It was true. The long, winding stairs were deserted.

"Next time I give you instructions, I expect you to obey them," said Master Owyn. "Perhaps I should put Smithson here in charge, instead, eh? Now get to bed."

There was a murmured chorus of *yes, master*. One by one, they began to file upstairs. Graves, as he stepped forwards, glanced at Finn, a glare on his face.

Finn knew well what it meant. There would be trouble again that night.

XIV

Within two weeks Finn had mastered the art of constructing the valves. He still wasn't as quick as the older artificers, the woman who had trained him and whose name he still didn't know, but his hands had learned all the necessary movements and he no longer had to think about what he was doing. The work had become boring and the long days in the Valve Hall with its thick muggy air wearied him to exhaustion each evening. At least calluses had formed on his fingers and he no longer felt any pain as he worked.

Also, despite the cramping pain in his neck and back as he bent over the table, he found he almost enjoyed the work. He was, at least, safe there from the taunts and blows of Graves and the others. There was order there and a sort of peace. He could spend hours with his own thoughts, uninterrupted, while his hands worked. It was a rare luxury.

He thought about how his life had changed. It had always been understood he would take over the forge after his father. In a sense, Engn had freed him from that. He'd always known he would make a poor blacksmith. Matt had been right about that at least. Finn loved to understand mechanisms and contraptions, but he just wasn't strong enough. The thought of bashing lumps of metal all day filled him with horror. When he'd helped his father, pumping the bellows to make the furnace glow white-hot, or lugging ingots of iron, he'd only ever made it through the day by being elsewhere in his mind, making up stories in his head, daydreaming.

He wondered whether his father had ever felt the same, whether he enjoyed the work he'd devoted his life to. Perhaps his father secretly did what Finn did, wandering in his mind while his great arms did the work of shaping and beating metal.

Finn would never know. That was all gone. His life consisted of constructing self-governing valves to keep the wheels of Engn turning. And that, at least, was something he could do. Sometimes he found himself settling into his new life, beginning to accept that this was it from now on. It really wasn't so bad. He climbed the spiral stairs to the dormitory filled with dread each night, terrified at the thought of Graves and Croft and Bellow, but other than that he was all right. He had food and shelter. He survived.

At the same time, he knew these were dangerous, seductive thoughts. He *had* to get away. The figure in the dome window had beckoned to him. Engn had to be destroyed. Connor would have plans; a trail would have been laid for him to follow. One way or another, he was being tested.

The problem was, as each day passed, it became harder and harder to remember his burning hatred of Engn and everything it had done. It was still unimaginable he would be there in forty years like the man he'd replaced. The thing was, it *was* imaginable he'd be there for just one more day. And that was all it needed. *One more day* would eventually become forty years, and some as-yet-unborn master would be tapping him on the shoulder, telling him to leave.

Finn sighed and glanced around the room, already so familiar. He knew hardly any of the other artificers but in his mind, he'd already given many a name, judging them by their similarity to someone he knew, or some quirk of their features, or something in their actions. The woman who had trained him on the first day he thought of as Scowl, because that was all she did, working away in a cold, drawn-out fury. Next to her was an older man he thought of as Sigh. Each time he picked up the pieces of another valve he sighed audibly, as if uncovering some fresh piece of bad news.

On the other side of Finn sat Tanner. That, at least, was his real name. Or at least a part of it: his family cured and prepared animal hides for a living. *Tanner* had become his name just as Finn had been transformed into *Smithson* when he arrived at Engn.

Finn had been wary of Tanner at first. No one would ever dare haul Tanner out of bed in the dark of the dormitory and kick him as he lay curled up in a ball. No one would call his mother a cow or a sow to his face. But there was a vulnerability about him, too, if you looked closely. Something in the movement of his eyes that hinted at troubled events in his past. He wasn't really like the others. And much to Finn's surprise, he and Tanner had become friends of a sort.

No conversation was allowed, of course. But, as Finn had noticed on the first day, there was a great deal of unspoken communication around the table. Some of the artificers mouthed words. Others appeared to employ a more complex sign-language, subtle but quite clear if you watched closely enough. An extra flourish as they slotted some pieces of the valve together, fingers pointing or formed into shapes. There were two pairs of people who were clearly couples judging by the winks and smiles they flashed at each other. Elsewhere there was animosity. That was clear enough every time he caught Graves' or Croft's or Bellow's glance. Either they would narrow their eyes and glare, or else they'd briefly mime out the blows they intended to land on him that night.

And there were the whispered conversations between people sitting next to each other. It had taken Finn several days to notice it but then Tanner had spoken to him, not looking at him.

"Fingers healing?"

Once, when Finn was younger, a traveling circus had come to the valley. One of the acts had been a voice-thrower, with brightly painted wooden figures that he picked up and made talk. Finn had loved it. The man was able to hold whole conversations with them, so you soon forgot he was really just talking to himself. The skill you needed to talk to your neighbour was something like that. You had to speak without moving your lips. The other trick was to speak in a tone that resonated with the background hum, hid within it. You had to keep one eye on the masters, too. After half an hour, Finn had replied. "Better, thanks." He'd seen Tanner's nod from the corner of his eye, but the older boy had said nothing more.

The valves still puzzled Finn. He examined the one he was working on now, turning it around in his hands. He could not see how they functioned. One of the brass wheels you could turn was clearly not connected to anything inside the device. Was it left over from some earlier version of the design? No one else appeared to have noticed, and he still dutifully attached the wheel to each one he produced. He also couldn't understand how the valve directed the flow of liquids around as Master Owyn had described. Although he couldn't see inside the valves, he'd formed a clear picture in his mind of the various cavities and springs that lay within. He pushed his calloused fingers inside now, feeling for the slot into which he had to attach a pair of jaw-like flanges. The holes in the valve interconnected but he could see no way in which a flow could be directed down three of them. Nor did it seem possible the various flaps and flanges would be water-tight or air-tight when they were in place.

Anxiety that he was constructing the valves incorrectly buzzed constantly in his stomach, making him feel sick. The day before, Master Owyn had made a boy stand up, showed him a valve, spat words into his face, then dashed him to the floor with a blow of his hand.

"Made it wrong," Tanner had said.

The scene had played on Finn's mind all night. Now, he could contain himself no longer.

"What happens if you keep making the valves incorrectly?" he asked Tanner. "What do they do?"

Tanner didn't reply immediately. Had he perhaps worked it out too? Was he debating with himself what to say to Finn?

"You can make one mistake," said Tanner. "One that doesn't work. If you mess up another, they take you through there." He indicated a small doorway in the corner of the room with a backwards nod of his head.

"Where does that go?"

"It's the postern gate. Takes you to the mines. Underneath Engn, where the coal and iron ore comes from. More people than they need there. They work you into the ground. Maybe nine months and you're starved or crushed or you just drop dead from exhaustion."

"You're sure?"

"Trust me. No one who goes through the postern is ever seen again. If not the mines, it's the furnaces. You're used as fuel."

Finn spent his days expecting Master Owyn to call his name out. He had to be assembling the valves incorrectly because they couldn't possibly function. The master strolled past behind his back. Finn didn't dare look up. He was merely aware of the looming mass of anger and threat as it floated behind him. The rustle of the cloak and the thoughtful, questioning clack of shoes. Finn imagined raising his hand and confessing what he'd worked out about the valves. But he dared not. Of course, he dared not. He wondered if the man whose seat he'd taken had worked it out, too. Had he spent forty years not daring to say something, or had he spent forty years not aware his efforts were futile? Finn couldn't decide which would be worse.

He set to work on his next valve. A trolleyman pushed a cartload of completed valves through the doorway behind him. Finn made a mental note of it. Several days ago, he'd calculated how many valves were produced each day. A brass trolley held 144 completed valves. On the wall directly in front of him, over Bellow's head, was the ancient metal clock that ticked and paused and ticked away at the eighteen hours they had to spend there each day. On average, four full trolleys were trundled through the doors behind him every hour. Finn took pleasure in performing the calculations in his head. That made 576 new valves produced each hour. In an eighteen-hour shift that made 10,368. Then with the night-shift that took over when their work was done for the day, that was a total of 20,736 self-governing valves assembled each day. It was a colossal amount. Engn was vast, of course, but even so, did it really need over seven million – the exact figure eluded his ability to work out the numbers – of the valves each year?

He also knew they were all being watched. Not just by the masters that prowled around the edge of the room. There were others. Finn had discovered that if he pretended to yawn and stretch while waiting for a completed valve to be picked up, he could cover the lamp hissing away above him with his hand and glimpse what lay above. The walls rose to a ceiling lost in the shadows but, high, high up, he could just pick out a fenced balcony or walkway that ran all the way around the walls. Catching glimpses as he came and went, he'd managed to ascertain that it ran the full circuit of the room, but also that there were no steps up to it from within the Valve Hall.

He had several times seen figures up there. They were indistinct, mere shadows, as tiny as small birds perched in the top of a tree. Occasionally there was a glint of light: a reflection from glass or polished metal. Finn was more and more sure they had telescopes watching them. It always put him in mind of the day the and Connor had seen the ironclads down in the valley, hunting for Diane.

Were the watchers up there looking at the artificers or the masters? Were they aware he'd noticed them? He felt constantly self-conscious as he worked, not daring to glance away from his valve for more than a moment, feeling the glare of the unknown observers as a physical weight on top of his head.

Finn completed his twelfth valve of the day and waited for the trolleyman to come and give him the parts for the thirteenth. He picked up his set of feeler-gauges from the table, fanned out the blades, and held them up against the lights as if checking them. The thinnest blade, so flimsy that it was more like paper than metal, was badly creased and crinkled. He pretended to flatten it out while really gazing up at the high balcony. There were people up there. He wondered if Connor was one of them.

And if he was, what was Connor expecting him to do? It was at least possible that Connor had arranged for Finn to work in the Valve Hall. If so, there must be a reason for him being there. But what? Was he supposed to escape? Or was he supposed to sabotage the valves, deliberately introducing a flaw so that some vital part of the machinery seized up or exploded? He imagined one of the great wheels tearing itself loose in a cloud of steam and rolling across the city, flattening everything in its way. But could a poorly constructed valve cause something like that? And even if it could, surely the sabotaged valve would have to be placed in just the right place at just the right time? They knew who made which valves from the numbers on them. So, was Connor diverting those Finn made to some particular usage where they could do maximum damage?

But if he introduced a flaw, how would Connor know which valve was the one?

For a time, Finn had imagined there was some special significance to the numbers on each valve. He'd thought about each carefully, trying to work out if there was a hidden message in it; if perhaps *this* one or *this* one was the valve he was supposed to sabotage. He would try turning the numbers upside-down to see if they spelled out a word, or he'd look for a number that might represent some important date. But he'd never been able to convince himself any was especially significant. Now he ignored the numbers.

In any case, he couldn't be sure he was supposed to sabotage the valves. Perhaps Connor had been trying and failing to keep him *out* of the Valve Hall when he'd spoken to Master Owyn on the first day. Perhaps the whole place existed to weed out the troublemakers and machine-wreckers, see who did produce flawed valves so they could be sent off to the mines. Perhaps that was the test: be a good worker. But if so, why did people spend their lives there, dutifully creating valves?

An hour before they were due to stop work, Tanner spoke to him again.

"Over here, behind me. Look."

Finn was stretching his back, trying to ease the stiff pain in his neck. He glanced past Tanner at a boy he thought of as Beanpole because he was so tall and gangly. Beanpole was standing in front of Master Owyn. He said something Finn couldn't hear, showing him the valve he was working on. Was there a problem with his work? Or had Beanpole also worked out the valves were useless and found the courage to say so? There was further conversation then the boy was led away. Not through the Octagon doorway, nor through the entrance the completed valves were taken. Through the postern gate. Beanpole and the master stopped before it. They were close enough that Finn could hear their words. It was suddenly very hushed in the great room, all clanking and clicking of metal muffled.

"I was mistaken, Master," said Beanpole. "Please. Let me continue working."

The master indicated with the briefest nod of his head that Beanpole was to go through the small doorway. Two of the ironclads had appeared from behind Finn and they now pushed Beanpole forwards by the shoulders.

What had the boy meant? Had he assembled a valve incorrectly? But then he wouldn't have said *I was mistaken*. His words suggested he'd said something about the valves. The thought of that filled Finn with a thrill of anticipation and an iron weight of dread at the same time. Part of him longed to do the same.

He watched the small door close on Beanpole. He wanted to ask Tanner about the valves, find out whether he, too, had worked out they were useless. But he dared not. You never knew who was a spy for the masters, who was really a friend.

He began work on his next valve and said nothing.

XV

They came for him again that night. Finn was drifting away to sleep, exhausted, his thoughts a jumble of hands beckoning to him and fists swinging at him. He heard whispers and sudden running feet. Before he could do anything, he felt his bed lurching onto its side. He was thrown onto the floor. Graves, Croft, Bellow and several others stood around him. They kicked at Finn as he rolled around on the ground.

"Have you managed to remember your own name yet?" shouted Graves. "Master Owyn's little pet."

"Let's use *him* as the ball," said Bellow.

Bellow had lost the tops of two of his teeth when Finn had tackled him on the flints of the Octagon. Since then the bigger boy had gone out of his way to make life miserable for Finn. He'd held him under the water of his bath, keeping him there even as Finn struggled frantically. When Finn had finally escaped, naked and spluttering, Bellow had laughed and walked away. Once, he'd nearly managed to push Finn down the spiral steps. Finn had only saved himself by grasping hold of the banister. Bellow had then tried to tip him over the side. Finn, terrified, had managed to kick himself loose and sprint away, half falling down the stairs anyway in his desperate hurry to get away.

Now, as he huddled on the floor, trying to protect his head from the kicks, he suddenly knew he'd had enough. He was powerless to fight all these bigger boys. Graves, who was supposed to keep order, was the worst of them. No one was going to come to protect him. The masters didn't care. It wasn't some game of scrum where there were rules of a sort. He'd hoped things would get better if he stuck it out for a while but he could see they weren't going to.

In that moment he found he no longer cared what happened to him. Didn't care about Engn or Connor or any of it. His heart pounded away but his mind was clear. He knew what he had to do. His father had told him not to take any messing from anyone. They were easy words to say and, so far, he hadn't dared follow them. Now it was time.

The alarm clock lay on the floor where it had fallen from beneath his pillow. Finn grasped it in his right hand. It was heavy, solid brass. With a shout he fought his way to his feet and turned to face his attackers.

"You dungbrains," said Finn. "Don't you see what you're doing? We should be fighting *them*. The masters. Engn. They're responsible for everything. Are you too stupid to understand that?"

"You see," said Croft. "Told you he was a wrecker. Told you he was one of them."

"Filth," said Bellow.

"Come on," said Graves. "Let's get him. Let's sort him out for good."

It was dark in the dormitory, but enough light slanted in through the window for Finn to see roughly where the other boys were. Graves, the tallest, stood right in front of him. Without a sound, clenching the brass clock, Finn swung his right hand at Graves' face.

He connected with a satisfying crunch. The boy's nose, perhaps. The taller boy screamed and bent over. Croft and Bellow charged at the same moment, pounding at Finn's head and back with their fists. But Finn vaulted over his upturned bed and ran a short way down the dormitory, between the lines of beds. His attackers were between him and the window. He could see their outlines clearly, but they wouldn't be able to see him nearly as well. He crept forwards. Graves' muffled screams came from somewhere nearby on the floor. Croft and Bellow roared that they were going to kill Finn when they caught hold of him. Finn crept up behind one of them – he couldn't tell which in the low light – and dashed the brass clock against the bigger boy's head. It was Croft, judging by the scream. He staggered backwards, roaring with rage.

Bellow charged then, his outline clearly visible against the window. Finn stepped aside and thrust out a leg to trip him up. Once again, as on the Octagon, Bellow was sent sprawling to the ground.

Finn stepped away from them, back around to his bed, awaiting their next attack. He'd been lucky, but he wouldn't be able to fight them off again. The bed gave him some sense of security and safety. He thought about trying to prize one of the iron struts free to use as a weapon. It was futile really. He'd had it now.

At that instant, once again, the electric light flicked on and Master Owyn stood in the doorway.

"What is going on in here?" A livid scowl contorted his face. Finn, kneeling by his bed, didn't speak. Graves, Croft, and Bellow, he could see, had all staggered to their feet, each clutching wounds on their face or head.

"It was Smithson, Master," said Graves, his voice muffled by the bloody hand covering his nose. "He attacked us."

The master glowered at Finn, still crouched next to his upturned bed.

"Is this true, Smithson?"

The master would surely find it hard to believe Finn had beaten the three bigger boys. He barely believed it himself. "No, Master Owyn. They were fighting each other. They turned my bed over then started hitting each other. I don't know why."

"You little…" Graves charged at Finn. But Master Owyn's voice stopped him dead.

"Graves! Come with me. You other boys too. It looks like you all need stitches."

The three boys filed out after Master Owyn, a trail of blood drops on the floor behind them. Each glared at Finn as they passed. Finn simply smiled back. It didn't matter now.

When they'd gone, he righted his bed and lay down. He put the clock to his ear. He could still hear faint ticking. Hopefully it would wake him up. He could hear excited conversation and laughter all around him as the other boys marvelled at what had happened. Finn ignored them and tried to sleep. He would be safe enough for one night. Even if Graves and the others came back before morning, they wouldn't dare cause any more trouble just then. They would bide their time, thinking they could get their revenge any time they liked. But they were wrong.

Finn's head pounded as he rested it on the pillow. It was a long time before he finally fell asleep.

The next morning, he was already awake when the little clock buzzed away in his ear. He felt stretched taut as if he hadn't slept at all. Graves, Croft, and Bellow were back in their beds, white bandages visible around their heads. Finn grinned at the sight of them. He had the strangest urge to walk over to them, shake them awake, taunt them. Or bludgeon them while they slept. It was delicious to think they couldn't touch him anymore.

His right hand throbbed from one of the blows he'd dealt them with the brass clock. It was swollen when he compared it to his left hand. He shrugged and dressed himself as quietly as he could. He slipped the clock and a few other possessions into his pockets before he left.

"Smithson! What are you doing?"

It was Boyle in the next bed. They'd become friends, of a sort. Boyle was clever, witty – but he suffered because he struggled with the valves and was useless at scrum. Finn wished he'd helped him more, stood up for him more.

"Nothing," said Finn. "Just pretend you're asleep."

"But you're taking everything. Where are you going?"

"Nowhere, okay?"

Finn set off for the dormitory door. After a few steps he stopped.

"Boyle, listen. If they give you the Sixth Bell duty next, make sure you look outside. Through the skylight."

"What do you mean?"

"Just remember that, okay?"

"Okay, Smithson."

At the door, Finn looked back at the dormitory and its rows of iron beds. It was only a few weeks yet it felt like he'd slept there for months and months, almost as if he'd always been there. Quietly, he closed the door behind him.

Instead of crossing to the other door up to the little attic, he crossed to the edge of the balcony and reached out for the rope that emerged from its slot in the ceiling. He'd tried previously and knew he could just reach the rope with his fingertips. He didn't dare look down as he leaned over the balcony, the iron rail digging into his waist. One foot left the ground as he reached. He clutched the balustrade tight with his other hand. Alarm flared inside him at what he was doing but he kept at it, wobbling on his tiptoes.

Finally, he had the rope in his fingers. He scrabbled it

into his hand then pulled it towards him. He began to haul it up onto the landing. Its length made it very heavy and he had to stop two or three times for the strength to return to his arms, but finally he had it coiled in a great mound beside him.

He pushed the end of the rope through the handle of the dormitory door and hauled it through. Then he threaded it through the handle of the door opposite, pulling the rope taut between them so that neither door could be opened from the inside. He knotted the rope to hold it in place then lifted the remaining coil back over the balcony. It unwound itself with an angry hiss before snapping back into place. Distantly he could hear the clock chiming the Sixth Bell. He was supposed to be ringing the alarm now to wake them all up. Instead, he walked slowly down the stairs. As he always did, he looked for the secret door, the one the clock-winder must have used. He could see no sign of it. The rope, when he reached the bottom, now finished twenty feet or so off the ground.

He wasn't hungry, but he knew he should eat if he could. Sitting alone at the long wooden table, he ate bread and butter and drank two cups of milk. Boys and girls from other dormitories clattered in, filling the air with the clinks and scrapes of cutlery and crockery. None of the boys from his dormitory arrived.

Before they could, he hurried across the Octagon and into the Valve Hall. He was a little early, but he could just wait inside until it was his turn at the table.

He worked for half an hour, assembling two complete valves, before Graves and the rest finally appeared. Master Owyn shepherded them inside, fury visible on his face. Bellow glared at Finn, eyes narrowed, as he sat down. Finn smiled back and even dared to wave. The master strode around the table to Finn. He was shaking with anger; Finn expected to be struck in the back, thrown to the ground.

Instead Owyn spat words at him. "Come to me when you have finished your work. You will pay for this, boy."

Finn nodded in assent, knowing he would do no such thing, knowing it didn't matter now. He worked for another hour, and then another, losing himself for a time in the comforting, humdrum familiarity of constructing the valves. He could put them together with his eyes shut now. Sometimes he did, just to vary what he was doing. He knew the weight and feel of each individual component so well he could feel them, sometimes, when he was asleep, his mind continuing to work on them all night long.

He put his tenth valve down on the table and murmured to Tanner beside him.

"Tanner. Listen. I'm going."

"Huh?"

"I'm leaving today. Now."

"Don't be an idiot, Finn. Of course, you're not. You can't leave." Tanner's eyes were suddenly fierce. "What are you talking about?"

"I mean it. I'm going to talk to Master Owyn. You know what about, don't you? You're no fool. You've worked it out too, right?"

"Finn, didn't you listen? I've told you what happens. The mines. You won't stand a chance down there."

"I don't think the mines are on the other side of that door. How do you know if no one ever comes back? I think there's something else. And I'm going to find out what."

"Finn, you fool. Don't do this!" Faces were turned to watch them, now. A low hubbub of muttering spread around the room. Finn could see Graves grinning, as if this were all some scheme of his own invention. The older boy still wore a white bandage around his forehead and ears. Bellow and Croft sat next to him, not understanding what was happening, but happy simply because they thought Finn was in trouble.

Tanner seized Finn and pulled him close to speak into his ear. "Finn, listen. I know a name. If you're going to do this, try and find Lud. He's your only hope."

"Lud?"

"The leader of the wreckers."

"How do I find him?"

"He'll find you if he wants to. No one knows who he really is."

Tanner released him and returned to his valve just as Master Owyn strode up to them. "What are you doing, boy? You're in enough trouble as it is."

"Master," said Finn, standing. "May I speak to you?"

"Are you ill? Can you not work?"

"I must speak to you."

Master Owyn yanked him away from the table, pinned him to the wall and all but shouted into his ear.

"What is it, boy?"

"Sir, it's the valves. I've known for a long time. They don't work. They can't work. They're all useless, aren't they, sir?"

Finn regretted his words instantly. They were, they should have been, unspeakable. He felt as if it were someone else saying them, someone he was simply listening to. But *he* had said them. They could not be unsaid. His heart thumped and thumped in his chest. He watched as Master Owyn stared at him, jowls bobbing, mouth opening and closing like a fish out of water, anger building to a sharp point in his pig's eyes.

And Finn understood, in that moment, that Master Owyn was not a part of the conspiracy. That he was not going to congratulate Finn for his cleverness. That he actually believed the valves worked as he had explained to them on the first day. Master Owyn's role was to cow the artificers with his bluster and brutality, keep them in line, keep them working. But he knew nothing. His ignorance, his piggish stupidity, was clear on his face. They called him *Master* but he was no master. He was a slave too, controlled by those who really controlled Engn. The Inner Wheel. Master Owyn was as much a cog in the machine as Finn was, scarcely above him in the great scheme of things. Despite everything, Finn found himself feeling sorry for him.

"I never would have thought it of you, Smithson," he said. "Bellow or Croft, perhaps, but not you." He spat out the words, his distaste clear. Finn had to stop himself laughing. What did it matter?

Croft is too stupid to work it out, he wanted to say. *Bellow too.* But he managed to hold his silence. One of the ironclads clanked up to him and placed a heavy gauntlet on his shoulder. He turned to look at the guard, seeing his darting eyes through the thin slit of his helmet.

Finn glanced around the room. Graves, Croft, Bellow, Tanner, Scowl, Sigh. He would never see any of them again. It was a wonderful, dizzying thought. He'd been happy there, in a way, but it was a prison.

So it was that, with a wide grin, the ironclad urging him forwards, Finn pushed open the postern door.

XVI

Finn strode through the postern door, refusing to look backwards. The door closed behind him with a gentle click. Thick, solid darkness consumed him. He stopped, waiting for his eyes to adjust. He would be able to see soon. But, after a minute, two minutes, he still could not. The darkness remained complete, except for faint lines of light around the edges of the door behind him. He experimented with closing and opening his eyes to see if there was a difference. Nothing. He thought about pounding on the postern door, asking to be let out again.

No. He wouldn't do that.

He felt around with his outstretched fingertips. A rough, stone wall on either side of him, nothing ahead but cold, empty air. He stood in a passageway of some sort. His arms held out in case he walked into something solid, he shuffled forwards on the dusty floor, feeling for each step with an outstretched foot.

The passageway twisted left and right so he soon had no idea in which direction he was walking. The air smelled muggy, as if he were being smothered by old blankets. The faintest humming noise sang from the stone walls around him, but otherwise the only sounds were the tapping of his outstretched toe and the rush of breath in his own chest. Occasionally his fingers found one of the glass orbs set into the walls. If they were lights, he could find no way of switching them on.

As he crept along, he thought about Tanner's stories of the mines and the furnaces. He began to imagine that, at any moment, he would step onto nothing and plummet into a pit, tipped into the flames or onto the sharp rocks of some deep cavern. On three occasions he came across an iron grill in the floor. Welcome cold air breathed up at him, clearing his head a little. He had no choice but to step onto them. Each rocked and boomed as he crossed but remained solid. Once he thought he heard distant voices from down below, calls or screams. He told himself it was just his own mind inventing things.

He walked for a long time – hours it seemed – but found nothing. He had to be going around in circles; eventually he'd find himself back at the postern gate. Still there were only rough stone walls on either side of him, nothing ahead but cold, empty air.

Weary, he lowered himself to the floor, his back against the wall. He longed for water. His mouth was dry, his lips cracked and sore. Why hadn't he smuggled food and drink out from breakfast? He could die of thirst and no one would know. He thought about all the others who'd been sent through the door. Were they all still in there, fumbling about in the darkness, or else reduced to clumps of bones? He tried to still his breathing and listen for a sound, any sound.

Nothing.

He thought about the name Tanner had whispered. *Lud.* Who was he? More importantly, where was he? Somehow, Finn had to find him. Or be found by him. Was that the plan? Had Connor deliberately arranged for Finn to sit next to Tanner so the other boy could pass on the name? Or did Lud already know about him? Perhaps it had even been Lud waving from the dome.

How could he know? How could he possibly know?

The questions whirled around in Finn's head, each chased by a further question rather than an answer. After a while, he fell into a fitful slumber, his tired brain full of confused voices calling to him, telling him to come quickly.

Sometime later he jerked awake, thinking someone had shouted his name. But he'd dreamed it; the darkness enfolding him was as still as ever. He couldn't tell if he'd slept for moments or hours.

Heaving himself to his feet he trudged on. He began to walk with his eyes closed. His mind repeatedly drifted into brief dreams where he walked along a precarious mountain path, or else was back inside the moving engine trundling across the great grass plain. So, it took him a few moments to understand what it meant when his foot clanged against something iron blocking his way.

It was another spiral staircase, this one leading both up and down. By feeling his way around the walls, he discovered that the passageway ended there. He had to go one way or another on the staircase. Was he allowed to go up? Or should he just accept his fate and descend? Was this one of the tests or had he already failed? He debated for long moments, then stepped onto the staircase to wind his way upwards. He had nothing to lose.

The iron spiral boomed like a cracked bell with each footstep. It also swayed, as if it only lightly anchored to the walls. Finn climbed step by step, his mind full of visions of the staircase collapsing, of his own body crushed within tons of buckled metal. He scraped off flakes of rust from the handrail as he climbed. How old were these stairs? Who maintained them, repainted them?

He grew more anxious and more weary as he ascended. He could no longer allow himself to sleep for fear of tumbling all the way back to the ground. Instead, several times, he sat on one of the steps, head in his hands, and waited for his breathing to calm.

Once when he was young, feverish with illness, he'd had nightmares of being on such a staircase. But it was unending, with an infinite gulf of space all around him, and in his confused state he lurched between being tiny and immense. He was pinned to the vast staircase, insignificant, unable to move.

It was a little like that now. Dizziness wheeled inside his mind. He hadn't eaten for a long time. Hours? Days? He could only go on. He hauled himself back to his feet and continued the climb. He began to think he wasn't moving; that the staircase wound downwards into the ground as he ascended, leaving him stationary. That he would ascend forever until he dropped dead from exhaustion and rattled all the way down to the mines or the furnaces at the foot of the stairs.

The third time he stopped, looking up, he made out a lattice-work of light filtering through the treads of the steps above him. He was finally getting somewhere. He stood up and hurried on before his strength failed.

The staircase finally delivered him onto a circular landing. An alcove in one wall revealed a small round window, glassless, from which the light shone. Finn peered through and could just make out, far, far below, the naphtha lamps and the great table where the artificers assembled the valves. He could discern one of the masters – impossible to say which – creeping around the edge of the table down there.

If he'd had paper, he'd write a note and throw it down to those left behind. If it didn't catch fire on the lamps, he could tell Tanner and the others he was safe, that he hadn't been cast into the furnace or condemned to the mines. But he wouldn't want the message to reach Graves or one of the others. It was only their ignorance that prevented them coming up the stairs after him. And in any case, he had neither paper nor pen.

He wondered if he was near the high walkway. Pushing his cheek against the cold stone and peering upwards he could see he was only about halfway to the top. The underside of the high balcony running around the walls of the hall was far above him. Still no way to get up there.

He turned. Opposite the alcove were three doors. The nearest was wooden, its ancient timbers lime green with rot. Finn hesitated for a moment, then knocked on it. There was no reply. He could feel a keen draught blowing around its edges. He rapped again, hard enough to make his knuckles hurt. When there was still no reply, he lifted the rusty iron catch of the door and pushed.

The rush of air took his breath away. He stood on a narrow shelf halfway up one of the towering walls. Three or four pigeons clattered away in alarm. The drop to the ground yawned open in front of him. He grasped hold of the door handle. The wind made his eyes water.

Machinery stretched into a distant haze, the pipes and pistons and wheels of Engn. Down below him he could just see a corner of the Octagon, crossed by insect figures. He watched as four of them, ironclads he thought, moved in a line over the flints. One stopped and Finn felt suddenly very exposed. It was too far to tell if the ironclad was looking up at him, but Finn stood very still, afraid any movement might give him away. After a few moments the ironclad resumed marching.

Peering to his left, not daring to lean out too far, he could just make out the edge of a dome, most of it obscured by the tower wall. He was higher than it but he was sure it was the same one he'd seen from the skylight. Did it look a little closer than it had? Perhaps he was going the right way after all.

Directly in front of him a vast beam engine nodded to and fro, like a giant's seesaw or a titanic set of scales, one end powered by a steaming, huffing cylinder the size of a large building, the other end turning a wheel, half-buried in the ground. A wide belt, driven by the wheel, ran through the air some way below him to power some other part of the machine. The belt was as wide as the lane back home and sandy brown in colour. He thought, briefly, about trying to jump down and land on it, in the hope of getting nearer the dome. Of riding the belt across Engn. But he knew he wouldn't dare.

As he had on the day he'd arrived, he tried to spot signs of wrecker activity. Burned-out towers or broken wheels. There was nothing. The machinery hummed and roared away in all directions.

He looked into the sky, up the tall wall of stone reaching away from him. He realized where he was. Set back into the wall was the face of a huge clock, its lowest curve just level with his own head. The long hand pointed down at him, accusingly. A tiny number, 72, was etched onto the face below the vast number eighteen. It was the clock, or at least another face of the clock, that he'd used every day to time his ringing of the Sixth bell. The little attic room had to be on the opposite side of the tower and farther down. He hadn't really come a great distance after all.

Leaning out as far as he dared, one hand clutching the handle of the rotting door, he tried to see what time it was. Halfway to the twenty-seventh bell. Assuming it was still the same day, he'd been walking for nearly twenty hours. He wondered what people were saying about him. He imagined Graves and the others laughing at the thought of him down in the mines. Back in the darkness he'd almost begun to wish someone *had* taken him there. At least he'd have known where he was. At least there would have been something to drink. Wandering around alone was terrible. Where was he supposed to go? What was he supposed to do?

He stepped backwards into the alcove and shut the door. He turned to the next door along. This one was heavier, metal, tarnished with a patina of rust. He pulled on the handle but it didn't budge. A catch mechanism was built into the handle. He lifted this with a finger and heaved hard. The door swung open easily, despite its thickness and obvious weight. He peered inside, wary of another great drop on the other side, but a passage led away, lit by flickering incandescent lights set in regular sconces all the way along. More silvery orbs were set into the walls, all dark. He stepped over the raised lip of the door and into the passage.

He was a few steps inside when he heard running footsteps and the familiar rhythmic clank of metal. He stepped backwards, wary of tripping over the frame of the heavy door. An ironclad ran around the bend up ahead, with another following close behind. They both shouted at Finn, muffled words he couldn't make out.

The ironclad in the front unslung a gun from his back and held it up to fire at Finn. It wasn't one of the muskets he'd seen them carrying previously. This was a more complicated contraption that looked like it fired a grapple about the size of Finn's hand. Twenty yards away, the ironclad stopped running to steady his aim. Finn stumbled backwards over the doorframe in his desperation to get away. He heard the crack of a shot and raised his arms to cover his face as he fell.

He heard a whirring, whistling sound coming at him very quickly. Something heavy and hard thudded off the side of his head, knocking him sideways. At the same moment he felt cold metal grip his arm, very tight, pinching his hairs painfully. A steel chain wound itself around his arm. He couldn't understand what was happening, the blow to his head blurring his senses. The weighted grapple had latched onto the chain wrapped around his arm with barbed teeth, locking itself into place. Another grapple on the other end of the cable revolved faster and faster around his arm as the chain wound up to his elbow. He held it away from his head so that the grapple didn't bash him again. It thumped into the muscle of his upper arm like a blow from a hammer. Once again, serrated teeth snapped out, gripping the chain, the links designed to interlock with the teeth. Some dug directly into his arm, punching a line of red holes in his soft skin. He shouted out in pain and alarm. The chain was locked fast to him. The device must have been intended for his legs, to bring him down like one of the cows on the Baron's farm, but it made little difference. They had him.

He felt his arm being tugged. A thin line attached to the steel cable led back to the ironclad who was hauling him in, back through the steel door. Frantically Finn tried to scrabble to his feet, but the ironclads kept him off-balance, jerking him forwards. The other ironclad began to haul on the cable, too. He had no chance of pulling against them. They hauled and strode forwards at the same time, lessening the distance to him rapidly.

Finn managed to catch one of his legs behind the half-open door. It was his only chance. With a roar he yanked his arm backwards, hoping to give himself a few inches of slack to play with. He felt the barbs embedded in his arm rip out of his skin. He screamed with the pain of it. He had just enough play in the cable to take a scrambled step backwards and get his other foot behind the door. He braced his feet against the door and, with a shout of effort, kicked it shut, slamming it in the faces of the approaching ironclads. It rang with a booming clang. Finn fell backwards, the thin-line attached to his arm severed by the heavy metal door.

He scrambled to his feet as quickly as he could. The ironclads would open the door again and be upon him at any moment. He couldn't face going back down the stairs again. He thought, briefly, about lunging back through the balcony door. At least the drop would mean a quick end. No. His only option was the third door. He ran for it, hearing the catch mechanism on the ironclads' door rattling at the same instant. If the third door was locked, he was trapped.

The door budged a little as he pushed it, stiff in its frame rather than locked. Frantic, he barged through shoulder first. Once inside he slammed the door shut behind him. Iron bolts were set into the top and bottom of the door. He worked them shut, skinning his knuckles on the stone doorframe as he did so.

He turned to look around, expecting to see more ironclads coming for him. There were none. He stood inside the clock. The cogs and weights and axles of it filled the great square room he found himself in. Wheels with sharp teeth *whirred* near his head.

In the centre of the room stood an old man with a shock of straggly grey hair, a familiar bushy beard. The old man, the clock-winder, looked up from the workings to peer at Finn through small, round glasses. Beside him on the floor stood the oblong bulk of his regulator clock.

"Ah, there you are," he said. "It's about time."

XVII

"The ironclads," shouted Finn over the whir and click of the clock mechanism. "They're after me."

The old man waved his arm dismissively. "Not allowed in here, boy. Delicate machinery."

Did the old man mean he, Finn, wasn't allowed in or that the ironclads weren't? Finn stood by the door, expecting his pursuers to start hammering on it at any moment. "I'm … I'm not even sure I'm supposed to be in here," he said.

The old man didn't reply. He adjusted something in the great clock's mechanism, delicately positioning a weight on a balance that rocked backwards and forwards. He glanced repeatedly at the oblong clock he'd set down on the floor. Finally, satisfied, he took out his black book and began to write.

"Clock seventy-two, Western Grand Tower, synchronized to master time."

"I came through the postern door," said Finn, not knowing what else to say. "Through the passageways. I got lost. I don't know where I'm supposed to go."

The old man kneeled and heaved the clock back onto his back. He stood on shaky legs and began to walk away from Finn.

"I mean, why me?" said Finn. "Why was I given the Sixth Bell duties? Was it deliberate?"

"Think you're special?" the old man said, not looking back.

"I just thought, maybe, someone picked me out. Because of the tests."

The man paused. "Tests? What tests?"

Was this the same man? The clock-winder and the gatekeeper? He couldn't be sure.

"I don't know," said Finn. "The gatekeeper mentioned them when I arrived."

The old man snorted but said nothing. He continued walking away.

"I brought you this back," shouted Finn after him. The man stopped again and glanced around. Finn strode forwards, holding out the small brass alarm that had woken him each morning. He held his left arm, the one with the chain locked around it, behind his back, not wanting the old man to see.

The man raised a caterpillar eyebrow. He held out his hand. Finn worked his way between the cogs and spinning shafts to reach him. He had to duck under a silver chain that buzzed through the air at head-height. He handed over the brass clock. The man examined it and held it to his ear. He nodded at Finn, as if he'd done the right thing.

"What sort of ironclads?"

"What do you mean?"

"What company were they?"

"I don't know. I thought they were all the same."

The old man sighed in an exaggerated way. "Come with me."

Despite his age and the weight on his back, the man was nimble. Finn had to break into a trot to keep up with him as they worked their way through the clock mechanism. They reached what looked like a wooden cupboard door set part way up a wall. The old man twisted a clasp and opened it. Crouching, he stepped through. The clock on his back banged against the top of the frame and he had to resort to crawling on hands and knees. Finn followed him, squeezing his shoulders through the narrow gap, to find another passageway, its floor two or three feet higher than that of the clock room. He recalled how the old man had vanished halfway up the spiral stairs to the dormitory. Perhaps there were secret doors like that all over Engn.

They set off now down a flight of steep steps, turning through ninety degrees every seventeenth. There were no windows visible but incandescent bulbs flickered at each turning. There were more of the unlit silvery orbs half-embedded in the walls. He asked the old man about them but received only a dismissive grunt as a reply.

Finally, they stood on a circular red-tiled floor, highly polished as if worn smooth by the passage of many feet. A set of wooden doors stood in front of them. The old man found another key from his jangling collection and unlocked them.

Inside was a round, echoing space, with a large gold circle painted upon it like the dial of some sort of clock. A great many symbols Finn didn't recognize were marked around the ring at irregular intervals, along with the standard numerals for the hours, one to thirty-six. He watched, amazed, as a vast pendulum swung across the space with a *whoosh* of air. The gold disc on the end of it must have been twenty feet across. Finn could feel the rush of it on his face as it swept past. The pendulum paused at the end of its arc then cut back through the air, across the middle of the room. The old man, not breaking his stride, walked directly across its path. It missed him by inches as it roared by, but he appeared not to notice. Finn, wary, followed the old man. He waited until the pendulum was at the very far end of its cycle before hopping across the gold line that marked its passage. If it hit him, it would swat him away like a fly.

They stopped outside a smaller door. The old man picked up a triangle of cloth from a peg next to it and tied it around his nose and mouth. He held out a second triangle for Finn. Finn took the cloth and copied the old man. It had the warm smell of dust. The old man unlocked the smaller door and they walked through into a room that clicked and clattered with the ticking of thousands of clocks.

Finn looked around, dazzled by the array of shining, whirring mechanisms, brass and iron and glass. Whichever way he looked the movement of some or other device flickered away in the corner of his eye. What were they all doing there? Some were in pieces, being repaired, but most looked to be in perfect order.

High up above his head hung something that wasn't a clock: a large, metal sphere suspended from the ceiling, spiked with hundreds of tiny tubes. Black cables led off in all directions from the spikes to disappear through the walls or ceiling. Against the background cacophony, he thought he could hear a deep hum coming from the sphere. He walked beneath it warily, half expecting it to drop on him. As he passed underneath, the hairs on his head lifted, as if the sphere were trying to suck him upwards.

The old man, meanwhile, had stopped at one of the benches. With infinite care, he lowered the regulator clock he bore into an empty space among a jumble of dismantled mechanisms. At home, their most accurate clock had been Mrs. Megrim's. The Switch House received a message on the trunk line each day at exactly twelve o'clock. If anyone else in the valley needed to know the precise time, they could ask the Switch House. Which meant that the whole world followed the time on a master clock somewhere in Engn. Was it one of these? Was it even the one carried around on his back by the old man? Had Finn lived his life by that clock's time without knowing it?

He tried to ask, his voice muffled by the mask he wore over his mouth and nose. The old man waved a hand at him, urgent, instructing him to be quiet. He turned and, free of his burden, walked on through the room of clocks. Finn followed, picking his way over broken cogs and chains and digits strewn about on the floor.

Then, with a vast clatter, all the clocks in the room began to whir and chime at the same moment, all of them reaching the twenty-seventh hour. The sounds clanged in Finn's ears, coming at him from all angles, seeming to echo around inside his skull. The noise was incredible, but the old man didn't appear to mind. He looked around at the clocks, nodded in approval, then unlocked a farther door. He walked through, and once again Finn followed. Outside, the old man took off his mask and indicated Finn could do the same.

"One breath in the wrong place in there and all the timings get disrupted," he said.

"What would happen then?" asked Finn.

The old man only shook his head in reply.

They stood in some sort of library. Books, sheaves of paper, and rolls of parchment cluttered every surface: shelves, desks, the floor. Pools of candle light illuminated the scene here and there, leaving most of the room in shifting darkness. The smell of dust and paper and age tickled Finn's nose, making him want to sneeze.

The old man crossed to a desk and sat at a stool. A large book lay open on the desk, each page the size of a child's cot.

"Your number?" he asked.

"My number?"

"Yes, your number, boy. Are you stupid?"

"I don't have a number."

"Nonsense. Everyone and everything in Engn has a

number. How else could we possibly keep track of it all?" The old man indicated the snowdrifts of paperwork surrounding him.

"I'm sorry. I don't know," said Finn. "No one told me."

The man sighed and shook his head in amazement. "Name then? Do you recall that at least?"

"Finn," said Finn. "Finn Smithson."

"Very well."

The old man took out his glasses and, his nose almost brushing the paper of the book, feeling his way across the lines of text with his fingertips, began to read.

Finn smelled freshly baked bread. On a low table next to the desk, a meal had been set out for the old man. A jug of water and a glass stood next to a dome of silver mesh. The old man, seeming to sense what Finn was thinking, waved a hand towards the food without looking up, telling Finn he could eat. Finn needed no more prompting. He was lightheaded with hunger, his mouth dusty with thirst. He poured himself water then began to consume the bread, dipping it in a beef stew that had also been provided. It was good. Very, very good.

As he ate, he studied the old man. He was more and more sure this was the gatekeeper. It was surely the same bushy grey beard he'd seen inside the little hut. He replayed the memories in his mind. And now, as well as gatekeeper and clock-winder, the old man appeared to be some sort of record-keeper, too. The masters gave him no end of menial tasks. Was he being punished for something?

The old man continued to read, his fingers spidering along the lines of tiny black letters. Occasionally he shook his head and a plume of powder billowed out of his shaggy hair to drift down to the table, as if his brains were slowly crumbling to dust and falling from his ears.

With a thrill of alarm in his stomach it occurred to Finn that perhaps *this* was Lud. Perhaps he'd been meant to come up here and find the old man. Finn suddenly wanted to tell him everything. Connor, the pact, all of it. He'd walked alone in darkness for too long. He'd had enough of secrets and of hiding; he couldn't keep them all in his head. He wanted to ask what he should do. Whether he was on the right path. Whether he was passing or failing the tests. What he was being tested *for*. How to join the wreckers.

He was about to speak when the old man, with a snort, finished his reading. He looked up at Finn. His eyes were so lifeless and cold that Finn suddenly couldn't speak. If this wasn't Lud, he might be condemning himself by even saying the name. The old man stood and crossed to a shelf of smaller ledgers, bound with red-leather. Finn said nothing. The old man's back was slightly crooked as he walked, bent forwards, as if he were still carrying the clock. With a practiced heave he pulled one of the books off the shelf, carried it back, and slammed it onto the desktop in a small explosion of dust.

"Here you are," said the old man. "Interesting."

It was the word he'd used the first time, by the gate. If it was him.

"What's interesting?" asked Finn.

"Thumb."

"Pardon?" asked Finn.

"Show me your thumb, boy."

Finn held his thumb out and the man began to inspect it closely, screwing a brass eyepiece into his eye to do so. Finally, he grunted, looked at Finn, and said, "Yes, you're definitely you. So, bright spark, are we?"

Finn wasn't at all clear whether the old man thought this was a good thing or a bad thing. He examined his thumb but could see nothing different about it.

"I don't know."

"Quick-witted. Clever with your fingers. Good head for heights. Punctual too, apart from this morning."

"That's all written down in there?"

The man held up his hand to quiet Finn. "Brave.

Understands the line-of-sights. Smart. Definite potential. *Definite* potential. But where are you to go, that's the question, eh?" The old man peered up at Finn, as if expecting an answer from him.

"I thought, perhaps, I should have gone down the spiral staircase, not up. Down to the mines I mean."

"Ah, you want to go to the mines, do you? That could be arranged."

"No, I … no. I just thought maybe I'd taken the wrong turning. I don't know if I've done the right thing coming up here."

"People your age never do the right thing. You're all as bad as each other, dim-witted and confused. It's a wonder any of you survive."

"I thought you said I was smart?"

The man grunted and stood, the legs of his wooden chair making a sharp, grating sound on the floor with the sudden movement. He plucked a candle from a sconce and crossed the room. He began to study yet another book. Looming shadows danced around him as he read. Then he returned to Finn, his face screwed up into a scowl of disapproval, beady eyes like those of a bird perched on the chair. He studied Finn through his eyebrows.

"Do other people come up here?" asked Finn. "I mean, through the postern gate and up the spiral stairs? Have there been others before me?"

"Think you're the first do you?"

"I don't know. I just wondered. There was a boy recently. Very tall and thin. Did he find his way up here?"

"No idea," said the old man.

"Then tell me this," said Finn. "How do people become masters?"

"Eh?"

The idea had come to him at some point in his wanderings through the tunnels.

"Is that it? The tests? The masters need to find *new* masters so they give people useless tasks to perform to see who questions it. Perhaps they find out who would make good ironclads at the same time too, people who obey orders without question?" He didn't add that they might also be weeding out wreckers by looking for deliberate acts of sabotage.

"Oh, you think you're going to become a master, do you?"

Perhaps. Was that Connor's plan? But Master Owyn clearly hadn't understood about the valves, so maybe there was more to it. Maybe you had to reach a certain Wheel to be told the truth. And if the old man was Lud, Finn saying he wanted to become a master was not going to help his cause.

"I don't know," said Finn. "I just thought." How could he tell what he should do? It had all been so simple back in the valley. Join the wreckers, destroy Engn. But how did he actually do any of that? It was much more complicated in reality. He could only do what seemed to him the right thing at the time.

The old man was still peering at him, as if reading all the thoughts in Finn's mind. Then he opened a drawer in his desk and took out a wad of yellow papers. With a metal pen he wrote something, very slowly, on the top one, before tearing it off and handing it to Finn.

"You're to go to the Vault. Take this to them. They'll know what to do with you."

"Is that what the masters said I had to do?"

"It's what the book says."

"But who writes the book?"

The old man ignored his question. "You'll have to look out for the ironclads on the way. Hide from them. If you can't hide, I'd suggest running."

"But can't you just tell them to leave me alone?"

"Me? I just wind the clocks. They don't take orders from me, boy."

"What is this Vault? I don't know where it is."

"Don't know much, do you?"

Finn shook his head.

"Three miles away," said the old man. "Towards the Hub."

"I don't know the way."

"Take the Grand Junction Walkway. That goes straight there. Obviously."

"But I don't know even what *that* is."

"It's a walkway, isn't it, boy? A big one. Dear, dear, dear, the people they send us these days."

"Can you at least tell me which way I need to go?"

"That door, that door! Up the Drop Tower. Take the lift. Now leave me in peace."

The old man returned to examining his book. Finn looked across the room in the direction the old man had indicated. He could dimly make out several other doors over there. He thought about asking the man if he could wait until tomorrow. Sleep there, safe from the ironclads. Weariness weighed him down.

"Hurry along," said the old man. "You're running out of time."

What did that mean? Was he supposed to perform the tests by a certain hour? Why would no one explain the rules to him?

He stood. At least he was being spared the mines. Unless the Vault *was* the mines. Before he set off, he hesitated, then grabbed more of the bread from the table. He gulped down more water. He didn't know when he'd have chance to eat again. The old man appeared not to notice.

Finn picked his way between teetering piles of books and papers to the distant doors. There were three the old man could have meant, each a different size, each heading off in a different direction from the angled walls. Finn pushed open the middle one. A narrow, curving room lay beyond, with yet another flight of stairs leading upwards.

He was about to step through, but he couldn't leave without asking the old man one more question.

"Please," he said, shouting through the gloom to the bubble of flickering light where the old man worked at his desk. "Did a master called Connor tell you about me? Was it he who told you what I was supposed to do?"

The old man didn't reply, simply waving his arm again without looking up. Finn sighed and stepped through the door.

XVIII

Finn closed the door behind him. At least he couldn't see any ironclads. But he couldn't face climbing more stairs. He was so exhausted it felt like the ground was sucking him into it. The old man had talked about a *lift*. Perhaps it was something like the hay lifts back home.

The tips of his fingers tingled and throbbed from the chain wrapped tight around his arm. He tried to prize it off but the barbed teeth of the grapple were completely interlocked with the chain's links. He succeeded only in slicing open the tip of his thumb. Perhaps he should have asked the old man if he had a key.

He sighed and set off, walking past the steps, around the tall, curving wall on his right. He could hear a wooden *clumping* noise coming from up ahead. A little farther around the wall the room ended at another doorway, although there was no actual door. Instead there was a wall that, incredibly, rushed upwards, giving Finn the dizzying impression that he was falling. A gap in the wall flashed by, revealing, momentarily, a small recess like a wooden box.

It, too, rushed upwards, and then there was more wall. Was this the lift? Surely he wasn't supposed to jump into the little wooden room as it flashed by? If he timed it wrong, he would be cut in two by the wall.

He thought about stopping where he was, sleeping the night there. He worked his way back round to the door he'd come through, thinking he could slip back inside and hide in a dark corner the old man couldn't see. But the door was locked and couldn't be opened from that side. And if anyone came down the steps he would be trapped. He had no choice.

Going back to the lift, he stood in front of it for long moments, rehearsing the leap he would need to make each time one of the alcoves shot past. The top of one rose into view. Without thinking what he was doing, he jumped.

He was too quick, if anything. He fell a short way to meet the rising wooden floor of the room. His knees buckled as he landed, tipping him forwards. He fell into the corner and huddled there gratefully, afraid of having a leg or an arm severed by the lip of the wall cutting downwards. The alcove shook as it hurtled upwards. It smelled of wax and oil. The feeling of rapid movement made his stomach lurch with alarm. Darkness swallowed him as the lift bore him upwards.

He wondered how he would know when to get off. Then a doorway flashed by, giving Finn a brief glimpse of a landing with two masters and an ironclad walking by. Was he supposed to have jumped out then? The lift had to be on some sort of belt. When it reached the top, it would wrap around and descend again. If he didn't leave would he be thrown into the workings or just turned on his head?

The rushing wall began to lighten again. Another doorway approaching. Finn prepared himself to leap out. He wasn't quick enough. He had a brief glimpse of another figure standing framed in the doorway, surprise and confusion clear on his lined face as he saw Finn. Another master, perhaps, although this one wore orange robes. The master plunged out of sight and the wall returned. This time Finn noticed a small metal plaque on it that said, simply, *Two*. The floor he was approaching or the one he'd just passed? He moved as close to the falling wall as he could and peered upwards, waiting for the light of another exit. He saw one coming, the wall lightening to grey. If it was the wrong floor he could always leap back and ascend farther. There was another plaque. *Three*. Finn threw himself towards the light as it sped by. He sprawled on the hard stone of a floor. He tucked his legs out of the way before they could be caught by the lift.

He scrambled to his feet and looked around, his heart pounding. He stood at the edge of a round room. Open arches all around the curving walls let in an icy wind. He looked to be very high up. Within the room, nine or ten people sat in a circle, huddled around a hole that dropped into darkness. None of them noticed Finn. The only other exit was a square doorway on the far side of the room. He began to creep towards it, hoping to skirt around the sitters without them noticing. He passed underneath one of the glassy orbs set high into the stone of the wall. This one, too, was broken. He could see only his own reflection in it, weirdly distorted as he peered upwards.

A stone channel had been carved into the floor around the lip of the hole: a channel with molten metal flowing around it. The sitters used delicate metal spoons to scoop up the metal then drop it into the hole. It made no sense. The red-hot metal spat and bubbled, and Finn saw one of the sitters gasp and drop his ladle. The man held the back of his hand to his mouth. His hands, all their hands, were mottled with red welts where the molten metal had caught them.

The man glanced across the circle at Finn as he sucked his wounded hand. He said nothing but Finn had the clear sensation of being studied, like the man had deliberately burned himself as an excuse to look up. The others paid no attention, continuing to ladle the red-hot metal into the pit, drop after drop. Finn continued to edge around to the doorway, hoping no one would stop him or call the ironclads.

The square doorway led outside onto the grill of a metal platform with five walkways fanning off from it. It was night and, away from the molten metal, instantly very cold. He was higher up than he'd ever been before. The lights and flames of Engn were all set out beneath him, twinkling away to the horizon like the stars reflecting on water. He felt like he was floating in the night air, all the roaring and pumping sounds of the machinery hushed by the distance, a little louder then a little quieter as the wind gusted.

What had the old man said? The Grand Junction Walkway. If these were the walkways, then he presumably just needed to take the biggest. But they all looked the same. And it was impossible to tell how far any one of them went. Whether they even went anywhere.

"Finn."

Finn span around. The man with the injured hand stood in the doorway, holding his ladle.

"Finn? It is you, isn't it?"

Something about the man was familiar: his voice, perhaps. He spoke a little like someone Finn knew.

"I ... who are you?" asked Finn.

The man glanced around, wary. He wasn't supposed to be doing this. "We were told to look out for you. You've done well to make it this far."

"Who told you? Who are you?"

"You don't know?"

"No."

The man strode up to him and took his hand. Finn looked up at him. The man looked weary, strands of greying hair plastered to his flushed face. But his smile was wide. For some reason it made Finn think of the red apples in their orchard back home.

"Who are you?" he asked again.

"You won't recognize me I suppose."

Finn shook his head. He felt very exposed. He and the man would be visible to anyone looking up at them. Surely they could be seen from all over Engn?

"My name is Rory."

"I'm sorry," said Finn. "I don't know you."

"No. I left before you were born. But my mother knows you."

"Your mother? I don't understand."

But even as the man spoke Finn did understand. He knew who this was. A memory of his own mother came to him, a day they'd picked blackberries together. *Tom and Rory*, she'd said. *Both full of mischief.* Mrs. Megrim's twin boys.

"Ah, I see you have heard of me," said the man.

"You've spoken to Mrs. Megrim, then? I mean, to your mother?"

The man nodded. "She sends messages and they are intercepted. We have a mechanism that allows us to glimpse them arriving. From afar. They're not encrypted as such, but there's an agreed meaning to the words used. A code, if you like. Unfortunately, we aren't able to send replies. But she told us about you, told us to look out for you. Described you, said you were very young. She likes you a lot, you know."

The thought of secret line-of-sight messages about him sent a jolt of alarm through his stomach. If the masters read them, they would know he wasn't to be trusted.

"We?" he asked.

"The wreckers. You know about us, of course?"

Finn didn't reply, not daring to admit what he knew. For all he knew, Rory might be working for the masters.

"Your mother gave you my name?"

"She did. Don't worry, we're very careful."

That was something. He might not know Rory, but he trusted Mrs. Megrim completely. "But if you can't reply, then she doesn't know you've even received the messages."

"No."

"She doesn't even know you're still alive."

"No, she doesn't. Still, she sends them, on and off. Always has, since the time Tom and I came here."

He'd had no idea Mrs. Megrim had been doing that. In the years they'd worked together she'd never mentioned it. Of course, she hadn't ever mentioned her children either.

"Is your brother here too, then?" Finn asked.

"I don't know. I haven't seen him in years. We were separated when we arrived and that was that."

The man took Finn's arm and examined the ironclad snare locked around it.

"I see you've had a few scrapes. These things are the devil to get off. You're lucky, really. Some of the companies just use muskets if they're pursuing someone. Wait there a moment."

Rory disappeared back into the tower. The wind picked up, buffeting Finn, knocking him backwards a step. He was very glad the metal walkways had handrails to stop him pitching over the side. He could feel the floor swaying beneath him. He glanced down. He could see through the mesh to the distant lights of the floor. It looked a very, very long way down.

"Here, let's try this," said Rory. He'd returned with a stubby knife that he now took to the clasp at the upper end of the chain.

"Are you sure you should be doing this?" asked Finn. "What if the ironclads come?"

"A master of the Second Wheel watches us, but she only comes up once an hour. She doesn't need to stay because they just count the bearings at the bottom."

"Bearings?" said Finn.

"That's what we're doing up here. The metal forms perfect spheres as it falls. The drop is so great that by the time it reaches the ground it's solidified and you have perfect ball bearings. They're collected and used in the machinery."

"We used bearings assembling the self-governing valves."

"Haven't heard of those. What do they do?"

"I don't think they do anything."

Rory nodded, as if that made complete sense to him.

"How long have you been up here?" Finn asked.

"Oh, fifteen years now. It's a good place to keep an eye on what's going on. On a clear day you can see the entire machine." He stepped closer to Finn and spoke in a whisper. "We had a wonderful view of the fires the other month. The rebellion. We thought that was going to be it, the destruction of Engn."

"The fires?"

"Weren't you here then? It was the wreckers. Managed to overload one of the main boilers, blew it into the sky. I've never heard such a noise. The explosion was like a solid wall hitting you. The whole tower shook. Fires raged for days; it was like daylight even at night."

"What happened?"

"They got everything back under control. The machines, the people. But next time they won't be able to. Next time we'll have them."

"How many wreckers are there?"

The man shrugged. "Who knows? A lot. We don't keep lists – too dangerous. The masters and the ironclads try to find us, of course, but they can't get all of us."

"I heard a name," said Finn. "Someone I'm supposed to find."

"What was the name?"

"Lud."

Rory nodded again but didn't speak. He continued to work away at the lock.

"Have you ever met him?" asked Finn.

"No, not that I'm aware of. No one knows what he looks like. Some say he's an old man now. Others say he's very young."

"But where is he? How do I find him?"

"I don't know. That's the way it is. But I'll put the word out you're looking for him. It might count for something. Most likely he already knows all about you. There!"

With a *snick* the grapple near Finn's elbow came away. Finn unwound the chain from his forearm. It pulled his hairs painfully. The skin of his forearm was mottled with spiralling indentations. It was wonderful to be able to scratch all the itches.

"Thanks," said Finn.

"Let's see if we can free the other end."

As he worked, Finn examined Rory's face closely. He *did* resemble Mrs. Megrim, there was no doubt about it. The same strong nose and eyes. Still, there was no knowing which side he was really on after so much time. Master Whelm had admitted to having wrecker sympathies once. Rory could still be just another test.

"Where are they sending you anyway?" asked Rory as he worked.

"The Vault."

"I've heard of that at least. Could be useful."

"I don't even know what it is."

"It's where they keep all the blueprints and plans. The designs for everything in Engn are there. Ach!"

The knife had skipped off the grapple and into the flesh of Rory's hand. He ignored the fresh wound and began to examine the clasp more closely.

"What will I be doing in this Vault?" asked Finn.

"Hard to say," said Rory. "Never been there. Working on the plans, I suppose; it's a key place to work. The word is we have several people there, ready to take action."

"Action?" said Finn. He had to be careful, not give himself away.

"Action to sabotage Engn. By amending the plans and making the machinery unstable. That's what we heard."

"The masters would be on the lookout for something

like that."

"They can't watch everyone all the time." Rory took a step backwards. "Finn, I'm sorry. I can't get the other end off. You need a proper key. Perhaps someone will have one at the Vault. At least your arm is free now."

The chain reached all the way down to Finn's feet. He picked up the other end and wrapped it, loosely this time, back around his arm so it didn't trip him up.

"Thanks. It feels much better."

"Look, I'd better get back," said Rory. "Like I say, they count the bearings."

"Will I see you again?"

"Probably not, Finn. Until the day we destroy this place. Then I'll walk with you back to the valley, okay?"

"I'd like that," said Finn. "So which way should I go now?"

"The middle walkway. It goes for miles, right over Engn. Who sent you by the way? Was it this Connor?"

"You know Connor?"

"Just the name. My mother mentioned him, too."

"I … I'm not sure," said Finn. "He might have been involved. But it was an old man who told me where to go. The man who winds all the clocks."

"Ah, him. Someone must have given him orders, though. Perhaps this friend of yours is a master already?"

Finn nodded. "I think he is."

"Be careful of him, then. You may think you know him, but people change when they join the wheels."

Finn nodded. "Have you seen anyone else from back home?" he asked. "My sister?"

"No. It's a miracle I found you. The machine is so vast these days."

"I'm glad you did find me."

The man clasped Finn close for a second. "And I'm sorry I can't help you more. Get to the Vault. You'll be safer there. It's dangerous out here on your own."

"Thanks."

"And don't let them win, Finn. Whatever happens, never give in to them, okay?"

Finn nodded. The man turned to leave, back into the red glow from the molten metal. Finn watched him for a moment. He wanted to call after him, ask him more questions, talk about home. But he knew he couldn't. It would be a danger to them both. With a sigh, he turned and headed for the central walkway.

The metal platform boomed and vibrated as he walked into the night air. It was impossible to see how the walkway was held in the sky. The wind whipped up his hair, buffeting him from side to side. He could barely even see the walkway itself except for the way the mesh made the lights down on the ground twinkle. He kept one hand on the rail and tried not to look down.

He reached a point where the walkway opened out onto an even wider metal road, so broad that he couldn't touch the handrails on both sides at the same time even with his arms outstretched. He debated with himself whether to turn left or right. *Towards the Hub* the old man had said. He tried to work out which way that was. Holding on tight with both hands, his fingers cold as they grasped the handrail, he leaned over the side of the walkway to peer downwards. The wind threw his hair into his eyes. Directly beneath him he could see a large orange circle, one of the great reservoirs filled with some bubbling oil. He could feel the heat coming off it on his cheeks, even from up there.

He tried to discern other details, work out where he was, but he recognized nothing. He could see no sign of the clock tower or the Octagon or the Titan Wheel. The dome where the figure had beckoned to him must also be somewhere in the darkness. But it did seem that more flames burned, more lights twinkled, more machinery roared, away to his right. Perhaps the centre lay that way. It was all he had to go off.

He stepped forwards, holding on to the rail with his left

hand, fingers numb now from the cold, fumbling as he ate his last few scraps of bread. The wide walkway skipped beneath his feet as the wind hit it. He tried not to think about how far down it was to the ground. He was just glad it was so dark. The distant ground seemed unreal, impossibly remote. He saw no one else on the walkway.

He reached a point where a telescope had been bolted to the rail, angled down to the ground. Similar, perhaps, to those he had glimpsed high in the Valve Hall. There was a low metal platform you stood on to peer into the telescope. He probably wouldn't be able to see anything, but he couldn't resist trying. What was it pointing at? Perhaps he could make out some detail he recognized. His frozen hands refused to work properly as he tried to hold the telescope still and adjust the focus. He set the other end of the chain on the ground and used both hands to hold the device. He began to make out shapes. People – tiny figures moving in front of incandescent lights or silhouetted against the red glow of the reservoirs. Shovelling coal into the red circles of furnaces. He panned the telescope around, trying to pick out some landmark he knew.

Spinning around to gaze back in the direction he'd come, he picked out the illuminated face of a familiar clock. It was the tower; he was sure of it. *The Western Grand Tower.* The clock he'd watched each morning from his little attic room. It already looked far away. He tried to make out the time it showed. He had to point the telescope downwards; it was incredible how high up he was. But the angle was uncomfortable and he couldn't hold the image steady.

Half sitting on the edge of the rail, legs locked around the stand of the telescope, he tried again. The yellow clock face shot through his field of view. He found it again and held the telescope steady as he read the time, holding his breath. It was the thirty-sixth hour. Midnight.

He heard the clang of a footstep and felt the rough

grasp of a hand all at the same moment. He turned to see a looming shape standing next to him. In the darkness it was impossible to see any detail but by the figure's size Finn knew it must be an ironclad. He could smell the leather and the iron and the sweat.

Desperately Finn tried to pull himself loose, grasping the tube of the telescope with both hands. The ironclad held him firm. Finn thought about letting himself be captured and then wriggling free later. In the darkness he might have a chance.

But the ironclad, gripping Finn's arm, didn't pull him forwards. Instead he began to push Finn over the edge of the railing. Finn's fingers slipped from the smooth tube of the telescope.

"No!"

He tried to grasp the ironclad's arm, tried to scrabble for the metal rail. His numb fingers wouldn't work quickly enough. He felt himself overbalancing, only that vice-like grip holding him up. Was this how the ironclads extracted information from people? By threatening to drop them? Finn tried to think of some story to explain who he was, what he was doing.

But the ironclad didn't speak. Instead, he released his grip. Finn plummeted with a sickening rush, the cold night air sucking the scream from his throat as he fell.

XIX

Finn's arm jerked sharply, wrenching his shoulder almost out of its socket. For a moment he couldn't understand what was happening. He swung there in the air, hanging by his arm, lights from the ground lurching around beneath him.

Metal bit into his wrist. The ironclad's grapple. It must have caught in the railings or the mesh of the walkway as he fell. He dangled there, his arm already tingling and numb. He thought about how slight the teeth of the grapple were. About the thinness of the chain that was stopping him plummeting to the distant ground.

Up above him, he could just see the shape of the ironclad against the orange glow of the night-sky, next to the telescope. He thought about calling out. But the ironclad wasn't going to just haul him up. His only hope was to stay very still, hope he wasn't seen. He spun slowly around, swaying in the gusting wind.

After long seconds the ironclad strode away, apparently satisfied. He made no sound, as if wearing rubber boots rather than the usual metal. Finn waited until the shape had faded into the night. By now, his shoulder throbbed alarmingly from supporting him at such an uncomfortable angle. It was hard to breathe, his chest squeezed by the weight of his body. He used his spare hand to reach up and grasp hold of the chain. He tried to pull himself up to the walkway, but it was useless. He didn't have anywhere near enough strength. Bitter, desperate tears came to his eyes. What was he going to do? He thought about trying to shake the chain free, let himself fall. The ground spinning beneath his feet was dark, but there would surely be some hard surface down there. At least, after a few bad moments, his torments would be over.

He did call out then, half sobbing, half crying. No one came. He wondered how long he could remain there, dangling, before unconsciousness overcame him. He almost wished it would.

The wind picked up again and sent him twisting around and around. He thought about their swing in the woods at home, the great leap off the bank over the treetops. If you had enough power you could get all the way back to safety. But if you didn't you could swing your way back by arching your body backwards and forwards in the right way. It was a chance. He could think of nothing else.

He waited for the wind to gust then kicked with his legs and waist. He began to swing. Agony shot through his shoulder. Perhaps he'd dislocated it. That had happened to one of the workers on Connor's farm while he was hefting hay bales up onto a wagon. Finn and Connor had watched from a hedge, fascinated, appalled. The man's scream of pain as they worked his shoulder back in had rung down the valley.

Another rush of wind hit Finn and he kicked again, swinging in a wider arc, gritting his teeth against the pain. If he timed it right, if there was another rush of wind at the right moment, he might just be able to grab hold of the underside of the walkway. A gust came and he kicked hard.

But he spun too, maddeningly, so that he faced away from the walkway. He reached up and behind with his free hand and just managed to touch the metal before he fell back down and away. His stomach flew and heaved from the swinging motion. He wondered how many goes he had before the chain or the grapple came loose and he fell.

The wind rushed at him again, a powerful gust, and he kicked once more. His left arm was numb now, just dead flesh. He held his spare hand forwards, reaching upwards for the walkway. He touched it again and hooked a single finger through the mesh but he couldn't hold himself. Again, he swung away.

He almost reached the walkway again at the other end of his swing. But instead of trying to grab hold he bent his knees and kicked off with all his strength. He thought perhaps the wind had dropped but then it gusted into him, propelling him forwards. The underside of the walkway loomed suddenly near to his face. He grasped onto it with his free hand and held tight. This time he didn't slip off.

He hung by his fingers for a few moments, waiting for sensation and strength to return to his numbed left hand. He needed to work his way to the edge of the walkway so he could climb up the side. He knew he couldn't hang on for long, but he would need both hands to work his way across. He breathed ragged, panicky breaths. If he fell, he surely wouldn't have the strength to swing back up again.

He reached out with his left hand. His fingers felt swollen and clumsy. He clawed them through the underside of the mesh a short distance away, took a breath and let go with his right hand. The fingers of his left hand started to slip immediately. With a gasp he grabbed back hold with his right hand, hurting the tips of his fingers as he grasped. But he'd made some progress; he was an inch or two nearer the edge.

In a series of desperate, panicky jerks, he worked his way across. At the edge, the wind gusted again, threatening to pluck him back into the night air. He held on while it died down then swung himself sideways up the railing, reaching with his right foot. He managed to hook his toes through. Hauling himself upwards he reached up and got a hand over the top of the railing. There was a brief moment as he teetered there, thinking he would fall, that all his effort had been in vain. Then he threw himself forwards onto the metal walkway, landing hard on his back.

He lay there utterly exhausted, arms burning with pain. The walkway spun and lurch beneath him. Exhaustion overwhelmed him. He closed his eyes and thought himself back on the swaying bough of an oak tree, clinging on after a leap between trees that he'd nearly missed. He slipped into unconsciousness.

"Finn!"

Someone shook him awake. He thought at first it must be Connor with his catapult, then the ironclad come back to hurl him over the side. But it was a kind voice, a worried voice, one he recognized. It was his father, cross at him for getting his clothes dirty again. Then it was Mrs. Megrim and he'd fallen asleep in the Switch House, a missed connection blinking away. But, no, it wasn't her, either.

"Rory?"

"I'm here, Finn. I came after you. I couldn't just sit there. I saw the ironclad and I thought he must have caught you."

"He threw me over the side. But the chain got caught up."

"Oh, Finn." The man kneeled and put his arms around Finn. Sharp pains shot through Finn's left shoulder.

"You shouldn't be here," said Finn. "They'll get you, too."

"No need to worry about that."

Finn attempted to stand, steadying himself with a hand on Rory's shoulder. "No. You should go back before the masters see you've gone."

"It doesn't matter."

"What do you mean?"

Rory stood and began to examine the chain, its free end still tangled up in the metalwork of the railing. "It's a miracle this held you up. Just think, if I had been able to free the other end…"

"What do you mean it doesn't matter?"

Rory looked up at him. "Finn, getting you to the Vault is the important thing now. If there are other wreckers there, if there's a chance you could help them sabotage the machinery, then that's all that matters. This could be our chance, don't you see? I've been biding my time for so long, waiting for the great moment to arrive. Perhaps this is it. Or perhaps it never will. I've got nothing to lose by trying."

"But if the ironclads catch you?"

Rory shrugged. "What if they don't?"

"You said you'd come home with me," said Finn. "Once Engn is destroyed."

"I know, Finn. But you have to get to the Vault and I have to help you. That's all there is to it."

"You can't endanger yourself because of me. I don't want you to."

"It's not because of you, Finn. Not only you, anyway. Now, enough arguing. Come on, we have to move." He sounded more than ever like his mother.

Rory turned and unhooked the grapple from the railing. It came away easily. "How does your arm feel?"

Finn flexed his shoulder. It throbbed more and more as sensation returned. Perhaps that was a good sign. He let Rory examine it, his fingers pressing into the flesh of his arm. With a gentle *click*, the other grapple, the one locked around his wrist, came away. Rory held it up to his eyes to examine it in the dim light. "Teeth are all bent. It could have come loose at any moment."

"Let me have it," said Finn. He stepped to the edge of the walkway and hurled the chain over the side. It was briefly visible in the glow from the ground, snaking its loops in the air.

"I'll help you to the Vault," said Rory. "Come on."

They started to walk, arm in arm, Finn peering up ahead for ironclads, terrified of seeing the shape of another against the distant lights.

"You do remind me of your mother, you know," said Rory.

"So do you," said Finn. "Of yours, I mean."

"How is my mother, Finn? How is she really?"

Finn thought about the last time he'd seen her, collapsed by the side of the road, defeated. And she wasn't well, Finn knew. Her absences from the Switch House had grown more and more frequent. He tried to decide how much he should say. "She hasn't slowed down much. Still running the line-of-sight network. Still bossing everyone around."

"That's good. She never says anything about herself. It's the way she is."

"I was terrified of her when I was young, you know. She used to teach me and Connor and we didn't dare to ever make a noise. Actually, I think everyone's a bit scared of her. Even my father."

"Your father? I wonder if I know him. As far as I know my mother never said who your mother married and you look so much like her, it's hard to tell."

"He's the blacksmith. I mean he does everything, really, but that's what people call him."

"Ah."

"What?"

"Oh, it's nothing. I'm just glad. I thought perhaps your father was someone else. There was a whole gang of us and there was another boy who was keen on your mother.

I thought perhaps she'd married him."

"You mean Matt."

Rory stopped and looked at him. "Yes, I do mean Matt. You know him? I'm glad you're not his. I didn't know your father that well. He wasn't really one of the gang, but he was a good lad, I could see that. There were depths to him."

"And you didn't like Matt?"

"Nasty streak in him. I wouldn't have wanted him for a father that's for sure. I wonder what happened to him?"

"You don't know what he did? Mrs. Megrim didn't tell you?"

"No. We don't manage to intercept all the messages. I have no idea."

They resumed walking, Finn recounting everything that had happened, right up to seeing Matt on the road from the moving engine. When he'd finished Rory was quiet for some time. The gusting wind had dropped and the rhythmic crashing of the machinery had grown louder, as if they were nearer the centre of Engn.

"Well," Rory said finally. "Now I'm very glad you're not his boy. You did well to stop him. We hear of people like him from time to time, sent out from Engn to spy on people."

"I wonder what will happen to him, though. I suppose I feel a bit responsible."

"Nonsense. He's to blame, Finn, not you. You didn't do anything wrong. As for Matt, he'll wheedle his way in somewhere and be just fine, I'll bet."

They walked on in silence for a time before Finn spoke again. "I don't understand it, though, Rory. The old man said I was supposed to go to this Vault. Those are my orders. Yet the ironclads tried to stop me, tried to kill me. Aren't they on the same side?"

Rory sighed. "It's complicated. They should be, but Engn is so vast these days it's sometimes impossible to coordinate everything properly. The ironclads are given their orders and they carry them out. Different companies get different orders. Some of us think we just have to sit and wait for Engn to grow so huge it collapses by itself. Or perhaps, I don't know, the orders that you were to go to the Vault hadn't reached the ironclad who found you."

Finn looked out over the fields of lights beneath them. "What's the point of it all, though? The machine is so vast and confusing and … pointless. I told you about the valves not functioning. Why do people go to so much effort doing things that simply don't matter? Why are more and more people being brought here?"

"Good questions. Perhaps there's no answer, and it's all because messages have become mixed up and garbled. Or, then again, have you heard the rumours of the hidden purpose, the original reason for Engn's existence?"

"What reason?"

"That's just it: no one knows. Something terribly important that's been kept a secret or even forgotten completely. Some say the purpose is more and more urgent, that things are nearing the point where the balance tips and the engine runs out of control. I don't know. Maybe that's just idle hearsay. And maybe that's why the masters are sucking in more and more people, draining the lands. They hope to find someone, anyone, who knows the secret and who can help them fix whatever it is that needs fixing."

"But who? And how?"

"I don't know. I truly wish I did; it might be something we could make use of."

Finn sighed. There was so much he didn't understand. "It's amazing how it all continues to function."

"Yes."

They'd reached another tower now, this one slender iron rather than stone. The walkway was slung from it by thick iron chains reaching up into the sky. A vast number of the electrical cables converged on the tower from all directions, swathing it in a thick cobweb of lines. A set of steps led down towards the ground.

"The Vault is down there," said Rory. "One of the main timing wheels is directly below us. They built the Vault into the base of it. We're not too far from the Hub."

"Do you think Lud is somewhere around here? Near the centre of Engn, I mean?"

Rory shrugged. "Perhaps. No one knows where he lives, what he does. He could be nearby and you wouldn't realize. They say he goes by other names, too, to keep his identity secret."

"So, I might have met him already?"

"Perhaps. Now you'd better go."

Finn set off for the steps. He wanted to have his feet back on the ground as soon as possible. His arm slipped free of Rory's.

"Aren't you coming down?" asked Finn.

"Best I don't."

"But what will you do?"

"I'll go back to the drop point. Perhaps they won't have noticed I've gone." He didn't sound convinced.

"Shouldn't you try and get away? There must be other groups of wreckers who can help you."

"Perhaps. The wreckers have to be so secretive even we don't know who we are."

"I could come with you. We could find them together."

"No. You have to get to the Vault. It's too good a chance to miss."

"But…"

"Go, Finn. Don't waste the chance. It could be our only one. I'll be okay."

Once again, they hugged a goodbye. One again Finn didn't want to let go.

"Hurry along," said Rory. "We don't want to be caught out here. Promise me you'll do what you can."

"I will."

"Off you go, then."

He sounded just like his mother, telling him to run

home after a long day at the Switch House.

Finn set off down the stairs, glancing backwards again and again. After a few moments he lost sight of Rory. The stairway descended steeply, each step very deep. Finn's thighs burned with the effort of it. The stairs wound around a stone column supporting the wheel. Spokes the size of tree trunks arced past Finn's head as he descended. A vast horizontal piston pumped the wheel round. The cam on the axle was the size of a boat on the millpond back home. One of the wide leather belts, gripped firmly by the serrated outer edge of the wheel, ran off to another, lower tower. From there, the belt was turned at an angle before heading off into the darkness.

Finn sighed. He would never understand any of it.

XX

The entrance to the Vault was unmistakable: two tall iron doors set into the base of the stone column. A pair of ironclads stood guard in front, unmoving. Finn watched them, unsure what to do. There was no way he could sneak past. He wanted to sit down on the stairs and close his eyes, shut everything out.

In the end he descended slowly, one step at a time, watching the guards in case they jerked into life and came for him. They didn't move. They must have seen him, but still they didn't react. Perhaps they weren't real, just statues or empty suits of armour. Or machines. The others back in the dormitory had told stories after dark of the automatons they'd seen stamping about Engn, breathing smoke and fire, their bodies cogs and chains. Or perhaps these ironclads weren't like those up on the walkway. Perhaps they were from one of the different companies Rory had mentioned.

Finn reached into his pocket for the yellow slip of paper the old man had given him. For a moment, heart thudding, he couldn't find it. He imagined it fluttering through the air from the walkway, lost when he'd been tipped over the side. But then he found it crumpled and creased in the corner of his pocket. He took it out, smoothed it open and walked up to the two ironclads.

They were definitely real. Their heads swivelled to watch him approach. Finn held the yellow paper out at arm's length as if it would protect him. When he was within touching distance, the two figures towering over him, one reached out a gauntlet. Finn flinched but the ironclad merely took the paper between metal thumb and finger. The other held something that made a grinding noise as he wound it up. Blue sparks flickered, then light flared from a small glass bulb attached to a thin metal tube. By its light the two ironclads examined Finn's scrap of paper through the narrow slits in their helmets.

After a moment, they stepped aside to let Finn through. Neither spoke. Finn hesitated, fearing some trap, then pushed open the iron doors. He expected armoured hands to seize him, alarms bells to clang, but there was nothing. He stepped inside.

He found himself on a balcony above an underground hall that stretched into the distance. Slender iron pillars supported the weight of the workings up on the surface. A web of wires had been strung between the pillars and hundreds of naphtha lamps hung down from them, suffusing everything in the hall with a bright, even glow.

In the distance, other halls rambled off in different directions, slanting at odd angles to each other as if fitting around the foundations of the machinery up above. The tall walls were lined floor to ceiling with metal bookshelves. To his right the books were all blue, while in the shelves on his left they were red. Away in the distance, around a corner, he could see sections of green and orange and purple. Countless thousands of books.

A framework of rails spanned each set of shelves, upon which something like a small, vertical engine shuttled up and down, backwards and forwards. Each time one of the engines stopped, it used metal grips to pull out or replace a book. The machines hissed and whooshed, carrying their cargoes up and down. Finn watched as a young woman operated a control box at the foot of the blue bookcase, dialling in some number then hauling on a lever to activate that shuttle, sending it shooting upwards and across the shelves.

A number of square tables had been set down the centre of the room at which many people worked, sketching drawings on huge sheets of paper. They copied diagrams from open books laid out on the tables, concentrating closely, measuring everything with callipers and rulers. At the nearest table, one of the sheets was being rolled into a scroll taller than Finn and handed to a young boy, who scurried off somewhere with it.

The girl who'd finished the drawing shut her book with a hollow *thud* that Finn could hear up on his balcony. She looked around and saw him staring down at her. Her eyes narrowed. Her hair was pure black, glossy like a blackbird's feathers. Finn smiled and the young woman raised an eyebrow in return but didn't smile back. She was, what, a year older than he was? He wondered where in the world she'd come from. Where they'd all come from. The young woman nudged the person working next to her, pointing out Finn with a nod of her head. Her neighbour, a young man with yellow hair, glanced up briefly from his work, pen poised over the paper.

Perhaps some sort of message had been sent by the ironclads at the door, because at that point two masters strode down the hall towards the balcony. One wore scarlet robes and the other white, a colour Finn had seen only a very few masters wear.

"You, boy," the white master shouted. "Come down here!"

Finn hurried down a spiral of worn stone steps. It was warmer down on the floor, muggy, the sound of the machinery louder. It reminded him a little of the Valve Hall. The bookshelves loomed tall over him as he walked. The steam shuttles whizzed overhead at alarming speed, looking like they could fly off their thin rails at any moment.

Finn made his way around the great square table where the black-haired girl worked. She'd started a new drawing, copying out the design of some wheeled contraption from another blue volume. She concentrated on the line of her pen but glanced up at Finn as he passed. She wore the same grey robes that all the workers wore. He smiled at her again, but she frowned and looked away, back to her work.

Reaching the two masters, Finn realized he didn't have the yellow slip of paper anymore. The ironclad at the door had taken it. He was about to explain when the scarlet master threw back his cowl and Finn saw who it was.

"I know this one," said Connor to the other master. "He's a good worker. He could be useful here."

The white master removed his hood, too. He was older, his head bald, a keen, calculating look in his eye, like a crow or a starling.

"He looks like he could drop dead at any moment."

"He's clever, though."

"How did you get here?" the older master asked Finn.

"I … I came along the walkway," said Finn. "I had a piece of paper."

Finn glanced at Connor. His friend had aged; his features were sharper, harder. He looked more like his father than ever. Connor scowled then looked away, back to the older master. Finn wondered what his friend had been through to get that far, what adventures he'd had, what sacrifices he'd made. He looked every inch the master now. If Finn didn't *know* he'd have been terrified of him. Rory had said becoming a master changed people. Finn could see just how much Connor had changed in order to play his part.

He wanted to say something, do something to acknowledge his boyhood friend. A smile, a wink, anything. But he dared not. Connor was playing a dangerous game, laying this careful trail. He mustn't do anything to give that away. He had to play along.

The older master stroked the lobe of his left ear between finger and thumb, thinking. Finn counted seven rings on his finger. First Wheel, very powerful. Only one step away from the Inner Wheel itself, the ultimate masters of Engn. Connor, he could see, wore five rings. He'd gone a long way in a short time. Did he also have Diane's ring hidden somewhere about him? It wasn't on his fingers, at least.

"Very well," the older master said. "Let him eat and sleep or he'll be useless. Tomorrow set him to work. The expansion works are progressing too slowly. But we can't afford any more mistakes, understood?"

"Yes, Master." Connor turned and with a nod of his head indicated that Finn should follow him. Finn said nothing and followed. Connor led him past the blue shelves and into a hall of orange books. At the far end of this, where three halls met, there was a raised wooden platform with a chair upon it and a wooden rail around it. Another master sat there, also scarlet, ticking off something on a roll of paper and occasionally glancing up at the activity in each of the halls. Connor nodded at this figure but he didn't stop. He led Finn towards the shadows at the end of one of the bookcases. There was a low doorway there, leading to a bare room lined with low, wooden beds. All but two or three were occupied.

"Sleep here," said Connor.

Finn nodded but didn't reply. He didn't dare speak in case one of the people in the beds was awake. Connor turned and led him through another doorway, into a long, narrow room. This was clearly where people ate: long tables stretched up the room with wooden benches like those in the Refectory. It was deserted. Finn glanced up at

Connor and could resist speaking no longer.

"Connor. Isn't it strange? I mean, here we both are." The image of the ironclads taking Connor away came to Finn. That terrible day he'd lost both his friends. It was only four years ago, but it seemed like an ancient memory.

"Eat in here," said Connor. "The others will tell you when. Understand, boy?"

"But Connor, I…"

"Enough. You have your orders. You'll begin work tomorrow."

"Yes, Master. Only, I don't know where to go or what to do."

Connor stepped closer to Finn so that he was only inches away. He sounded angry when he spoke again. "You will be shown the way, boy. Do what you are supposed to do and all will be well. Understand?"

For a moment, the briefest moment, it was the old Connor standing there. A look of recognition in his eye. Then the stern master's scowl returned, and Connor turned and stomped away.

Finn watched him go, wondering if he'd imagined it.

XXI

Finn slept deeply in his wooden bed, and could have slept for twice as long, but a shake roused him from his slumbers. It seemed to be the start of a shift; people stretched and yawned and dressed all around the room. Finn did likewise, then followed the others into the long room where food had been set out: wedges of bread and cheese with hot tea to drink. He ate, feeling more and more hungry with each mouthful. There were no masters in sight. He looked around, hoping to pick out a friendly face, but saw no one he knew.

"I'm Aelth. You're to come with me."

The blond-haired man from the night before had walked up behind him and now strode off without waiting. Finn rose and followed, his mouth crammed full of bread and cheese. Aelth led him back to the blue shelves.

"What is this place for?" asked Finn. "I mean, I don't know what to do."

Aelth glanced aside at him. "Runners come in from all over Engn with the code numbers of the drawings they need. Each mechanism, each component, each detail has its own master drawing. It's our job to transcribe the required design at full size onto one of the rolls of paper. Then a runner can take it away to where it's needed and a new part of the mechanism can be built. Or a worn-out part repaired. But any mistake, however small, can be disastrous. Got it? The whole mechanism depends on us transcribing the designs correctly."

Finn nodded. He thought about the self-governing valves. Was the design for those somewhere here? Was it possible, then, that a simple mistake had been made in the copying of that design, perhaps years ago? That the valves really were, or should have been, fully functional? But surely someone would have noticed?

"Watch," said Aelth.

A runner arrived, out of breath and clutching a slip of paper. Aelth took it, examined it, then showed it to Finn.

"It's a D code, see? That means structural, so it's in the blue books, one for us. Red is wiring; black, water, and steam; green for the timing controls, and so on. It'll all make sense soon."

"So, you dial this code into the book shuttle?" said Finn.

"That's it. But first you dial in your own code, so they know who has pulled which design, then the code for the drawing. The machine gets it, you transcribe it, then you put the book back. Think you can do it?"

"I don't have a code."

"You just use the one they gave you when you arrived."

"I don't have it. I mean, they didn't give me one."

The man looked puzzled for a moment, as if Finn were a contraption he'd never come across before.

"Are you sure?"

"Well, yes."

"Everyone has a number."

"So I've heard. But I don't."

"Are you sure you're even supposed to be here?"

"Well, I don't know really. I think so."

Aelth examined Finn closely. "Well, we'd best see if we can get that sorted out first."

He led Finn back past the blue shelves towards the raised wooden platform. Another scarlet-robed master sat on the chair, ruffling through a sheaf of papers. They stood and waited at the foot of the stairs for the master to look up. The wood of the steps was worn smooth, almost shining, by the passage of so many feet.

Finn wondered what, exactly, he was *really* supposed to be doing there. What Connor's plan was. Perhaps the idea was to sabotage some vital piece of the design. He could see how that might work. It wouldn't have to be much. Some tiny but vital detail transposed or confused. An easy, innocent mistake and one of the bigger mechanisms could be made to flood or explode. Finn imagined fires spreading, explosions triggering further explosions like a chain of firecrackers. It would be dangerous, though, very dangerous. How would they destroy the mechanism without endangering everyone inside?

The master rammed a wad of papers onto an iron spike on his desk, then looked down at them.

"Yes?"

"Master, this boy has no number," said Aelth.

The master looked at Aelth, and then at Finn. He scowled.

"That's impossible. What happened to it, boy?"

"I was never given one," said Finn.

"Of course you were given one."

"Then no one told me it, Master."

The master stood and descended. Finn though he was going to strike him, but instead the master pushed past and strode away to converse with a master in white some distance away. The two conversed for some time, their heads nodding. Finn couldn't tell if they were arguing or laughing together. Eventually, the master came striding back, a slip of paper in his hand.

"Here's your new number, boy. I had to go to a lot of trouble to get it. Don't lose this one as well."

"I … I won't, Master."

"Make sure you don't."

Finn and Aelth made their way back to the blue shelves. Aelth spoke when no one else was close enough to overhear. "How *did* you manage to lose your old number? That's only supposed to happen when you die."

"Like I said, I didn't know I had a number," said Finn. "That's the truth. But there was an accident yesterday. I don't know, perhaps they thought I was dead."

"You've been lucky, then. If you haven't got a number it's usually easier for them just to kill you to keep the records straight."

"Really?"

"Really. Tell me: that master last night said he knew you. Was he a friend?"

Finn wondered what to say. "We just grew up in the same village. We didn't know each other very well."

"I see."

"Why do you ask?" said Finn.

"Oh. No reason."

Back at the tables, Aelth showed Finn how to operate the book engine. Finn tried it for himself, dialling in the codes then pulling on the lever. The lever refused to budge.

"You have to wait until the machine is idle," said Aelth. "It can only store two codes, the current and the next. It's locked out at the moment. If it had three codes it would go haywire."

"What would it do?"

"Best you don't find out."

When the machine was ready, Finn pulled the lever again. This time, the shuttle clattered up and across its cradle of rails, billowing steam, to pluck out a volume in the high, far corner of the bookcase.

Once he had the book in his hands, Finn crossed to the

table Aelth directed him to, and set to work copying the required plan. It was very simple: a right-angle shaped piece of metal that looked like it slotted into something. He copied out the design carefully, drawing it life-size by using the scale marked on the drawing in the book. His first two attempts went badly wrong. On the first, he scored holes in the thin, crinkly paper, right through to the wooden table. On the second, his calculations went wrong and two lines that should have met didn't. The black-haired woman, working next to him, glanced across to give him an instruction as he worked on his third attempt.

"Don't smudge your lines as your draw. Rotate the paper if you have to."

"Okay."

"Check that angle is ninety degrees. If you draw it wrong, they'll construct it wrong."

"Okay."

His third attempt, when he finished it, looked perfect to Finn. The woman – who introduced herself as Ciara – cast a glance over it and nodded her head. It would do. Finn rolled up the design into a tube, and a runner came to take it from him. Finn heaved the great blue book back to the shelf and typed in the code to return it to its correct slot.

The next design Aelth assigned him to copy was more complicated, a spiral-shaped structure, part of a pump perhaps. This time he only took two goes to copy it accurately, and Ciara only had to correct him once.

Occasionally, he looked up from his work and flexed his right hand to relieve the cramping pain from holding the steel pen. He took the time to study the others around him, just as he had back in the Valve Hall. Apart from Ciara and Aelth, three others worked at their table: a woman and two men, all of them older. They looked like they'd been there for many years. After maybe an hour the woman had glanced up to meet Finn's gaze, her eyes narrowed as if trying to remember something about him.

"I'm Maeve. This is Garvin and this is Colm." She'd said no more, returning to her work with a frown.

He worked for eight hours, the only respite the walk to and from the bookshelves. He soon learned to make the most of that, walking slowly, taking his time to wait for the shuttle. Back at the table he worked methodically and in a week was copying the blueprint designs without mistakes.

His table mates kept themselves to themselves as they worked, rarely speaking, only stopping occasionally to stretch fingers or backs. As far as Finn could tell, they each copied their designs flawlessly. Ciara, despite her age, appeared to be responsible for all of their work. Each time one of the others completed a piece they would show it to her, and she would approve it or tell them what needed fixing. Clearly, she was in a position of some power. Finn thought about that as he worked. If one of the others introduced a deliberate flaw into their work, she would know about it. If, on the other hand, *she* made a mistake, deliberate or otherwise, no one would know. No one checked her designs.

He also noticed she and Aelth communicating silently, flashing glances full of meaning at each other, indicating someone or something with a nod of a head. One of the masters strolling by or some detail of a diagram. It was subtle, but clear if you looked carefully. Perhaps they were together, a couple. Or perhaps they were scheming, waiting for the opportunity to act. Wreckers, maybe. On the other hand, they might have been placed there by the masters to keep a close eye on everyone. He had to bide his time, find out more about them all.

One evening, trudging back to the side room where their wooden beds were laid out in a line, Finn found himself walking alongside Aelth once more.

"So, how long have you worked here?" he asked, trying to sound as if he wasn't really that interested. He stretched his fingers, staring at them as if they were what really occupied him.

"Oh, a year or two now."

"Were you somewhere else before this?"

"Why do you want to know?"

Finn shrugged as if it didn't matter. "Just wondered. I used to be in the Valve Hall; I wondered if you'd been there too."

"No, never. I think Maeve said she'd been there once."

Finn glanced around. No one else was near. Over the clatter of the shuttles, no one else would be able to hear them.

"Assembling the valves?"

"No, delivering a blueprint. Sometimes when there isn't a runner handy, we have to take them ourselves."

"But in the Valve Hall they just assemble the parts already made by someone else."

Aelth shrugged. "Maybe they wanted to check something was correct, then."

"So, Maeve and the others, Garvin and Colm, they were already here when you came?"

"Yeah. Been here years, those three. So long they've become sloppy. That's why the masters made Ciara their supervisor."

"You mean they make mistakes? In the diagrams?"

Aelth looked at him for the briefest moment, eyes narrowed. Finn could see he was wary. "There was trouble some time back, some mistakes were made. That's when they appointed the table supervisors."

"Ciara."

"Yeah, Ciara."

"She seems very smart."

"I suppose so."

Weeks went by. Aelth and Ciara gave Finn more and more complex diagrams to copy out. Ciara rarely had to correct him at all. He began to settle in. At first, he expected the ironclads to come for him and drag him away. Either that or he feared one of the boys from the Valve Hall arriving, Graves or Croft or Bellow. In the flashing of the skylight, outside on the roof, he had scratched a message. *Don't believe the masters. The postern gate is the escape.* Sometimes he regretted that, fearful that one of the others would see it and follow him. He wasn't sure which would be worse: that or the ironclads.

But no one came and, slowly, he became more relaxed. Ciara, Aelth, and the others were friendly enough, although no one talked that much. They weren't like the boys back in the dormitory at least. Most of the time he was left alone, which suited him fine.

As he worked away each day, he thought more and more about what he was supposed to do. It looked like Connor had gone out of his way to ensure he, Finn, worked in the Vault. *You will be shown the way, boy. Do what you are supposed to do and all will be well.* Wasn't it likely, then, that he'd placed Finn at *this* particular table for a reason? One or more of the five must be wreckers. Finn studied them all as casually as he could but came to no conclusions. He longed to talk to one of them about it but didn't dare. Not yet. One word to the wrong person and the ironclads would come for him. He surely wouldn't be able to escape again.

He sometimes thought about making a deliberate mistake, something small but dangerous. But the problem was knowing what change to make. They transcribed plans for individual components of the machinery so that it was hard to know what was a vital piece and what wasn't. Also, it was impossible to know which were real, working components and which were dummies like the valves. And what would Ciara do if he did introduce a fatal flaw? Would she correct him or let his mistake through? But if she did that she'd be just as much to blame as he was. He tried to catch her eye as he showed her each completed plan, to hint that he was ready to act, but she never appeared to notice.

Eventually, he stopped paying much attention to the others' work, stopped looking for deliberate mistakes, and consigned himself to waiting for the right moment. He saw Connor occasionally, sitting on his wooden platform or strolling round the room. They didn't speak, didn't acknowledge each other. Perhaps there would be a sign when the time was right. He just had to be patient.

He could see Connor now if he glanced down the hallway, discussing something with the older master in the white robes. It had been a busy day in the Vault, runners scurrying around constantly, carrying completed plans off into the workings. Thankfully Finn's shift was nearly over. He felt lightheaded with hunger.

He rolled up the plan he'd just finished, an intricate locking mechanism with some very detailed slots inside. Somewhere in the room, presumably, was the design for the key that fitted it. He looked around for a runner to take his design but none were there. Ciara, rolling up her own scroll of paper, saw his confusion.

"No runners around," she said. "We'll need to take them ourselves."

"Where to?"

"Both of these need to go to the Foundry."

"I don't know where that is."

The truth was, he didn't want to go outside. He hadn't left the Vault since he'd arrived. He felt safe there. He didn't want to meet up with any more ironclads.

"I'll show you," said Ciara. "Then you'll know for next time."

She turned and strode off, away towards the stairs.

Finn looked around, unsure whether he was even allowed to follow her.

Maeve watched him from across the table, seeing his confusion. "Go on, go after her. Then you'll know the way."

"But is it allowed? To go outside?"

"Of course. If you're delivering plans from the Vault you're allowed to go anywhere. You go wherever the plans are needed. Now hurry before you lose her."

Finn, turning away, scurried after Ciara.

They climbed the spiral stairs up to ground level. The two ironclads guarding the doors stood aside as they emerged into the open air. Finn looked around, amazed at how bright the light was. It was towards evening, the sun casting long, slanting shadows from the wheels and domes and towers. An electrical crackle filled the air. Squinting upwards, he could see the walkway he'd come along the night he'd arrived. It looked no more substantial than a mesh of fine threads hanging in the sky.

Ciara nodded up to it. "We'll take the walkway."

"Isn't there another way?" Finn asked.

"Afraid of heights?"

"No. I just don't want to go up there again."

Her eyes narrowed as she studied him, but she didn't ask for details. She shrugged. "Okay. There's a tunnel we can take instead. There's an entrance in the Hub."

"Can't we just walk on the surface?" It was good to be outside, in the open air. Despite his earlier fears he suddenly didn't want to be back underground.

"Too dangerous. There's a lot of fast-moving machinery around here."

She led him past the wheel and the flight of stone steps he'd descended when he'd arrived. An area of the machine he hadn't seen before lay ahead. Either he'd been too preoccupied to notice it, or it hadn't been illuminated that night. Now he saw a vast cube of a building, perhaps the biggest single structure he'd seen in Engn. Each side of the cube was pierced by an immense horizontal shaft. The top, too, had a shaft pressing down on it, connected to the arm of the biggest beam engine he'd seen. A great many of the chains and belts and cables led to the wheels powering those shafts, but none of them appeared to be in use any more. The mechanism was rusted and silent.

Ciara led him directly towards it. With each step the scale of the cube became clearer. It loomed over him, growing and growing as he approached. The horizontal shaft penetrating the nearest wall of the cube was easily fifty feet above him. Finn felt wary walking beneath it. It had to weigh hundreds of tons.

Ciara pushed open a door in the cubic building and stepped inside. Finn followed her, then stopped to take in the sight before him.

Light filtered into the vast, echoing space through the circular holes cut in the walls. He could see, now, that six shafts entered the building; another rose up through the floor from some underground engine. As the shafts approached the centre of the cube, they gradually tapered. By the time they touched, what had been a shaft wider than a tree trunk was now as fine as a steel pen. Finn knew enough about mechanics from his father to understand that the pressures exerted on the tiny point in the centre would be absolutely vast. If the machinery was operating.

"What is this place?" he asked.

Ciara shrugged. "It's the Hub. They say it marked the middle of Engn once. But now it's not used."

"But what was it for? What were they trying to crush in the middle?" There was surely only room for the tiniest, dice-sized cube between the tips of the six shafts.

"Don't know," said Ciara. "We never have to work on the blueprints for any of this. Just some old part of the mechanism."

They walked directly across the echoing hall, around the shaft rising up from the floor. That, too, was marked with lines of rust. Peering upwards, Finn could just make out a grey cube of something held pinched between the shafts. Everything looked corroded and long broken.

Nearby was a square opening in the ground. A flight of metal steps led down, presumably allowing access to the buried engine. Ciara lifted a light-globe from a rack to the right of the opening and cranked it into life. Finn followed her down the steps. The light threw off a flickering purple glow as they descended. The air smelled of damp and mould. At the bottom of the steps stood a riveted iron door, locked, but Ciara ignored it and instead turned to head into a tunnel that led away into the darkness of the underground. They moved along in a bubble of light, Ciara's shadow shifting and leaping on the walls around them. Drops of water *tapped* and *plipped* on the stone ground as they walked.

Now that they were alone together, he wanted to say something to her. Surely no one would hear them down there. He was more and more sure she was part of the plot, that she'd worked her way into a position of control for a reason. She and Aelth still spent a lot of their time whispering over diagrams, drawing phantom lines on them, nodding or shaking their heads and looking thoughtful. If they caught him watching them, they scowled and returned to their work. They *must* be debating which was the right diagram, the right component, to introduce their vital flaw into. And he wanted her to know she could trust him to help when the time came.

They walked for long minutes, neither speaking. Occasionally the tunnel branched or came to a crossroads. At each junction, arrows had been painted onto the stone walls, each with a number underneath. Even the rooms in Engn, it seemed, had unique codes. E-0001 seemed to be the Hub: all the arrows pointing back the way they'd come bore that number. But there were countless other codes as well, far too many for him to remember. Apart from the numbers, and the occasional lifeless, glass orb, the walls were completely featureless.

"What number are we looking for?" he asked.

He thought she wasn't going to reply. She wound up the light-wand again, the purple light snapping back into brightness.

"District ZN, then room 1211."

"Is it far?"

This time she didn't answer but tapped an arrow on the wall by her left shoulder. The writing underneath said ZN-1001. Presumably they were near.

"It's all so complicated," he said. "Engn, I mean. It's amazing the machinery carries on working at all."

It was as much as he dared say.

"That's why we're here," she said. "To make sure everything does."

He nodded, even though she couldn't see him. He thought about her words, wondering what, if anything, he should read into them. She was only saying what any master would say, that their job was essential to Engn. On the other hand, she was acknowledging the machinery was vulnerable if a flaw was introduced. Was she sounding him out, perhaps? Or just showing her allegiance to Engn? He couldn't decide. He was still pondering when she stopped at another low door, the code ZA-1211 painted next to it in fading letters.

"This way," she said.

She heaved the door open. A blast of hot air hit Finn on the face as he followed Ciara inside. A line of towering metal constructions, eight or ten of them, tall as trees, bulky as buildings, dominated the room they had entered. Fearsome heat slammed out from them: far hotter, even, than his father's forge back home. This heat felt like a solid wall clashing into him. He didn't want to go anywhere near the metal towers. The air was thick, more like a liquid as he laboured to breathe it.

They walked down the centre of the room, the raging furnaces on either side. Workers swathed in thick, reinforced clothing and iron masks operated each furnace, tapping gauges, turning wheels. Finn watched as one heaved open a small hatchway, revealing the roaring, vivid red of the fire inside, too bright to look at directly. Finn looked away, feeling his eyes prickle from the intense heat.

A metal platform ran around the edges of the room, past the gaping hoppers on the top of each furnace. Finn watched as a swathed figure up there pushed along a heavy trolley on little wheels. The figure stopped at one of the furnaces, docked the trolley into some sort of mechanism and, with the turn of a spoked wheel, tipped the contents into the furnace.

At the far end of the room, Finn could see a doorway guarded by an ironclad. Another trolley was being pushed through and onto the high walkway. Finn knew, then, what must be in the trolleys. There would be four every hour on average. Five-hundred and seventy-six valves, each carefully constructed by someone sitting at the table down at the other end of the tunnel. He was nearly back at the Valve Hall. Just through there, maybe even in sight if he looked, would be Tanner and Graves and all the rest of them.

He had the perverse urge to run past the guard and back into that familiar room. Into his old life.

"What's wrong with you, Finn?"

Ciara had to shout to make herself heard over the furnaces. He had stopped and was staring up at the next trolley being pushed towards one of the hoppers.

"The valves," he shouted back to her. "It's just – I used to make them. Look what they do with them!"

Down at ground level, a worker pulled a lever that sent a river of blinding red metal spitting down a channel and into a mould. A set of twelve identical casts, each about the size of a heart.

"Those are the pieces," Finn continued. "Don't you see? They melt them down and make new parts so the people in the other room can construct more valves. Over and over again."

"You had no idea?" She had to shout to him, her mouth close to his ear.

He shook his head. "I had no idea. I worked out the valves were useless, but I never imagined this."

She looked at him for a moment. She looked as if she were calculating some tricky sum in her head.

"Come on. We need to deliver these blueprints." She strode off towards a waiting master in another scarlet robe.

Back in the hush of the tunnel, Finn leaned against the cold wall, breathing deeply, while Ciara locked the doorway shut. The skin on his face felt dried and cracked, like dead old paper.

"What did you think they did with the valves?" she asked as she turned to look at him.

Finn, exhausted by the heat of the Foundry, sank down on the floor. Ciara looked as though she was about to tell him off, hurry him along back to the Vault, but she said nothing. Instead she shook out her hair and retied the strip of cloth that held it back out of her eyes. Her face was flushed red.

Finn shrugged. "There was a man who left the day I arrived. I took his seat. He'd worked there for forty years making the valves. It was his whole life. And all for nothing."

"Yes," she said.

"But why? It makes no sense."

She shrugged. "It's the way things are."

"It's like they're testing people for some reason."

"Yes," she said again.

She didn't sound quite as cross with him as normal. Perhaps she was just tired. She held out a hand to haul him to his feet.

"You think they're trying to find out who would make a good master?" he asked. "Or who is really a wrecker?"

She paused before she replied. She didn't look at him. "Could be either of those."

Finn spoke before he had chance to stop himself. "Because I think it's both. I think they're looking for people who can work it out, but also for those carrying out deliberate acts of sabotage. For wreckers. I nearly did that myself. But it's too obvious, isn't it? Too easy. You've got to be cleverer than that to really have a chance to destroy Engn, haven't you?"

She looked at him sharply. He knew immediately from her face that he'd made a terrible mistake.

XXII

Ciara stared at Finn, looking as if she was going to reply. But instead she took her lamp, wound it furiously, then marched away down the stone tunnel.

"We need to get back," she called over her shoulder.

Finn raced after her. "Ciara, what is it? I'm sorry."

She didn't reply. Instead she hurried on ahead of him.

"Ciara, I don't understand," said Finn. "Look, there's no one else down here. You can tell me."

"Oh, you'd love that, wouldn't you?"

She turned abruptly so that he almost ran into her. The light cast her features into eerie shadows, making them shift and flicker, as if her whole face was warping and writhing.

"What do you mean?" asked Finn.

"Was that the plan, you and the masters? Befriend us all, check us out, try and get us to admit we belong to the wreckers, that we're plotting some terrible crime?"

"No!"

"And in return, what? You get to be made a master

too? Is that how it works? One ring for each wrecker you name?"

"Ciara, I don't know what you mean."

"Course, you don't even need any proof. You just say someone's guilty and that's it, they're never seen again. It doesn't even matter what I say, does it? How much I deny being one of them."

She turned and set off again, back towards the Hub. Finn, angry now, grabbed her by the shoulder, making her stop. "Ciara, I am not working for the masters. I'm a wrecker too. I promise I am. I hate this place."

"And you would say that, wouldn't you?"

"It's the truth."

"Then you're going to be in big trouble when I tell them all about this conversation."

"You can't," said Finn.

"Oh, I think I can. Because if I don't, I'm just admitting my supposed crimes, aren't I?"

"But I want to help. Changing the blueprints could be our only hope to break the machine."

Once again, she was about to say something but stopped herself. That was the plan, he could see it in her expression. But she couldn't admit to it without trusting him completely. And she obviously didn't.

"Ciara, please," he said.

"I'm not stupid, Finn. Arriving in the middle of the night like that and all of a sudden that master's looking after you, getting you a new number. Do you think it isn't obvious what's going on? That you're their little spy?"

"It isn't like that. I mean, yes, I knew Connor before. But he's not like the others. He's one of us, I swear. We're working together. He arranged things so I could come here, but only to meet you. So, I could help."

He regretted his words immediately. He only suspected she was a wrecker. If she was really working for the masters, for Engn, he had just condemned Connor.

"Is that right?" said Ciara.

He thought about retracting his words. Perhaps he could pretend he was just trying to lure Ciara out into the open with wild claims. But what would he do then? Just go back to how he was? He'd be stuck in limbo again, perhaps for good.

"Listen, you mustn't tell anyone I said that," said Finn. "It's a secret agreement. Only three people in the whole world know about it, and the other one isn't even in Engn."

Her eyes narrowed as she looked at him. "And what makes you think you can trust me?"

Finn shrugged. "I don't know. I just thought if I didn't say something, I'd just end up staying here forever, wondering who my friends and who my enemies really are. Perhaps you *are* working for the masters and perhaps they'll set the ironclads on me when I get back. But at least I'll have tried."

She went very quiet. The purple light faded to an inky blackness. She didn't wind the torch back up.

"We should get back," she said after a while.

"What are you going to do? What are you going to say?"

"Nothing."

"Then you do believe me."

"I didn't say that."

"But if you were working for them you should report all this to them immediately."

"Perhaps I'm stringing you along to see who else is part of the conspiracy."

"Look," said Finn. "I'll prove it to you, okay? I'll prove I'm a wrecker. Then you'll have to believe me."

"And how will you do that?"

"I don't know. Destroy some of the machinery. Change a blueprint so that something breaks or explodes."

"And then when they find out I'm responsible for checking your work, I get the blame. Is that it?"

"No."

"Come on. I'm leaving."

She wound the brass handle on the light again, flooding them in the harsh purple light. She set off, pulling herself away from him. Neither spoke again until they reached the Vault. He watched her warily as they strode past the tables, expecting her to go up to one of the masters and tell them everything. Instead she made her away to the side room where she and the other women slept, not even looking back at him.

Finn worked diligently for the next few days, saying little or nothing to anyone. He exchanged a few words with Aelth, but only ever about some detail of the blueprints. No masters, no ironclads came for either of them. Ciara and Aelth continued to exchange meaningful glances every now and then. Once he caught Aelth watching him, his pen in his mouth, pensive. Maeve and the others behaved as they always had, getting on with their work, not talking.

The question was, how could he convince Ciara and Aelth they could trust him? The puzzle occupied his days and nights. He turned it over and over in his mind as he copied out the plans by day and as he lay on his low wooden bed at night. Ciara would be held responsible if he introduced a deliberate mistake, yet if he didn't do something, they would never accept him. The best he could hope for then would be for their scheme to work. But as far as he could tell they didn't have one of the masters on their side. It might be years before they were ready. And by then they might have convinced themselves they didn't need to try.

It came to him a week later what he should do. He was returning one of the volumes of blueprints to its slot halfway up one of the towering metal bookcases. As Aelth had shown him, he waited for the shuttle to return so he could dial in his new code. He gazed around the room for a moment.

The workers were huddled over the tables, concentrating on their blueprints, paying him no attention. Up above them, strung between the bookcases, was the mesh of cables from which the array of naphtha lamps hung. There were pipes, too, running along and down some of the cables to feed the liquid fuel to the lights.

Finn was thinking back on Aelth's words, about the dangers of overloading the shuttles. He wondered what would happen if you tried. Would the mechanism just break? Or would it explode? Perhaps the shuttle would shoot out of its mounting. The mesh of cables supporting the lamps would probably stop the machine flying too far, but it would do some damage to the lights, the pipes, everything.

He knew, he was sure he knew, what Connor's plan was. What it was he, Finn, had been brought there to do. He didn't need to join the other wreckers; he could do it all himself. Connor couldn't tell him, of course – that would be too dangerous for him. He had just waited for Finn to work it out. He stood there for long moments, heart beating, face flushed, while he thought about it. It was only when Maeve, standing behind him for her turn on the shuttle, tapped him on the shoulder that he realized the book-engine was sitting waiting for him.

"Are you just going to stand there?" said Maeve. "Or are you going to do something?"

"Sorry, sorry," said Finn and dialled in his number.

He waited a week, refining his plans in his mind. He'd only get once chance; he had to get it right. That night, the working day over, he pretended to go to sleep like everyone else. Instead, he stayed awake, eyes closed, stomach churning with dread at what he was about to do. He slipped in and out of a half sleep from time to time. Confused dreams came to him. Shireen, still looking as she had on that long-ago day in the clearing, spoke to him in urgent tones, but he couldn't understand what she was trying to say. She looked worried about him. Her words were just becoming clear when a blaring horn in the distance made Finn jerk awake with a gasp.

He sat up in bed, looking around, listening. He could hear only the gentle breathing of those around him and, beyond that, the hiss of the naphtha lamps in the Vault. When things were busy people worked at all hours, like in the Valve Hall. Three shifts of twelve hours. But it was quieter just now, and the night shift wasn't running. No one was allowed into the book halls. Which made it the perfect opportunity.

He stood up and dressed as silently as he could. His heart thudded; it seemed incredible that no one else could hear it. He ran through his plan one more time. If it worked, it would all be over. This would be the end of Engn. It might even be his last day there. The prospect was alarming and delicious at the same time.

He padded across to the bed where Aelth slept, just a shock of hair in the low light. Finn touched his shoulder and roused him, very gently.

"Hmm? What is it?"

"Aelth, it's Finn. It's okay. But I'm going to do it now."

"Do it? Do what?"

"Show you. You and Ciara. And Lud. I'm going to show you I'm on your side. I'm going to show you how to destroy Engn."

"What? Finn?"

Aelth, still fuddled by sleep, was having trouble understanding. Finn stood and left him there. They would know it was him at least. He crept to the doorway and peered around the corner. Out in the Vault, a few lamps burned above the tables but there was no one in sight. The steam shuttles were silent, their boilers cold.

He made his way along the foot of the towering bookcase, red for wiring, and peeped around the next corner at the raised platform where the masters sat. The chair was bathed in a pool of light but no one sat there. Finn stood and listened. Perhaps the masters walked the Vault at night, keeping an eye on all the precious books. He stood for a minute or two, straining to hear footsteps on the hard stone floor. Finally, resisting the urge to just go back to bed and forget the whole thing, he set off through the main hall.

He'd decided the blue books would be best. No one slept anywhere near them. No one apart from him would be in any danger. The others would be able to flee in time. There were several exits to the surface. He had seen it all in his mind, how it would work. There was no need for anyone else to get hurt.

He reached the blue bookcases. He stood for a moment beneath the shelves, looking upwards, considering. Then he began to climb.

The books took up most of the width of each shelf, giving him only a thin toehold to stand on. His left foot slipped off one of the low shelves, but he held on with his hands. If he placed his feet sideways, he could get more purchase. It made climbing awkward, an effort, but no worse than some of the trees back home. He worked his way upwards, pulling himself higher by grasping the edge of each shelf above him. He tried not to think about what would happen if someone back on the ground started up the shuttle and sent it skittering along its rails. Instead, as he climbed, he talked to himself, telling himself over and over he was doing fine, he was going to be okay.

He stopped when he was near the top, level with the wires that fanned out to support the naphtha lamps. He held onto the nearest cable. It was thicker than he'd imagined, bolted onto the metal frame of the bookcase so that it couldn't come loose. A small pipe, running down from the roof, recessed into a slot in the bookcase frame so the shuttle didn't hit it, led out along the cable, strung underneath by a series of metal clips.

Waiting for his breathing to return to normal, Finn looked around. The hall beneath him was still deserted. Each of the great tables was illuminated by a single lamp, but otherwise the floor lay in shadow. For a moment he remembered the day, long ago, when he'd helped his father in his workshop. He'd stopped at the top of the ladder then, too, enjoying the strange perspective of looking down on the world. He liked the fact that someone walking through the hall might not even see him up there, high up in the gloom, clutching the metal frame. He liked the feeling of being detached from the world.

Still, he couldn't stay there forever. The longer he delayed the more likely it was he *would* be discovered. He would never get this chance again. Hooking one arm around the frame of the shelf he leaned out to undo the first clip on the naphtha piping.

"Finn! What are you doing?"

He'd thought it possible that Ciara and Aelth would come and find him. But to his surprise, someone else stood in the shadows at the foot of the bookcase, calling up to him.

"Maeve? What are you doing here?"

"That's what I'm asking you."

"I'm showing everyone how to destroy Engn, of course."

"You can't, Finn."

"I can. It's easy. You don't need to introduce a flaw in some vital diagram. You don't have to do anything so clever. The answer was here all along."

"Come down, Finn," said Maeve. "This isn't the way."

Was she one of the wreckers after all then? Or was she working for the masters? It didn't matter. He just had to act before anyone stopped him.

"Where are Ciara and Aelth?" he asked, still working away on the metal clip.

"I told them to stay behind. No point endangering them, too. Climb down, Finn, before any real harm is done."

"They take orders from you?"

The metal clip was stiff. He had to work it loose with his nails. It gave, skinning the tip of a finger as it sprang loose. A moment later, he heard it *tinkle* to the floor. He reached out to the next clip, having to reach out farther along the cable. It swayed and thrummed under his weight but he thought it would support him. He reckoned he'd need to remove three of the clips altogether.

"Ciara and Aelth are young and headstrong," said Maeve. "Full of wild ideas. I try to keep them from harm. Their hearts are in the right place, but they're too impulsive. Like you."

The second clip jumped loose, shooting away to bounce off the books and down to the ground.

"It doesn't matter now," said Finn. "I'm about to destroy everything."

"And what if your plan doesn't work, Finn?"

"Then at least I'll have tried."

By reaching right out he found he could just touch the third clip. He had to stretch farther to be able to work it loose. He hooked one leg around the metal upright of the bookcase and let go of it with his arm. He stretched right out along the cable, supporting his whole weight on one hand, his body at forty-five degrees. Now he had a spare hand he could use. He tried not to think of the gaping fall of air, the hard ground down there beneath him.

"Finn, listen to me," said Maeve, calling up to him. "We believe you, now, okay? You're one of us. But can you come down so we can talk about this? This isn't the way, believe me."

He glanced down at her, her upturned face visible in

the light now. For a moment, he thought about agreeing. He had made friends, won them over.

"No," said Finn. "It's too late. I'm nearly there. You should get away while you can."

With a *ping*, the third clip sprang free. The pipe sagged down from its wire. There should be enough play in it now. He pulled himself back and began to flex it backwards and forwards. It was some soft metal, lead in it, malleable for bending around corners. It wouldn't take long to fracture.

Down on the ground, Maeve turned and hurried away.

The pipe cracked where he was creasing it and a thin spray of pressurized liquid naphtha fanned out from it, its smell pungent. He tried to make sure none of it got on him. Working the end of the pipe free, he held it out and sent a stream of fuel spraying out over the books. The pressure was enough to send the naphtha ten or twenty feet, spreading out in a fan. He worked for a minute or more, until he was sure all the paper he could reach was soaked. Then he let the free end of the pipe gush down the wall of books to the floor.

He stepped sideways, away from the pipe. He couldn't avoid getting the oil all over his hands. When he was far enough away, he tried to rub it off on his trousers so that he didn't slip as he descended. The air was rich with the smell of the naphtha now, thick and dangerous, filling his lungs and his head. He felt dizzy, felt the world lurch and reel about him. He had to get back down to the ground.

He reached down for the next lower shelf and found it with his toe. Gradually he stepped his way back down to the stone floor, his eyes shut as he descended. The bookcase seemed to go on forever. More than once he opened his eyes to see how much farther he had to go.

Finally back on the floor, he found himself surrounded by a widening pool of naphtha. He had no choice but to step through it to get to the book-engine.

He didn't need to fire up the boiler. That would take

too long anyway. But there was a priming mechanism built into the base of the unit that would suffice. He'd studied the mechanism carefully over several days. The spark from a sprung flint trigger ignited a fine jet of naphtha fed from a reservoir, with a fire valve making sure it didn't ignite the whole pipe. The flame heated the coals in the machine's boiler. Once they were hot enough, they boiled the water that sent the shuttles whizzing up and along on jets of steam.

Making sure his fingers were dry and as free of naphtha as possible, Finn turned on the oil in the priming mechanism. He shut his eyes once more. If any naphtha was touching the mechanism, the flame would shoot along it in a moment, engulfing him and all the books. He would have no chance. He wasn't even sure whether the air, now heady with fumes, wouldn't itself burn once he made the machine spark. Perhaps, if something like that did happen, it would be quick.

Taking a breath, he flicked the trigger with his thumb. Nothing happened. He probably hadn't pressed hard enough. He tried again. This time, the jet of oil from the priming tank took, burning with a tongue of orange-yellow flame. There was a valve to adjust the amount of air being consumed. He turned it carefully, a tiny cross-hatched brass wheel, until the flame roared an angry blue. He swung the arm holding the burner around to let it play across the coal in the machine's boiler.

He waited. All he needed was a single red-hot coal and he could carry out his plan. He needed only a few minutes without someone coming. The future of Engn depended on this. The coals began to fume and give off lead-grey smoke. Finn looked around. He knew he would be easily visible to anyone looking into the Vault now, but he could only wait. A few more moments and he would be ready. He wondered where Connor was, whether he had seen what was happening.

The coal nearest the flames was starting to glow

orange. He had only to ignite the naphtha and it was done. Finn fished it out with the tongs that hung on the side of the machine's boiler. He stepped backwards, holding the flaming coal out at arm's length. He made sure he stood outside the widening pool of naphtha on the floor. He stamped his feet to shake off as much of the oil as he could. He had to hurry. The coal was already darkening back to grey. It had to be now.

He hurled the smouldering coal into the middle of the pool of naphtha on the floor.

For a moment he thought it wasn't going to take; that it had all been for nothing. Then with a *wumph* the pool of oil on the floor caught fire. He felt the blast of heat from it on his face. He stepped backwards. A flame-devil whipped and whirled on the surface of the naphtha, green and blue, spreading and growing. He stepped farther back until his legs pressed against the square table. The table where he worked. Coils of heavy, dirty smoke in the air made him cough and retch.

The flame found the cascade of oil from the fractured pipe. A line of blue fire shot upwards, up to the high shelf where Finn had perched. It was a living beast, sniffing out the naphtha trail left for it. It pounced on the books with glee, growing to engulf all the volumes he had sprayed with oil. Soon, all the blueprints began to burn.

He had done it. The plans for Engn were being destroyed and no one, surely, would ever be able to recreate them. Whatever happened to him now, his plan, Connor's plan, had succeeded. Succeeded where so many others had failed.

"Finn!"

He turned to see Maeve standing twenty yards away. Her face glowed in the light from the fire.

"It's done!" Finn shouted to her over the roaring of the fire, his throat prickly from the fumes. "We've done it. You see?"

He could see her shaking her head in the shifting air.

"No," called Maeve. "I told you. This is not the way."

Another noise came to him then: an angry hissing noise, loud, from somewhere up above. He peered up through the roiling smoke. He could see a sheet of something like glass up there. He stepped around the table to gain a better perspective. Not glass, a milky liquid. It sprayed onto the burning books from other pipes strung along the cables. Where it struck, it fizzed and thickened into a white foam, coating every surface, smothering the flames. Plumes of steam hissed off the blue volumes where the foam clung. But the fire would surely win; there couldn't be enough to douse all the flames, could there?

The foam continued to spray out, thicker and thicker. Now it filled the air, raining down like heavy snow, the taste of it acrid. It began to cover the floor, blanketing the pool of naphtha. Soon the whole bookshelf was coated. All around, the smothered flames licked and writhed and died, leaving behind only black smoke and silence.

The foam continued for a few moments longer then cut out. After a pause, the clicking of some mechanism, torrents of water began to spray out instead. The water washed away the foam, sending it pouring down the books in an avalanche to the floor. Finn peered up through the spray, desperate to gauge the extent of the damage. The fire hadn't burned for long, but surely he must have destroyed a lot of books. And even *some* would be enough, if they contained vital designs.

But as the foam sluiced off the shelves, he saw the familiar wall of blue leather. A few volumes looked singed brown, but there they still were. Alarm thumped through him. The books were fireproof. Or they hadn't burned for long enough. In any case, they were undamaged. He stared upwards in stunned silence.

"Finn."

Maeve still stood there, watching him rather than looking at the books. Her face wore its familiar glower.

"I thought I could destroy the blueprints," said Finn

uselessly.

"No," said Maeve. "You can't."

"I don't know what to do."

"There isn't anything you can do," said Maeve.

"Why have you come back? Where did you go?"

"I went to get help."

"From the wreckers?" said Finn. "If Lud learns what I've done perhaps he'll take me in, hide me from the masters."

Maeve turned away from him and began to pace up and down, as if pondering some deep mystery. Occasionally she glanced back up the hallway. "Lud isn't going to do that. And Lud already knows all about you and what you've done."

"He does?"

"Of course. Word gets around. The wreckers hear about everything and everyone, sooner or later. There have been whispers about you, from outside as well as in here. The Valve Hall. The Drop Tower."

"And what have they heard?"

"That you might be on their side. And you might not be."

"But Lud will hear about all this, too," said Finn, indicating the books, the pools of water. "Then he'll know which said I'm on. Why do you say he won't hide me?"

"Because it doesn't suit the wreckers' purpose. You're too dangerous. You can't follow orders. You can't be trusted."

"And how do you know Lud thinks that?"

"Haven't you worked it out, Finn? I thought you were supposed to be clever."

Realization struck Finn like a blow. "You mean…"

"That's correct. You understand now. I am Lud."

"You can't be."

"I am. The current one, at least. Lud is just a name. A figurehead. There have been many before me."

"But I don't understand. Why won't you help me? Why

did you tell me to stop? Why didn't you even talk to me before? We've worked at that table for weeks and weeks and you've barely spoken."

Maeve stopped pacing to study him. "I wasn't sure about you. You wouldn't be the first puppet of the masters trying to infiltrate us."

"Well, now you know the truth. Now you know I'm on your side. And look, we could still do this, don't you see? We could disable the foam and try again. Destroy the blueprints properly. You and I."

Maeve shook her head. "No. I told you. This isn't the way. There are other plans."

"What plans?" asked Finn.

"I can't tell you. We have to bide our time, await the right moment."

Finn felt suddenly furious. Sick of the lies. Sick of fighting. Maeve should have helped him. Should have been on his side. Should have done *something*. He'd imagined meeting Lud a hundred times. Imagined being embraced by the wreckers, heard them cheering as he joined their ranks. Saw them marching together on some vital piece of the machinery. But now here was Maeve – Lud – refusing to help him. Refusing to do anything.

"And how long have you been waiting?" he said, shouting now. "How many years? How many decades? Because Engn still looks functional to me. I don't see much of it wrecked." His words tailed off into a spluttering cough. The taste of oily smoke filled his mouth from the smoke. His head was throbbing.

"You don't understand," said Maeve. "Breaking the wheels, wrecking the machines. What does it actually achieve?"

"The destruction of Engn," said Finn. "That's why you're here. That's what the wreckers are for."

"Of course, of course. And it's a noble aim, one we hold dear. But it's impossible to achieve in the short term. And little acts of sabotage like yours will only ruin everything."

"Good! Because that's exactly what we need to do. We need to ruin everything. We need to destroy Engn."

"But it won't work, don't you see? And it's far too dangerous. Far better to concentrate on giving people hope, a cause to believe in. That's something we *can* do."

"No."

"I'm afraid so. And one day, the time will be right."

"But the fires. The acts of sabotage. That wasn't you?"

"People acting alone. I do my best to protect them. Stop them harming themselves. And others."

Finn couldn't reply for a moment, trying to take in Maeve's words.

"Then you're no better than the masters," he said at last. "In fact, you're worse. At least people know the masters are against them. You make me sick."

Maeve shook her head, looked genuinely sad. "You just don't understand."

"I understand perfectly," said Finn. "Tell me, when did you stop believing, working away here at your safe little job? When did you betray everything you ever stood for?"

"I haven't stopped believing, Finn. I came here the same as you. Determined to destroy it all, refusing to be beaten down. And one day we *will* win. Perhaps not in my lifetime, but one day. Led by some other Lud."

"Is that what you tell yourself so you can sleep at night?" said Finn. "It's a fantasy, Maeve. You have to *do* something, not just sit around waiting. You're not fit to be called a wrecker. You're not fit to be called Lud. You disgust me."

Maeve didn't reply, just shook her head again. At that moment, footsteps clattered down the hall. A group of people approaching at speed.

"Who is that?" said Finn. "Who did you call?"

"I'm sorry," said Maeve. "I had no choice. We have to protect ourselves."

"What have you done?" said Finn.

Connor strode into the light, then, hood back, a grim look on his face. Behind him came a phalanx of ironclads. Only they weren't ironclads. Their armour wasn't the familiar grey and black metal. These shined like mirrors; their armour polished to a sheen decorated with swirling etched lines around the joints. In the flickering light from the remaining naphtha lamps they looked like dazzling creatures of silver and glass.

"Here he is, Master," said Maeve. "He tried to burn the blueprints."

Complex expressions played across Connor's face. Anger. Doubt. Sadness. He didn't speak. Deciding on a course of action, no doubt. A plan. Finn stood there. He had no idea what to do. Could they claim it was all an accident; that Finn had discovered the fire and was trying to put it out? Would the other masters believe that?

"Connor?" said Finn.

Connor motioned the guards forwards. They surrounded Finn in a moment. There was no possible escape.

"Take him to the cells," said Connor. "The Inner Wheel will meet in the morning to pass judgment on him."

The guards grasped hold of Finn and pulled him forwards. Finn screamed. Maeve stepped aside, staring down at the ground to avoid Finn's eye.

Finn wanted to shout at Connor, ask him what it meant, what he was supposed to do. But Connor was gone.

XXIII

They took him from his cell in the morning. Finn had passed the night huddled in the corner of the small stone room, its walls running with rivulets of water that fanned out into triangles of green slime. The only light came from a high, barred aperture in the ceiling that he would never be able to reach and would never be able to squeeze through even if he could. He lay there alone, curled up on his side, eyes open. He shivered, from the cold, from fear. He felt hollowed out. His cell reeked of the naphtha soaked into his clothes. His head swam from the fumes, but he had no strength to move.

Now, another of the silver ironclads stood in the doorway, impossibly tall, beautiful to look at. "Stand up. The Inner Wheel awaits."

"Are you an ironclad?" Finn asked, his voice a croak.

"A silverclad. The private guard of the Inner Wheel. Now come with me."

Finn worked his way up to stiff legs and followed, struggling to keep up with the figure. They walked up the stone corridor he'd been led along the previous night, the line of metal doors all the same, all locked. His head thudded with pain at each step.

They climbed back up to ground-level from the underground cells. Outside, Finn blinked in the painful light. They were far from the Vault. He'd been escorted by the silverclads across Engn, marched for an hour or more to the tall metal tower, perfectly cylindrical, that he now stood outside. The building shone like the silverclads: utterly impregnable, utterly beautiful. He wanted to stroke its shining surface but instead the silverclad pushed him forwards.

"Start walking."

"I don't know the way," said Finn. "I don't know where we're going."

The silverclad pushed him again. "Just walk."

They worked their way through a forest of the vertical cylinders. They were all, he saw, functioning mechanisms. A part of the machine. Some were connected by pistons pumping to and fro. Some appeared to be working on their own, disconnected apart from the cables and ducts strung between them. Blue electricity sparked and crackled from others, making the hairs on Finn's arms stand on end.

The silverclad steered Finn with an occasional prod to one of his shoulders. Finn soon felt weary, drained of all energy, his mouth parched to sandpaper. He hadn't had food or water for many hours. He didn't dare say anything.

"Stop here," said the silverclad.

They stood in front of a spherical building, its surface also gleaming. He could see his reflection in it: distorted, bloated. Rails ran along the ground out of the spherical building and off into the distance. A machine shot along them, solid balls of smoke huffing out of it. It looked something like the moving engine that had carried him to Engn but bigger and much, much faster. It roared towards them. Finn was sure it was going to crash into the round, silver building where the rails ended. Instead, venting off angry clouds of steam, it slowed to a halt and crept inside.

"Onto the shuttle," said the silverclad. Finn did as he was told. It would be pointless to run, even if he could manage it. Two or three times on their way there they had met ironclads who had stepped aside to let them pass, even bowing their heads.

The shuttle pulled an open carriage with seats inside it, slatted wooden benches that were speckled with spots of soot from the engine. Finn stepped in and sat, the silverclad behind him. The ironclad operating the engine began to turn valve wheels. The shuttle jolted forwards, making the wooden bench dig painfully into the bones of Finn's spine. They picked up speed. Finn was soon traveling faster than he had ever gone in his life. His eyes watered and the cold morning air streaming by bit at his ears. For some reason, despite the air rushing at his face, he could barely breathe and had to turn his head to one side to gulp in air. A blur of waterwheels and engine-mountings flashed past, each too quick for him to focus on. The effort of it made his head thud more and more. In the end he settled for closing his eyes against the onslaught of air and waiting until they stopped.

After ten or twenty minutes the shuttle decelerated sharply, throwing Finn forwards against the wooden seat in front. They approached another silvery, dome-shaped building, the rails leading into it like a long tongue into its mouth. Again, he thought they would crash, but the ironclad controlling the engine timed it perfectly and they kissed into the springs at the end of the rail with the gentlest of jolts.

"Out," said the silverclad.

A wide, circular space lay beyond the shuttle station. It was the biggest open expanse Finn had seen anywhere in Engn, far larger than the Octagon. Masters, silverclads, and ironclads strolled to and fro across the stone flags, many of them deep in conversation, carrying papers or studying small mechanical devices of some description. Most walked to or from the building erected at the very centre of the great circle: a tall spike of a tower with windows winding up it in a spiral. It, too, shone like polished glass. It could only be where the Inner Wheel, the masters of Engn, met. Ciara had said the Hub had once been at the heart of Engn, but this had to be the centre now. The place everything was controlled from.

They set off towards the tower. Some of the masters glanced at Finn as he walked by, their eyes narrowed. Most paid them no attention. He saw no one he recognized. He wondered where Connor was.

It was cool and dark inside the tower. He stood for a moment while his eyes adjusted. A spiral staircase wound around the walls, following the line of windows. Square beams of sunlight radiated down like the spokes of a wheel, illuminating the stone floor at the entrance to the building. More masters and soldiers strode across the open space, each footstep reverberating with a solid *clack*.

Finn's silverclad pushed him towards a doorway that led into the inner keep that filled the centre of the tower. An ironclad guard on the door stood aside to let them through. Inside, Finn found himself in another narrow room, its only feature the metal door in front of him.

The silverclad didn't followed him inside. The ironclad guard shut and locked the outer door, leaving Finn alone again.

He stood and listened. He could hear the murmur of voices through the inner door but couldn't make out any words. His heart pumped at the thought of the Inner Wheel of Engn waiting for him in there. He felt sick now, his stomach fizzing and lurching. He retched once, but his stomach was dry and empty and nothing came up. His stomach muscles cramped with a sharp pain. He wondered whether Connor was inside, explaining what had happened, defending Finn.

He was just about to slump to the floor to wait when

the inner door was pulled open. A silverclad – impossible to say whether it was the same one – beckoned him inside.

The court of the Inner Wheel of Engn was perfectly circular. He'd expected more of the gleaming metal, more bright light, but the room was dimly lit, the light from many white candles making solid details shift and flicker. The masters sat in a ring of carved stone chairs set into the stone walls, as if the entire room, walls and chairs, had been carved from a single, vast rock. He could smell the age and dust of the place.

Twelve masters sat around the ring, settled back into the shadows of their great thrones so that only their knees were visible. Twelve masters from the twelve mechanical guilds, the Duodecad. Above each chair, a series of stone faces had been carved, larger than life size, one on top of the other. The faces at the bottom were smooth, worn away almost back to flat stone. Higher up, the faces' features became sharper and sharper. Finn peered up at one of the columns, counting more than thirty effigies before they were lost in the shadows. Former masters of the Inner Wheel. He wondered how far the column went.

Scraps of Mrs. Megrim's teachings came to him. The faces at the bottom had to be the effigies of the defeated leaders of the Clockwork War. The masters of the twelve upstart guilds, defeated by the armies of the twenty-four older guilds that the twelve had tried to supplant. That was all before work had started on Engn, of course; the beaten leaders of the twelve had been exiled to the wastes of the plain from the ruins of their city-states, the construction of Engn a punishment or some sort of recompense. The carved faces of those ancient masters looked almost alive in the shifting light. He could feel the crushing weight of their gaze upon him, pressing him down to the ground.

Connor stood in his master's robes in the centre of the circle, not moving. One of the seated masters raised a hand, a flash of grey flesh, briefly visible. He waved his hand as if flicking Connor away. Connor turned and strode towards the door Finn had entered by. What had he told them? What story had he given? Sickening alarm thudded through Finn. He had no way of knowing what Connor had said to the masters. What story he should give. He watched Connor's face as he strode by, hoping for some clue, some sign as to what he should do. Connor's gaze flicked sideways, briefly, at Finn. A weak smile flashed across his face. Something else too: fear or regret. Then he was gone. The metal door boomed shut, leaving Finn alone with the masters.

"Come forwards."

An old man's voice, creaking like a machine in need of oiling. Finn walked into the circle. The blood-red tile floor was worn and scuffed, its centre inlaid with the design of a single cog. Finn stood there and waited, trying desperately to think what he should say. His mind had gone blank.

Another of the masters spoke, off to his right.

"So, Finn Smithson. You decided to try and destroy the blueprints in the Vault and so prevent any further work taking place on the machinery. Is this correct? You intended to destroy Engn?"

Alarm hammered into his stomach like a physical blow. He didn't know what to say. They knew everything. But he couldn't bring himself to admit to them what he had done. He managed only to stutter out a stream of confused words.

"No. I didn't … I mean, it wasn't like that. I was in the Vault, but not to destroy it. There was a fire and…"

He stopped, knowing he was convincing no one. If only he knew what Connor told them.

"Let me tell you what is really going on here," another master said from the shadows of another of the thrones. "Just so you aren't left wondering what is to come. Thousands of people come to Engn each year, from all over the lands. Some are strong, some are skilful, some clever. All have a part to play in the great construction. But how do we know who is best suited for each task? And how do we know who we can trust and who, secretly, isn't harbouring some lunatic desire to destroy what has been built? Hmm?"

"I … I don't know."

"No. Well, we test them. We set them to work and we see what they're good at, see what they can work out, what they do."

"You mean the valves?" He regretted saying it immediately. But surely these masters, the Inner Wheel, would know that particular truth.

"The valves, yes. That and other things. Some people need to be merely occupied, you see, made to feel important. Places like the Valve Hall serve a purpose, creating a little world into which newcomers can be placed. Some never leave that. Others we have higher hopes for and we give them other opportunities, to test them out. People, you see, are just like machines. You have to test out a new engine to discover how powerful it is, whether it runs true. It's the same with people."

Finn swallowed and said nothing. He wondered how much they knew.

"Now, you we weren't sure about. Clever, undoubtedly; skilful, resourceful. But where did your heart really lie? Were you secretly working on some scheme to destroy us? You could have been a master, but were you really a wrecker? We had to know. And now, clearly, we do. You have been scheming to destroy Engn all along."

"No," said Finn. "No. I wasn't. I'm not."

"Perhaps you think you're the first?" another voice continued, slow and hollow with age. "Perhaps you think no one else has ever come here harbouring such dark intentions. I can assure you you're not. Your little rebellion is only the latest in a long line. There have been hundreds of them over the years. We let them happen so we can judge people's true mettle. Most get no further than your petty act of vandalism. Occasionally a larger uprising flares up, but Engn is never threatened."

Finn wondered if they knew about Maeve, knew who she really was. Did the masters and the wreckers secretly work together? Perhaps that was why she'd told him the truth of her identity. But what about Ciara? He was sure *she* at least was a true wrecker. He didn't care what happened to Maeve, but the thought of Ciara and Aelth being blamed for what he'd done was suddenly unbearable. In the night, he'd considered telling them about Maeve being Lud. But, no. He wouldn't descend to that level.

"I acted alone," said Finn. "I mean, there were others there but they weren't involved. They must have heard the flames, but they had nothing to do with it, I swear. You must believe me."

There was another pause as the masters considered his words. Finn wondered, briefly, whether even this was a test. Whether they were aware of everything that had happened and were simply trying to get him to admit it. He didn't know, couldn't know. Perhaps by admitting his guilt he was damning Connor too; perhaps Connor had invented some unlikely story to explain Finn's actions. But what could he do?

"Yes, we accept that," the first master said. "There *are* others in the Vault that are being watched, but in this rather pathetic act of destruction it is clear you were acting alone."

That was something, a weight off his shoulders. He let out a deep breath that he appeared to have been holding in for some time.

"What happens to me?" he asked, his words catching in his parched mouth.

Another master spoke, leaning forwards into the light so that his lined face, leathery skin stretched across a skull, became visible.

"How many people would have been injured or killed if you'd succeeded, do you think? How many years of toil would have been destroyed?"

"I don't know. I mean, I didn't want to harm anyone."

"And what made you think you had the right to even try? To destroy all this?" The master sounded genuinely puzzled.

"I … I hate this place," said Finn, mumbling over his words.

"I beg your pardon?"

"I said I hate this place. Don't you understand? I hate it. Everyone here hates it. Don't you know?" It didn't matter what he said now. He had no hope of being rescued.

The master looked amazed, his brow furrowed as if he was trying to understand some difficult idea.

"But why?"

"Because … because you took my sister. And then you took my friends. Because you take everyone. And the people you bring here you change into something else, something *not them* anymore. I wish I had succeeded in destroying the blueprints. And one day, someone will."

The master looked sad now, disbelieving, as if Finn was to be pitied. He sighed. "Finn Smithson, you have been tested and you have failed. You could have been a master, could perhaps have joined the Inner Wheel one day. But instead you have rejected us and everything we offered you. You are to be sent to the mines immediately to work out the rest of your days."

The master sat back, his face disappearing back into the shadows. Finn looked around for someone, anyone to help him.

"No, please."

The masters of the Inner Wheel of Engn spoke no more. Finn's arms were seized, a silverclad soldier on each, and he was half dragged, half lifted out of the stone circle, out of the chamber.

He was taken through another metal door and down into a cramped room somewhere beneath the masters' chamber, bare except for a large circular hole in the ground, like a well. A well or a mine shaft. The silverclads thrust him towards it. Finn tried to struggle, briefly, but it was no use.

He peered into the hole. The lights in the room illuminated a sloping chute that led steeply down into the darkness. He felt heat blasting up at him from somewhere down there, as if the chute were used to tip coal into some deep furnace. Distantly he could hear sounds, *clanks* and *bangs*, the thin shouts of people from far below him.

He struggled again, but the silverclads were too strong. They pushed him forwards and Finn found himself half falling, half sliding, spinning and crashing, down into the darkness of the mines of Engn.

XXIV

Mrs. Megrim stopped to lean on the stone wall of the blacksmith's cottage. Her hips always ached first thing in the morning. They hadn't been the same since her fall. The day Finn left. Maybe she'd cracked some bone and it had healed askew. Still, it hardly mattered now.

While her breathing slowed, she studied the garden in front of her. They'd been gone only six months, Ida and Dan, but with the summer riot of growth and colour left unchecked, the garden was now a tangled mass of greenery. She doubted the two of them would ever return. They'd wait there forever outside the walls of Engn, hoping for some glimpse or mention of Finn or Shireen. Not that she blamed them. She'd thought about doing the same when Tom and Rory had been taken. But in the end, she'd decided she'd be more use at home, running the line-of-sight.

She sighed and, leaning heavily on her stick, set off up the lane. As it curved round a bend, she half expected Finn to come careering round into her. She smiled to herself at the memory of that day, Finn so wide-eyed and out of breath, terrified at the sight of her. She felt the familiar pang of loss. She missed the boy almost as much as her own children. She'd taught him all she knew, but it wasn't enough. Was he dead by now? It was possible. The messages back from the wreckers were so scarce. Years could go by without a reply, and even when she did hear something, it was some unimportant scrap of information about someone she didn't know. Still, they kept one another informed, all the operators on her line. All those they trusted. And just occasionally, a scrap of useful information got through, and someone somewhere in the valley would learn the fate of a loved one. They were still alive; they were dead. People were grateful for the news either way.

She had never heard a whisper about either of her own children. It was a cruel fact, especially when people accused her of knowing everything that went on. She'd had a few mentions of Finn in the year he'd been gone. Sightings, reports of him making his way in the machine. Then it had all cut off. Six months ago, at about the time his parents left. There was some talk of a sabotage attempt, a fire, then nothing. He'd disappeared. She sighed again. She'd tried everything to protect him, but she'd failed, just as she'd failed to protect her own children. Maybe she should go and camp outside the walls along with all the others after all. She wasn't achieving anything back there, was she? A few secret messages. They were hardly going to bring Engn crashing down.

The first few workers were already out in the Baron's fields, wading through the early-morning mist, scythes over their shoulders to begin the day's harvesting. She hadn't protected Connor, either. Although she'd always had doubts about that one. Could never tell if he was his father's son or his mother's. A strange pairing, those two, but love was love. They'd stayed together despite everything. The Baron who despised Engn and whose family had a long history of sympathy for the wreckers. His wife from a family with ancient connections to the original builders of the machine. The victors and the losers in the wars. And where did that leave Connor? Which side was he on? Finn had trusted him completely. She just hoped the boy hadn't been misguided. Connor had done well in Engn, by all accounts, risen rapidly through the ranks in part because of his mother and her family. But what his real attitude towards Engn was, she had no idea.

She could only imagine what an open sore Connor's loss was between his parents. Still, it was none of her business.

The autumn sun was peering out over the mountain tops now. She welcomed the first rays of warmth on her face. Her bones gave her less trouble in the summer heat; it was the long, cold winters she dreaded. Some nights she stayed at the Switch House, sleeping up there on a makeshift cot, rather than facing the morning walk through ice and snow. Flane kept the roads in good order now, to be sure, but she didn't trust her own limbs any more. She couldn't heat the Switch House for fear of warping the lenses, but enough layers and she could keep warm enough. And she wasn't the first to camp up there. Shireen had loved to do that when she'd first helped out, thinking herself so important guarding the Switch House overnight.

Mrs. Megrim smiled at that memory, too.

Of all those who had been taken, only Shireen was still alive, so far as she knew. News she'd only just heard. It had been such a stroke of luck for the girl, being taken directly into the Directory. It happened, sometimes. A clever girl, of course, just like her brother. It was just a shame Finn had ended up among the masters and their ridiculous games. But maybe Connor would be able to look out for him.

Maybe.

She began to shuffle her way up the spiral path to the

Switch House. The poplar trees at the edge of the fields cast vast shadows right across the hill and the hut. It looked like a sunny day at least. Something to be grateful for. At the top, she unlocked the door and stepped inside. She glanced around the familiar, gloomy interior, checking everything was in order. Then she set about opening the view ports and lining up the 'scopes, ready for the day.

The first message came through from Engn almost immediately. As happened every day, she felt a thrill of combined anticipation and dread. Perhaps today she'd hear something. News about Rory or Tom. Or Finn. But, as ever, it was just the automatic timing message, the one broadcast to all Switch Houses so that everyone across the land operated on master Engn time.

She adjusted the wheels of the little clock on her desk, then sat and waited for the first calls to route. Within minutes, they started to come through. The familiar, humdrum messages about the weather, and the harvest, and who in the valley had been seen walking out with whom, and who had fallen out with whom.

She worked dutifully away all day, making sure each message reached its intended recipient.

XXV

"Get up. Get up and dig."

The ironclad whipped his cane down onto Finn's bare back. Finn grunted but barely moved as he lay there in the dust, one eye to the ground. The pain was sharp, his back red raw, but one more cut made little difference. In any case he was too exhausted, too sick. His body cried out for him to rest, sleep, but the ironclad wasn't going to let him. They couldn't stop working because they were ill, nor because they were injured or starving. They had to dig and dig, and if they stopped, they were beaten until they started again or died from the injuries inflicted on them.

With a raw grunt of effort, teeth clenched, Finn rocked over onto his knees and, eyes still shut, lifted his hand axe to hew at the rock-face in front of him. He had no strength; the metal axe head skittered off the rock and down uselessly to the ground.

"Harder! Fill the trolley with ore."

Another stinging crack across his back. Finn didn't respond, didn't look up. He heaved up his axe again and threw all his strength into hacking at the rock in front of him. This time it gave way, a small landslide of dust and stones tumbling down to engulf his knees. Despite the filthy rag around his face he tasted rock dust, parching his mouth even more. He sometimes thought the dust would dry him out completely, leaving him a desiccated husk of bones on the cavern floor.

"Again!"

With a snarl, Finn attacked the wall, angling the end of his axe upwards at the unsupported, overhanging rock. He had learned, over the months, that this was the way to do it. Once you had the initial breakthrough at the foot, the rock above it came loose more easily. The risk was that it all came down at once and engulfed you. More than once he'd been set to work on a rockfall like that, picking away at it until he found the soft body entombed within.

"Faster. I want this trolley full when I return," the ironclad said. He strode away down the line of diggers, following the chain that anchored them together along the face. Sometimes the chain was the lifeline they used to haul a digger from a rockfall. Sometimes they even came out alive.

Finn swung again, without the strength to angle his blade properly this time. He hit lucky; another flood of dust and rock crashed to the ground, engulfing him for a moment. He worked his way backwards, coughing, spluttering. With an effort he rose to his feet. The cavern lurched around him. He lifted a head-sized boulder and began to lurch towards the waiting trolley.

Halfway there he collapsed. He must have lost consciousness. One moment he teetered along, the next he lay in the dust, his forehead throbbing where he'd struck it. The boulder he'd dropped was sharp beneath his belly.

He felt someone reach under him to haul the rock out. It would be the ironclad. This would be the end. He was too sick and too weak to care. They would whip him and whip him but there was nothing he could do but lie there and take it. He hoped it wouldn't take long. Perhaps if he bashed his head against the stone floor some more, he could knock himself out again and he wouldn't know anything about it.

"Finn, here, let me do it."

But it wasn't an ironclad; the voice was soft, muffled, familiar. Finn felt the boulder being hauled out from beneath him.

"No, Tom," Finn said, his voice a dried whisper. "No. You can't do my work, too. You have your own."

"My trolley's full," said Tom. "Full enough, anyway. I'll load what I can into yours, okay? You can't work, Finn. You're sick."

Finn looked up to see Tom's dusty boots walking away from him. The metal trolley boomed as he dropped the boulder into it. Finn crawled back towards the rock-face to collect more ore. Tom easily overtook him.

"No, Finn. You'll kill yourself. Look, keep a look-out. Rest and tell me when the ironclad is returning."

Finn looked up at Tom. The man was just walking bones himself. They all were. His face was dust and his clothes, rags. He smiled, briefly, down at Finn, wrinkles cracking the grime about his mouth.

Finn conceded defeat. He couldn't make his limbs work however much he wanted to. He nodded but said nothing. He lay with one eye sighting along the chain that stretched across the uneven floor of the cavern, watching for the return of the ironclad. He coughed constantly, just as they all did, each cough a sharp pain in his lungs. He forced himself to stay awake. He was just lucky that Tom had been next to him today. Usually when a digger collapsed or died, their companion took their ore and saved themselves a few hours' labour. He'd done it himself. Anything to survive. He was just lucky it hadn't been Graves next to him. Graves would have seen Finn struggling and taken advantage. Yanked the chain to trip him up or called the ironclads.

Life had been better, a little better, before Graves arrived. The worst of it was, the older boy blamed Finn for his ending up down there. It was Graves who'd eventually found Finn's message scraped into the lead around the skylight. He'd made his way through the tunnels only to be caught by the ironclads. Graves had been there a year now himself, taking his anger out on Finn whenever he could. It was fortunate, in a way, that they were so exhausted all the time. Graves rarely had the strength to do him any real harm.

When their shift was finally over, Tom half carried Finn away from the rock-face. Their two trolleys were both piled high; somehow Tom had managed to fill them both. Finn just hoped he would have done the same had Tom been sick.

They trudged into the main cavern, passing the line of diggers coming in to replace them. No one spoke. Boyle was among them, staring down at his feet as he shuffled along in the line. Strange, but you could never tell who would survive the mines and who wouldn't. The ones who looked strong often died quickly while the stick-thin ones somehow struggled on. It was a constant surprise to Finn that he had survived. He'd been sure, in those first gruelling days and weeks, that he would not. He wasn't strong enough; he wasn't cruel enough.

But he'd survived and Boyle had survived. So far. And the boy he knew only as Beanpole was somewhere about, too. Yet Bellow, for all his muscles and his malicious eyes, had lasted only a few weeks before a fall of rocks had crushed him. He'd been one that Finn had helped dig out. Finn had felt sure that Bellow was going to be alive under the rock. A part of Finn hadn't wanted to rescue him, wanted to leave him safely entombed there. But, of course, the ironclads had wanted the pile moving. The landslip got in the way and the rocks had to be lugged to the waiting trolleys. They'd dragged Bellow's body, purple and bleeding, his chest clearly crushed, to one of the furnaces.

His front teeth were crooked, broken that day on the Octagon.

Croft, too, had come and gone. Beaten to the ground by the ironclads for some offense. Beaten so badly he hadn't got up again. It was just a shame Graves was too smart to do something similar.

Now, Finn and Tom fell to the ground, their tattered blankets laid out in rough rectangles on the hard floor in a corner of the main cavern. The great round lights, like trapped constant suns, swayed to and fro far above them, giving everything multiple shadows.

Food and water had been wheeled out to them: a vat of porridge and a tank of the gritty, metallic water. The diggers thronged around it, fighting with their remaining strength for their share. Finn sat back and watched, too exhausted to join in. He'd seen many diggers die just because they were too ill, too injured, to fetch their own food and water. But he didn't care. He just needed to sleep.

Tom emerged from the crowd, fighting through with two metal bowls and two metal cups in his hands. Finn nodded his head at the sight, grateful but too tired to say so. Tom kneeled and tipped water into Finn's mouth from one of the cups, parting his sealed lips so none was wasted, before glugging back great gulps himself. Tom ate his gruel. Finn sipped at his but his stomach lurched at the taste of it, and he handed it back to Tom to eat.

They'd known each other since the day Finn had landed in a broken huddle at the foot of the chute. Tom hadn't recognized him, of course, but Finn immediately saw who he was, despite the grime and his thick, matted beard. Tall and slightly bent over, he had the same open, clever face, the same knowing expression in his eyes. Finn had called to him by name as they sat in the semi-dark a few nights later.

"It's Tom, isn't it? Rory's brother."

Tom had been eating then, too, sitting alone and

shovelling gruel into his mouth with determined, machine-like motions. Finn's words had stopped him dead.

"You know Rory? Is he still alive?"

"He is. At least, he was a few weeks ago. He helped me."

"Why? Why did he help you?"

His food forgotten, Tom had shuffled over to sit beside Finn. Finn hadn't been sure Rory was still alive, of course. There was a good chance he'd been caught by the ironclads by then. On the other hand, Finn hadn't seen him down in the mines. Which didn't mean he wasn't there somewhere. The diggings were vast. Still, he liked to think Rory was free, somewhere up above them in the workings. He'd told Tom everything he could recall about his brother.

"So, you've seen my mother recently, too?" Tom had asked.

"She taught me how to operate the Switch House. And lots of other things. We worked together. She was well, the last time I saw her." As with Rory, he didn't mention his last sight of her, collapsed in a heap at the side of the lane. "She was well. Bossing me around as much as ever."

Tom had grinned. "That's good."

Over the next weeks and months, they'd slowly recounted their stories to each other. They were often too exhausted, too sick, so it took time. And they both rationed what they said, out of wariness at first, but then because neither wanted to use their memories up quickly. Each fresh episode, each tiny detail of life back in the valley, was a precious moment lighting up grim days. Finn looked forwards to his conversations with Tom like nothing else. He'd been wary, at first, about discussing Connor, Diane, the wreckers. In the end it didn't seem to matter. What more could the masters do to them? He and Tom shared all their secrets, huddling close to each other on the hard rock.

Most of Tom's recollections were of life back home.

He'd known Finn's parents, of course. Finn loved to hear those stories. Tom's time in Engn had been less dramatic than Finn's. He'd told his story in just a few words, early on in their friendship.

"Rory and I were separated when we got to Engn, and I didn't see him again. They put me to work in the line-of-sight tower, because I used to help out my mother, I suppose. But they were obviously keeping a close eye on me. The first hint of something wrong, a message or two mis-transcribed, and they pulled me away and brought me down here. Said I'd failed the tests. I've been here ever since. I suppose they have to be very careful with the messages."

"The line-of-sight tower? Where's that?"

"You can't miss it; it's one of the highest. It needs it for the range, you see."

"Your brother said they could intercept messages, somehow."

"Did he? Good. But I hope they're careful. The masters are clever. You think you've got away with something and they really know all about it."

"Yes."

Now, Finn opened his eyes to glance across at Tom. His friend was one of the longest survivors of the mines. His face had the sickly, green tinge they all had. Finn had never been able to decide whether this was because of the unnatural light or the result of some disease.

"Thanks," he said. "You saved me." He began to cough. Tom shrugged, too busy eating to reply. Finn nodded his head as if everything now made sense and he turned back to gaze out across the cavern.

The size of it had always amazed him. Some said it was a natural cave that had been extended and deepened over the centuries by generations of diggers. Others said the whole thing had been dug out by axe and hand, countless thousands of people scraping and scraping away at it. Whatever the truth, the underground space was huge – far,

far greater than any hall or vault up in Engn, far greater than any room possibly could be. Pillars of rock had been left throughout to support the weight of the rock above. They looked delicate, but if you walked up to one they were titanic, curved columns like stalactites and stalagmites that had met in the middle, far broader than any tree. Finn often wondered how many people on the ground above them knew that Engn was built on that yawning space, all the workings supported by those few pillars of rock. He thought, too, about how many trolley loads of coal and ore had been cut from the rock to build the machinery. How many hands had worked away there over the centuries. It was impossible to calculate.

As he gazed out, the pillars of rock began to lurch around. It was only his exhausted mind playing tricks on him, but it looked like the whole place was coming crashing down. Just then he didn't care. So long as he could sleep. He closed his eyes, still sitting upright, his last thought the vain hope that tomorrow he would have more strength. That, somehow, he'd be able to make it through one more day in the mines.

XXVI

The next day passed in a blur of noise and pain for Finn. He awoke still exhausted, shivering and sweating at the same time. He was aware, distantly, of an ironclad standing over him, a kick in his side, a voice bellowing at him to get up. He knew he could not and knew that meant he was no longer any use to them. Neither thing seemed terribly important.

Then he heard Tom speaking as a strong arm hauled him to his feet. "He'll be fine. He'll come around."

"He'd better."

The ironclad strode away. Finn tried to support himself with his own legs, but they'd turned to grass. He lay back on the ground while Tom dribbled more water into his mouth. He felt it trickling down inside him as if he were hollow.

"Come on, Finn. You just need to get to the rock face."

Finn nodded, lacking the strength to reply. Tom pulled him back to his feet and, surrounded by the other diggers, they worked their way along the shaft to the seam of ore.

Kneeling, Finn tried to work the rock, swinging the axe he could barely lift. The walls lurched around in front of him, seeming to be both near and distant at the same time. Sometimes a flurry of dust and rock came away as he struck. More often, he dropped the axe completely. He lost track of time. He'd been working there for moments and for years. He saw the rock face before him and also saw himself from above, looking down on his weak, useless swipes at the wall. He coughed and coughed, but the pain in his chest felt distant, as if it belonged to someone else.

Once, his father tapped him on the shoulder. "It's all right, Finn. You've done very well. Let me dig for you now."

Finn often imagined his parents coming for him, rescuing him, as they always had in the old days if he was in trouble. But when he looked around and up it wasn't his father after all. It was someone he only vaguely recognized.

"Let me cut into the wall, Finn. Then at least it will look like you're working."

Finn shook his head, refusing to let go of his axe. People would steal anything down there. Without an axe he was useless.

"It's okay, Finn," said the man. "It's me, Tom. I'll give it back to you once I've started the cut. I promise."

Finn nodded and let go of the axe, too exhausted to argue. He sat back, waiting for the next thing to happen. The man – Tom – hacked out an undercut in the rock-face, then handed the axe back to Finn. "Here. It won't take much to make it fall now." Finn tried to lift the axe and make it hit the wall in front of him. On his third attempt, a small rattle of rubble and dust fell to the ground in front of him.

Delirious dreams filled him all day, filling the cave around him. He saw familiar faces in the markings on the rocks. They called to him in voices that made him feel sick. He was back in the valley helping his father beat red-hot iron in the forge. He was on the swing in the forest, the tree trunks lurching around him. He was back inside the moving engine, lying on his back, jolted around as they trundled along the valley lane. He was in the mines with Tom shaking him as an ironclad walked by, and this was the real world, not a nightmare.

Somehow, without Finn knowing how, his trolley filled with ore. He tried to make it look as though he was working each time Tom roused him but couldn't keep it up for more than a few minutes. Numerous times the whip stung across his back, but the pain felt mercifully distant. Each time he managed to work on for a little longer, until the ironclad strode away. He panted deep breaths, as if he'd been running for miles.

He didn't recall the trudge back to their beds at the end of the day. Tom said nothing. A little later there was another trickle of cool water in his mouth. Then he felt the scratch of his rough bed against his cheek and he knew he could close his eyes and sleep at last.

A week later, Finn and his gang of diggers were roused by the ironclads and told to prepare for a march. The week had passed in a confusion of exhaustion and sickness for Finn, but he'd survived thanks to Tom. He was slowly recovering, gaining a little more strength each day. At some point – he couldn't recall when – he'd fallen badly and ricked his back, making it difficult for him to stoop or even walk. Yet, strangely, that seemed to help; it gave him something to focus on so that he forgot how sick he felt. But the thought of a long march through the mines filled him with dread again.

"You're needed at the top-end," said the ironclad. "The wheels need re-caulking. Gather your belongings; we leave now."

A murmur of delight passed through the diggers at this. Re-caulking the wheels was a rare privilege. It was dangerous work, but less so than digging, and any change to their gruelling routine was welcome. Finn just hoped he could make it that far. It was miles to the wheels. At least they wouldn't be chained together. If someone fell and couldn't stand again, it took too much time to unshackle everyone.

Soon, the gang of thirty of them were filing down onto the main cavern floor, each carrying their bundle of bedding rags. They headed towards the nearest of the supporting stone pillars. The ground fell slightly as they trudged along. Finn's ricked back hurt constantly, jarred by each step. He sucked at the gaps in his gums as he went, a habit from when his teeth had started to fall out. Another was loose now. No one knew why that happened, but it was the same for everyone. You could tell how long someone had been down there by how few teeth they had left. Tom had three.

Two or three hours into the first day of the march, they skirted around a depression in the ground. Water pooled within it. Drops fell from the distant roof, great fat globes of water that reminded Finn of something – the ball-bearings that Rory had made perhaps. One of the drops fell onto the top of his head, instantly cold and wonderful. The ironclads let them stop and drink, refill water bottles.

"Where does all that water go?" he asked Tom. They could talk so long as they kept their heads down and spoke in a hushed whisper.

Tom glanced across at the nearest ironclad, checking they weren't being watched.

"Drainage hole. A tunnel leads away deeper into the rock. It's filled with water; no one knows how long it is."

"Has anyone ever tried to escape this way? Through the water?"

"You don't give up, do you, Finn? Enough of this.

Why don't you just accept you can't beat them, can't escape, can't change anything? Don't even think about it."

It was a long debate between them. Finn spent hours and days puzzling over ways to escape the mines. When he thought he had a scheme he would report it to Tom who, invariably, explained why it was unworkable. He had seen it tried, knew it was impossible.

"I can't just give up," Finn always said.

In truth he was often tempted to do just that. It was hopeless and he often despaired. Destroying Engn was utterly impossible. But then some spark would reignite inside him and he knew he wouldn't give up even if it was pointless. He would never give in.

"So, no one has tried to get out that way?" he asked.

Tom sighed. Finn thought he wasn't going to reply at first, but then he answered. "Saw two people try it once. Just dived in. The ironclads sat on their horses, doing nothing. One of the two stayed down for a couple of minutes before bursting up, gasping for breath."

"What did the ironclads do?"

"Hauled him out and made him find a boulder. They chained it to him then threw him back in."

"What about the other person?"

"Came back eventually. His body did, anyway. Bobbed up to the surface after an hour or so, blue and lifeless."

Finn nodded, making careful note of the information. There *had* to be some way. The chutes they pushed people down were no good. His memory of crashing and clanging down from above was confused, but he did clearly recall the smooth metal sides he scrabbled against to try to slow himself down. Even if you could reach one of the chutes protruding partway up the walls, it would surely be impossible to climb up to the surface without at least a rope let down for you.

There were doors, of course. The ironclad guards came and went through them each day. But they were heavy iron slabs, locked from the other side and constantly guarded.

They were only ever opened when a troop of ironclads was passing in or out, and it would surely be impossible to sneak through then.

It was rumoured there was an unguarded door somewhere in the caverns, beyond which a simple flight of steps led up to the surface. People sometimes claimed to have glimpsed it in the distance, but neither Finn nor Tom had ever seen it. It was just some crazy story. A desperate fantasy to give people hope.

Finn sometimes dreamed about bashing through to a forgotten tunnel as he laboured away at the rock face, a sudden blast of cold air on his face, a glimpse of sky. He knew that was impossible. They were too far underground; they could dig for ever and never see the surface. Still, it was a glorious thought. Perhaps *this* blow. Perhaps *this* blow.

He knew that no one ever escaped the mines. The only way out was into the flames of the furnace, when you were too exhausted or broken to work anymore. But that didn't prevent him puzzling over the problem constantly.

Partway through the second day of their march, one of the diggers in front of Finn staggered and collapsed. It was a man he didn't know, a recent newcomer, his hair still quite short, all his teeth showing. His eyes were shut as he lay there on the ground, chest heaving rapidly.

Finn stopped to try and haul the man back to his feet. He felt Tom's firm grip on his arm, pulling him along. "You can't stop, Finn. They'll beat you and make you run after us. You can't do anything."

"We can't just leave him there to die."

"We have to."

Finn caught Tom's intent glare for a moment. The man lay on the ground, unmoving. One of the ironclads had spurred his horse forwards and trotted towards him.

"You didn't just let me die the other day," said Finn. "All those other times."

"No, I didn't. Because I could do something about it.

And because we're friends. There's nothing we can do for him, not out here."

"So, if I fell here and couldn't go on what would you do then? Leave me, too?"

Tom didn't reply for a moment. They both heard the fallen man whimper as the ironclad kicked him to try to rouse him.

"I'd have to, Finn. And you'd have to do the same to me. Understand?"

"I don't believe you."

"You should. How would it help getting us both killed?"

Finn looked from the fallen man and up at Tom. Tom looked away. Finn saw that he meant what he said. They walked in silence after that.

Over the next two days, they wound their way around twenty-four of the vast stone pillars, each far wider at its base than Finn's house in the valley. From a distance the pillars looked slender, and Finn fantasized about hacking away at one, bringing the whole cavern, the whole of Engn, crashing down. But up close he could see how impossible that would be. It would take a whole gang of them years and years to do it. Gazing up to the distant ceiling, Finn wondered if there were spy-holes up there, masters with telescopes gazing down as they had in the Valve Hall. If there were, they were too tiny to see.

They arrived beneath the wheels late on the second day. They were exhausted, barely walking, but they'd lost no one else on the way. Graves, unfortunately, had survived. They'd met two other gangs crossing the cavern floor, each person haloed by four, five, six shadows from the enormous swinging orbs up above them. Finn had seen no one he recognized. With all the grime and dust, it was hard to identify anyone.

The ironclads leading them pointed at a patch of the stone ground where they were to lie. Finn and the others trudged across, the last few paces almost too much. They fell to the floor, sitting or lying, utterly spent. Finn just hoped they weren't expected to work without sleeping and eating first. He knew he wouldn't be able to.

From his position on the ground he gazed up at their reason for being there. The line of six wheels filled the upper end of the great cavern. Their immense creaking and groaning had been audible for miles, slowly drowning out the normal background noise of the mines: the *clink, clink* of axe on stone, the scuffling of feet, the squeak of trolley wheels, the cries. The cavern was lower there, floor and ceiling sloping together. Even so, only a part of each wheel was visible. Their lower curves ran inside deep channels in the ground, the course of the underground river that flowed beneath Engn. The En. The spray from the gushing, foaming waters filled the air, making every surface slick. The wheels scooped it up and, by doing so, kept the mines from flooding. The tops of the wheels were also invisible: protruding through great cuts in the ceiling of the caves, the surface-level of the machine. Somewhere up there they tipped their water into a vast reservoir: to drink, perhaps, or to feed the pipes that led to the steam engines. The wheels were a marvel to see. Finn, exhausted as he was, still out of breath, tried to work out how they'd been constructed, how they'd been set in place. His father would have been fascinated by them.

Each wheel was wooden, held together by a spider's web of black iron rods and plates. Finn could see chains driving them, looping down and around their hubs from up on the surface. They were steam-powered, clearly; the force of the river would never be enough to lift its own water up so high. From a distance they appeared to turn slowly, reluctantly, but that was just an illusion because of their great size. Up close they rolled at an alarming rate, the great scoops shooting up into the air, dripping cascades of water. Their speed and power dizzied Finn. The nearest wheel, however, wasn't in use. It rotated very slowly, without any water pouring off it.

"How do they work?" asked Finn. Tom had worked on the wheels more than once in the past.

"They control the flow with sluice gates," said Tom without opening his eyes. "When they need to maintain one of the wheels, they close off the flow to it. Then we can work on it, repair the rotten wood, re-caulk them so each bucket's waterproof."

Finn nodded. He watched as a gang clambered out of one of the buckets of the wheel, iron tools in hand. Just that one scoop looked as big as a barn, effectively a wooden room enclosed on all four sides, with a floor but no roof. It swung freely on its own axis so the water didn't spill out as the wheel turned. Some mechanism up on top forced each bucket to tip over at the right moment, spilling the water out to be collected. The power needed to operate the whole thing was incredible.

Finn lay back and thought of the times he'd helped his father re-caulk their own waterwheel back home. It had been one of their regular late-summer tasks, when the water was low and the wheel could be stopped for a few days without anyone minding the loss of electricity. It was a job he'd never enjoyed. Still, he wished he was back there with his father now.

"If all the wheels stopped at once the mine would flood?"

Tom eyed him suspiciously, afraid he was hatching another plot. "I suppose so. They say this is where Engn started. The first wheel was put into the En to power the wheels they needed to keep these delvings from flooding."

"What were they even digging for?" It occurred to him only then that he'd never asked the question. They hewed at the rock to extend the mines, but he'd never known why.

"Iron and coal at first," said Tom. "When I came here, we were also told to look out for specks of a greyish mineral flecked with silvery sparkles. We were told not to touch it if we saw it but to tell the masters immediately. I've never seen any and the masters appear to have forgotten all about it. Come to think of it, I've never seen any seams of coal or iron either. We dig because there are mines, that's all there is to it."

"But..."

A shadow fell over them. "You. Get up." An ironclad stood there, interrupting their conversation. He kicked one of the nearby diggers. "All of you, move."

There was a chorus of groans. But they weren't being made to start work on the wheels. Instead, food and water had been brought for them. Finn rose and staggered forwards, Tom next to him, to get his share. The gruel was warm, as if it had been made somewhere nearby. But the water was icy cold, scooped up, presumably, from the underground river.

When they had eaten and drunk, they were finally allowed to sleep. Gratefully, Finn closed his eyes and curled up on the bare, damp rock. He hugged his bundle of blankets to his chin and fell into deep slumber.

The next morning, they were instructed in what they had to do by one of the ironclads, shouting at them over the roar of the water and the deafening creaks of the wheels. "Cut away any dead wood and replace it with fresh laths. Understand? Then the entire inside of each bucket is to be re-caulked with tar. It must be completely waterproof."

The ironclad indicated a cauldron of black, acrid liquid bubbling away over a fire. A path of black splashes from countless thousands of spills led away from it and up to the wheel. A worker ran up, clanking an empty bucket. Spots of black spattered his head, the skin red and angry. The worker climbed onto a step and ladled out more of the tar before lugging the bucket away, struggling awkwardly with its swaying weight.

The buckets on the wheel being repaired were locked in place so they didn't rotate around their own axis. That had puzzled Finn at first but now he saw why. As the wheel turned, the scoops turned with it rather than pivoting to remain horizontal. If they hadn't been locked the workers wouldn't have been able to reach up the sides of each bucket. As it was, they could climb in as one bucket descended towards the floor and set to work on its lower wall while it was still horizontal enough to stand on. As the wheel turned, they could then move on to the base of the bucket and, as they rose back into the air again, the other wall. Rickety wooden ladders had been strapped to the frame of the wheel to allow them to climb in and out.

"Listen out for this bell," continued the ironclad. "When it rings you are to leave the bucket immediately. Understand? If you don't, you'll be tipped out by the turning wheel. You have until the bell rings to complete each scoop, then you start work on the next one."

They filed away towards a rack of iron axes and scrapers and large leather brushes that were used to apply the tar. Finn took one of each and, following Tom, walked up to the wheel. Graves, some way ahead in the line, glanced back at him. Finn looked away. He had more important things to worry about.

They worked all that day, stripping and re-caulking three room-sized buckets. The wood was green where the water had washed away the old layers of tar and some of it was mushy and soft. The stench of the treacly, black liquid made Finn retch and cough as he worked. He tried to keep his mouth shut as he scraped and brushed, but it made no difference. The smell crept inside him. They had to work fast, before the tar cooled and solidified in the bucket. That inevitably meant they all got splashed with it.

At all times they listened for the bell. The slow, inexorable tilt of each bucket was alarming. Finn felt safest when the wheel was at its lowest point, the high wooden walls on each side reassuring. As the wheel continued to turn, the floor became steeper and steeper and they had to step down onto what had been the wall. Eventually this became horizontal, then continued to tip with nothing to stop them being pitched out. The ironclad watching from the ground below made sure the scoop was completely re-caulked before ringing the bell. Several times they had to work away as the angle of the floor became almost too steep to cling onto. Below them was just the gaping vault of air and the fall to the distant ground.

Finally, they were allowed to rest, clambering onto the rickety ladders lashed to the wheel's frame. As they trudged back to their camp, another crew of workers stood in line, waiting to take their place. Finn's head throbbed from the fumes he'd been breathing in all day. He drank three cups of water but, unable to face any food, lay down to sleep as soon as he could.

Bells awoke him, the same urgent clanging note, over and over. Something was wrong. He sat up, wondering how long he had slept. It was impossible to say in the eternal twilight of the caves, but he had the impression hours had passed by.

A group of workers stood at the base of the wheel. An ironclad clanged the bell nearby. Everyone looked upwards. Finn, following their gaze, saw that one of the workers hadn't climbed down in time. He now dangled from the lip of the tilting bucket, holding onto some ridge in the wood with one hand. Finn watched as tools and then a tub of tar slid down the wooden side of the rising bucket to fall to the ground.

For a moment he thought the worker up there would survive. He managed to get a grip with his other hand and began to haul himself upwards. Perhaps he could wedge himself into the framework of the wheel until it turned full circle. But that wasn't his plan. Instead, he began to swing his body to and fro, building up momentum. Then, his legs at full extension away from the great wheel, he let go and catapulted himself into the air, away from the wheel. For a moment he hung there. He surely had no chance of surviving, but Finn thrilled at the sight of him. The man turned like a leaping fish and dove towards the ground.

Except, he wasn't aiming for the ground. A trickle of water still ran in the channel under the wheel. The sluice gates were not fully water-tight. The water wasn't deep, three or four feet at the most, but at least it was softer than rock. That was what he was aiming for.

His aim was nearly perfect. He arrowed vertically down to the water, very fast, surely too fast for such shallows, but on target at least. Then he overbalanced and began to wobble in the air. His side banged into the lip of the channel. He was suddenly a crumpled huddle of rags rather than a diver. He disappeared out of sight. Nearby workers clustered around the channel, peering down. Finn, standing, ran to join them.

"Stop! Into the next bucket!" The ironclad continued to ring the bell as he shouted at the workers. "You're losing time. Begin work immediately!"

The others stopped and walked back to the base of the wheel to begin their shift. Finn carried on, hoping he would be allowed to rescue the man since his shift was over. The ironclad let him. They probably needed to know whether they'd lost another worker, anyway.

Finn knelt at the side of the channel and peered down into the dark. The spray soaked Finn's face, making it hard to see detail. He could just make out a formless shape there, bobbing in the water, not moving.

"Here. I've got a rope."

Tom stood behind him. Between them they let the rope down, dangling it near the shape as if they were fishing.

"Grab the rope!" Finn shouted down. "We'll pull you up."

The body in the water didn't move.

"Fall must have killed him," said Tom.

"No. I'm going down to check," said Finn.

He hauled the rope up and tied it around his waist. He wound the other end around one of the vast wooden stays that supported the wheel-housing.

"Lower me down," he said to Tom.

"What about your back? You could barely walk yesterday."

"It's a lot freer today. I can do this."

In the confined space of the channel it was instantly darker, the roaring and banging sounds from up above echoing weirdly off the sheer walls, making them seem immediately distant. The stone was thick with green slime. Finn wondered, briefly, whether this was a way out. The water flowing under the wheels had to go somewhere. There had to be a channel leading away underground. Was it like the soak-hole back in the middle of the cavern, completely flooded? Or could there be an air gap? Could you bob and gasp your way through?

But when he reached the surface of the underground water, he could see it was useless. The river entered an underground tunnel, the waters swirling angrily around as if fighting to escape. It was possible the tunnel opened out eventually, but there was no gap, no air to breathe. That wasn't the answer.

"Keep going," he shouted up to Tom.

The cold water made him cry out as the rope dipped him into it. He couldn't recall the last time he'd been immersed in water. The body bobbed nearby, but it was hard to reach in the whirlpool at the end of the channel. Finn floundered around trying to grab hold of a leg before, finally, snagging it by its loose clothes. He pulled himself nearer. The man was on his back at least, face to the air. Hard to tell whether he was still alive. Finn thought he saw movement in the hands, a faint gesture, but it may have been the current. Treading water, he untied the rope and fastened it under the arms of the man. He had to hurry. He was already weary, fatigue making his legs leaden.

"Pull him up!" he shouted to Tom.

Finn found a notch in the stone of the wall he could wedge one foot into and another higher up he could hold onto while he waited. Slowly, jerk by jerk, the sagging, dripping body was hauled back upwards to the light.

After a long, long time, so long that Finn began to think Tom had forgotten him, the end of the rope came back down. Finn tied it around himself and, walking up the slimy side of the wall, doing his best to place his weight in footholds in the rock, he too ascended.

Back on the surface, Finn kneeled and gasped air back into his lungs. Coughing fits made sucking in enough air hard. A short distance away, four of five people stood next to Tom, also breathing deeply at the exertion of hauling the two of them up. The man they had rescued lay on the ground, unmoving. The ironclad in charge stood nearby, watching. Finn didn't know the ironclad's name, of course, but he recognized him as one who often manned the wheels. The swell of his stomach stretched the black leather of his armour taut and he wheezed sometimes as he walked. It had occurred to Finn more than once that all the diggers together could easily overwhelm him and make their escape. The problem, of course, was that it wouldn't do any good. There was nowhere for them to run to.

Finn crawled across to the man they'd rescued. Long, straggly hair covered his gaunt face. Finn pushed it away, thinking to breathe air into the unmoving figure's mouth.

Bring him back to life. It was then that he saw who it was they had pulled from the water. Saw that it wasn't a man after all but a young woman. In the mines it was hard to tell the difference; they were all just half-starved, filthy skeletons.

"Well, is he dead or not?"

Finn sat her up and, working from behind, tried to pump water from her lungs. The ironclad grew impatient, smacking his cane against the leather of his boots. He wouldn't wait for long. Just then, the woman coughed and spluttered, retching up mouthfuls of water that splashed onto the stone floor.

"He's half-dead," said the ironclad. "Furnace would be best for him anyway."

"No," said Finn. "*She'll* be fine. Just needs a night's rest and she can get back to work on the wheels tomorrow."

He looked up at the ironclad. The man's eyes were invisible inside his helmet. Finn thought he wasn't going to allow it. Then he seemed to relent.

"He or she, what does it matter? She can rest until her next shift. If she can't work by then we'll dispose of her."

Between them, Finn and Tom carried her back to the beds and laid her down on their own bundled rags. Tom looked questioningly at Finn, seeing that he knew who she was. But he didn't say anything, simply looking on while Finn tried to make her comfortable. Finn did his best to check her for injuries. There was a great red mark where her hip had bashed into the lip of the rock as she fell. Other than that, she appeared to be uninjured.

As he worked, she opened her eyes to look at him. She raised her hand and put it to Finn's cheek, stroking him with a feather touch.

"Oh, Finn. Look what they've done to you. You were such a fine-looking boy."

Finn took hold of Diane's hand and cried with laughter.

XXVII

They sat together in the hours before Finn had to work, Diane lying on the floor, unable to get comfortable, Finn propped against the rock wall beside her. Tom had gone back to bed, saying nothing, once Finn had explained who Diane was.

"He's really Mrs. Megrim's son?" asked Diane.

"One of them."

"He doesn't seem as bad as his mother."

"He's not. I mean, neither was Mrs. Megrim really. Once you and Connor had left, I got to know her well."

"They came for Connor too?"

"You didn't know? Of course. That's why they were there in the valley that day. They hadn't come for you — they came for him."

"Ah."

She stared up at the cavern ceiling for a moment, as if trying to remember everything that had happened. "You lost both of us at the same time. On the same day."

Finn nodded. She had too, of course. They all had. It

occurred to him only then that this was something else he had in common with Mrs. Megrim, who had also lost two beloved people to Engn on the same day.

"I'm sorry, Finn," she said. "I had to leave. I had to try and stay ahead of them. I thought they were coming for me."

"I know."

He glanced down at Diane's face, cast into half-shadow by the great spokes of the nearby wheel. He was delighted to see her, more delighted than he could begin to say. But the sight of her was also a sharp blow, like being punched in the stomach. He could see she'd been through a lot. He'd thought about her often, imagining her still running free outside in the wilds, always one step ahead of the ironclads. Or maybe even settled down somewhere, a place far away where the soldiers of Engn never came. He had invented this whole story: her peaceful, happy life deep in the distant woods. Because, somehow, if she was still free, part of him was still free, too. Only now it wasn't.

"Here," he said. "I've still got this. Remember that day you made them?"

He prized a knotted twist of metal from the seam of his jacket: wire that had once been a ring. "It's a bit battered, I'm afraid. I've kept it with me ever since."

She flashed a bright smile at him. He couldn't remember the last time he'd seen someone smiling. She still had all her teeth. She looked so young and alive. He felt as if, briefly, a light had been switched on inside him. A flood of forgotten, glorious emotions ran through him. For a moment, he was Finn again. The real Finn.

"Still got mine, too," she said. She fished inside her tunic for a piece of string, pulling it out for Finn to see. "I wore mine until they captured me. Hopefully no one will see it on this chain."

"When did they catch you? How long have you been here?"

"About two weeks."

"Two weeks! But that's fantastic. So, all this time you have been out there, living free. I used to imagine that, and me there with you. It helped, you know."

"It wasn't always a lot of fun. They never let up. I had to keep moving. Still, it was better than being here."

"And they brought you straight down into the mines?"

"Yeah. I guess because I'd run. What about you? Have you been down here all the time?"

The portly ironclad strode by, casting a glance at them, looking as if he was about to say something. Then he shrugged and walked on. If they wanted to waste their sleeping time talking that was their problem. So long as it didn't affect their work.

"It's a long story," said Finn, whispering more quietly. "And you should sleep. We both should."

"No, tell me everything that happened to you. I can't sleep. I used to imagine what you were up to as well. I thought *you* had the ideal life, that wonderful cottage with your mother and father, all the food you wanted, safe and secure. The thought of you, you and Connor, kept me going too, I guess."

Finn shook his head at the irony of it. "Okay," he said, and he began to relate to her everything that had happened since the day she left.

She was silent when he finished, so silent that Finn thought, at first, she'd fallen asleep after all.

"I'm sorry," she said finally. "For everything you've been through."

Finn shrugged. "It doesn't matter now. We've just got to get out of here. Now that we've found each other we can escape together. Don't you see? Perhaps this was supposed to happen. Perhaps we were meant to meet down here."

"Meant by who, Finn?"

"Well, perhaps it's all part of the plan. Connor's plan, I mean."

She leaned up on one elbow, wincing at the pain in her side. "You're not seriously saying you still believe all that, are you? You still think he's that boy you grew up with, that he's still on your side?"

Privately, he'd had doubts, of course. When he was half-dead from hacking at the rock walls or lying awake in the middle of the night too exhausted to sleep, he'd sometimes think he'd been abandoned down there. But finding Diane had given him hope again.

"Well, yes. We made a vow."

"You're such a child, Finn. Don't you see what's happening here? Connor's making a name for himself up there. You and I are just an embarrassment to him, a threat. He's not going to want anyone to know about his pact to destroy Engn, is he? If there is a plan it's just to get us out of the way. He made sure you ended up here, set you up, and he probably made sure I got brought down here, too."

"I don't believe it," said Finn. "Connor wouldn't do that."

"He's done it, Finn. He did it years ago."

"No. He's got a plan and this is all part of it. I know it seems he's left me to die here, but he hasn't. There's a reason for me coming here, for everything that's happened. I know there is."

Diane shook her head. "People change, Finn."

"Yes. But they also stay the same, deep down. You didn't know him long. I did. We grew up together. And besides, if we don't do this, no one else will. I explained about the wreckers and Lud. I don't think they're ever going to really *do* anything."

Diane sighed and lay back down, closing her eyes. Finn looked away. Perhaps she was right. His eyes prickled with fatigue. He wanted to sleep but it would soon be time for the start of his shift. If Diane was right then there was no hope. There was no escape and they would die down there: he, Diane, Tom, all of them.

He thought back to the day in the tree, the day of the avalanche. In the blur of misery and fatigue he'd lost track of the passage of months, but that memory seemed clearer and brighter all the time. The day he and Connor had started out as enemies and become friends. He gazed over the scene in front of him, the huddled lines of workers lying in their rags like giant moth cocoons. The vast, turning wheels beyond them. The food trolley trundling along its rail towards them. The master ringing the bell to call the workers down from the buckets to end their shift. Soon it would be Finn's turn. He was exhausted, utterly exhausted, but he was used to that. He would get through the hours somehow. Caulking the wheels wasn't as bad as digging. You were hidden a lot of the time, inside the buckets where the masters couldn't see how hard you worked.

As he gazed, he suddenly saw what the answer was, how they could escape the mines. He glanced around, then down at Diane, his stomach fizzing with anticipation. It could work, it really could. They would need luck, but there was a chance. Diane was a good swimmer; that would help. A memory of a day at the millpond flashed through his mind, her long legs slipping under the water as she dived in, a memory that often drifted through his mind.

"Will you at least come with me if I leave?" he asked her, lowering his head to be very near hers.

"Leave? There is no way out, Finn. Everyone knows that."

"No," he said. "There is a way. This time tomorrow, I'm going. We can escape together. It's what we're supposed to do."

"It's not possible, Finn!" In her anger she spoke too

loudly, and one or two of the other workers stirred, scowling at being woken up before necessary. Sleep was their only refuge. Diane dropped her voice back to a whisper. "Haven't you seen what's up there? The size of it? It isn't some stupid pile of twigs; it's vast, it goes on forever. You can't destroy all that. We never had a chance."

"No, you're wrong," he replied, trying to keep his voice down. "It is possible. To get out, I mean. And then, after that, we'll see. Come with me and I'll show you."

"It's hopeless."

"At least say you'll try to escape. Please? You've got nothing to lose by staying here, believe me."

She studied his face for long moments. Then she shut her eyes.

"Okay, Finn," she said. "We'll escape the mines of Engn tomorrow. Whatever you say."

Finn sat deep in thought, thinking over the details of what they would have to do. He glanced over at Tom being kicked awake by an ironclad guard. They would need a diversion, someone to stay behind. Could he really ask Tom to do that? He tried to think of some alternative until the bell rang for them to start work.

Finn waited until the great wooden bucket was at its lowest point on the wheel before talking to Tom. The ironclads sometimes perched at the top of one of the ladders to watch them, but if there wasn't one there you were safe to talk for a moment. Tom worked in one of the corners, splashing tar onto the freshly exposed wood. Spots of black speckled his face. Finn, cutting away decayed, soggy wood with a saw and a file, worked his way across. The others in the gang were some distance away. He talked quickly, in hushed tones.

"I need your help. I'm going to get out tomorrow morning."

Tom carried on working away, slapping the thick, sludgy tar onto the wood. "Are you now?"

"I've worked out how to do it, you see. This time it will work. Diane gave me the idea. It's easy. The only problem is I need something to distract the ironclads for a moment and…"

He tailed off. He was asking Tom to stay behind. Strong, reliable Tom. He was asking him to sacrifice himself so he and Diane could escape. He'd take Tom, too, if he could. He'd take all of them apart from Graves. But it wasn't possible. But if two of them could escape, maybe they could wreck the workings and set everyone free eventually.

"No, Finn. I'm sorry," said Tom, not looking up from his work.

"We'd take you if we could, Tom. You know that. But we need someone we can trust to stay here. Just for now."

Tom shook his head. "You don't get it, do you? I'm not going to help you because I'm not going to let you get yourself killed. I've kept you alive all this time. Whatever you're planning, it isn't going to work."

"But it will, I know it." He'd raised his voice now. A few of the others glanced over at them, frowning. It wasn't unknown for fights to break out when the ironclads' gaze was elsewhere, and any trouble often meant punishment for them all.

"It won't," said Tom. "And if I have to put up with you getting angry at me to save your skin again, then that's fine. But I won't help you."

"Please, Tom."

But the older man would say no more. Soon an ironclad climbed up the ladder to oversee them and Finn worked his way away from the corner, attacking the rotten wood of the floor with feverish anger. Without Tom they had no chance.

Diane was still asleep when he returned. She stirred as Finn lay down nearby but there was no chance to talk. The ironclads were already urging the new shift to begin. Diane struggled to her feet, clearly in pain. She set off to follow the others but the portly ironclad waved her back. She wasn't fit yet, would be a danger to others. Finn knew, as Diane surely did too, that they wouldn't wait forever. If she wasn't ready for work soon, they'd give up on her. Finn just hoped she'd be mobile enough to escape with him.

Finn watched her for a time, picking her way around the scattered piles of rags where the others from her shift had slept, trying to work some movement back into her back. He wanted to say something to her, tell her about Tom, but he couldn't. Too many guards milled around. One of them directed her to push the empty meal trolley away. Finn slipped into a troubled slumber as he tried to think of a way to distract the ironclads long enough to put his plans into action.

He awoke feeling barely rested, a knot of anxiety fizzing away in his stomach. The other shift was coming down from the wheel and soon he would have to climb back on to begin work. He glanced up at the curve of the great wheel, checking out which bucket the others had completed while he slept. His calculations of two days earlier were correct. The wheel was almost completely re-caulked now; today might be their last day on it. He and Diane had to leave now.

He looked around and saw her helping to push the new food trolley towards the camp. She grimaced with the effort and pain of it, but she was moving a little better.

That was something. She looked up at Finn, catching his gaze. Finn nodded to her, telling her now was the time – be ready.

He looked around for Tom, hoping his friend had relented and was somewhere nearby ready to help them. But Tom was queuing up for the morning's gruel, his back turned to Finn.

Someone kicked Finn in the side, a sharp blow that made him recoil with pain. He turned expecting to see an ironclad urging him to work. But instead it was Graves standing over him.

"Leave me alone, Graves," said Finn. "I'm not afraid of you anymore."

"You should be. Because I know all about your plan."

"My plan?"

"Oh, yes, I heard the two of you arranging it all. Well, you're taking me with you, Smithson. It's your fault I'm down here so you can get me out."

"What makes you think I would ever do anything for you, Graves? You can rot down here for the rest of your life as far as I care."

Graves grinned. "Because if you don't take me, I'll tell the ironclads what you're planning."

"They won't believe you."

"Won't they? Sure about that? Maybe they'll cart you off to the furnaces just in case I'm right, eh?"

Finn thought quickly. He doubted the ironclads would believe Graves, but if the older boy did tell them what he'd heard it would make it impossible for Finn and Diane to slip away. And they might never make it back to the wheels. He had to act now.

He looked at Graves, grinning away at his own cleverness. Except, he wasn't clever, was he? He was brighter than Croft or Bellow, maybe, but that wasn't saying much. He'd ruled the dormitory because he was the strongest, the tallest, the meanest. And he had no idea what Finn's plans actually were. He hadn't explained them to Diane or Tom. Finn saw, then, what he should do, how to engineer the distraction he needed.

He slumped his shoulders and sighed, feigning defeat. "You win, Graves. We'll take you. But once we're back on the surface, we go our separate ways, yes? You're on your own and we never see each other again."

Graves nodded. "Suits me. So, what's the plan? What do we do?"

Finn nodded over at the metal trolley that brought them their vats of gruel each day. "Know where that goes when it's empty?"

Graves shook his head, eyes narrowing as he tried to understand Finn's plan.

"I found out," said Finn. "They make the slop upstairs, on the surface. There's a little cage they haul up and down on a chain, over at the end of the rail. It's big enough for those metal churns so it's big enough for one of us. That's the plan. We go up one at a time."

"The ironclads will see us. They must guard it."

"No, that's the beauty of it. See, Diane's been pushing the food and water over there, checking it all out. The ironclads don't inspect the trolleys. All we have to do is take the empty churns out and there'll be room for me – for the two of us I mean – inside. Diane can just push us along. When the shift starts the ironclads are too busy watching the wheel to see us. We just take turns ascending in the cage. We can be up and out in minutes."

Croft looked doubtful, seeing problems with the plan. Finn wasn't surprised. It sounded wild and unbelievable to him even as he made it up. He carried on talking before Graves could object. "I'll go up first, make sure the coast is clear, then send the cage back for you."

"You think I'm stupid, don't you?" said Graves. "I'll go up first, understand?"

Finn frowned, pretending to calculate. "And why should I trust you?"

"You haven't got much choice, have you?"

Finn waited a moment more, then sighed. "Okay," he said. "But make sure you send the cage back down. You'll need me up there. I've seen a lot more of Engn than you have."

Graves grinned, and Finn knew he planned to leave the two of them stranded down there once he was free.

"Of course," said Graves. "But where do we hide the churns?"

"That's easy," said Finn. "We just stack them over by the wheel, carry them over as if we've been told to by one of the ironclads. They often get taken over there for cleaning in the river. The ironclads won't suspect anything; they don't count them or anything."

Finn turned to set off. There were only a few moments before the bell rang for the start of the shift and he didn't want Graves to have too much time to think about the plan.

"Where are you going?" called Graves as Finn walked away.

"I'll distract the ironclads while you move the churns. I'll keep them talking about something and make sure they don't see you, okay?"

It was a nice touch. In reality Graves would be the one causing the distraction for the guards. He just had to hope Graves wouldn't see that.

"Why don't I talk to the ironclads and you move the churns?" asked Graves.

"If you like," said Finn. "Doesn't really matter. Only, I've got this whole story worked out, one to keep them occupied for a few minutes. If you'd rather do that bit then feel free. But you'll need to keep them busy for long enough or we'll never get away."

There was only the briefest pause while Graves considered. "No, you do that, talk to the ironclads. I'll lug the churns over to the wheel. Just make sure you keep them distracted."

"Will do," said Finn. "Once you've cleared the trolley,

jump inside. Make sure there's room for me. When it's clear I'll hop in and Diane can push us out of here. Got it?"

"Got it," said Graves.

Finn walked away, towards the masters who stood near the foot of the wheel, watching the workers climbing down at the end of their shift. He allowed himself once glance back to see Graves lifting the metal churn out of the trolley and rolling it, in a great booming clatter, towards the river. Finn grinned. If the noise of all that didn't get the ironclads' attention, one of them was bound to notice Graves crouching there inside the trolley, waiting patiently to be wheeled away.

Finn hurried through the throng of stirring workers, stepping over and around those who still clung to sleep. Diane was over by the wheel, as agreed. Tom stood up ahead of him a short way, watching him approach. For a moment, Finn thought Tom had relented, that he was going to help after all. But no. Tom looked away, lowered his head. Finn stopped when he reached him, bending down, pretending to pick up some bit of rag.

"Goodbye, Tom," he said. "Thank you. For everything. I'll get you out of here, I promise I will."

Tom shook his head. "You won't, Finn. You'll just get yourself killed."

Finn turned to go. They had to leave, now.

"Finn?" said Tom.

"Yes?"

"Thank you, too."

"For what?"

"For your stories. For everything. You've kept me alive, too, you know."

Finn was about to reply when a cry went up from the portly ironclad. He'd spotted Graves trundling the empty churn towards the water. Perhaps he suspected some escape attempt. Perhaps he just saw a worker doing what he wasn't supposed to. In any case, blowing his metal whistle, the shrill piping sound echoing around the cavern, the ironclad lumbered over to Graves. From all around the wheels other guards converged too, carrying whips or muskets or grapples, ready to suppress the trouble, the riot, whatever it was. Finn caught a glimpse of Graves, stranded in the open as the ironclads converged on him, comically clinging on to his churn. He wouldn't live long after this. Finn felt neither remorse nor jubilation. Escaping was all that mattered.

He had to hurry. He walked briskly towards the wheel, dodging past all the workers who were hurrying to see what was going on. In a moment, Finn reached Diane standing at the wheel. She looked nervous, shaky, unsure of herself.

"Come on," said Finn. "We don't have much time. Follow me."

He led her around the wheel they had been re-caulking and on to the next one. This ran at full speed: immense, terrifying, churning through the water of the river, lifting the great, streaming buckets of water upwards towards the surface. They ran around to the far side, the camp out of sight. Spray lashed into their faces. Finn tried to dry his hands on his sodden clothes.

"Up there," he said. "We need to climb the frame."

"What?"

"Hurry. Come on, we can do it. It's just like climbing a tree."

He pulled himself onto the lowest spar of the wooden framework that supported the great wheel. Although the frame of the wheel and the drive mechanism were made of metal, the cradles in which the wheels were mounted were all wood: a nest of thick, round beams lashed together with ropes or pinned with iron rivets the size of Finn's arm, reaching all the way up to the roof of the cavern. He could feel the framework swaying and creaking in time to the turning of the wheel. He reached down to haul Diane up. The stretch of it clearly hurt her but she pulled herself onto the lowest beam. Finn set off, shinning his way up a diagonal spar.

"We'll never make it to the top," said Diane. This close to the thunder of the water and the wheel she had to shout to be heard.

"No need!" replied Finn. "We just need to get up a short way. It'll be safer then."

They climbed for several minutes, Finn helping Diane as much as he could, repeatedly glancing down, expecting to see the ironclads. They were still within easy range of a musket. He tried to climb faster but the smooth wood was slick with water. They were taking too long. They had to try it now.

He helped Diane onto a horizontal beam and stood for a moment to catch his breath. In front of them, so close he could reach out and touch them, the vast wooden buckets full of frothing water roared past his face.

"There," he said. "This is it."

"The buckets? You plan to grab hold of one and ride it up? That's crazy. You could never hold on long enough."

He turned to look at Diane. She was soaked, her black hair plastering her face.

"No, that's not it," he shouted. "You don't need to hold on. If you time the jump properly you can jump into the bucket. Then you'll be taken all the way out of the caves, up to the surface."

She looked upwards, then back to him. "But you don't know what happens up there. Where the water goes."

"It must empty out somewhere. There's so much of it with all these wheels running, it can't just be sent straight to the boilers can it?"

"It's a terrible risk, Finn. I don't like it."

"It's the only chance we've got. It's this or die in the mines. Believe me, I've never found another way out in all this time."

He tried to sound as confident as he could. In truth, he was racked with doubts himself, and terrified at what he was suggesting. If they missed their jump they would be mangled by the wheel. And of course, he was only guessing what happened up on the surface. They could easily be crushed or drowned or boiled. But it was their only chance. Diane glanced between wheel and ground, unsure, terrified of either prospect.

"We have to try it now," said Finn. "It's our only chance. Let's hold hands and jump. Then at least we'll stay together. Whatever happens. Okay?"

She thought for a moment more, then nodded. She grasped Finn's hand. He could feel the tension in it, the way it shook. Or perhaps it was him shaking.

He watched the buckets on the wheel, each rising rapidly towards and past them, trying to judge the best moment to jump. The expanse of water in each was clear as it rose at them. They just had to reach that. But if they timed it wrong and caught the lip of the bucket, they'd be scissored in two as it cut past the spars of the framework. They stood there for long moments, repeatedly twitching at what seemed like the right moment, not daring to jump *this* time as each bucket roared past them and upwards. It reminded Finn of something, an old memory, but he couldn't think what.

A cracking sound near his ear distracted him for a moment. He thought the wood was splitting, perhaps, giving way under their weight. But that couldn't be right; surely they were insignificant compared to the wheels. The diagonal spar near his head had a great gouge cut out of it, fresh looking. It hadn't been there a moment ago. He looked down at the ground, confused, and saw the ironclad down there aiming his musket up at them. The shot had been inaudible against the roaring and creaking of the wheel.

"Now!" Finn shouted, gripping Diane's hand tight. "Jump now!"

He leapt into space, tugging her with him into the air. They seemed to fall for a long time. They must have missed the bucket; they would tumble among the wooden spars before smashing into the ground. But then water engulfed him. Finn shot under the surface, his breath taken away by the freezing chill of it. He struggled, confused, kicking out but suddenly unable to work out which way was up. He could see nothing around him except a blur of brown and blue. He no longer held Diane's hand. Had she made the jump too? He had to get to the surface and find her. They had to be ready for the bucket to reach the top of the wheel so they could get out. He had to breathe. He had forgotten to take a breath as he jumped and his lungs were already screaming in alarm.

He kicked out, hoping he was swimming upwards. He hit something solid with his knee – a wall or the floor? – and tried to push off from it, up to the surface.

For a moment he broke through into the air, a confusion of wooden spars rushing past nearby. He sucked in a gulp of air but he was pulled back down again and swallowed water instead. Then everything went black. Was that what it was like to drown? The swirling black water tossed him around and there was nothing he could do.

XXVIII

A hand grasped Finn's shoulder and Finn, clutching at it, kicked upwards. He broke out of the water and sucked in gulps of air. Diane was there, her head visible and invisible between the waves. Light flooded down from above, brighter and brighter as they soared up to the surface. They were near the top. Somehow the water would be emptied out of the bucket before hurtling back down to pick up more. They just had to escape with it.

"Ready?" he shouted across to her. She was too busy trying to stay above the water and didn't reply. Finn could see blue sky now, blindingly bright. They soared past the ground level, past a blur of buildings and towers, the skyline of Engn, and still upwards. The wheels were vast. If they were tipped out of the bucket now, they would fall a long, long way.

Distinctly, Finn heard a metallic *chunk* sound. He recognized it from down in the mine.

"The pivot lock," he shouted, trying to explain to Diane what he'd just understood. "It must get applied automatically up here. As the wheel turns, we'll be tipped out!"

Panic surged through him. Already he could see the water was no longer horizontal within the bucket but angled towards the far lip as the wheel descended. They were hurtling back towards the ground inside a water-filled bucket that was about to pitch them out. He screamed; wanted, suddenly, to stay inside, go back round, anything to avoid what was to come. Water filled his mouth. Coughing, he reached out for the tarred wooden wall and tried to grab hold of it. Of anything solid. But the wood was too smooth and wet and he could get no grip.

The water tipped over the far side of the bucket, then began to flood out. There was nothing he could do to stop himself. Their arms flailing uselessly, he and Diane were hurled into the air, falling inside their own, brief waterfall down towards the ground. He could make out no detail as he spun around. The water would be collected somehow but for all he knew they would be dashed against a grill, or there was a narrow pipe they would simply miss. He tried to scream out but couldn't.

Then deep water engulfed him once again. He was about to start swimming when his head clashed against something solid. Reality faded into the distance and darkness overwhelmed him.

"Finn! Wake up."

A hand shook him roughly. He opened his eyes but could see only white light. It filled his head as pain: sharp pain. His stomach heaved and he retched, turning to kneel up as he vomited water from his stomach.

Squinting with one eye he looked to his side. Diane was there, one hand on the back of his head. She looked worried. Exhausted too, her shoulders heaving up and down.

"We made it," said Finn between breaths.

"Next time you have an escape plan you're going on your own, hear me?"

"What happened?"

"It tipped us out into a channel underneath the curve of the wheel. Didn't you see?"

"I hit my head."

"The channel emptied out into this reservoir. I thought you'd drowned. I towed you here to the side."

Finn looked around, the light a little more bearable now. They were on the steeply sloping stone bank of a manmade lake. Nearby he could see six circular entrances, great plumes of water cascading out of five of them in regular surges. Above them were the wheels, the five churning around and the one stationary. Beyond them, and all around the lip of the reservoir, were the familiar towers and wheels of the machine.

"Ironclads," he said. "Have you seen any ironclads?"

"None. They probably thought no one would be stupid enough to try what we just did."

He grinned at her through the pain. Her words were angry but there was a warmth to them too.

"It worked though," he said.

"And we nearly died in the process. I thought you *had* died."

Finn stood to shaky legs and held out a hand to pull her up.

"I would have drowned without you," he said.

She shrugged and stood too, holding her back and wincing at the pain. He wondered what it had cost her to swim ashore and pull him along.

"And I'd still be stuck down there without you. Forget about it. The question is, where to now?"

Finn looked around. They must be visible for miles, two black spots on the grey rim of the lake. They'd probably been seen already. "We can't stay here. They'll have raised the alarm down in the mines."

"Come on," said Diane. She led him upwards towards the lip of the reservoir wall. It was hard to climb the steep slope and keep his feet, dizzy as he was. Eventually, grasping for the wall at the top, he lay down to peer over the lip.

The outside world lay before them, the stone ramparts of the reservoir sloping almost vertically down to the ground some thirty or forty feet below. The builders must have decided this was all the wall they needed there. They were right. It would surely be impossible to climb that smooth expanse of stone. At the foot of the wall, far below, the ground was dried mud and then the grass plain began. On the horizon, rising through distant haze, ran a line of snow-topped mountains he didn't recognize. He thought he could discern a cluster of towers in a gap in the mountains. One of the other guild city-states. A string of line-of-sight towers strode across the plain towards it.

"It's too far to jump down," said Diane. "We'd break our legs."

She looked thoughtful, glancing up and down the wall. She must have faced many such adventures in the years the ironclads had pursued her. Finn was glad, very glad, she was there with him.

"What's that over there?" she asked. She set off running along the top of the steep bank, half crouching and keeping one hand on the wall. Farther along was a chain, one end embedded in the bank, its other lost beneath the waters of the reservoir. The two of them half slid down the bank to reach the point where the chain was bolted to the stone.

It was as thick as Finn's arm and very rusty, but it would easily support their weight if they could haul it up and lower it over the side. Finn walked down the chain to the water's edge, hoping to see a corroded link at which they could break it, but there were none.

"Let's see if we can pull it up," said Diane.

Finn returned to the anchor point and the two of them lifted the chain to try and heave it up. They couldn't move it.

"Let's try nearer the water," said Diane.

They skidded and slid down to the reservoir's edge. The chain disappeared into the rippling waters, its rusty links vanishing into the murk after a few yards. If it was attached to something, there was little they could do.

Again they heaved, Diane wincing at the pain it caused her. This time the chain moved, two links coming out of the water.

"Keep going," she shouted.

They pulled again and more of the chain rattled out of the water and up the bank. It took a lot of effort; the chain was heavy and soon very slippery. They were both weak. But at least the chain didn't appear to be attached to anything. After a few minutes of hauling and resting and hauling, the other end was revealed. A hook was attached to the end that must, once, have been attached to something beneath the water.

They paused for a moment to get their breaths back. A sharp pain thrummed in Finn's shoulders but he knew they couldn't stop. He grasped the hook and began to climb the steep slope of the reservoir. Diane joined him. It became harder and harder as they towed more and more of the chain. Between them, leaning into the slope, they inched their way upwards.

He didn't think they were going to make it. Twice he slipped over and the chain rattled back down the slope a short way. They must have been heard by now even if they hadn't been seen. But finally, Diane grasping the top of the wall with one hand, gritting her teeth, they managed to get the hook over the lip of the wall. Then it was a matter of hauling more and more of it over, link by link, until it reached a point where the weight of chain hanging down to the ground was enough.

"Look out!" Diane shouted.

The chain suddenly had a life of its own, rattling over the top of the wall at greater and greater speed in a cloud of dust. Then it stopped, held taut by the anchor point halfway down to the water.

Finn peered over the edge again. The chain was more than long enough to reach the floor. Its other end lay in coils on the dusty ground.

"I'll go first," said Diane. "Keep watch."

She climbed over the edge of the wall and began to descend. The chain swayed as she worked her way down. She'd be completely vulnerable if the ironclads came now, but there was no sign of anyone. Perhaps they really were going to escape.

Diane dropped the last few yards to the ground and looked up. "Come on, Finn. You now."

Finn swung his legs over the edge and hooked an arm through one of the links. The chain swung around, bashing him against the wall, almost jarring him loose. He began to work his way down, feeling for each foothold. The muscles in his stomach and arms quivered from the effort of it. He had to carry on; he didn't have the strength to climb up again. When he was near enough the ground, he let go and landed in a heap beside Diane.

"They'll know what we've done," she said. "There's no way we can get the chain back up."

Finn nodded. "We'll have to get away as far as we can. Hope they don't see us."

Diane looked doubtful now. "I don't think we're going to get very far. You can see for miles across the plain. A few ironclads on horses will catch us up easily."

Finn said nothing, gazing around at the scene, trying to come up with a clever plan. He looked back at Diane. She looked exhausted, close to tears. He must look worse. But they couldn't just give in now. They'd come so far.

"There's one place they wouldn't think of looking for us," he said.

"Where?"

"Back inside. They'll assume we've fled across the grass."

"Finn, no. I'm never going back in there. In any case, what are you going to do, shin up the chain?"

"No. But we could, I don't know, walk around the walls, maybe find another way inside."

"Well, I'm going to try and get away. I don't care what happens."

"But we can't just leave."

She turned on him, angry now. "Listen, Finn, I know you've got these wild ideas in your head of destroying Engn, all these dreams you cling to of Connor and our silly game. But it's not real, do you hear me? None of it is real. You can't destroy all that. They're going to try to catch us and kill us. And I'm going to try to get away. At least I'll die free, in the open air."

She turned and strode away, away from the walls.

"Diane!" Finn called after her, but she didn't glance back.

He hurried after her. He could let her go, but the thought of losing her again after all that time was too much. Perhaps she was right. At the very least, they needed to get out of sight, stop and think.

"Look, you can't just walk across the plain in the open like this," he said. "You'll have no chance."

"I like it better than your plan."

"Okay, but look. Let's head for the line-of-sight towers."

"The towers?"

"We can hide in the nearest one. Wait there until it's dark, come up with a plan. Perhaps we can walk from one to the next, at night, so they won't see us."

"What's the point? They're bound to check them."

"Maybe, but it's better than walking across the plain in full view isn't it?"

She stopped, then, and turned to look at him. "You'll

come too?"

He'd thought she'd wanted to get away from him. Now the look of frank fear in her face told him otherwise. What must it have been like all those years on her own, living in the wilds, always running?

"I might," he said. "I don't know. But we can't stay here."

"Let's go then."

They broke into a jog, heading for the nearest line-of-sight tower. It would take them an hour or more even if they could maintain the same pace, and they'd be visible from the walls all the way. As they jogged, Finn looked backwards, constantly expecting to see pursuit. There was nothing. But even if the ironclads knew where they were, they'd have to leave Engn by a gate. They were probably galloping towards them even now, around the curve of the wall. He and Diane had to get out of sight.

He spurted forwards to try and hurry them on, although he didn't have the energy to keep it up and soon slowed again. Diane jogged along beside him, panting heavily. When had they last eaten? He couldn't remember.

From the reservoir wall the grass plain had looked featureless, stretching uninterrupted to the distant mountains. Now he saw there were undulations in it: dips and rises that became surprisingly steep when you tried to cross them. They reached the bottom of one of the dips and, looking backwards, Finn found he could no longer see the towers and wheels of the great machine. They were out of sight for the moment.

"This way," he said, turning sharply left and following the line of the little valley. Perhaps it would confuse anyone following them.

"It won't make much difference," said Diane, her words punctuated by her laboured breathing. "They have dogs. They'll track us."

"Perhaps we'll find water," said Finn. "A lake or a river. Remember how you used the Silverburn to hide your trail when you came to the valley?"

She didn't reply, too out of breath. Finn wondered how bad her injuries from her fall from the wheel were. They ran on for some way, going parallel to the walls of Engn. Sooner or later they would have to leave the fold of earth that hid them and strike out, towards the tower. He was just about to suggest it when the fold rounded a bend to reveal a ramshackle collection of wooden huts, five of them. Each had been cobbled together from branches and planks and sheets of rusting iron.

They stopped, glancing at each other, neither sure what they should do.

"I can't see anyone," said Finn. The houses looked deserted, roofs hanging off at angles, doors banging and banging in the slight breeze that blew up the valley. "Perhaps we could hide here until dark."

"No. They'd still sniff us out," said Diane. "Anyway, who lives here?"

"People looking for their loved ones," said Finn. "I saw another village like it when they brought me in. Perhaps they're dotted all around."

"Let's go and see."

They walked down towards the huts, always wary that someone could burst out at them. There was no one. They stood in a rough square surrounded by the broken hovels.

"Perhaps we should look for food?" said Finn.

"No. Let's get away. We'll just be trapped here if they come."

They set off, leaving the hovels behind them. Only then did they hear a thin voice, a hiss almost, calling out to them. "You two, come here. Quick."

They turned but there was no one in sight. The wind continued to lift and release loose roof-sheets and bang doors. Except that one of the doors didn't swing shut. Finn was sure he'd seen it move but now it was held open. Inside he could see nothing but shadows.

"They might be able to help us," said Finn. "Let's see

what they want."

Diane looked doubtful. "I don't like it. Whoever they are they'll probably just try to hand us over to the ironclads."

"But perhaps they can hide us. Perhaps they're friends."

She wanted to think they were, he could see, but her fear of being caught again was too great.

"Tell you what," he said. "I'll go and talk to them. If it's okay, I'll wave to you. Otherwise just get away, head for the tower."

She looked doubtful but nodded her head in agreement.

Finn walked back towards the hovels, towards the one whose door stayed open. It was, he noticed, the best-repaired of all the huts, its roof intact.

"Hello?" he said, approaching the open doorway. "Who are you?"

"Come in, quick, before they see you."

Finn pushed the creaking door farther open and peered inside the darkness of the hut. It smelled of damp and rot. A grim place to live. Cracks and holes in the walls let in thin beams of light and Finn was reminded of the Switch House up on the hill, and Mrs. Megrim telling him off for being late.

"Who are you?" he said again. He stepped just inside the doorway.

"Running from the ironclads, are you?"

"No," said Finn.

"Course you are. Why else would you be out here? Come on, I can hide you from them. You and your frightened rabbit of a friend."

"Hide us? How?"

The voice collapsed into spluttered coughing for a moment. "I know how to hide from them. They ride through here but they never see me, never smell me out."

"How? Who are you?"

A face loomed out of the darkness then: sunken and wrinkled, like that of someone worn down by years of heavy labour.

"Come on," said the man. "I won't harm you. I've no love for the ironclads either."

"Who are you?" Finn repeated. "Why are you here?"

"My son was taken inside," the man said. "I came here to wait for him."

"When did they take him?"

The old man looked down at the ground. "Oh. Years ago, now."

"And you can hide us? Help us get away?"

"Oh yes. There's a way. That's how we come and go, you see."

"Who?"

"Lots of us here, living outside the walls, waiting and watching."

"But how? How can we get away?"

"Down the well, see. The tunnels, the underground streams."

"What tunnels?"

"Been here hundreds of years, the tunnels. We've found them all. Wells all over the place and the tunnels connect them, see. The first builders used to live out here and they dug wells, all around. Deep tunnels and caverns. You can use them to travel and not be seen."

"Show me how to get down there," said Finn.

"You walked right past it!" The man seemed delighted. "There, right out in the open."

Finn looked back. A mound of rotting wood lay piled in between the houses. The man looked warily all around then stepped out of the house. He walked to the well and started lifting sheets. Underneath lay a circle of worn stones set into the ground, the lip of a shaft descending downwards. From a distance, not moving, Diane watched them warily.

"Hurry," said the man, pointing down the shaft.

"They'll see you. Get down quick before they come."

"You're sure?" asked Finn. "You can escape that way?"

"Yes, yes. Head away from the machine. There's another well shaft farther on. Climb up there, they'll never track you then."

Finn stood, debating what to do.

"We want to get to the tower," he said. "The line-of-sight."

"Yes, yes. Go that way. Through the tunnel and you'll be there. Upstream. Left, left, right, straight, right, left. No time to teach you the song now, you'll just have to remember the words. Hurry, before they come."

"Left, left … I don't understand. What song?"

"I told you. Tunnels everywhere down there. If you don't know your way you could come up anywhere. Or nowhere. We use the song-maps to find our way around in the darkness."

"Tell me it again."

"Upstream. Left, left, right, straight, right, left. Now go, before they come here."

Finn came to a decision. They had little to lose anyway. He waved to Diane, telling her to come.

"How many years?" he asked

"What?" said the old man.

"How many years have you waited out here for your son?"

The man paused before he spoke. "Nearly forty now."

"I'm sorry," said Finn. "I hope you find him soon."

The old man didn't reply. Finn turned away crouched by the well. The old man disappeared back into his hovel as Diane approached.

"What did he say?" asked Diane. "What are you doing?"

"We can get away down here," said Finn. "There are tunnels."

"You're sure?"

"That's what the old man said."

"Can we trust him? Perhaps he's just sending us back to Engn?"

"If he'd wanted us to get caught, he could have just let us wander around the plain on our own."

A line of iron hoops cemented into the wall of the well led down into the darkness. Finn turned to let himself down. He could feel cold air breathing up at him, hear the distant chortle of running water from somewhere underground.

"Come on," he said. "Hopefully it's not too far."

He began to descend. His breathing sounded heavier, rougher in the enclosed space of the shaft. He looked up at the circle of light, at the silhouette of Diane as she climbed over the edge of the well to follow him down. He felt for each rung with the tip of an outstretched foot, testing each one in case it had worn loose. It was easier than the chain, at least. He could see nothing below him. The rungs were slick with water or slime. He concentrated on taking each step downwards.

"They'll see the well," said Diane. "They'll know we've come down here."

She sounded very close in the confined space, her voice hollow.

"He'll cover it up again."

"They'll still be able to follow our scent. The dogs."

"Not down here. It sounds like there are loads of tunnels. Streams, too. They won't know where we're going to come up."

"And you do?"

"The man gave me directions."

"Did he now?"

Finn's outstretched foot dipped into cold, flowing water. Letting himself down farther he found the hard stone of the bottom. He stood knee-deep in the underground stream. Looking up, the entrance to the well was just a distant circle.

"I'm at the bottom."

"Is there a tunnel? A way out?"

Finn felt around with his hand, the stone rough and crumbling beneath his fingers. Upstream. His hand found the lip of the tunnel down which the water flowed. It was low; they would have to stoop, but there should be room to squeeze through.

"It's here."

Diane splashed into the water beside him. He could see nothing of her. But the rush of her breathing was loud and he could feel the warmth from her body.

"Where?"

Finn fumbled for her hand. It felt cold from the iron of the rungs. He drew her gently forwards in the dark and showed her the low opening.

"How far is it?"

"He told me what turnings to take. Left, left, right, straight, right, left."

"What?"

"That's what he said. Remember it too in case I forget it."

"Okay, say it again."

Finn repeated it several times until they could recite the list of turnings together.

"Apparently, they sing it," said Finn.

"I'll just remember it, thanks."

"Ready?"

"Ready. And if we end back up inside Engn, I will kill you, okay?"

Finn grinned although she wouldn't be able to see. "Agreed."

She went first. She gasped as she bent down to duck into the tunnel, her side hurting her. She didn't say anything.

"You feel along the left wall and I'll do the right," she said. "If we miss a turning, we've had it."

"Shame we don't have a ball of string to find our way back."

"Just make sure you don't miss a turning."

Crouching painfully, the icy water lapping over their thighs, splashing into their faces, they sidled forwards. The tunnels were regular, manmade, dug out and lined. They smelled of earth and rock. It was utterly dark. Finn opened and closed his eyes but it made no difference. He'd been in tunnels this dark before. When was it? Back home? No, he remembered now. The day he'd walked through the postern gate to leave the Valve Hall. It seemed like someone else, or just a story he'd read.

They laboured forwards, stopping occasionally to rest by kneeling in the water. They were soon both shivering. At least there was plenty of water to drink. Finn scooped up a handful, feeling the cold of it trickling down inside him.

"Here's a crossroads," said Diane from up ahead.

"Okay. So, left."

"Stay close. We mustn't get separated."

They stumbled on and on for an eternity. For long stretches of time they found no other tunnels and Finn began to think they were lost. It was impossible to know which way they were heading. There was just the numbing chill of the water flowing against their legs and the rough stone on their hands. His back stung sharply with the effort of stooping down. He could only imagine what Diane, her side already painful, was going through.

Eventually, encouraging each other, having to stop more and more frequently, they reached the last turning of the sequence the old man had given them, the last left.

"What now?" asked Diane.

"We get to another shaft I suppose," said Finn.

"Okay."

They set off again. They could do nothing but go on. Finn wanted to stop and rest, lie down and sleep. They crept along in the darkness, their hands scrabbling along the roof of the tunnel for fear of massing the shaft that would take them back up to the world. After another long,

long trudge, doubts began to fill Finn's mind. The old man had tricked them. They had missed a turning. They were lost and would die down there, where no one would ever know. His parents, Connor, Mrs. Megrim: none of them would ever know. He was too exhausted for the thought to seem particularly terrible.

"Here," said Diane. "I think it's here. Feel."

Finn reached the place where she stood and felt air above him instead of the low earth ceiling. There was a hole in the tunnel roof, wide enough for them both to stand up in. It was glorious just to be able to stand straight. Finn felt around the walls of the shaft.

"There are rungs to climb up."

He peered upwards. Dimly, he thought he could see a lightening of the dark above him. Was it there or was he imagining it?

"You go first," said Diane. She sounded utterly exhausted. "I don't want to fall onto you if I let go."

"Let's wait here for a bit. Get our strength back."

"No. Let's get out of here. I don't want to stop now."

"Okay."

They stood next to each other in the narrow shaft, bodies touching, her warmth delicious. He wanted to say something else to her but couldn't think what. Instead he reached up for the first rung and hauled himself upwards.

They worked their way upwards slowly, stepping from rung to rung. It definitely grew lighter as they climbed. Soon, Finn could see the rusting iron rungs and the rough stone of the wall in front of his eyes. Eventually he reached up and hit the wooden planks that capped the shaft.

"We're here."

Diane was still some way below him, pulling herself up one rung at a time, stopping to get her breath back between each. She didn't reply. Holding tight with one hand, trying not to think of the shaft beneath him, the fall if he let go, he began to pull the wood aside with his spare hand.

The wood slid aside and light slanted into the top of the shaft, temporarily blinding him. Squinting, he peered up over the lip of the well, expecting to see the boots of a ring of ironclads there, waiting for them.

XXIX

But the grass plain stretched away unbroken at Finn's eye-level. No people, no houses were visible. Wherever the ironclads were, they weren't there. Finn and Diane had emerged in another deep fold in the ground. Not far away, beyond the rising earth, just as the old man had promised, he could see the top of a wooden line-of-sight tower.

The light had seemed very bright at first, but now it was actually twilight: dusk, or dawn. He had no idea how long they'd been down beneath the ground. The low sun glinted off the glass lenses of the 'scopes in the tower.

"We're here," he called down to Diane. "We made it."

He heaved himself out and lay on his back. After a few moments, the top of Diane's head appeared from the hole in the ground. She pulled herself out and they lay there like fish pulled from a hole in the ice, gulping and helpless.

Diane stood first. "Let's get into the tower. We're too visible out here."

Hand in hand, they made their way up the grass slope to the tower. They could soon see Engn rising behind them. They sky beyond the great machine glowed with an orangey, sulphur light. The sun was setting. Was it still the same day? Or the next day? Finn was too exhausted to think straight. Even lying down there by the shaft already seemed strangely distant.

They each peered around nervously as they reached the top of the rise in the ground, conscious they would be visible for miles around, terrified of seeing a troop of ironclads galloping towards them. Still they could see no one. The only thing moving were lines of smoke rising straight up into the still air from here and there on the plain, blazing yellow higher up as the setting sun caught them. There had to be hovels dotted about everywhere.

The relay line-of-sight tower was huge, seeming to swell in size as they neared it. A framework of lashed timbers, something like the one holding up the wheels, zigzagged upwards to support a wooden hut housing the 'scopes. A ladder led up to a trapdoor in its floor. Beyond it, the line of mountains looked familiar. He'd seen that sight before, or one very like it, when they'd first transported him to Engn. The valley lay that way.

"It'll be manned, won't it?" said Diane. "Someone must operate it."

"No, it's just a relay station. It doesn't switch, it just picks up signals and sends them on brighter so they don't decay."

When they got near enough, they could see the ground around the tower was freshly churned up by horses, their hoof prints like large letter C's, quite clear in the mud. They looked at each other. The ironclads, or someone at least, had been there recently.

"They must have come this way while we were underground," said Diane.

Finn nodded, saying nothing. The thought of their pursuers riding around somewhere above their heads while they laboured through the tunnels made him shiver. They could only hope the ironclads had started looking farther afield now.

"Let's get inside," he said. "Whatever happens, we can't go any farther just now."

He felt very exposed climbing the ladder, more and more of the wide sweep of the plain opening up around him. Thankfully the darkness was thickening. They might be invisible in the shadows if anyone happened to be looking. So he told himself. The trapdoor at the top of the ladder was padlocked shut with an iron hasp. He hadn't thought about that. Diane waited for him as he jangled the lock, hoping it might come free.

"What is it?"

"Locked."

"Can we open it?"

Finn yanked hard on the padlock. The screws holding it to the trapdoor ripped out of the wood a short way. The wood was rotten, poorly maintained.

"I think I can pull it free."

He hooked an arm through the ladder to stop himself falling and pulled down as hard as he could. With each tug, the wood gave way a little. Finally, in a shower of sawdust, the padlock came free in his hand. He pushed upwards on the trapdoor, swinging it open into the darkness of the line-of-sight tower. Once inside in the dusty comforting darkness, they closed the trapdoor shut and sat together on the bare wood of the floor.

A light flickered in the one of the 'scope lenses, the rapid flash of a message being sent out from Engn. He couldn't interpret it. Either he'd lost the ability to read them or it was encrypted. There was a whole bank of 'scopes: an array of twelve by twelve, enough for 144 messages to be routed to and from Engn at the same time. As he gazed up at them, more and more lit up, flickered for a few moments, then winked out. It was beautiful to watch, like looking up at the stars twinkling in the sky. He wondered if any of the messages were about *them*, the two who had escaped Engn. Instructions, maybe, to all the ironclads and masters out there to be on the lookout. *Catch them. Return them. Kill them.* If so, there wasn't a lot they could do about it. If they blocked the messages, maybe misaligned the 'scopes, the masters would soon know someone was in one of the towers.

Finn shut his eyes, listening for sounds from outside, dreading hoofs or voices. There was nothing. The only sound was Diane's peaceful breathing. He sighed and rested his head on her shoulder.

"What do you think it's all for?" he said. "Engn, I mean. What does it do? Why is it here? All that machinery, all that clever complexity. All that effort. I mean, what's the point of it all? Why did the twelve guilds go to so much trouble? Rory said there was a hidden purpose, but I don't know. It's like they went a bit mad after being defeated all that time ago."

He waited for an answer but there was none. Diane was already asleep.

He thought he should keep watch while she slept, peer out of the 'scope ports for anyone approaching them. But weariness weighed him down, overwhelming him before he could move. Soon he, too, fell asleep.

In the glowing morning light, he thought, briefly, he was in the old barn back home, he and Connor and Diane sleeping out there for the night amid the prickly straw. He luxuriated in the still warmth as he emerged from wonderful dreams.

He flickered one eye open. Diane was there, lying a few feet away from him, still asleep. Connor wasn't there, of course. They weren't in the barn. Memories of where he really was, of everything that had happened, came back to him like a series of blows to his stomach.

He stirred and, walking on his knees, crossed to peer out of one of the unoccupied 'scope ports. Outside it was bright sunlight, a hot day on the great plain. Shimmering in the distance he could see the next relay tower partway to the blue mountains. The shifting air would play havoc with the line-of-sight images. A day like today meant slow messages. There was a good chance someone would come to recollimate the lenses. He peered to each side of the tower, the tiny holes affording only a very restricted view. He could see no one. So far, at least, they had survived. It was incredible. They had escaped Engn and lasted a night without being caught. As far as he knew, that had never happened before.

He crossed the dark, dusty interior of the wooden house, careful not to nudge any of the 'scopes, to peer out the other way, back towards Engn. The great machine stretched from horizon to horizon in the sunlight as if nothing had happened, as if unaware he and Diane had fled. Smoke rose from its stacks and vents. Sunlight glinted off its housings and wheels. Nothing at all had changed.

"What's happening?" Diane stirred in the darkness behind him, her voice groggy.

"Nothing," he replied. "No sign of anyone. We're safe so far."

"Good."

Finn turned to stare back into the dark interior of the hut, Diane invisible in the gloom after the bright exterior. They still hadn't agreed where they should go next, of course, what they should do.

"We need to drink and eat," he said.

"What time do you think it is?"

"Hard to say for sure. The sun's well up. Mid-morning maybe?"

"It's too dangerous to go out there during the day. We should wait until it's dark, then set off for the next tower. Perhaps that way we can get all the way to the mountains. Maybe find food and water along the way."

Finn didn't reply. He busied himself working his way around the room to peer out of the other ports.

"Finn?"

"Yeah."

"Do you agree? That's what we should do?"

Finn shrugged. It was pointless, he knew. She couldn't see him.

"It's a good plan," he said. "It's the only way to get across the plain. But I'm not going, Diane. I'm going to try and get back inside."

"But it's madness, Finn. They'll just catch you again. I don't know what they'll do to you this time, but it will be worse, far worse, than the mines."

She might be right. And he didn't have any idea about how to get back inside, let alone about destroying the machinery once he was there. For some reason none of that seemed to matter. He had made his mind up. Made it up a long time ago.

"Finn?"

"We can't do anything until it's dark," he said. "Let's wait here until then. It'll give us a chance to rest properly."

"But I don't understand why you want to do this."

He sighed. Perhaps it was because their pact meant there was some meaning to it all. Some hope. Clinging to that had allowed him to survive. He understood why people gave in, too powerless to fight back, but he'd refused. Each agony and humiliation had just made him more determined. Going with Diane, as much as he longed to, would be like admitting his life in Engn had been a lie all along.

"You ran for all those years, Diane, avoided the ironclads, lived free. I don't know how far away you got, but they still found you, didn't they? They still brought you back here. I don't think your plan is much more sensible than mine."

"I'm not going back in there. I'm sorry."

"And what if you're part of what we have to do? What

if you're meant to be there? What if Conn needs you?"

"I'm not. He doesn't. Don't you see? That's all just in your head. It's not real. It's never been real."

He didn't reply for a moment. He was tempted, of course, to give in, run off with her to the mountains. He couldn't bear to lose her again. He had already lost everyone else.

"Well," he said eventually. "Let's rest until it's dark. Best we keep as quiet as possible."

She sighed but said nothing more. Her silhouette was just visible now as his eyes adjusted. A black outline in the deeper blackness. She sat against the wall of the hut, not moving. They would have this day together, at least. That was more than he had ever expected.

Finn turned to examine the machinery of the relay house. The 'scopes were unfamiliar to him, their lenses and controls very different from those back home in Mrs. Megrim's switch house. Still, he thought he could work them. He peered all around the nearest one, careful not to nudge it out of alignment. The numbers were entered by pressing buttons that advanced one of the ten dials by a digit each time. Still, the principle had to be the same. He was sure he could make it work.

The idea had come to him in the middle of the night, a moment of half-waking. He knew immediately that he had to try. It was pointless, probably. Foolhardy, too. But the shimmering heat of the day had encouraged him. They wouldn't suspect if a few messages got lost and had to be resent.

"What are you doing?" asked Diane.

"I'm going to send a message home."

"What? Is that safe?"

"It should be. I think this is one of the relay towers on our line; it's heading in the right direction for our mountains. They won't know anything about it in Engn. I'll just take one of the 'scopes offline for a few minutes and type in my own message from here. They may not even notice the line has dropped. If they do, they'll just think something blocked it somewhere so long as I set everything up properly again afterwards."

"Are you sure? They might come and investigate. Find us in here."

"I doubt it," said Finn. "Messages need to be repeated all the time. Especially trunk messages. It'll be safe enough."

"But what are you going to send? A message to your parents?"

"No. Not directly anyway. I'm going to talk to Mrs. Megrim."

"Surely someone could intercept the message and read it."

"They can intercept it but they won't be able to read it. I remembered it, you see. The code she gave me."

"What code?"

"The day I left the valley. You know I said she stopped the ironclads, stood in front of them and made them pull up. She gave me a piece of paper. I thought it was going to be a letter but it was just ten digits, nothing more."

"An encryption key for the line-of-sight network."

"Exactly. I lost the note pretty soon afterwards. But I memorized the digits in case I ever needed them again. I think she gave me them so I could communicate with her if I got the chance."

As he explained he busied himself setting up the rig he would need. The relay house had two banks of 'scopes, pairs on each connected by a cable. The receiving 'scope interpreted a message, sent it down the wire to its sister machine, which translated it back into a sequence of flashes to send on its way. One day, some people said, cables would be laid everywhere about the land, so that they wouldn't need 'scopes at all. He doubted such a thing was possible. But Mrs. Megrim had made sure he understood how it all worked. Her lessons had been very clear on that. Although the relay devices were fully automatic, they were essentially identical to the manual machines he was used to. As well as the encryption code dials, each had a set of keys that could be used to punch in a message, essential when the collimation of each device was being tested.

"You think she's been sitting there all this time waiting for a message from you? For all we know she's not even alive anymore. She was already ancient."

"I have to try," said Finn. "If she's alive I think she'll be there waiting, keeping one eye open for an encrypted message with the right key. I'll bet she's had a 'scope set up for it all this time."

He pictured her there in the dark of the Switch House, one of the spare 'scopes permanently set up with the number dialled onto it. Did she reset it each night so no one could learn the code? It was what he'd have done.

"So she can relay a message to your parents? Tell them you're still alive?"

"Yes. But I think she gave me the code for another reason too."

"Her own children."

"I'm going to tell her they're both still alive as far as I know. Alive and well the last time I saw them."

Being careful not to touch any of the others, Finn disconnected the cable from one of the 'scopes that pointed away from Engn. He had watched them very carefully to see how they were used. The device on the bottom left received the heaviest usage. If that was active, a second concurrent message used the next in line, and so on. Most of the time only half the 'scopes were actually lit up. By using the device on the far right of the twelfth row, there was a good chance no one would ever notice he'd taken it offline.

"Can you watch the 'scopes on the top row for me? Let me know if any messages start to come through on them?"

"Okay."

Kneeling on the wooden floor, he set to work. A bank

of keys was attached to each device by another, smaller cable, so that messages could be punched in without vibrating the 'scope and knocking it out of alignment. The letters were represented by finger-sized brass buttons, arranged alphabetically in a square. Carefully, his fingers stiff and clumsy, Finn dialled in the address for Mrs. Megrim. It was slow going in the low light. When he'd entered the address, he typed in the encryption key he'd memorized. Then, finally, he began to type out his message.

"What are you saying to her?"

"I'm telling her to sweep the floor and dust the lenses."

"Huh?"

"It's what she always told me to do. It became a sort of joke between us. Then she'll know it's really me."

When the message was sent, he kneeled there in the dark, waiting. The message would reach the valley instantly, of course. But was Mrs. Megrim there to receive it?

They sat together in silence for long moments. The only sound was the gentle clicking from the other 'scopes as encrypted messages were routed through.

"How do they look?" he asked, not wanting to take his eye off the one lens, looking for the tell-tale flicker of white light.

"The eighth row lit up just now."

"Good. Hopefully I won't have to reconnect this 'scope."

"If you do and she sends, they'll get her message in Engn."

"I know. They won't be able to read it though."

"Unless they have her key."

"Yeah. Hopefully they'll just think it's a normal message that's got garbled and request a resend in plaintext."

"The eighth row is lighting up again. Now the ninth and tenth rows, too. Finn, they'll be using your 'scope any second. You have to reconnect it."

Finn glanced aside at the other devices. The bottom eleven rows were all lit now. One after another, the twelve 'scopes on the top row began to light up too. Still he waited, giving Mrs. Megrim as long as he could, not wanting to give up on her.

"Finn. They're all lit up now. Engn will soon get suspicious."

"Just a couple more moments."

"Reconnect it, Finn. This is too dangerous."

"A couple more moments."

"Finn!"

"There!"

His hand was already lifting the pairing cable to reconnect the 'scope to its twin. But light had begun to flicker in the 'scope's eyepiece.

"Is it her? What does she say?"

Finn studied the paper tape rolling out of the device as each character was burned onto it. He had to hold it up to one of the unused ports in the wall to see what was written there. He just hoped he could still remember how to read them.

"It says, *And keep one eye on the bank wall, boy*. It's her, all right. That's what she used to say."

He glanced at the array of 'scopes. The top line was only half-lit now. Had the last one been offline for too long? Would Engn have noticed?

"Let me know if the lights come close again," he said. He began to type out the long message he'd already written in his head.

When he'd finished, he sat down against the wall, next to Diane. For some reason he was out of breath. "I told her about you, too," he said. "Perhaps she'll be able to relay a message down to your own village."

Diane hooked her arm through his. "So, what do we do now?"

"Wait. It might take her a while to reply."

Diane nodded but said nothing. He rested his head on hers. They waited together, watching the 'scopes, terrified they'd all light up again but knowing, now, they wouldn't reconnect the top right one until Mrs. Megrim replied.

They snoozed away most of the day inside the relay house, waiting for the reply. The atmosphere became warm and thick as the day wore on, more dust than air. They both longed for water. Finn imagined himself swimming in the cool waters of the lake. But they dared not leave until it was dark. Occasionally, one of them would stir and peer out of the ports to see if anyone was approaching, although they could do nothing if anyone did. They saw groups of ironclads in the distance, marching in lines across the plains, passing to and from Engn. None came near them.

They spoke only rarely, each aware they would be going their separate ways soon. Occasionally one would ask the other about some detail of what had happened to them over the years. Then they would fall silent again.

"Perhaps she's not going to reply. Perhaps she's been found out," said Diane at one point in the afternoon.

Finn shrugged. "Perhaps."

They watched the array of 'scopes in case they filled up again, but in the drowsy heat it soon became too much effort to keep their eyes open and stay awake.

It was early evening, the air cooling down at last, when the paper roller attached to the top right machine chuntered and rattled into life. They both stirred and, careful not to knock any of the machinery, crossed to see what Mrs. Megrim had to say. The familiar smell of singed paper filled the air. The first words were just becoming visible on the thin strip of paper.

"Bless you, bless you, my dear boy…"

It was a long message, revealed word by word over the period of an hour or more. Mrs. Megrim had been busy. They sat back down next to the machine, heads close together, and consumed each new word by the light of an unused 'scope port.

When they had finished reading, neither spoke for a time, lost in thought. Finn's head whirled with all the information. It was hard to take it all in. He was lightheaded from the suffocating heat and hunger. He was having trouble understanding it all. He'd thought she'd taught him everything she knew. Clearly, she hadn't.

"Shireen's your sister?" asked Diane.

"Yes. I haven't seen her since I was tiny. I thought she was dead. She was taken to Engn long ago but I never saw her there."

"And she's been communicating with Mrs. Megrim?"

"Looks like it. Or someone else has."

"What is this *Directory* she mentions? I've never heard of it." Diane sifted through the coils of paper nesting on the floor. "Here. *Shireen is in the Directory. The true controllers of Engn. Find her. She will help.*"

"I don't know," said Finn. "The masters run Engn, obviously. And the Inner Wheel controls them. I've never heard of a Directory."

"Do you even believe her?"

"What do you mean?"

"I don't know, it all seems so incredible. Perhaps she's gone, you know, a bit bonkers. Sounds to me like she never got over losing her children. She could be inventing the whole thing, imagining plots that will bring them back to her."

"Rory said there were wreckers receiving messages from her. I think it's all real. I'll bet there's a whole network of people like her, using the line-of-sight network against Engn."

"But the wreckers are disorganized. Powerless. They're

not what we hoped they were at all. Perhaps it was different once, but this Lud doesn't seem to be in any hurry to do anything. It sounds to me like she's enjoying her position of power. She'd rather talk about destroying the machine at some vague point in the future rather than actually doing it."

Finn didn't reply.

"You really are going to go back in, aren't you?" said Diane.

"I have to. Shireen's in there, in this Directory. And now Connor too. It's all coming together. There's a plan, I'm sure of it, but they need me. They need us."

Diane didn't reply, thinking about his plans or thinking about something else entirely.

"I'm sorry about your father," he said. "At least your mother knows you're alive now."

"Yeah."

Mrs. Megrim had sent messages down the valley to Diane's own village, to whatever their Switch House equivalent was. He had the impression of a whole network of Mrs. Megrims, communicating in secret, safe because they were the ones who were supposed to monitor the line-of-sight network. He wondered if she'd planned to include him in it all once he was older.

"I'm sorry about your parents," said Diane.

They'd left the valley a year back, never able to settle after the loss of both their children. Even Mrs. Megrim and her spider's web didn't know what had happened to them. He thought about his mother's enveloping softness, his father's bull-like strength. He was responsible for what had happened to them. If the ironclads hadn't come for him, they'd still be there now, weeding the vegetable patch, working the bellows in the forge. He tried to imagine the house abandoned, overgrown, but couldn't.

"Will you come now?" he asked. "I know we don't have much chance, that Engn is too big, too strong. But there's a hope, at least. Maybe with Shireen's help, or

Connor's…"

"It's madness," said Diane. But she sounded less sure of herself.

"Please," said Finn. "You read what Mrs. Megrim said."

"I don't know. It all sounds so incredible."

"Tell you what," said Finn. "You come with me to find Shireen through this tunnel Mrs. Megrim mentioned. But if we can't find it, if it doesn't exist, I'll give up and come with you."

"And what if we're caught trying?"

"What if we're caught escaping? It's dangerous whatever we do."

She sighed and said nothing for a time. Finn thought she'd fallen asleep again.

"Give me your ring," she said.

"Huh?"

"Your ring. The one I made for you that you managed to squash."

"Here."

Finn fished out the knot of silver wire and handed it to her. Working in the near-darkness, Diane teased it back into a straight piece of wire, working out its kinks as best she could. Then she began to weave and knot it again until the ring, the original ring, was there again. Only then did she speak.

"Here, put it on."

She took Finn's hand and pushed it onto his finger, twisting it around to get it over his knuckle. Then she untied the string around her neck and handed her ring to him. He looked at her in the darkness.

"I don't understand."

"You're supposed to put it on my finger. Idiot."

"But…"

"Put it on me."

Finn did as he was told, sliding Diane's ring onto her finger. They held them up so a thin beam of light caught the silvery metal.

"Okay," she said. "I'll come with you. We'll try. And then, if it doesn't work, when it doesn't work, we'll leave and never come back. Agreed?"

"Agreed."

The sudden touch of her lips on his was as unexpected as it was wonderful.

When it was finally dark, they lifted up the hatch in the floor and peered outside. There was no one in sight. They'd checked all around using the 'scope ports. Nobody had come near them all day. The glow from the machinery lit up the night, the incessant roaring and clanking filling the air. Hopefully they could cross the dark plain without being seen and reach the walls of Engn.

"We should go to the well first," said Diane. "Get some water. We're both dying of thirst."

Finn nodded. There had been an old leather bucket tied to a rope there that had been used, at some point, to draw water. They could probably haul some up with that. He just wished they had something to eat. How did the people in the hovels out there, the old man who had helped them, survive? He wished he'd been able to bring some food with him, but he couldn't see how it would have worked. They just had to hope that, once back inside Engn, they could find something to eat.

So that no one could read the printout of Mrs. Megrim's message, they tore it into tiny pieces then scattered the scraps to the wind. They set off back the way they'd come, holding hands again. Neither saw the shadow that lifted itself off the ground behind them. As they walked towards Engn, the figure floated after them, a patch of darkness against the night. Finn heard nothing and saw nothing until a blow to his head sent the ground lurching up to hit him in the face. He turned over, tried to rise. A man stood there, club raised, silhouetted against the whirling stars. Another blow came and Finn knew no more.

"Hello again, young man."

Pain hammered through Finn's head, dwarfing the distant voice. He recognized it, though. Thinner than it had been, sharper, but a familiar voice from his past. Who was it? He squinted open an eye briefly but the throbbing in his head redoubled and he shut them again. He tried to speak but couldn't make the words come out, his parched lips sealed together.

Something cut into his back. He tried to wriggle away. Rough rope dug into his wrists. His hands were tied to something behind his back. He tried to speak again, shout out. He felt water being dribbled into his lips, seeping into his mouth, wonderfully fresh and cool. It made no sense. The person had knocked him out, tied him up.

He opened one eye again. The figure was a blur, right in front of him, watching him. More water was tipped into his mouth. He gulped it down. He looked around. Diane was next to him, also bound. They were back at the line-of-sight tower, tied to one of its legs.

"Thought you'd got rid of me for good, didn't you, eh? Afraid not, young man. Here I am, large as life."

He looked much older, his podgy features sunken down to the lines of his bones. Finn's mouth worked now. He whispered the name of his attacker.

"Matt."

"Ah, so you do remember me? Good, good."

"How did you get here?"

"Me? I've lived here for years. Nowhere else I could go, was there, once you had me thrown out of the valley? See, I know what you did, you and your father. Had plenty of time to work that out."

"What do you want? Why are we tied up?"

"I wondered if it was you. The descriptions were vague but I thought to myself, perhaps it *is* him. Him and the girl, escaping from Engn. You always were slippery. So, I came to see for myself. And here we are, just like old times."

"I don't understand. What do you want?"

"What do I want? Isn't it obvious, young man? I want a life. I want a house and a bed. I want everything I had before, everything I was promised. And with you to trade, the masters of Engn will give it all to me."

"You're going to turn us in?"

"Waited years for a chance like this. I never thought it would actually happen."

Finn closed his eyes again, trying to think of what he could say, of a way out. But the pain in his head was too large and there was no room left for thought.

"Let Diane go at least," he said. "I'll come with you."

"Such a fine, noble lad. Your father's son, eh? But no. I think the price will be much better for the two of you. The two escapers captured. The masters will be very grateful."

"They weren't grateful to you before. They just left you to die out here."

The blow across Finn's cheek stung briefly. The worst of it was the way it sent his brain thudding with pain again.

"Now, now, there's no need for that, is there, young man?" said Matt. "I'm just setting things straight. I've been wronged and you've escaped from Engn. This will put everything right."

"We won't cooperate," said Diane. He turned to look at her. Dried blood matted her hair where she'd been struck. She scowled from the pain throbbing in her own head. "You'll have to drag us to Engn."

"And if I threaten to cut some bits off you with my knife here?"

"So what?" she said. "It's nothing compared to what will happen to us inside."

Matt snorted with laughter, as if Diane had said something funny. "Good point, young lady. How about this then? If you don't cooperate, I'll take the knife to Finn here. And if he doesn't come, I'll cut you up. Oh yes, I've seen you together, holding hands. Two right little lovebirds, aren't we?"

"If you touch her again, I'll kill you," said Finn.

"No, you won't," said Matt, delighted at Finn's outburst. "You really won't. Because I'm going to turn you over to the masters of Engn and be richly rewarded. And you will never be heard of again."

Matt rose and walked behind them to work on their ropes, untying them from the leg of the tower.

"Right, up you get. Time we were leaving. It's a good day's walk to the gate. We can be there before they close at dusk."

He yanked on a rope that was tied around both of their waists.

"Up you get or I'll start using the knife. The masters want you alive, that's all. But they won't mind if a few parts are missing."

Finn and Diane worked their way to their feet. Their hands were still tied behind their backs and their legs were bound together, too, so that they could only shamble forwards in tiny steps. No chance of running.

Matt walked away ahead of them, hauling them forwards by the rope. They half stumbled and followed after him, unable to catch up, not daring to stop. Desperately, Finn tried to think of a way of escaping. Perhaps they could overpower Matt as they walked. Grab the knife and cut themselves free. But he couldn't see how. They were too tightly bound.

As they stumbled their way towards Engn, Finn tried to

understand what had happened. Had Mrs. Megrim betrayed them? Sent a message through to Matt, told him where they were? Or perhaps she wasn't alone back there in the Switch House. Perhaps there were ironclads with her, waiting for Finn to try communicating, telling her what to reply. But that made no sense either. If the ironclads knew where he and Diane were, they wouldn't have sent Matt. They'd have come themselves.

Must have been the old man then, the one who'd shown them the tunnel. He'd betrayed them. Told everyone what he'd seen, what he'd done. He knew where they were going, anyone could have worked out where they were hiding. He told Matt and Matt had simply waited for them to come out. It was strange. They'd been so terrified the ironclads would catch them. It had never occurred to him the old lengthsman from his boyhood would get them instead. He hadn't even thought about Matt for years.

Eventually they reached the gathering of huts where they'd met the old man the day before. It was a lot nearer than Finn had imagined: the route they'd taken through the tunnels must have taken them far out of their way. Was that all a part of the old man's plan? Delay them so he could set about betraying them?

Finn saw the old man squatting next to a smouldering pile of ash as they approached, the remnants of the night's bonfire. The smoke was a thin column of grey climbing vertically into the still air. At their approach he looked up, startled, his hand reaching for a stick lying beside him on the ground. His response puzzled Finn. He carried on clutching his stick as they approached, as if frightened of Matt.

"What do you want here?" the old man asked. He stood up tall and straight, trying and failing to look fierce. He looked as if one blow from Matt would crumple him to the ground.

"Oh, nothing from you, old man. We're just passing

through. A bucket of water from the well is all we need."

The man's eyes were on Finn and Diane now.

"Why are these two tied up? What are you doing with them?"

"That's none of your business, now, is it?" said Matt. "You just sit there quietly and say nothing and we won't have any problems."

The two men seemed not to know each other after all. They certainly didn't appear to be working together.

"He caught us," Finn blurted out. "He's going to take us to Engn, turn us over. Please, help us."

Matt laughed and gave the rope a vicious yank, sending both Finn and Diane sprawling to the ground.

"Now, now," said Matt. "This old bag of bones isn't going to be able to help you. No one is. We'll take our water and be on our way to Engn. The gates will be opening soon."

Finn scrambled back to his feet, Diane helping him upright. The old man stood there, clenching and unclenching his staff, his hands like the talons of a giant bird. But he did nothing to help them.

Matt made them haul up a leaking bucket of water from the well. He filled a flask, took a drink. He didn't give any water to them.

"Well," he said. "Let's be getting you to Engn, shall we?"

They set off again, over the grassy rise of ground, the pumping and whirring of Engn suddenly louder. Finn could see the six wheels, all of them turning now, looming beyond the wall.

They skirted around the edges of more and more clusters of houses. They seemed to huddle beneath the walls of Engn, sheltering from the winds, perhaps. Near the ramshackle communities, Finn saw a few places where the land had been tilled and planted with vegetables. He also saw traps set out here and there like those back on Connor's farm. Rabbits or rats. With what they could catch and their meagre crops and the water from the underground streams, the people here scratched out a living. This was how Matt must have been living all this time, seeing the gates to Engn open and close each day, waiting for his chance.

After a couple of hours of stumbling progress, Matt stopped and gave them each a sip of water. He took great gulps of it himself, spilling more to the ground than he let either of them have. Finn thought about his long journey to Engn, sitting inside the moving engine. Now here he was again, being taken to Engn, helpless. And this time there would be no bed or meal waiting for him. His stomach churned with anxiety at what lay ahead. For Diane as well. Somehow, they had to get free, but he could see no way. They had nothing sharp they could use to cut the rope. Even if they did, Matt looked in better shape than either of them. He would soon catch them again. If they could incapacitate him, somehow, knock him out, then perhaps they could get far enough away. But he could think of no way of doing it. He glanced across at Diane, hoping she might have an idea, some plan to escape. But her head was down, watching the ground in front of them as they trudged along.

They stopped at around midday, the sun high in the blue sky, its heat pinning them to the ground. He could feel his skin burning. Too used to the dim chill of the caves. Matt had a rough hat, little more than a floppy cloth, that he draped over his bald head to keep the sun off. He gave them a few more sips of water and then began to chew on a lump of something he pulled from inside his jacket. He didn't offer any to them.

Up ahead, the wall of Engn climbed upwards: a sheer, smooth cliff of grey rock. Another cluster of the little houses must be there too. It was invisible behind a rise in the ground but Finn could see another line of smoke, rising against the dark stone even in the noon heat. Why burn fires in this heat? It made no sense.

Glancing backwards he saw that all the other fires still burned too: indistinct plumes of smoke all across the plain. Most were solid lines but some had breaks in them where something had interrupted their rise. Realization of what they really were came to him at the same moment as he saw the hulking, black figure atop a nearby rise. Another silhouette, but this one had the bulk and height of an ironclad. The figure stood unmoving for a moment and then, weapon in hand, strode down the slope directly towards them.

XXX

Finn slumped to the ground, Diane with him. Matt had let go of the rope but neither thought about running. They were too exhausted. Matt would hand them over to the ironclads and that would be that.

The figure broke into a run, racing towards them down the hill, brandishing a metal club. He cried out in fury. "I should have killed you when I had chance, Matt Dobey!"

Finn looked on in amazement. He recognized the voice immediately. It was no ironclad. Was it possible? His father wasn't as tall as he remembered but there he was, charging down to rescue them.

Matt fumbled for a knife from inside his jacket and held it forwards, but he was too slow. His father, swinging his club, smashed Matt's arm to one side, sending the knife flying.

"Please, no. I can help you," said Matt, cowering to the ground. "I have friends in Engn." His father swung again, connecting with the side of Matt's head, sending him crashing to the ground where he lay still.

His father dropped his weapon and ran across to them. He hugged Finn into his chest, nearly crushing him. "Oh, my boy. My beautiful boy."

His hands still tied, Finn could only stand there, his eyes closed.

"And this must be Diane," his father said, looking over Finn's shoulder.

"Yes. You know her?"

"Mrs. Megrim told us everything."

"I should have told you myself. I'm sorry."

"It doesn't matter now."

"We? Mother is here too?"

"She is. And Badger. I'll take you to them now. It's not far."

"But how did you find us?"

"I saw Bran's signals and wondered if it could be you. It looks like Matt saw them too."

"You mean the old man's fire? The smoke?"

"There's a whole language to it if you can read it. We're just lucky it's a still day."

"I thought the old man had betrayed us."

"No, no. He just put the word out. It's what people do. I knew Diane had been captured recently and I thought, I hoped, the two of you had somehow managed to escape. And here you are. It's a miracle."

"Matt was going to take us back. Buy favour with the masters."

"I know. Don't worry about him. He can't harm you anymore."

"Is he dead?"

His father knelt down to examine Matt. The ground was stained red beneath his head. His father looked up. "Like I say, you don't need to worry about him anymore."

Finn nodded.

"Come on," said his father. "Let's get you to your mother. It'll be safer inside the hut. And there's a lot to talk about."

His mother didn't speak when Finn ducked into the low hut. But Badger leapt at him in uncontained delight, all tongue and paws and wagging tail. His mother simply clutched him to her and rocked him from side to side as if he were still a baby. He didn't protest. When she finally let go his eyes had adjusted to the gloom. She looked pinched, sucked dry, but the smile on her face was his mother's old smile. She stroked his cheek as she studied him. "Oh, Finn. Look at you."

They sat on the ground in a circle in the quiet darkness of the hut. Badger rested her head on Finn's legs and closed her eyes. They ate freshly baked bread. It was the most delicious thing Finn had ever tasted. How did they manage to even make it out there? It was one more miracle.

When he had eaten his fill, he sat back and looked around in contentment. For the first time in many months he felt safe. Felt he could relax, sleep safely. It was a glorious feeling. But, at the same time, he knew it was an illusion. They couldn't stay there. Sooner or later the ironclads would find them. He was only endangering his parents. If his father and Matt had read the smoke signals, Engn could, too.

"We'd better not stay long," he said. "The ironclads will find us."

"It's safer here than trying to cross the plain," said his father.

"I'm not going to cross the plain. I'm going to get back inside."

"Finn, no," said his mother. "You can't do that."

"But I have to," said Finn. "Diane too. It's the only way. We won't be free or safe until we destroy the machine. Destroy everything."

"Oh, Finn," said his father. "You must know by now

that's not possible. You've seen how vast it is."

"I think there's a way."

"What way?"

"I don't know. I mean, I don't know the details. But I'm sure it's possible. A plan put in place. I've been talking to Mrs. Megrim. She's told us about a tunnel back inside. A secret tunnel. A way to get in touch with both Shireen and Connor."

"Shireen? She's still alive?" said his mother.

"You didn't know?" Somehow, he'd imagined Mrs. Megrim or the wreckers inside Engn would had kept them informed.

"No. Tell us," said his mother.

"She's alive and well. She's in something called the Directory."

"How do you know all this?" said his father. "How have you been talking to Mrs. Megrim?"

Finn recounted Mrs. Megrim's words as best as he could remember, Diane chipping in with details. Fear and hope fought on his mother's face while his father simply frowned as he listened, deep in thought.

"Don't you see?" said Finn when they'd finished. "This is our chance. Our only chance. With Shireen's help we can find Connor and do … whatever it is we need to do."

His father shook his head. "It's crazy, Finn. You can't really do this."

"I have to try, Father. You brought me up to always do the right thing. That's what I'm doing."

"But you'll just get yourself killed," said his mother. "That's not going to help anyone, is it?"

"Look," said his father. "Idealism is all very well. But when you get a bit older you learn you can't change everything. You learn you have to accept some things as they are."

"You don't understand," said Finn.

"I understand very well," said his father.

"I don't think you do," said Finn. He was suddenly

angry with his father. With both of them. He'd expected them to help him, support him. "You had your safe life back there in the valley, far away from Engn. You didn't know what it was like to see your friends taken one by one."

He regretted his words immediately. Of course, they knew. They had lost both their children to the ironclads. And others. He thought his father was going to be furious with him, but instead he only sighed.

"I do understand, Finn. I really do. In fact, I tried to do something similar, myself, once."

"You?"

"Yes. Long before you and Shireen. You remember I was an unbonded artisan as a young man? I travelled among the towns and cities circling the great grass plain, learning what scraps the guilds would teach me. I stayed longest with the Ironmasters and the Wheelwrights, but most of the guilds were happy to teach outsiders a few basic skills, in the hope of recruiting them, I think. One time, heading home for the valley, five or six of us actually marched onto the plain intent on destroying the machine. We were going to smash it to pieces with our sticks before it could take any of us."

"You did?"

"Oh, yes. Connor's dad was there, too. Actually, I think it was his idea. He liked to think he could tell us what to do, and for once we listened to him." Finn's father smiled at the memory, a smile with no humour to it.

"So, what happened?" asked Finn.

"You remember I said I'd seen Engn once? That was the time. We were idiots; we had no idea about the size of the machine. Half a day out from the foothills we realized how foolish we were. The following day we turned around and went home. I don't think Engn ever knew anything about it."

"If you hadn't turned back, Shireen and I wouldn't have been born," said Finn.

"No. I know. Still, I've often regretted it. Regretted it every time someone gets taken. And when Shireen was taken and then you were taken, I saw how much we'd failed you."

"Then you understand why we have to go back inside," said Finn. "Because otherwise it just goes on and on doesn't it? Some other child. And some other parent."

"We don't care about other children," said his mother. "We care about you and Shireen."

Finn looked into her eyes and caught a clue of what it must have been like for his parents all this time, not knowing if either of their children had survived. And facing the prospect, now, of losing them once again. The truth was he hadn't thought much about their feelings all that time. He'd longed to see them, fantasized about them coming to rescue him, take him home. He'd never stopped to think what they must be going through.

"I'm sorry," said Finn, kneeling before his mother. "But we have to try. We're in danger whatever we do. If there's a chance to destroy the machine we have to take it. And perhaps we can rescue Shireen, too."

A look passed between his mother and father. An unspoken conversation, like in the old days.

"Rest here for a few days, at least," said his mother. "You're both dead on your feet. There's no need to rush into anything."

"But it's not safe," said Diane. "Like Finn says, the ironclads will find us and then they'll take you, too."

"Don't worry about that," said his father. "We'll hear the signal if any of them come near. And there's a shaft not far away you can slip down."

"He's right," said his mother. "You'll be safe enough here for a little while. We can teach you the song maps so you can find your way underground."

Finn looked at Diane. Another unspoken conversation. He could see she wanted to stay, also that she wanted to get away as quickly as possible. In the end exhaustion won, and she acceded with the slightest nod of her head.

"We could stay a day or two, if you think it's safe," said Finn. "But we won't endanger you. Any sign of the ironclads and we'll leave."

His mother smiled. "Then it's agreed. Make yourselves at home."

The next three days were a golden interlude, another period Finn would remember fondly. His parents tended to their wounds, fed them, made them rest. As well as fresh bread, they were brought chicken and fresh vegetables and fresh water from the wells to drink. He and Diane spent their days in the quiet of the hut, swapping details of their respective adventures, remembering their time together back in the valley. The day Finn and Connor had found Diane in the clearing and she'd threatened them with her knife. The barn she'd slept in. The way they thought no one knew what they were up to.

Finn's parents came and went, giving them the peace they needed. But in the evenings, after dark, they all sat together outside, eating and talking. Swapping stories. Finn loved to sit under the stars, his back to Engn, gazing into the far distances.

"What are they saying about us?" he asked his father on the second evening. "Everyone out here."

"They're all talking about you," said his father. "Two people escaping Engn. It's unheard of. You've given them all hope, I think. Made them believe they might see their own loved ones again."

"But where do the ironclads think we are?"

"Some say you had horses ready and galloped across the plain for the mountains, heading for one of the old guild city-states maybe. The ironclads have been seen fanning out in all directions. Others think you're here somewhere, hiding."

"Does anyone know you're connected to us?"

"No, no. People are good at keeping secrets here."

"But if they're searching, they'll find us eventually,"

said Diane. "Perhaps we should disguise ourselves. Change our appearance."

"Wouldn't do any good," said Finn. "They have all our thumbprints on record. They can identify you from that. It happened to me once."

"There are thousands and thousands of people out here, scattered for miles around," said his mother. "They can't search us all immediately."

Finn nodded and went back to watching the sparks from the fires dancing up into the air to join the stars.

They heard the distant whistle late the following day, a long, falling note. Badger awoke immediately, her ears pricked. Finn looked at Diane, wondering what it meant. Then his father and mother came in. The alarm on their faces was clear.

"Ironclads coming this way," said his father.

"We should go," said Diane. She looked at Finn. Finn nodded.

"You're going to do this?" said his mother. "Try and get back inside?"

"We are."

"Perhaps the wreckers will be able to help you. Look out for you."

Finn shook his head. "We can't rely on them. Some of them helped me but their leader betrayed me to the masters."

"Their leader?" said his father.

"They call her Lud," said Finn. "Although her real name is Maeve as far as I know. In any case, we can't trust her."

His mother sighed. "Then just … just promise us you'll be careful."

"We will."

"I'll come with you now, as far as I can," said his father.

"The thing is," said Diane. "We don't know where this tunnel is. Mrs. Megrim didn't know."

"No," said his father. "But Bran will. He remembers the oldest song maps, the ones made up by the first builders. Songs that have been passed down for generations because they're too dangerous to write down. If anyone knows where this tunnel is, he will."

"Will he help us?"

His father considered. "He might. We can ask."

They packed in haste. His father peered out of the hut first, then looked back inside. "The smoke says they're still some way away to the south. Half a mile or so. If we hurry, they won't see us."

Finn hugged his mother again. She clutched him tight but said nothing. Finn smiled at her, stroked Badger and stepped outside. Diane followed. A late-afternoon glow filled the air, making everything blaze with a vivid light, beautiful to see. A slight breeze picked up. Finn watched it ruffling the great expanse of grass, like waves blown on the waters of a pond. It also scattered the lines of smoke rising up into the sky, scrambling their messages irrevocably. As he stepped forwards, he had the clear sensation of picking up old burdens, of old weights on his shoulders.

"Follow me," said his father. "We'll keep to the dips. We'll need to move quickly and silently."

They reached Bran's little scattering of huts without seeing anyone. His father stood by the fire in clear view and gave a whistle, a rising note, completely different to the warning about the ironclads. After a moment, Bran came out to meet them. He looked warily all around as he approached but looked pleased enough to see them.

"I'm sorry I didn't help you," he said to Finn and Diane. "Twenty years ago, I'd have taken him on. The man who caught you. But now … there was nothing I could do to stop him."

"You did plenty," Finn's father replied. "Without your signals I'd never have found my son again."

"And now you're spiriting him away somewhere? Getting him safely out of the way, him and his pretty friend?"

"Finn and Diane are going to try and get back inside Engn."

"No." Bran looked stunned. It took him a few moments to reply. "But why? Why would you do that?"

His father looked at Finn but didn't reply.

"There are others still in there," said Finn. It seemed they could trust Bran but, still, there was no point in telling him everything. "Others we might be able to get out."

"Ah," said Bran, nodding, as if it all now made sense. "Did I tell you my own son is in there?"

"You did," said Finn. "What's his name?"

"Owyn. I heard he was a master. Did you ever come across him at all? He was short, like me."

Finn could suddenly see it. There in Bran's face, unmistakably, were the features of Master Owyn staring back at him. Perhaps if things had been different Owyn would have been different, too. More like his father. The masters were victims as well, in their own way.

"Yes," said Finn. "I knew him. A year or so back. He was … alive and well then. A master, like you said."

"Ah!" The old man simply looked at Finn, a look of pure joy on his lined features.

"The thing is, Bran," said Finn's father. "We need your help to find a tunnel."

"A tunnel?"

"It goes directly into something called the Directory,"

said Finn. "Do you know it?"

Bran looked thoughtful for a moment. He said nothing but his lips moved. Finn had the clear impression he was singing a song to himself. Finally, the old man nodded. "Yes. I know it. But you shouldn't go that way. A few have tried and most haven't come out again."

"Will you tell us where it is?" asked Finn.

Bran considered. "I couldn't help you before when I should have. But I will help you now. For that and because of the news about my son."

"We have to hurry," said Finn. "There are ironclads looking for us."

"Let us go then," said Bran. "The sooner we go the sooner I can be back to keep watch for Owyn."

The four of them set off in a line, away from the warmth of Bran's fire towards the looming bulk of the walls of Engn. They walked for an hour or more, none of them speaking. Three times they heard whistles, but always in the distance. Each time they stopped and listened in absolute silence, Finn dreading to hear the thunder of hooves charging towards them.

They clung to the shadows, threading their way between the fires. Only the lights from Engn illuminated their path. Finally, they stopped at the top of a steep bank, a depression in the ground on whose slopes grew thickets of scratchy bushes. A jumble of boulders lay all around the bottom of the pit, as if it had once been a quarry. They were very close to the walls. Finn could feel the familiar thrumming and booming noises through his feet. It was strange – he had almost missed them.

"It's down there," said Bran. "It's well hidden. There's a stone cap you'll need to pull aside."

"But there must be hundreds of boulders down there," said Finn.

"The one you want is halfway down the slope, hidden in the bushes," said Bran. "It's big. You'll need to be strong to budge it."

"I can do that," said Finn's father.

"Why is it there?" asked Diane, suspicion clear in her voice. "If the ironclads know there's a tunnel here why don't they seal it up? They must guard it at least."

"No, no," said Bran. "The ironclads don't know about it. You won't find any of them at the other end. This takes you to the Directory. No ironclads there, are there?"

"How do you know that?" asked Diane. "And why haven't you used the tunnel to get inside yourself?"

"I know that because I have used the tunnel myself."

"You?"

"Many years ago, now. I crept inside looking for Owyn. Then I crept right out again when it became clear he wasn't there."

"But that makes no sense," said Diane. "You could have looked for him in the rest of Engn."

"No," said Bran. "You don't understand. The Directory is isolated. You can't get anywhere else from there. It's the secret heart of Engn. The centre, the control. And the ironclads aren't allowed in."

"But the masters control Engn," said Finn. "And the Inner Wheel governs them. Everyone knows that."

"Then they know nothing," replied Bran. "The masters just do what they're told by the Directory. Always have. Even the Inner Wheel is just a tool of the Directors. They're the real power in Engn. The masters carry out their instructions."

"So, there'll be silverclads there?" asked Finn.

"No, not them neither! The Directors don't allow them, don't allow anyone. No one goes in or out, don't you see? The Directory has walls all of its own inside the walls of Engn. It's the inner sanctum, the brain inside the body."

"Yet they have this tunnel people can crawl through to get inside," said Diane. "And they let you get in and escape again. How can that be?"

"You'll see why, young lady. It's not a tunnel to them, is it? It can't possibly be a tunnel. I escaped because they didn't think escape was possible. Or even meaningful."

"That makes no sense," said Diane.

"Still, you'll see what I mean when you're inside."

"You said others have used the tunnel," said Finn. "Has anyone else ever escaped this way?"

"None I ever heard of," said Bran. "I was lucky I suppose. I didn't hang around when I saw how things were. If you're going, go now, before the ironclads find us. Plenty of them out here at least, especially with you two on the run."

Bran was right. They couldn't stand there all night debating what to do. Finn began to scramble down into the dip. He worked his way awkwardly through the dense, stubborn boughs of the bushes. He could see nothing around him and had to feel his way, reaching with his hands to pull aside the bushes, using his feet to feel around for the stone cap. His father and Diane followed him. Bran stayed where he was, up on the lip of the hollow.

Finn stumbled over the entrance halfway down the slope. A round boulder half-embedded in the earth. It was certainly in the right place. A tunnel behind it would lead directly towards the walls.

The three of them set to work. Wrapping their fingers around the edge of the boulder they began to pull. The stone *was* massive, but Finn could feel it moving slightly as they pulled. It was awkward standing partway down the slope, slightly off-balance. He imagined the rock coming suddenly loose and the three of them tumbling down the slope in an avalanche of soil and stone.

"Rock it," said his father. "Rock it loose."

They worked away for some time, getting into a rhythm

of pulling the stone aside then letting it fall back. Slowly it began to work free.

"One more heave," said his father.

They put all their strength into it, Finn grunting with the effort. The great stone budged and came forwards. For a moment it balanced in its end, deciding which way to fall. Finn grasped one of the thicker boughs around him and tried to swing out of the way. The stone came to its decision and toppled forwards, down the slope, crashing between the boughs of the bushes to land at the bottom of the hollow.

"Have you found it?" Bran shouted down. He sounded distant, as if he'd walked some way away.

"I think so," called Finn. He kneeled at the place where the stone had been and felt the ground. There was a hollow there. He reached forwards and touched stone-lined walls, leading away under the ground. It was low; they would have to crawl on hands and knees.

"How long is the tunnel?" Finn shouted up. "Do we need directions like before?"

"No directions, no turnings," called Bran. "Just go straight and you'll get there."

"How far?"

But the old man didn't answer.

"You'd better go," said Finn's father.

They hugged again, almost overbalancing and sending themselves after the boulder. Then Finn let go and crouched down at the tunnel entrance.

"You don't have to come any farther, Diane," he called back. "You said you'd come with me this far. I can go in alone."

"Oh, no," she said. "You'd only mess everything up. Look how long it took you to escape last time."

She was trying to make light of it, but he could tell she was terrified. He was too. His insides fizzed with fear at the thought of going back inside.

"I'll wait here as long as I can," said his father. "In case the tunnel is blocked."

Finn felt his father's hand on his shoulder, his grip strong. Finn squeezed it, then began to crawl forwards into the darkness.

XXXI

They crawled for a long time, the sound of their laboured breathing filling the narrow tunnel. Finn's knees soon ached sharply; it felt as though his bones had worked their way out of his skin to jut against the stones of the floor. The tunnel was utterly dark. Every now and then something tickled his face: the fronds of a tree's roots or a spider's web. For a while his father called to them, asking how they were, his voice hollow and sounding strangely near. But now, when Finn called back, there was no reply. His father had gone. Perhaps the ironclads had been sighted nearby.

The air grew warmer and thicker. It was impossible to know how far they'd travelled. Somewhere up above them were the walls of Engn: those massive stone ramparts pressing down into the ground. He imagined he could feel their crushing weight. He thought the tunnel sloped down slightly but it was hard to be sure. Perhaps it burrowed down to get under the walls. He thought about Bran's words, the tunnel not really being a tunnel. It made no sense but he was already too weary to try and work it out. He couldn't think straight. He had to just keep going.

"How much farther do you think?" Diane sounded exhausted behind him. Her knees must be in agony too. He was probably more used to crawling around in caverns than she was.

"Don't know. Do you think the tunnel is sloping?"

"I thought it was," She spoke in short bursts, between breaths. "Now it seems level."

The ground was certainly muddier, with little pools of chilling water here and there. They were very welcome, numbing Finn's knees. But soon the ground hardened back to stone. The tunnel seemed to be climbing once more. What was above them? What great mechanism was up there above their heads? The deep *whumping* sound through the ground grew louder and louder. It felt as if the whole tunnel shook with each thump. He tried not to think about the ceiling giving way, the tunnel collapsing.

They crawled on and on, neither speaking. Twice Finn thought about suggesting they turn back, that the tunnel was endless, in some sort of loop. Perhaps that was what Bran had meant. But there wasn't enough room to spin around in the cramped passage and the thought of reversing all that way was too much. They could only grind onwards. He closed his eyes as he went, drifting into a half slumber, the pain in his knees and hands filling his mind, his whole universe. Worried he might be missing something, some side passage, he forced his eyes open again and again, but he could never see anything. Then his eyes would slip shut and the nightmare crawl would continue.

So it was that he was momentarily confused when his head struck a solid wall of earth and stone in front of him.

"What is it?" He felt Diane's outstretched hand on his foot.

"The end of the tunnel. There's a wall."

"Is there a way out?"

Finn felt about with his hands, to the sides, above his head, but felt only stone and soil. "Perhaps we missed it in the darkness," he said, trying to keep the panic from his voice. Perhaps, after everything, the tunnel was a dead end. A trick.

"Here. It's here," said Diane from behind him. "There's a wooden door in the side of the passage. We crawled right past it."

"Is it locked?"

He heard Diane grunting with the effort of pushing and pulling the door. The end of the tunnel was slightly wider. There was enough room to turn and go back to help. He found her arms in the darkness, and then the door. Between them they tried to push it open.

"It's moving," said Diane. "It's just swollen in its frame."

Finn turned so his feet were against the door, back braced against the tunnel wall. He pushed with all his strength. With a sudden flurry of loosened soil and pebbles that made his heart leap in alarm, the door gave way. Light burst in. Diane was surprisingly close to him, her face covered in grime. Through the door they could see a flight of stone steps leading upwards. One after the other they crawled through. Tentatively, peering upwards, they set off up the stairs to the surface.

They emerged at the end of a passageway, tall enough to walk down. Electric lights strung along the ceiling provided a flickering illumination. The walls were of square-cut stones, well-made. There was no one in sight. He'd expected guards at least.

"Do you think we're back above ground?" he asked. Diane stood beside him, brushing herself down with her muddy hands.

"I suppose so," she said. "There's no lichen on the walls. Come on, let's see what's down the passage."

The corridor snaked left and right as they edged forwards. There were no other doors leading off it. They could only go one way. They emerged, suddenly, into a large, airy room, windows providing bright illumination. A woman sat at a large desk in the centre, working on a contraption of iron wheels and electrical wires. A generator or something similar. The pungent smell of solder filled the air, instantly familiar to Finn from his father's workshop back in the valley. Strange how smells took you back across the years. The woman appeared to be constructing the device, scribbling notes into a large book as she slotted parts of it together. She looked confused when Finn and Diane stepped warily into the room.

"Are you lost?" she asked. She had brown hair, cropped very short so it didn't get in the way of her machinery. For the briefest moment Finn thought that it might be Shireen, the sister he hadn't seen for so many years. She would have changed, of course, and she certainly wouldn't recognize him. But her strong-boned face didn't look remotely familiar. Without waiting for an answer, she turned back to her work, attempting to fit a cogged wheel into something like a gearbox.

"We're just … on our way through," said Finn.

"Where from?" she asked without looking up at them. "You're both covered in mud."

"We came along the passageway," said Diane. "The tunnel that leads … away from here."

"Tunnel?" The woman looked even more confused. Worried, even. She set down the pincers she'd been using and looked at them again. "What do you mean 'tunnel'?"

"Back there," said Finn. There seemed little point in trying to invent a story. "It runs underground from the foot of the steps."

The woman shook her head as if trying to dislodge Finn's words. "You're making no sense. There's just an empty room there. And how did you get past before without me noticing?"

Finn glanced at Diane, who looked as unsure as he was what to say.

"We didn't come past you," said Diane. "We came through the tunnel, like we said."

"Why would you invent something like that?" the woman asked. She looked alarmed now. "Is this some sort of test?"

"No, no," said Finn. "We're telling the truth. There is a tunnel, leading out of Engn."

"Outside?"

They glanced at each other again. Diane shrugged her shoulders. "Yes."

"Ah, I think I understand," said the woman, visibly relaxing. "You've recently been in the Sanatorium, yes? They've been looking after you there until you're … better."

"The Sanatorium?" said Finn. "No, I don't think so."

"Well," replied the woman, ignoring his words, "I think it's perhaps best if we send you back there, don't you? They'll look after you, help you to see the world more … clearly." The woman looked visibly relieved at this explanation.

"You've never seen the tunnel?" asked Finn. It seemed utterly incredible. She worked just a short walk from an unguarded passageway out of Engn that she could crawl along any time she wanted. "You've never been tempted to see where it goes? Get outside?"

"Now, I think that's enough of that talk, don't you? No wonder they took you to the Sanatorium. They're very good there, I'm sure they'll soon cure you."

Diane shook her head, her brow furrowed in puzzlement. "Okay, we'll just head on back to the Sanatorium. Like you said. Could you tell us which way it is?"

The woman looked satisfied at Diane's words, as if everything now made sense again. She turned to the wall behind her and pushed a button that, somewhere distantly, made a bell ring. "I'll summon someone to take you there," she said. "Don't want you wandering around the

Directory all alone, do we? No knowing what trouble you'll get up to."

Finn was about to object, argue, when a cowled figure entered the room. He or she wore red robes, a sort Finn hadn't seen before. The figure turned its shadowed face to look at the woman.

"Take these two unfortunates to the Sanatorium. And tell them not to be so careless with their patients in future."

The cowled figure nodded, beckoned to Finn and Diane, then turned to leave. Finn glanced at the woman, engrossed in her machinery once more, then followed.

The hooded figure led them out into the glaring light of a courtyard. High walls encircled them, peeking over which Finn could see the familiar workings of Engn. The roar and thump of the machinery filled the air but it was muffled by distance. The air smelled cleaner than usual.

Many other red-robed figures walked to and fro across the courtyard and Finn and Diane had to hurry to stay close to their own. They could, Finn thought, easily slip away to hide; the figure they followed didn't seem at all concerned about losing them.

"This place is weird," said Diane. "They don't seem surprised to find us here."

"I know."

"Perhaps we should just run."

"Where would we go, though?" said Finn. "We might as well see where this one is taking us."

"Okay. But I don't like it. It makes no sense. I understood it when the ironclads were after us."

They entered a tall oblong building with round windows and a single door at its base. Inside it was dark and hushed, the thick walls muffling all the sound of the machinery. They passed through rooms of empty beds, each surrounded by comfortable chairs and an array of shelves. None were occupied. Beyond the bedrooms was a bright, spacious room with tall windows leading out onto a wide balcony. The robed figure leading them talked into an iron grille in one of the walls, through which Finn could discern a face. The conversation continued for some time, then the robed figure walked past them and left, still without speaking to them.

"Well, well," said a man emerging from a doorway near the grille. He also wore red robes but his cowl was hanging down his back, revealing his features. He had a handsome, friendly face. His head was shaved completely bald and his cheeks dimpled as he smiled at them. He wore a metal stud through one of his earlobes, as if someone had fired a rivet into him. "So, who have we here?"

Finn tried to invent some names on the spur of the moment, but his mind went blank. "I'm Finn. This is Diane," he said. The man held a rectangle of metal on which was clipped a piece of paper. He wrote something with a steel pen. Finn felt sure the man would realize who they were, but after a few moments he looked back up at them, still smiling.

"Very good. I'm Nathaniel. Let's go and sit outside and have a little chat, shall we? It's a lovely, warm day."

He hauled on one of the tall windows, which slid on some sort of ball bearing mechanism to open like a door. Outside, chairs had been set out. Morning sunlight glowed in the air, the smoke and steam of Engn giving everything a misty glow. Over the high walls, Finn could see the tops of the wheels and towers of Engn. He wasn't sure where in the workings they were but one distant tower looked distinctly like the Drop Tower. Spindly lines led off from it through the air, presumably the walkways.

"Good, good," said the man. "Now, tell me how you came to be here." He sounded genuinely interested to know their answer, delighted at the prospect of hearing a favourite story.

"We came through a tunnel," said Diane. "Crawled all the way underground."

"A tunnel? How fascinating." He wrote more words.

"So, where was the other end of this *tunnel?*"

Nathaniel's friendly manner was disarming. Finn found himself telling the man the truth. He couldn't think of anything else to say. "It was outside. We found it on the great plain, hidden in a little hollow in the ground overgrown with bushes."

"I see," said Nathaniel.

"There was a great stone covering the entrance," said Finn. "We had to haul it aside to get in."

"And then you simply crawled all the way in, popped up and here you are?" asked Nathaniel.

"Well, yes," said Finn.

"I see, I see. So that's why you're both so mucky?"

"Yes," said Diane.

Nathaniel looked thoughtful for a time, peering at the both of them as if they were a puzzle. He wrote down more on his sheet of paper then looked up at them again. "I'd love to hear more about this *outside* you mention. Can you describe it to me?"

"All of it?" asked Finn. "But it's vast. I mean, it's outside, it's everything. How can we describe all that to you?"

"Yes of course, of course," said Nathaniel. "I can see it would be difficult. Why don't you just tell me a little for now. Then, when you, ah, remember more of it, you can tell me that. We've plenty of time."

Finn looked at Diane, who wore the same puzzled expression as before. He shrugged. "Well, there's the great plain outside Engn. The grass stretches for many miles, in all directions. Engn is in the middle of it, obviously."

"I see. And what is beyond this grass plain?"

"Well, everything, the whole of the world. Mountains and forests. The city-states around the edge of the plain and all the towns and villages in between. The sea, some people say."

"The sea?" The man sounded as if the word was unfamiliar.

"Yes, you know, like a lake, only much, much bigger. Although, I've never actually seen that."

"Much bigger. Yes." The man scribbled furiously now, appearing to write down everything they said. He turned his sheet of paper over, clipped it back into place and carried on writing. "And this grass plain. People live there?"

"Some. They wait outside the walls of Engn and send smoke signals to each other with their fires."

"Do they? And why are they there? What do they do?"

"Well, generally they're waiting for someone inside. Or they want to try and get inside themselves."

"Of course they do, of course they do." The man reached the end of his sheet of paper. He reread what he'd written then peered at Finn and Diane. "Well, this is certainly fascinating. I'd like to spend lots of time with you and hear everything about this wonderful world outside Engn. Would that be okay?"

"Sure," said Finn.

"But we don't want to wear you out," continued Nathaniel. "You look exhausted. Shall we resume tomorrow?"

"Okay," said Diane, shrugging. "So, where should we go until then?"

"Oh, stay here of course. We have plenty of room. Comfortable beds and I'm sure you must be starving after your long journey underground, yes? I don't suppose there's much food to be found out there, is there? Outside Engn?"

"Well, no," said Diane.

"No. Good. Well, follow me and I'll show you around. Then tomorrow we can talk some more. I'll be sure to bring lots more paper with me."

The man ushered them back inside and up some stairs. Finn felt sure he was playing some terrible joke on them, that they'd find themselves surrounded by the ironclads at any moment. But, instead, they were shown to a room dotted with numerous round tables. Food and drink was brought to them on wooden plates, all of it steaming hot and delicious-smelling. They both ate hungrily, Nathaniel watching them all the time, a look of delight on his face. When they sat back, he grinned. "Well, and now you'd like to rest, I'm sure. I'll show you where you can sleep."

They were taken up two more flights of steps to a narrow corridor off which led a series of doors. Nathaniel opened the nearest two. Each revealed a large, L-shaped room, a bed along one wall and two chairs around a round table beside it. Around the angle of the L was a bath and sink, each fed by hot and cold water, along with a flushing toilet. In the wall over the bath, one of the round windows let in a shaft of bright sunlight.

"I'll give you adjacent rooms," the man said. "That way you can talk but you'll have solitude and quiet if you need it. There's a little grille in the wall you can slide open if you want to communicate."

"Thanks," said Finn sitting down on the bed. It felt very soft and springy. He seemed to sink into it.

"I will have to lock your doors of course. For your own safety."

"Our own safety?" asked Diane.

"Yes. Just until you're better. Once we've got you sorted out then you can go back to your old lives in the Directory. But until then, it's best we keep you safe and secure. Don't want you wandering somewhere you shouldn't."

"We won't go anywhere," said Diane. "You can leave the doors unlocked, can't you?" Finn narrowed his eyes at her but she refused to return his look.

"Oh, I wish I could," said Nathaniel. "But really, it's for the best. Then, tomorrow, we can go outside again and talk. Would that be all right?"

She was thinking about running, Finn could see, weighing up the odds of being able to escape the building, the Directory, the whole city. He couldn't blame her. None of this made any sense at all.

"Now, now," said Nathaniel, also reading Diane's expression. "I can summon help if I need, as I'm sure you know. But we prefer not to here at the Sanatorium. We like to do everything very gently, very peacefully. You'd prefer that, wouldn't you?"

On the wall outside his room there was a button like the one the woman had used. Nathaniel could summon help any time he liked. Diane, it seemed, came to the same conclusion. There seemed to be little harm in staying for a time. Nathaniel seemed to have no idea who they really were.

Diane lowered her head in assent and followed the man into the next room. Finn heard their muffled voices as he showed her around, then the *click* of the two doors being shut and locked. He lay on his bed, letting its softness engulf him. Somehow, he didn't mind the door being locked like that. It was an illusion, no doubt, but it made him feel safer. His own room, his own bed. He loved the thought of all this *space* being his, his alone. The thought of having a hot bath made his skin tingle with anticipation. He was so tired, though. Perhaps a snooze first would be a good idea.

"Finn!"

It was Diane, whispering to him through the grille. He slid open the cover on his side and, through it, half obscured by thin metal bars, he could see Diane's face. "Finn, what the hell is going on here? What's wrong with them all?"

Finn shook his head. He whispered back in case they were being listened to. "Beats me. They seem to think *we're* mad."

"They think we're just making it all up. Everything outside Engn. They don't believe it's real."

"The walls around this place are very high. I don't think you can see the plain or the mountains. Perhaps they just don't know about them."

"But that's crazy. They can see the sky, the sun, the stars. What do they think *they* are?"

"Don't know," said Finn. "It makes no sense. The good thing is they're convinced we belong here. There isn't an outside so we can't have broken in. They think we're supposed to be here but just have these delusions."

"You're suggesting we play along?"

"For a while at least. Food, hot water, comfortable beds. I have to be honest, I think I like it here."

"And I don't trust them. Not for a moment."

"No, but I think we're safe for now. It doesn't seem to occur to them the ironclads might be looking for us. Perhaps we can find Shireen and work out what's really going on."

"Shireen? That's what really worries me."

"Why?"

"Don't you see? If she's one of them she won't believe there's anything outside Engn either. She won't believe you're her brother. She won't believe in Mrs. Megrim. Not any of it."

Finn lay back on his bed and thought about that. Within minutes he fell asleep and began to dream troubled dreams. The ironclads pursued him around and around a circular corridor with no exits. He ran as fast as he could to get away from them. But he succeeded only in catching them up from behind, and then it became he who chased them.

XXXII

They spent the next morning explaining the world to Nathaniel.

"So, let me see if I have this right," said Nathaniel after a few hours. "You arrived in Engn very recently. You especially, Diane. Before that you were elsewhere, and then you both found your way here. But most of your lives have been lived a long, long way away, in this other world."

Finn shrugged. "Yes." He'd done most of the talking and was trying to ignore the growing feeling his answers sounded ridiculous. Fantasies he was making up. Nathaniel never said anything to show he doubted them, but he was clearly delighted at the detail of their invention. He wrote everything they said carefully down.

"You don't believe us, do you?" said Diane. It was the first time she'd spoken for an hour or more. "You think we're crazy."

Nathaniel looked shocked. "I certainly wouldn't use that word."

"But you don't believe us."

"I believe you believe what you say."

"But why are you so interested in all the details of the outside world if you think it's made up?"

Nathaniel didn't reply. Instead he looked down at his paper and began to write again. Finn had the clear impression he was doodling rather than writing actual words. Nathaniel looked back up at them, playing with the metal stud in his ear-lobe.

"I'll tell you why," said Diane. "It fascinates you, doesn't it? The thought of everything outside the walls. That's why you're asking us these questions. Secretly, you're worried it's true and that all you know is a lie."

Nathaniel shook his head. "We're not here to talk about me. I'm not the one in need of help."

Diane pressed on. "Really? Because I bet you've read all the accounts of the other patients you've had in here. I bet you sit alone at night and imagine yourself outside, running free."

Nathaniel was about to reply, then stopped. A frown flashed across his face. "I think we'd better leave it for today," he said. "You must still be tired. We can resume tomorrow."

"But I'm not tired," said Diane. "Shall I tell you about the smell of a summer meadow? Or the crunching sound fresh snow makes when you walk across it? Or the view from the top of a mountain when it feels like you're standing on top of a cloud? Shall I tell you about all the things you've missed out on?"

"No!" Nathaniel's face flushed red. He half stood, scattering his papers to the floor. Then he controlled himself and sat back down. "No. I really think it's best you go back to your rooms now."

He stood and pressed a button, summoning a guard. Diane stood to leave, a look of satisfaction on her face. Nathaniel knelt to pick up his papers. His hand, Finn noticed, was shaking.

"What did you say all that for?" They lay on their beds, separated only by the wall and the grille. "We shouldn't draw attention to ourselves."

"He annoyed me," said Diane. "This whole place annoys me. How can they think the outside world doesn't exist? How can people spend their lives not seeing what's right in front of their eyes? It's ridiculous."

"Lots of people believe ridiculous things," said Finn.

"Well I'm not going to play their game anymore. Next chance I get I'm going to run for it."

"Where to?"

"Out. Back to the tunnel. Before I also start to believe the world out there doesn't exist."

Finn stared up at the ceiling of his room and didn't reply.

That evening, they were brought medicine: a viscous, milky liquid carried in clinking, metal beakers by another cowled figure. For a moment, Finn thought it might be Shireen come to find them at last. But when the newcomer threw back her hood it was a woman he didn't recognize. He was beginning to think his sister wasn't there after all.

"I'm Matilda," said the woman. "You must drink this; it will make you feel much better." Her face was wrinkled all over so that Finn couldn't tell if she was smiling or frowning.

"I'm not drinking it," said Diane. "I'm not ill."

"But you must," said Matilda. "It's for your own good."

"What is it?" Finn asked. "What does it do?"

"It helps you sleep," said Matilda. "Nothing more."

"We don't need help to sleep," said Diane.

Matilda didn't reply for a moment. She looked confused. Finn expected her to press the button, summon help to force the liquid down their throats. He spoke before she could act. "Let me try it first. I'll take some and then if I'm okay tomorrow, Diane will too."

"No, Finn. Don't do this," said Diane.

"It's okay," said Finn, looking at Diane, conscious of Matilda's gaze upon him. "I'm happy to try it. And I did have trouble sleeping."

Finn nodded at Matilda and she handed over a beaker. He sniffed. It smelled creamy and minty at the same time, but not unpleasant. With a shrug he swallowed it down.

"Very good," said Matilda, looking relieved. She turned to Diane. "And perhaps tomorrow you'll both take it?"

"Perhaps," said Diane. But mistrust was clear on her face.

The crisp sound of footsteps in the hallway, a key rattling in his lock, roused Finn from deep sleep. He lay for a moment with his eyes closed, enjoying the warm sensation of being bundled up in his blankets. He heard more footsteps, a jangle of keys as Diane's door was unlocked.

Then there was a wordless shout, the clang of a door being thrown wide, running footsteps outside.

"Finn!" It was Diane, shouting to him from the corridor outside. "Come on! Let's get out of here."

Finn sprang to his feet, heart pounding, and hauled open his own door. The cowled figure who had come to rouse them lay sprawled on the ground. Diane was racing away towards the stairs. Finn thought, briefly, about staying behind. Then he hared off after Diane. They had to stay together.

They careered down the stairs, jumping three or four at a time. Past rows of empty beds to the corridor on the ground floor they had arrived in two days earlier. Diane reached the door first and tried to haul it open by its iron handles. Finn arrived to help her and between them they pulled and pushed the heavy door.

"It's locked, I'm afraid," said a voice from behind them. Nathaniel. "We always lock it when we have visitors."

"Let us out," said Diane, turning to face him. Three cowled figures stood behind him.

"I can't do that," said Nathaniel. "You're not cured yet." His face was full of regret, as if he really wanted to set them free.

"Look," said Diane. "Come with us to the tunnel entrance. We'll prove to you we're telling the truth. We'll show you the way outside. But if it isn't there and you're right, we'll return with you and carry on with our treatment."

Nathaniel shook his head. "I'm sorry, but I can't do that. I don't like to go outside."

"We're not asking you to come through the tunnel," said Diane. "Just see it for yourself."

"You don't understand. I mean I don't like to go outside the Sanatorium."

Diane looked at Finn, desperation clear in her eyes.

"You could still let us go," said Finn. "We won't tell anyone. We'll slip away and be gone."

"No. I can't let that happen, can I?" said Nathaniel. "You'll end up hiding somewhere in the Directory causing trouble. I really can't let you out until you're better. I'm sorry."

Finn spent the rest of the day answering more of Nathaniel's questions. Diane sat in a sullen silence while he talked. Perhaps when they were alone again, they could come up with another plan. For now, they had to play the game. So, Finn found himself explaining at length the plants his mother kept in their garden, the layout of the woods and fields near his home, the intricate workings of the line-of-sight network.

The only detail he left out was of Connor. It seemed dangerous to draw him into the story. Did Nathaniel know Connor? Finn didn't dare ask. Fortunately, Nathaniel didn't bring up the subject of Finn's childhood friend. He continued to dwell on seemingly irrelevant details of their former life, as if trying to catch them out.

Only as they stood up to leave, the sun already low over the walls, slanting into their eyes, did Nathaniel mention the events of the morning. "Oh, and Diane. I'm sorry you felt so upset this morning. I really do think you should take the sleeping medicine I've prescribed for you."

"I won't," said Diane. The first words she'd spoken all day.

"I'm sorry to hear that," said Nathaniel. "Very sorry. I'd hoped you would start to trust us by now."

"No."

"Well," said Nathaniel, "in that case I'll send the Sanatorium's Executive along tonight with your draughts. She can be very persuasive. In the past she's had great success with helping our guests. We'll see if she can persuade you, shall we?"

"It won't make any difference," said Diane. She looked startled, though, alarmed at what this *Executive* might do. Once again, Finn could see Diane's clear desire to run, run *now*, before they could get to her.

That evening, the knock on his door made Finn's heart leap within his chest. Opening up he expected to see a phalanx of ironclads at the very least. Or a master he recognized from elsewhere in Engn, one who wouldn't play the Directory's ridiculous game, who would see Finn and Diane for what they really were.

Instead there was just a lone figure in red, taller than the others who'd come. The Executive moved forwards and Finn found himself stepping back automatically. It was only when she pushed her hood back that Finn saw who it really was.

She had changed, of course: her face slightly lined, her hair short. She looked like a cross between the sister he remembered and their own mother, the mother from his youth, back in the valley. She didn't smile though. Finn said nothing, could think of nothing to say. Here was Shireen, not seen since that half-remembered day years ago when the ironclads came for her. His beloved elder sister. He'd imagined meeting her again so often: embracing her, laughing with her. As it was, he simply stood there, unmoving, not speaking.

"I've brought your medicine," said Shireen. "For you and the other one. You are going to take it, aren't you?"

Finn tried to think what to say. Did his sister even recognize him? Had he changed that much? He wasn't aware of having changed at all, but maybe had had. His time in the mines had taken their toll. Or perhaps Diane had been right; perhaps Shireen was the same as the others now, not believing there was an outside world any more.

She held out the minty liquid for him. He looked into her eyes. Not a flicker of recognition or warmth. He took the cup and gulped the whole thing down in one.

"Good," said Shireen. "Now let us hope your companion is this reasonable." She picked up the tray and turned to leave.

"I found the clearing again," Finn blurted out as she swung his door shut. "The secret place you took me that day. When the ironclads came for you. I found it again. I did what you said. I thought about you, about everything."

The door stopped, just shadows beyond it, his sister

invisible. Then it began to creep open again. The woman, his sister, stared hard at him, a calculating look on her face. She glanced over her shoulder, stepped into the room. She set the tray down and only then flung her arms around him.

"Oh, Finn, Finn, it is you. Look at you, all grown up. I didn't know. I didn't know it was you, didn't know if you still remembered me."

"Yes," he said. "Yes." For a while, he couldn't think of anything else to say. He held her at arms' length to look at her again. He was taller than she was now. For a moment he saw her as she'd been that hot day in the clearing, the sun sparkling through her chestnut hair.

"And your friend?" she asked, speaking very quietly, indicating with a nod of her head.

"She knows everything," said Finn. "You. Mrs. Megrim. Everything."

"I see," said Shireen. She breathed out sharply, a nervous breath as if both excited and alarmed at what was about to happen. "Very well. Let us go next door where we can all talk."

She picked up the tray and led him from the room.

Diane looked up with wary eyes as they entered. Her room was identical to his own except for everything being the wrong way around, a mirror image. Finn sat down on one of the chairs. His sister took the other.

"Diane," said Finn. "This is my sister, Shireen."

Diane nodded but still didn't speak. She regarded both of them with calculating eyes.

"Diane, this is it, don't you see?" said Finn. "Our chance to get out of here and do what we came to do."

Diane spoke then, still looking intently at Shireen. "Then tell us what's going on here. Tell us why no one believes us. Tell us about the world outside Engn."

"Outside?"

"Yes. The world outside. Or do you think we've invented it all as well?"

Shireen was about to speak, then stopped. She looked down at the stone floor.

"You can't, can you?" said Diane. "You don't believe it either, do you? You're just like the rest of them. What have you told yourself? That it was all a childish fantasy? A game? A story?"

Shireen looked troubled at Diane's words. Finally, she spoke in a whisper. "No. It isn't that. It's just … I haven't talked about any of it for years. Not to anyone. To do so is madness, unthinkable. You've seen what it's like here. In the Directory, no one talks about outside because they know there isn't one."

"But why?" asked Finn. "It makes no sense."

Shireen sighed, trying to shape her thoughts into words. "Outside, in the rest of Engn I mean, everyone follows the orders we give them. That's the way it has always been, since the earliest days. The masters and the ironclads and all the rest obey us. But they don't know why. Only we know why. The Directory guards all the secrets of Engn, the true purpose of the machine. That's how it was set up, all those years ago. I think we were sealed off from the outside so that the secrets couldn't get out and, over the centuries, the people here simply stopped believing there even was an outside."

"So, what is the secret?" asked Diane. "What is the machine for?"

Diane frowned. "I don't know. But the secret is kept here. Possibly only the Director himself knows the truth."

"The Director?" asked Finn.

"He's the ultimate power in Engn," said Shireen. "He controls everything."

"Nathaniel really does think we're deluded?" said Finn. "That we're just making it all up?"

"He does. Nathaniel was born here and has never been outside. The same with most of us. He genuinely thinks you're ill and need his help. He's a good person."

"You like him, don't you?" asked Diane.

His sister looked down at her feet, saying nothing for a moment. "I do. But it could never work out. Helping people with their delusions about Engn – as he sees it – means everything to him. He's devoted his life to it. We could never really be honest with each other."

"Have you asked him?" said Diane. "I wouldn't be so sure."

"What do you mean?"

"I think he secretly wants to believe the stories are true. He just can't bring himself to admit it. I feel sorry for him."

"No," said Shireen. "He was born and raised in here. His parents ran the Sanatorium before him. This is his whole world. He's happy here. Outside he's … not so good."

"But how did you get in here?" asked Diane.

"Very occasionally, they need people from outside. The population of the Directory is small and closed off. They need fresh blood from time to time. I was very young when I came here, young enough for them to mould me. Also, I had the recommendation from someone back home. A friend of Engn with contacts here."

"Who?" asked Finn.

"Connor's mother. Her family has some connection with Engn, with the Clockmakers and Timecounters Guild. Did you know I used to read to her sometimes, when you were still a baby? She's never been well, spends all her time in bed, staring out of her window. She always used to say how much she loved my visits. She never had a daughter, of course. Then, when I was taken, she sent a message about me to Engn, and when I arrived, I was brought to the Directory."

"All this time you've had to pretend you didn't believe in the outside?" asked Finn.

"Yes. To be honest, I often doubted my own memories. That's why I find it so hard to talk about it all."

"You could have left at any time, you know," said

Diane. "There's a tunnel."

"I know. What would be the point? The ironclads know very well the outside world is real."

"Why should we believe you?" continued Diane. "Everyone here is lying to us. You're probably still doing what they tell you, trying to befriend us. Playing some game."

Shireen shook her head. "I'm not. I understand why you would say that, but I'm not. Believe me. This place, all of this, I despise it."

"Why?" continued Diane. "Look at you. You're trusted here. You're important. You have a comfortable life. Why should we believe you're ready to destroy it after all this time?"

"Mrs. Megrim said she was with us," said Finn to Diane.

"Mrs. Megrim is miles and miles away," said Diane. "She doesn't know what's really going on here. She doesn't know what your sister is like now."

"You're right," said Shireen. "You don't know you can trust me. But I assure you, ever since I came here, all those years ago, I've done what I can to bring about the destruction of Engn."

"Why?" said Diane.

His sister reached out to stroke Finn's hair. A memory came back to him of her doing just that when he was a boy. "Don't you see?" she said. "Don't you understand what Finn meant to me? I was his sister, of course, but I'm a lot older. I was more like his mother at times. I looked after him when our parents were busy. He was my boy, my baby. I loved him more than anything in the world. And they took all that away from me. His growing up, everything. I thought I'd never see him again, and I hated them."

Finn looked into her eyes. It had never occurred to him she would have missed him. Too concerned for himself. He couldn't think what to say. At least he'd had their parents, their home, all those years she'd been here.

He touched her hand and she smiled at him. He wasn't that little boy any more. She'd never really have him back now. "They're still alive," he said to her. "Our parents. They're here, outside the walls. They came for us."

"Ah," she said, nodding. Tears filled her eyes. She looked at him for a moment, a fond smile on her face. Then she turned back to Diane, wiping her eyes with the palms of her hands. "Come on. There's something I want to show you. I know you don't trust me, but I can at least prove to you that I believe in the outside still."

She stood and picked up the flask from the tray on the table. "We'll pour this down the sink to keep Nathaniel happy. It really is just a sleeping draught like he said."

Diane nodded.

"And I'll lock your doors in case anyone comes by," said Shireen. "If we make a hump in your beds with a pile of clothes and towels anyone glancing in will think you're both asleep."

"How far are we going?" asked Finn.

"Not far. We'll only be gone a few minutes. Best be careful though."

She opened the door, stepped outside and turned to look at them. "Coming?" She was looking mainly at Diane.

Diane paused for a moment then followed her outside, Finn right behind her.

They walked down the familiar bare stone corridor, but instead of descending to the ground-floor when they reached the stairs, Shireen began to climb. Neither of them had been up there before. Finn suddenly felt they were in very dangerous territory. If they were seen, would his sister be able to protect them or would they all be in danger? They climbed the stone stairs as quietly as they could, listening out for voices or footsteps. The only sound was the distant, muffled hum of Engn; the hum you only noticed when you made an effort to listen. Once, a door slammed shut somewhere down below, but they saw no one.

They climbed past three or four identical landings, corridors leading off to rows of rooms like their own. They all looked deserted. Had they once been full, all those rooms? Perhaps, in the old days, there had been many in the Directory struggling with their delusions of an *outside*.

Finally, they reached the top floor, a dead end that led only to a final line of doors.

"We need to go higher," said Shireen. She looked up to indicate a square cut in the ceiling, barely visible. "It's a hatchway that leads on up to the top of the tower. They don't like anyone going up there. You'll see why."

"How do we get up there?" asked Finn. The ceiling was high above them, with no way to climb up.

"It's a bit tricky. If you climb onto the banister you can just about reach up with your fingers and open it."

"You're serious?" asked Diane.

"It'll be easier with the three of us. Ready?"

Diane looked unconvinced, as if all this was some elaborate ploy.

Shireen, seeing this, stepped up onto the rail of the balcony, leaning with one hand on the wall to steady herself. She pushed off from the wall to stand upright on the narrow handrail, balancing as if on a tightrope. She began to make small, sideways steps. She took it slowly, deep in concentration, wobbling a little. If she fell forwards onto the landing, she would be fine. If she fell backwards, she would either hit the flight of steps or plummet down the central shaft to the distant floor. Finn wanted to reach out and hold onto her but was too afraid he'd overbalance her. Both he and Diane watched in silence as she edged her way along.

Finally, reaching the hatch, she reached carefully up and pushed. The square lifted and she worked it sideways, revealing a dark hole in the ceiling.

"Mind out," she called down. "I'm going to jump up and haul myself in."

Shireen sprang upwards, legs flailing around as she got an elbow then her arms up through the hatchway. She hauled herself upwards. Finn was impressed. The thought of teetering on that narrow banister, the great drop gaping beneath him, filled him with alarm and reminded him of too many other events. Shireen had clearly done it on her own, and more than once by the sound of it. He thought he'd been the one for adventure and getting into trouble. Perhaps they were more alike than he'd imagined.

He looked across at Diane again. "Do you believe her now?"

"Maybe."

"Here," called Shireen from above. "This will make it easier."

The end of a rope snaked down towards them, its end bent slightly like a snake's head as it searched for them. Finn grabbed hold and climbed onto the banister. When he was underneath the hatch he began to climb, feeding the rope between his legs and working his way upwards. Through the hatch, he found himself in a dark, hushed room that smelled of stale air and dust. Shireen was a disembodied voice beside him.

"Let's get the rope down for Diane. We're safer once the hatch is shut. No one will know we're here then."

"What if they find out we've gone?"

"We'll be okay for a while. They don't think we can really *go* anywhere after all."

"Okay."

Diane clambered up next and Shireen lowered the hatch back into place. Once more they found themselves in utter darkness.

"Where are we?" asked Diane.

"The Sanatorium has a steeple," said Shireen. "I began to wonder whether you could get up inside it, right up to the top. That was when I found the hatch."

"We can go higher?" asked Finn.

"There's a ladder. It's pretty old and rickety. We should

go up one at a time.”

“How far?”

“One hundred and fifty-three rungs.”

“And what’s at the top?” asked Diane. “Why are we going up there?”

“There’s just a little platform. Nothing much. A part of the scaffolding they used when they constructed the building, I suppose. But there should be room for three of us up there.”

Shireen climbed first, Finn holding the bottom of the bowing, swaying ladder as she ascended. As his eyes adjusted, he could just make out a dim light filtering down. Not enough to see by, but he could make out Shireen as a shadow, occasionally eclipsing the glow as she climbed. Once she reached the top, she called down to them.

“I’ll go next, shall I?” said Finn.

“Sure.”

The wood of the ladder was soft and soapy beneath him. It sagged alarmingly. He wondered how long it had been there. He could see nothing save the glow from above, but he had the clear sensation the walls were closing in around him as he climbed. At the top, Shireen reached down for his arm to guide him up. She knelt on a little wooden platform right in the apex of the spire. A series of small, semi-circular openings at floor-level, like half-open eyes, were set around the platform letting in the dim light. Finn huddled up next to his sister and called down to Diane to follow. The top of the ladder began to buck as she came up after them.

When they were all together, Shireen spoke. “You know, you were right not to trust me, Diane,” she said.

“Why?” asked Diane, wariness clear in her voice.

“You thought I’d forgotten about the outside world, that I’d convinced myself Engn was everything. The truth is, I have often thought that. Living in the Directory, it’s hard not to. No one tells you what to think but everyone assumes there is no outside world. They don’t even try and persuade you; they simply assume you think the same way. It's strange how persuasive that can be. There have been times, quite a few times, when I've doubted it all, too. So, I come up here."

"Why?" said Diane again.

Shireen lay down on the small circular platform so that her eyes were level with one of the semi-circular openings. She peered through.

"I come here to remind myself. See for yourself. It looks stormy over the mountains today. The Silverburn will be in full spate tomorrow."

Finn and Diane lay down alongside her to peer out through the openings. They were very high up. He could see clear across the walls of the Directory, out over the steaming, turning, pumping workings of Engn, out across the great grass plain and all the way to the steel-grey mountains he recognized. Somewhere over there, beneath those storm clouds, he had been born and raised. Somewhere over there was home.

"I couldn't see any of you, of course. But I could come up here to remind myself it was all real. That you were all real. So far as I know this is the only place in all of the Directory you can see the outside from."

Finn craned his neck around, trying to see more familiar detail. Through the machinery he could see the Drop Tower. Some way beyond it, glimpsed through the spokes of a vast turning wheel, a dome that looked very much like the one near the dormitory, where the figure had beckoned to him all that time ago.

He peered downwards, to the stone ground just visible over the Directory walls. Knots of ironclads and masters worked their way among the engines, some of them accompanying blue-clad workers.

He sat up and looked at his big sister. Had she ever seen him out there? Glimpsed him as a distant dot, coming across the plain perhaps, or making his way along the walkway the night the ironclad had hurled him off?

Probably not. Still, it pleased him to think she might have been there all along, watching over him.

"Right," he heard Diane say quietly beside him. "Let's talk about how we go about destroying Engn."

XXXIII

"Not now," said Shireen. "We should get back. The longer we're up here, the more likely someone will notice."

They took turns to work their way back down the sagging ladder, then dropped through the hatchway onto the landing. There was no one around. Shireen led them back downstairs and locked them in their rooms. Finn lay on his bed. He stared at the ceiling and thought about everything that had happened. Diane, burning with enthusiasm now, lay on the other side of the grille and talked. It was good to hear the excitement in her voice, but he was in no mood for conversation. Probably the medicine. Diane was still talking as he drifted off to sleep.

Shireen didn't come to them the next evening, nor the next. Diane now took her sleeping draught without objection. Matilda, watching her glug it down, smiled with satisfaction. Diane simply smiled back as she placed her cup on the tray. Even so, after two days of seeing no more of Shireen, they both began to worry. Perhaps someone had found out about their excursion up the spire.

"What do we do if she doesn't return?" Diane whispered through the grille.

"We need to find Connor," said Finn. "He's the key. He must be here somewhere. Perhaps we could climb the spire and try and spot him. If we took turns one of us might see him."

"Let's give Shireen one more day. Then we'll try it."

"Okay."

The following day, Nathaniel returned to the subject of Connor's father. It was something that clearly fascinated him.

"So, this Baron. He tells people what to do?"

"Not really," said Finn. "It's just an old title. It doesn't mean much anymore."

"But someone must be in charge. Someone must give the orders."

"No. It's not like that. Nobody's in charge."

Finn's words seemed to trouble and fascinate Nathaniel in equal measure. He paused for thought. "But somebody has to control everything. Like here in Engn with the Directory and the masters. Otherwise it would be chaos."

Finn shrugged. "No, everything works okay. Sometimes people gather at the Moot Hall to decide things, but that's all."

"I see. And tell me, do you think this is a better system than the one here?"

Finn hesitated. He could see where this was going. Nathaniel clearly thought these supposed fantasies were dangerous; the result of a desire to destroy Engn perhaps. He had to be careful. "No, I ... it's just different."

Nathaniel regarded him in silence for several moments. He looked unhappy, as if Finn had disappointed him.

Finally, he returned to his notes, filling several more pages while Finn and Diane sat there in silence.

That evening, it was Matilda and not Shireen who came with their medicine once again. They both became more worried still, convinced their plot had been uncovered. Perhaps Shireen was being held somewhere, grilled, interrogated. They began to talk about spending three hour shifts up at the top of the spire, watching for Connor. Perhaps they could claim to be ill during the day then sneak away to spend some time up there. They went to sleep with nothing decided. Despite the medicine, Finn slept less well, waking repeatedly, his stomach fizzing with anxiety.

The following day, when they arrived for the day's interview, Nathaniel stood with his back to them, looking out of the window. Finn and Diane sat down but Nathaniel didn't move.

"Is there anything wrong?" asked Diane.

Nathaniel turned to look at the two of them. He looked tired, as if he hadn't slept well either. "In truth I'm worried I may not be able to help you," he said. "Your delusions are so deep-seated, so detailed. It may be that I can't return you to full health."

"And what happens then?" asked Finn.

"It has happened on occasion," said Nathaniel. "In the end it becomes too dangerous to have such people around. For everyone else I mean. I'm sure you understand."

Finn glanced at Diane. They could both see where this was going. They had to do something. They needed to stay in the Directory, not be thrown back into the mines. Or worse. "But we are making progress," said Finn. "Truly. Telling you all these stories has helped me ... understand them. Put them in perspective."

Nathaniel's brow creased as he considered Finn's words. "You begin to accept these are just stories?"

"You must have had similar fantasies yourself," said Diane. "Everyone must. Dreams of impossible worlds and imaginary lands."

Nathaniel regarded her with something like alarm, as if Diane had touched a raw nerve. Who would he go to, Finn wondered, to discuss such things?

"Of course, everyone has idle dreams," said Nathaniel. "It's perfectly normal."

"Talking to you is certainly helping us understand that," said Finn, choosing his words carefully.

"It is?"

Finn nodded. "Definitely." He glanced at Diane, prompting her. She nodded too.

Nathaniel let out a sigh of air. "Well, that's good. Let us proceed then." He strode over to his chair and picked up his sheaf of paper, ready to begin the day's questions.

That evening, finally, it was Shireen who came to them with their sleeping draughts. She looked calm, smiling as she pushed back the cowl on her hood. All Finn's gnawing fears for her melted away.

"I'm sorry," she said. "I came as soon as I could."

"What do you do here anyway?" he asked. "What is an Executive?"

"I simply execute various functions in the Directory. Helping Nathaniel is one such duty."

"So, Nathaniel isn't the Director?" asked Diane.

"No, no. He's in charge of the Sanatorium, nothing more. That's why he's so fascinated with you two. There's actually no one else here."

"We noticed," said Diane. "Why is that?"

"It was busy once, when a lot people came in from outside – from Engn I mean – but these days that doesn't happen much. So much of the machine is automated now."

"Connor got in," said Finn.

"He did. Being his mother's son helps, as I say. I think he was picked out to come here a long time ago. Chosen as a candidate because the existing Director is so old. Or maybe they thought he knew something important about the secret purpose."

"So, Connor is in the Directory? You've met him?"

"No. I mean, I haven't met him. I only know he's here because I heard it over the grapevine, as you did."

"Then you have a line-of-sight?" said Diane. "How can that be when no one believes the outside world even exists?"

"Our line-of-sight is only used to relay instructions to other parts of Engn. It's not connected to the outside world. But sometimes we get news that way. Then things get passed around on the grapevine. Word of mouth. Whispered messages as people brush by each other."

"What do you know about Connor?" asked Finn.

"That secretly, despite everything, he's supposed to be one of us. Although others doubt this and are wary of him."

"Mrs. Megrim said we had to find him. Do you know where he might be?"

Shireen frowned and didn't speak for a moment. "Before we talk about that I need to know more about him. I don't remember him from back home; he was too young. I've never spoken to him. The question is, can we really trust him? You both knew him better."

Finn glanced at Diane, who met his look with troubled eyes. She still had doubts about Connor, he knew. She'd come because he'd asked her to, perhaps for no other reason.

Shireen saw the uncertainty between them. "You're not convinced about him, are you, Diane? We have to be absolutely sure before we make a move. There will be no going back, no second chance. Connor is an important man now. One word from him and it will be the end for all of us."

Finn sighed, rehearsing in his mind all the arguments he'd had with himself about his boyhood friend. All the episodes from their life he'd run through in his mind again and again. Sometimes he found himself asking questions of Connor, the younger Connor in his mind, seeking reassurances. Going over details again and again. Just like Nathaniel in a strange way.

"I believe in him," said Finn. "I do. Look what I've been through. Despite all that I still believe in him. We were friends and we agreed to destroy Engn. I'm sure that is still his intention."

Shireen stared into his eyes, as if trying to gauge the truth of his words. "And if he's changed? Grown up, become part of the machine?"

Finn shrugged. "I don't believe it. But if he has then it was all meaningless anyway. Everything that's happened. None of it will matter."

Shireen stood and walked across the room to the little window. She stared out, deep in thought. Did he really have such confidence in his old friend? It sounded so convincing when he said it out loud. In his mind it was nowhere near so simple. What must it be like for Diane, who barely knew Connor, and Shireen, who had most to lose and who'd never even spoken to him?

"You don't have to be involved, Shireen," said Finn. "I understand. Help us find him and we'll do the rest."

She turned and smiled at his words. "Ah, Finn, I've missed you so much. You were always a serious little boy. If you made a solemn promise to do something, you did it even if it took you all day. In some ways you haven't changed a bit."

"So, what are you going to do?" he asked.

Shireen looked at Diane. "What do you think? You're somewhere between us in all this. You have the perspective of distance. Is this childish madness? You two could escape, slip back down the tunnel and I could go back to my life. With a bit of luck, we might all survive into old age."

Diane glanced between them. Finn could see the replies forming in her mind, all her doubts and hopes. This was the turning point. If Diane said no now, they would have to leave, have to try and survive outside Engn. Everything would go back to how it was. He didn't speak, didn't want to say anything that might encourage or discourage her.

Diane sighed. "I came this far. This may be the only chance anyone will ever get. I don't really trust Connor, it's true. I don't know him, not now. But I do trust Finn, and we did make a promise. I'm with him."

"Very well," said Shireen. "Then so am I."

Finn realized he'd been holding his breath. He exhaled, looking at both of them. He wanted to hug them both.

"We must still be very careful," said Shireen. "Nathaniel may seem easy-going, but anything out of place will make him suspicious. He thinks you're harmless and deluded. If he thought you were a threat, things would be very different. You must carry on as before until it's time to act. Do you understand?"

"Can't you talk to him?" asked Diane. "I'm sure he has feelings for you, too. Can't you make him see the truth?"

"I've wanted to, often," said Shireen. "Believe me. And he would listen to me, I know. But I don't want to give him that dilemma. Of having to treat me or banish me."

"Do you know where Connor might be?" asked Diane. "Can you get us to him?"

"I think I do," said Shireen. "That's part of the reason I haven't been here. I've been looking around and listening."

"And?"

"The whispers are quite clear. He was a master of the

Inner Wheel before the Director himself recruited him as his apprentice."

"So, Connor is in the one place he can really organize things, change things. That must have been his plan all along. Be like them, be one of them."

"I hope so," said Shireen.

"How do we find him?" asked Diane.

"In the middle of the Directory is a square building. They say that's where the Director operates."

"Connor must be in there," said Finn.

"The problem is, the building has no doors or windows. No one knows how he comes and goes. Secret tunnels, I suppose. I'll try and find out."

"But if you're caught," said Finn.

"There's no other way. It seems the point of everything has been to get the two of you to Connor."

"So, what should we do?" asked Diane.

"What you've been doing. Don't attract suspicion and I'll find out what I can. Okay?"

"Okay."

At the door, Finn and his sister hugged each other again.

"Be careful," said Finn.

"And you."

Shireen didn't return the next evening, and once again they began to worry things had gone wrong. Diane became more and more subdued. They ambled through the familiar daily routine, trying not to look anxious or alarmed.

The following day, strong winds sent heavy rain slashing diagonally across the world outside. They sat with the windows shut, raindrops dashing against the glass like handfuls of rice. Nathaniel seemed subdued, too. Worried about something. He fidgeted constantly with the stud in his ear.

"Now," he said, "you told me you had a sister back in your former home, Finn." He leafed back through his notes. "Shireen. Is that correct?"

"Yes." Alarm thudded through Finn. He tried to look relaxed. He didn't dare glance across at Diane.

"Can you tell me what happened to her?" asked Nathaniel. "You didn't mention her in any of your later adventures."

He thought about what he should say. He didn't know how much Nathaniel already knew. He could only think to tell the truth. "She was taken, too. When I was very small. The ironclads came for her and took her to Engn."

"That must have been very upsetting."

"I suppose. I was very young."

"And, of course, she never returned to the valley. Do you know what became of her?"

"No," said Finn. "I've never seen her. I don't think I'd recognize her now."

He regretted saying that even as he spoke. It sounded too much like an attempt to justify his lie. He felt his face redden slightly. Nathaniel paused for a moment, regarding Finn, then began to scribble away.

"But she must still be here somewhere?" he said when he'd finished writing.

"I suppose so."

"Perhaps we should try and track her down. See … what she remembers of those old days, back outside."

"Yes. We could try."

"If I may say so, Finn, you seem very reluctant about this. I would have thought you'd jump at the chance."

"Yes. I would. It's just, if she is still alive, she might not even remember me."

"Ah. Perhaps so." Nathaniel scribbled again, several long sentences. Finn waited, anxiety fizzing within him.

Did Nathaniel know Shireen's true identity?

"And tell me," said Nathaniel at last. "Was anyone else from your old home brought here? Apart from yourself, Shireen, and Diane?"

Finn tried to recall what he'd said in their previous sessions. Had he ever even mentioned Connor? He had to be careful. Nathaniel could spot inconsistencies by checking back on his notes.

"No one I can think of," said Finn.

"No one at all?"

"No."

"I see."

More scribbling. Nathaniel turned the sheet over and continued to write. Finn glanced at Diane. Her face was taut with worry. Nathaniel finished writing, looked back up at them and smiled. "Very well. Interesting, interesting. I think that's enough for today, yes? We'll resume tomorrow."

Nathaniel stood to lead them to the dining hall. This time, two cowled figures accompanied them. They stood guard by the doors as Finn and Diane ate in silence.

Back in their rooms they whispered through the grilles.

"He knows, doesn't he?" whispered Finn. "About Shireen. I know he does."

"Perhaps he was just seeing how much you'd make up," said Diane. "I mean, he can't know everything since he doesn't believe there is a valley outside Engn."

"No. But he might know Shireen is my sister. What's he going to do, question her? He might uncover all *her* delusions then."

"If he is in love with her, he won't want to. Won't want to put her through it. That may protect her."

They were silent for a time, both lost in their thoughts. The light faded as, somewhere over the Directory walls, the sun sank behind the mountains. All colour, all detail leeched out of the room. Finn could hear nothing apart from the deep, ever-present hum of the machinery.

"I think we should get out of here," said Diane.

"Now?"

"Now. If Shireen doesn't come tonight then I think it means they've caught her. What do you think?"

"I think you're right," said Finn. "But where do we go? What do we do?"

"Find this Director's building. Try and get to Connor. I wonder though…" she trailed off, lost in thought.

"What?"

"I wonder if she has tried to contact us but couldn't. Maybe she knew someone was onto her and sent us a message."

"But we haven't had a message. How could she?"

"What would you do if you were her and you needed to tell us something?"

"I don't know. Write a note and hide it in one of our rooms I suppose."

"No good. Anyone could find it then."

"Then where?"

"If I were her, I'd leave a note at the top of that ladder. No one else goes up there and only we know about it. If she had time she could have gone up before they came for her."

"If they did come for her."

"Yes. But it's worth checking."

"We need to get out of our rooms then. They're always locked."

"Not always," said Diane. "Haven't you noticed? When the other woman – Matilda – brings us our sleeping medicine she opens your door, gives it to you, opens my door, gives it to me and then locks both doors."

"So, if I sneak in behind her while she's in your room…"

"Exactly. Hit her over the head, knock her out and we can lock her in while we escape."

Finn didn't reply.

"Can you do this, Finn?"

Could he? He wouldn't have been able to, once. But his time in Engn had changed him.

"Yes," he said. "I have to."

"Good. Try and get her before I drink. And try not to take yours, too. We don't want to be falling asleep up there."

"Okay."

"Get something ready to hit her with. She'll be coming around soon."

"What?"

"A chair leg," she said. "See if you can work one loose. It's heavy enough."

Finn turned one of his chairs upside down and tried each of the legs. Even as he worked, he heard the jangle of keys, the clink of beakers. He leapt back onto his bed as his door swung open and lights flicked on. A cowled figure stood in his doorway. Perhaps it would be Shireen after all and everything would be well.

But it was Matilda's dry, unfriendly voice that greeted him. "Here's your draught. Now drink up."

Finn, trying to remember what he normally did, sat up on his bed and waited while she poured the liquid into the little beaker. He threw back his head and gulped it down, put the cup back on the tray and nodded.

"Very good," said Matilda.

Finn lay back on his bed as if preparing to sleep while she crossed back to his door. When she disappeared around the corner Finn leapt up and ran to his sink to spit out his medicine. He crept to the door, unlocked and slightly ajar, and peered out. Matilda was in Diane's room. Picking up the entire chair, Finn stepped after her.

Peering through the open door he could see Matilda with her back to him. Diane seemed to be stalling, complaining about something. He had to do it now. He stepped forwards into the room, desperate not to make a single sound.

"Come on now, drink up, there's a good girl."

"But it smells funny tonight."

Two more steps and he was there. Matilda had heard nothing. He lifted the wooden chair up over his shoulder to get in a good swing. His arms flinched, the start of a swing. Diane tried not to look at him. He swung for real, clattering the wooden chair against the back of Matilda's skull.

He thought that was all he'd have to do. She would crumple neatly and silently to the ground. Instead she screamed and spun around to face him. He hadn't swung hard enough. He took a step backwards, raising the chair again. This time he would have to swing at her face. He was about to do it when there was a hollow *clunk* sound and Matilda's eyes shut. She collapsed to the floor. Diane stood behind her, a chair leg in her hand.

"That's how you do it," she said.

Finn smiled, mostly out of relief. "I weakened her. You just finished her off."

"The question is, what do we do with her now?"

"Tie her up. Lock her in."

"You know what we should do…"

"What?" asked Finn.

"Whatever we do she'll get out sooner or later, make herself heard."

"You're saying we should finish her off? Kill her so she can't raise the alarm?"

"It's the sensible thing to do."

They both looked at the prone body on the floor, a heap of red cloth with, comically, two white shins sticking out from one end.

"How would we do it?" said Finn.

"Suffocate her I suppose. That's the quietest way."

"I don't think I can."

Diane looked up at him, then back down at Matilda. The cut on the back of her head was clear, glistening blood in her matted hair.

"No. Okay then. Let's just tie her up. Maybe no one

will hear her up here anyway."

They took Matilda's keys and bound her wrists together with the cord from her own cloak. She still breathed, shallow, almost peaceful.

"Come on," he said. "We need to hurry."

They ran from the room, locked both their doors and sped away, up the stairs, leaping three at a time to reach the top landing.

Finn, who was slightly taller, went first. He shook as he strained upwards with his fingertips to reach the hatch. Diane, anchoring herself against the banister, held him around the hips to stop him falling backwards.

"I can't reach," he called down.

"Shireen managed it and you're taller. Just do it."

"I'm trying."

"Stand on my shoulders."

The extra height allowed him to haul himself up through the hatch. He marvelled at the fact Shireen had done it by herself. He lowered the rope down for Diane to climb up. When they were both inside, they shut the hatch and began the climb the ladder.

"Do you see anything?" Diane called up when Finn, climbing first, reached the top. "Any note?"

"Nothing. Wait. There's something here, written on the wall. It's very faint."

"Was it there before?"

"I don't remember it."

"What does it say?"

"There's an arrow pointing at the window below it. Something about the building with no doors."

Diane arrived at the top of the ladder and knelt beside him to examine the hurried, scribbled writing. "The Director's building, then. Can you see it?"

Finn peered through. He had to rest one cheek on the dusty floor. Down between two metal spires with wires crisscrossing between them he could see, in the middle of an open square, a low building, squat and square. "I think so. I still don't see how we get inside if there are no doors."

"There's more written here. I can't quite make it out. Something about going underground."

"We knew we'd have to do that," said Finn.

"Shh. Also, something about clocks. *Fellow, no, Follow the clock-winder.* What does that mean? There's a time too."

"The clock-winder. Of course."

"Of course what?" asked Diane.

"I told you about him, remember? He goes everywhere in Engn setting all the clocks. He has keys for everywhere. He must have a key for the Director's building, too. If we can find him, perhaps we can follow him inside."

"It must take him months to go all round Engn. The chances of coming across him now are tiny."

"Shireen must have known that. Maybe she knew he'd be here soon and left us the note."

"Or maybe she expected us to come up yesterday and we've already missed him."

Finn crouched next to Diane and examined the scribbled writing again.

"Does that time look like 34:00 to you?"

"Yeah. I think so. But it doesn't say which day. It could be tonight or tomorrow or yesterday. I don't see how it helps us."

"I suppose she didn't have time to complete the message. Still, it doesn't matter. It's our only chance. We can't just go back to our rooms, can we?"

"Come on then."

Back on the landing they peered over the banister at the stone staircase falling away beneath them. No one was in sight. The Sanatorium was as deserted as ever.

"We could go and take her cloak," said Diane as they descended.

"Whose?"

"Matilda's. If one of us wears it we might not get stopped if anyone sees us."

"She might have woken up by now."

"I don't hear her shouting."

"Perhaps she's … you know."

"Let's go and see. We should have thought to take it when we could."

"Okay."

Finn listened at Diane's door but could hear nothing. Perhaps Matilda had gone; perhaps everyone was searching for them even now. He peered through the grille. The woman lay there in the middle of the room, just where they'd left her.

He slid they key into the lock, watching her all the time, expecting some trick, expecting her to leap up and grab him. Strange how their roles had reversed. But she didn't move. They stepped quietly to her and knelt down. The blood on the floor was smeared, suggesting she had moved a little. He couldn't tell if she was breathing in her baggy cloak. Holding his own breath, he knelt down and put his ear to her mouth.

"She's alive. Let's take her cloak off and get out of here," he said.

"I'll do it," said Diane. "You hold the chair leg ready in case she wakes up."

"Okay."

"If she does, hit her properly this time."

Finn nodded and stood at Matilda's head, chair leg held ready. But, apart from murmuring something inaudible, Matilda didn't wake up. Diane pulled the red cloak up over her head, revealing a grey cotton shift underneath. Finn had to half lift Matilda so they could wrestle the cloak over her shoulders.

"You should wear it," he said. "She's more your height."

"Walk ahead of me. If we meet anyone, they might think I'm escorting you somewhere."

"Okay."

They backed out of the room, still wary of Matilda, still

expecting her to leap to her feet. She didn't stir. Finn clicked the door shut and locked it again, finally releasing his breath. He turned to look at Diane.

"What are you doing?" The sudden, loud voice from the corridor made Finn's heart pound. Nathaniel stood in the corridor, blocking their way. Diane held Matilda's cloak in her arms.

"We're … leaving," said Finn. "We're going to leave Engn. Get outside." Perhaps if they played the role of the deluded patients Nathaniel wouldn't be so suspicious. Perhaps, somehow, he hadn't noticed Matilda's cloak, didn't realize what it meant.

"She's your sister, isn't she?"

"Who?" asked Finn, briefly, puzzled. "Matilda?"

"Shireen. I checked into the records after they'd … after the questions were raised. I thought I knew all about her but there it was, clear as day. Brother, Finn Smithson, deceased. I'm not sure which I was more surprised about. The fact that you're her brother or the fact that you're dead." Nathaniel looked bemused – frightened, even.

"They're wrong about me being dead," said Finn. "Perhaps they're wrong about her being my sister, too."

"Are they? I can check your thumbprints if necessary."

He had a point. "Okay. She is my sister. Although it's true we haven't seen each other for a long time."

Nathaniel said nothing for long moments. More than anything he looked confused. His duty to Engn was clear. He should press the button and summon guards to take them away. But so far, he hadn't done so.

"You love her," said Diane.

Nathaniel looked startled. "What?"

"Shireen. You're in love with her."

Nathaniel sagged a little, nodded his head. "I suppose I am, yes. From afar. But she's always been distant with me. I don't think she likes me. She's made that quite clear."

"What have they done to her?" asked Finn.

"Nothing yet. They're still asking questions. They'll get

answers from her one way or another."

"If you help us, we can protect her," said Diane.

Nathaniel shook his head. "No, you can't. More delusions."

"No," said Finn. "You're wrong about that, and you're wrong about Shireen. She does love you. She explained. But she doesn't want to lie to you. Doesn't want to have to pretend there isn't a world outside Engn when she knows there is. Because she thinks the same way we do."

Nathaniel looked even more lost at Finn's words. "If she believes that then I will never see her again."

"Unless we can save her."

"How could you possibly do that now? It's hopeless."

"With the help of the Director's apprentice."

Nathaniel shook his head, refusing to accept such a crazy notion. "Him? Why would he help you?"

"Because we're old friends. You must have checked the records about me. You must know we're connected."

"I know you knew him many years ago, outside the Directory. I don't see how that helps you now."

"There's a chance we can help Shireen, help a lot of people, if we can get to Connor," said Diane.

Nathaniel still stood there. He still hadn't pressed the button. "But I can't let you go. Not after this." He waved towards Matilda's cloak.

"We haven't harmed her," said Finn. "I mean, she's just unconscious. She'll be all right."

"Even so. I couldn't allow it." His words were clear, but Finn could see a different story on his face. A part of Nathaniel wanted to believe them. Believe he might see Shireen again.

"Unless you never saw us," said Diane.

"What?"

"If anyone asks you can say you weren't here. We escaped by attacking Matilda. Stole her keys to get outside. No one would blame you."

Nathaniel's eyes narrowed as he debated with himself.

His hand flinched towards the button to summon the guards. Then he stopped.

"You really think you can help her?"

"We have a chance. That's all."

Nathaniel sagged visibly and nodded his head. "Wait here." He turned and strode down the corridor and into one of the other rooms. A moment later he returned with another cloak, neatly folded over his arm. "Take this. It's all I can do for you. Once you leave here, you're on your own. I'll deny it if you tell anyone I knew."

Finn took the cloak. "Thank you. And, Nathaniel, I think you should climb to the top floor when we're gone. There's a hatchway there, and a ladder, and some high windows. Go there and you'll see. There is a world out there. Whatever happens you should know the truth."

Nathaniel looked alarmed, but he nodded his head in reply. Together, Finn and Diane ran for the stairs, working their way into their cloaks as they descended.

XXXIV

"Which way?" said Finn.

It was fully dark outside. Despite the Directory's high walls, a cold wind, sharp as metal, cut into Finn's cheeks. He spun slowly around, trying to orientate himself, the cowl over his face blinkering his vision.

That late in the evening everything was quiet, although one or two figures still hurried to and fro, heads down, arms crossed inside their cloaks for warmth.

"Come on," said Diane.

They skirted the wall of the Sanatorium and set off across an open space, paved with a swirling pattern of cobble stones. Finn glanced up and backwards at the spire to orientate himself. He tried not to appear too conspicuous. If anyone saw them their cloaks would protect them, but they had to be careful.

"There. Let's go that way," he said.

He'd seen what he was looking for. To find the clock-winder they needed to find a clock. He'd been looking for some high tower like the one near the Valve Hall, but instead there was a small, round clock on a building wall up ahead, its thirty-six digits picked out in gold. Two incandescent bulbs flickered beneath it, the clock's single hand casting a long shadow up the wall.

"If it's *this* thirty-four he'll be here soon," said Diane.

"We need to get inside," said Finn. "He must adjust this clock. He has a regular route, ticks each one off in his book as he goes around."

"Okay."

The clock building at least had doorways. The first they tried was locked. They walked as slowly as they could to the next one, trying to look as if they'd made a simple mistake and really knew where they were going. A solitary cowled figure strode across the square but said nothing to them. They tried the next door. This one swung open, leading into deeper darkness. They stepped inside, Finn tripping over a lip of stone in the doorway. He stood, waiting for his eyes to adjust, hoping there would be enough light to see by. Then electric lights snapped on. Diane stood beside him, one hand still on the switch. She shrugged as Finn looked at her.

"Let's find the clock mechanism," she said.

They hurried upstairs and along stone corridors, seeing no one. Occasionally they passed windows and Finn glanced outside, partly to work out where they were in relation to the clock, partly to see if any throng was searching for them.

"It must be about here," he said. Each door bore a number embossed on an oval metal plate, but had no other indication of what might be inside. Finn expected ironclads to burst out of each. None did. Eventually, by listening at each for the ticking, they found the door that led to the clock mechanism.

Finn tried to open it but it was locked. For all they knew the clock-winder had just left or was about to arrive. He looked at Diane.

"We'll have to wait here for him," she said. "Let's try

and find somewhere to hide."

They worked their way along the corridor, listening at the doors, rattling their brass handles, all pretence of belonging in the Directory gone. Eventually Diane found one that opened. She peered through the crack then stepped inside. Finn followed.

"Leave the door open slightly," said Diane. "Then we can watch for him."

The room smelled of dust and old paper. The walls were lined with hundreds and hundreds of wooden drawers. While Diane watched the corridor, Finn opened a few of them at random. "They're just full of old books. Plans and diagrams. They look ancient."

"Perhaps they're the original plans for Engn. Before they built the Blueprint Hall."

"Maybe. There are lists of names too, like old records of who lived here. Hundreds and hundreds of them."

"Strange how it's all so deserted now."

"I suppose it's like Shireen said – they have machines controlling the machines now."

"I suppose."

Finn leafed through some of the old papers, trying to make sense of the closely written tables, the abbreviations and symbols. He could make nothing of them. They appeared to be written in a language he didn't recognize. Shutting the drawers and, fighting back a sneeze from all the dust, he wandered farther into the room. There was another doorway at the back. He could hear no sound coming from that way. He pushed it open and felt for the light switch inside. It was another room lined with thousands of small drawers, metal rather than wood. They tinkled as he pulled one open. Instead of papers each held an array of slim metal cylinders, each about the size of a pen, 144 of them to a drawer. Finn picked one up, trying to understand what it was. It was solid metal and had tiny grooves etched all the way over its surface. It was like some very fine file. Perhaps it was just a decoration.

Perhaps it didn't do anything, like the valves. But then why were they all being stored so carefully?

"Finn!"

Diane's whisper roused him from his thoughts. He shut the drawer and walked back to her as quietly as he could. He peered out through the narrow gap in the doorway. The old man was twenty yards away, bent almost double, trudging his way along the corridor. His head was invisible, thin legs protruding from the oblong regulator clock he bore on his back. They watched as he selected a key from the ring on his belt, unlocked the door and went inside.

"We're in luck," said Diane. "It's *this* night."

"I suppose," said Finn.

"What?"

"It just seems unlikely. And odd that Shireen didn't say which day it was, too."

"She didn't have time."

"Maybe. Or maybe there's another reason. Maybe he comes this way every day."

"Because the clocks in the Directory are more important?"

"I suppose. Perhaps they're just older and need more adjusting."

They waited in silence for the old man to emerge. Finn, fearing the clock-winder had left by another door, was about to suggest they creep into the corridor when the old man reappeared. His wild grey hair first, then the clock, almost horizontal on his bent back. The old man locked the door behind him and continued on down the corridor, away from Finn and Diane.

"Come on," whispered Diane. They stepped out of the room and crept after him.

They followed along corridors, down steps, across rooms, not daring to get close but terrified they'd lose him if they let him get too far ahead. Finn well remembered the old man's habit of disappearing through secret doorways no one else could find.

They were soon underground, the rough stones of the walls thick with blooms of green algae. Finn lost all sense of direction. They could be moving towards or away from the Director's building. Perhaps the old man had already been there and was now leading them to the next clock on his list, elsewhere in the Directory, or even somewhere else in Engn. Which was an interesting thought. The Directory was supposed to be sealed off. Yet, clearly, the clock-winder knew tunnels that allowed him to come and go.

Diane's hand on his shoulder froze him. He hadn't been paying attention. Up ahead the old man stood outside another opening: a rough stone lintel above a rusting metal door. Next to it, part way up the wall, was a tall rectangular alcove. The old man stood with his back to this so that the clock was inside the alcove, then pulled his arms free, leaving the clock there. It fit perfectly. He stepped away, arms on his lower back as he stretched himself. He looked much taller standing properly upright. He stood before the iron door, picked another key from his jangling collection and slid it into the lock.

"This must be it," said Finn. "The Director's building."

The clock-winder pushed the door open and stepped inside. He left the door ajar. Finn and Diane shared a look then crept forwards. Was Connor there, somewhere inside? And the Director too? They walked forwards to the doorway.

"Why didn't he take the clock in with him?" said Diane.

"And why has he left the door open?"

Through the doorway, a flight of stone steps led upwards, curving around into brighter light. Something flickered and hummed up there, some mechanism they couldn't see.

"We need to hide inside," said Diane. "Until we can speak to Connor. Let me go first. If he sees you, he might recognize you."

"I doubt it. Not now."

"But if he did, he might raise the alarm. At least he's

never seen me. I'll sneak up and see if there's somewhere I can hide. Wait a bit and follow me up."

They were both whispering, feeling very exposed in the deserted corridor. Diane set off, treading carefully on each step so as not to make a noise, peering upwards in case someone came down. She disappeared around the bend in the steps. For some reason he couldn't understand, Finn found himself counting slowly upwards. When he reached thirty, and Diane hadn't reappeared, he set off himself. He wondered what the old man was doing up there. Perhaps he had to report to the Director about all the clocks he'd corrected. They'd have to wait and hide until they were alone with Connor. Assuming Connor was even there at all. Perhaps the grapevine wasn't reliable after all. They didn't know for sure he was there. They didn't know anything. Finn's heart hammered in his chest as he stole upwards into the light.

At the top of the stairs he hid behind a stone pillar that supported a high roof. Blue light flickered out from a large room up ahead. From the glimpse he'd had of it, he guessed it was the interior of the Director's building. The size and shape seemed about right.

Holding his breath, he peered around the pillar again. A younger man bent over a line of glass orbs, the light from within making his features glow, flickering shadows across his face. It was Connor.

In the middle of the room, staring vacantly around as if awaiting instruction, stood the clock-winder. There was no sign of the Director. But Finn could see Diane. She'd worked her way behind a screen of pillars to the far side of the room, a spot where Connor could see her if he looked up. She waited. For that moment the three of them, Finn, Connor and Diane stood in a perfect line.

Connor glanced off to the side, towards Diane, then stood up straight, his back to Finn.

"You can come out now, Diane."

Finn watched as Diane stepped forwards, her gaze

switching between the clock-winder and Connor. If Connor would just tell the old man he was no longer needed then they were there, they had succeeded. The three of them together in the control room of Engn.

"Kill her," the old man said. He waved a hand towards Diane.

Connor dipped his head in acknowledgement. "Yes, sir."

Connor drew a small, metallic device from inside his robes. With Connor in the way, Finn couldn't see it clearly, but he could tell from Diane's expression, her wide-mouthed shock, what it must be. Connor stepped towards her. Diane, her eyes on Connor's face, on the gun he held in his hands, stepped backwards. But only to reach the stone wall behind her. She lunged suddenly to the side, trying to get away. The booming *crack* of the gun echoed in the confined space. Diane flopped to the floor in mid-stride and lay in a shapeless huddle on the ground.

Connor walked up to her, the old man following. They appeared to speak, too quietly for Finn to hear. Finn stood stunned, his mouth open, his useless shout of warning still unuttered. Connor had killed Diane. The old man had told him to and he'd done it.

He could run, he knew. He could fall down the steps, get back outside, maybe reach the tunnel and get away from Engn forever. He saw that path very clearly. It was probably the wise thing to do. But something else stirred inside him, a clear determination not to just give in. There was the machinery that controlled all of Engn. Switches and dials and levers filled the walls of the room. Connor and the old man stood over Diane's body. How much damage could he do in the few moments before they stopped him? Perhaps enough. He strode into the control room, picked the biggest and most important looking controls he could and began to twist and press and pull, hoping that somewhere in Engn he was sending vital parts of the machinery into overdrive. One particularly large brass lever caught his eye. The knob on its end was polished smooth as if it had been pulled many times over the years. It had to be vital. Using both hands, Finn grabbed it and began to heave.

"Finn."

It was Connor, behind him, speaking calmly. Finn ignored him. The lever wouldn't budge. Finn swung all his weight onto it, trying to force it down.

"Finn," said Connor again. "You can't move it. It's pointless."

Finn let go and returned to the other controls he could see, twisting and pressing again. He'd lost track of what he'd already done. Perhaps he was just setting everything back to how it was. He carried on anyway.

"Finn, stop. You're not doing anything to harm the machine. The control mechanisms are locked out. You're not affecting anything."

Finn turned to see Connor standing in the middle of the room, the old man behind his shoulder. Connor held the gun in his hand, pointing it directly at Finn. He smiled warmly.

"It's good to see you again, Finn. I wasn't sure you'd ever make it here. You've done well."

Finn didn't speak for a moment, trying to understand what was taking place. "Then this ... this was the plan all along?"

"Oh yes. You've played your part well."

"And it's true Engn is controlled from here?"

"It is. We call this the Panopticon. It's the one place where you can see everything that is taking place, control everything. See for yourself. It's only fair."

Finn looked down at one of the flickering glass orbs, identical to those he'd seen all over Engn. He could see an image inside it, a black-and-white picture suspended, somehow, in the middle of the sphere. He studied it closely; it looked familiar. A quadrangle with a floor of hard flints. Incredibly, the picture moved as a huddle of apprentices walked across the scene. He knew where it was, then. The Octagon.

"But that's miles from here," said Finn. "Are these some sort of line-of-sight?"

"Something like that," said Connor. "But much, much better. They send pictures rather than words. We have eyes all over Engn, watching what is happening, relaying the pictures here."

"It's incredible."

Finn stepped slowly around the room, looking into each sphere. There was the Valve Hall, unchanged since he'd laboured in it all that time ago. There was the high walkway above it, the whispering gallery. There was the top of the Drop Tower, the Blueprint Vault, and countless other places he didn't recognize.

"The mines? Are they here too?"

"All here, Finn."

"So, when I worked down there, wondering if you were still alive, wondering what had happened to you, you were watching me?"

"Yes."

"You saw me when I nearly died down there? And when we escaped on the water-wheel?"

"Yes."

"And you control it all from here? The bells, the machines, everything?"

"The flow of water and electricity. The regulation of the furnaces and the wheels. The speed of the beam engines. All of it is governed from this room, Finn."

"Then that means we can do it, doesn't it, Connor?" He glanced at the old man, expecting him to look alarmed. Instead the expression on his face remained unmoved. "That's been the great scheme, hasn't it? Pretend to work for Engn. Become the Director's apprentice. Because from here we can finally destroy it, can't we? The right knobs turned, the right switches opened, and we can make the furnaces explode and the water flood. That's it, isn't it,

Connor?"

It was a glorious scheme. Connor had been true all along. Everything, everything had been worth it. Yet still, there was the simple fact of Diane's body on the ground. And of the gun barrel pointing at him.

Connor looked thoughtful. "And you still think, Finn, that we should do what we promised all those years ago? Those three ignorant children with mud on their faces."

"Yes. I do," said Finn.

The old man, the clock-winder, stepped forwards then, to stand next to Connor. "And what of all the people who live here, who work here? You would destroy all that? You could destroy everything from here, it's true. But how many people would be killed if we did that?"

"And what of all the people not yet born who will be forced to waste their lives here?" said Finn. "What of all the children who are out there now, playing in the fields and woods, unaware of the ironclads marching from Engn to collect them?"

The old man looked calm, unconcerned. He had a look in his eye Finn had glimpsed there before: a keen-eyed intelligence. With alarm pounding away inside him Finn suddenly understood who this old man was. He wobbled his way all over Engn, seeing everything, keeping an eye on everything, and no one paid him any attention.

The Director of Engn.

A trail *had* been laid for Finn, but it wasn't Connor's trail. It was the Director's. The old man who'd met him at the gate on the day he'd arrived in Engn, who had sent him on his way to the Blueprint Vault.

"It was you beckoning to me from that dome, wasn't it?" said Finn to the old man. "It was you all along."

"It was."

"Why?"

"You know why. To test you, as was explained," said the Director. "To see where your heart really lay. But you failed long ago. The day you set fire to the blueprints."

"So why am I still here? Why was Diane?"

"To test Connor, of course. Don't you see? You're *his* test. You and Diane over there. That's all you are. I wanted to know which side he is really on, his mother's or his father's. Who he'd choose when it came down to it. Me or you."

Finn looked at Connor, his old friend's familiar eyes in that older, sadder face.

"Connor?" said Finn.

"Kill him, Connor," said the Director.

"Yes sir," said Connor.

Connor raised his gun again. The bright light blinded Finn for the briefest moment before the shot knocked him backwards and he saw no more.

XXXV

"…and this is the master time signal generator. It all depends on this, understand? Everything comes down to this. The other generators about Engn get their time from here so everything is in sync."

"I understand," said Connor.

Finn's chest roared with a vast pain. Some terrible injury. How had he survived? The floor was hard beneath his back. He didn't understand why he wasn't dead.

Somewhere nearby he heard the familiar jangling of the old man's keys.

"And this is the key to activate the control panel. Small and unimportant, isn't it? No one would ever imagine it governs the whole machine. You'll need the code as well. Insert the key and I'll type it in. You must watch and remember it. Never write it down, hear me? Never."

Finn didn't dare move. Didn't want to explore his wound, afraid of what he'd find. His head throbbed, but it was a lesser pain, drowned out by his chest. He flickered an eye open and shut. He lay on the cold ground of the

Panopticon. Across the room, Connor stood with the Director, the two of them leaning over some of the controls. Finn recognized the object of their attention immediately; he'd seen one like it before. A large, silver sphere, not glass like the image line-of-sights, but metal. Hundreds of cables led off from it, a thick sheaf of them snaking into a duct.

He heard the *plunk, plunk, plunk* of buttons being pressed.

"There," said the Director. "Sixteen digits. Got them?"

"Yes," said Connor. "But what if I forget? Or if something happens to me. What if something had happened to you?"

"Then the whole system would need to be reset. Engn shut down, recalibrated, a new code entered and everything started again. *Weeks* of disruption to the schedule. Don't let it happen. There are two people in Engn who know how to do it apart from us: the silverclad general and the master of the Inner Wheel. Neither is allowed in here, of course. Just make sure you don't forget the code."

"I won't," said Connor. "I promise."

"There," said the Director. "Now we have control. Normally you don't have to touch anything. Like most things in Engn, it's self-regulating these days. Not like the old days. If you *do* need to fix it, take manual control and reroute the timing signals to the backup device over there. Only then is it safe to deactivate. Got it, boy?"

"Yes. It's very clear what I have to do."

"Good. Type in the code to lock it up again. That's it. Now an *8*. That's it. Doesn't matter if you make a mistake. Just pull this lever and start again. There, you have it. Excellent." The old man let out a long sigh. "So. Think you're ready?"

"Yes," said Connor. "I'm ready."

"Your mother will be very proud of you."

"I hope so."

"And of course, only a few among the masters and the silverclads will know who you are. Think you can handle that? Sometimes it is difficult to remain silent."

"I'm good at staying silent when I have to."

"Very well. I've shown you everything. It's up to you now, Connor."

"And what about them?"

"Your friends? Call the silverclads to have them removed. They're not supposed to come into the Directory, but they will if you give them a direct order."

"And what will you do?"

"This transition of power is long overdue. I'm old and weary. But I'll still be around. Keeping an eye on things."

"You must be sick of lugging that old clock around."

"It has its uses. You can sit here and gaze into the orbs all day but if you really want to know what's going on out there you have to go and see. Still, that's up to you now. You'll do it your own way, I'm sure. Here."

More jangling. Finn flickered his eyes open again. He watched as the Director, the old Director, handed his great bunch of keys across to Connor.

Footsteps clipped across the room. Finn shut his eyes again and lay still, thinking they were coming to check on him. But they moved away again. It was the old man, heading for the stairs.

"Director?" Connor's voice sounded strange, strained.

"Yes, Connor?"

"You haven't told me everything."

"I believe I have."

"You haven't explained *why*. Why all this exists. What Engn is for."

"For, Connor? It isn't *for* anything. It just is. An end unto itself. The vast and glorious machine. Why does there have to be a reason?"

"But you must know. I thought you of all people would know. The Hub, I mean. It all comes back to that. What did it do?"

"The Hub? There's nothing there, boy. It's unimportant. You mustn't believe all you read in the old records. I've told you everything that matters. Everything I was told by the previous Director. Now I must go."

"But what happened to the first three Engns? Why were they destroyed?"

"Ancient stories, boy. They aren't important."

Finn had the strange impression Connor was asking questions he already knew the answer to. "But the *Event*. Every 317 years. What is it? What happens then?"

"Nothing happens. All that matters is that the machine is kept running. And now I'm going. Look after it all."

"Director? One more thing."

"What now?"

"I'm sorry. You've failed the test."

The third roar of the gun made Finn wince. He expected more pain but there was none. He looked again. Connor stood in the middle of the room, gun held out, smoke or steam coiling off it, a chemical tang in the air. Over at the edge of the room, by the door, the old man lay in a heap on the ground. Face up, an expression of confusion frozen onto his face. For a moment nobody moved. Then Connor, letting the gun clatter to the floor, ran over to Finn.

"Finn, Finn. Are you okay? Tell me you're okay."

Finn looked up into Connor's face, looming suddenly large over him. The look of worry told him everything he needed to know.

"You always were a terrible shot," said Finn. "With a catapult or a gun."

"Can you stand?"

"I don't know. My chest feels bad."

"You'll be bruised, that's all. It was the only thing I could do. Two dummy slugs and one real one. I had to be sure to fire in the right order."

"So, Diane?"

"She'll be okay as long as I didn't hit her in the head."

"And the Director?"

"I made no mistake about him."

Finn struggled up to lean on one elbow. Sharp pain shot across his chest. He felt with his hand, expecting there to be blood, a gaping wound, but there was nothing.

"I'm sorry, Finn," said Connor. "Sorry for everything. I know what you've been through. The mines, everything. It was the only way. They knew all about us. I had to convince them."

"Help me up."

"That day in the Inner Circle. You threw me then. I never expected you to try setting fire to the blueprints. Incredible. But I had to sacrifice you. What else could I do?"

"It's okay. I never doubted you."

"Never?"

"Well, sometimes."

"I didn't dare do anything to give you a hint. It wasn't safe. I had to pretend I was trying to finish you off."

"You did a good job."

Between them they hobbled over to Diane, who still hadn't moved. Finn expected a pool of blood. There was nothing.

"Diane? Can you hear me?"

Finn hesitated then placed a hand onto her breast. He could feel her chest inflating and deflating. "She's still breathing."

Connor nodded, relief bright on his face. "We need her to come around. Once we start disrupting the timing signals, Engn will blow. It'll be cataclysmic. We won't want to be anywhere near."

"We head back through the tunnel?"

"That's the plan, but we can't pull her. She'll have to be able to crawl on her own."

"I'll try and rouse her. How long will it take you to break everything?"

"Not long. Once the timing signals are stopped

everything will spiral out of control. Too much fuel or too little pumped, engines starved or flooded, wheels going haywire."

"You're sure Engn will be destroyed?"

"I'm sure."

Finn thought about all the people he'd worked alongside, on the surface and down in the mines. Rory and Tom and all the others.

"The people down there. And up here. They won't have a chance."

Connor sighed, looking troubled. He ran his hand through his hair. "They'll have some chance. There are alarms. One the machinery starts failing bells will go off across Engn. People will have time to evacuate. A little time."

"But there's no way out of the mines."

"No. I know," said Connor.

"People will get killed. Perhaps a lot of them. It's inevitable."

"Yes," said Connor. "Are you saying you don't want to do this? After everything you've been through?"

Finn found he suddenly didn't know. The thing he'd wished for all this time, the thing that had kept him alive. But now it came to it, could they really do it? Destroy so much? Did they have the right?

"You think we should?"

"We have to." Diane sounded woozy, distant, but her words were clear. Finn knelt back over her.

"You're okay?"

"I think. A bit sore. Glad to be alive."

"Connor shot us with dummy bullets. Then he shot the Director with a real one once he'd got the codes and the key."

She sat up, looking around as if confused about where she was. "So, we can really do it? Destroy the machine?"

"Yes," said Connor.

"What about all the ironclads?" said Finn. "They aren't

just going to stand by. Can't they operate the machinery, shut it down safely?"

"They might try," said Connor. "But it's all so automated. And the ironclads aren't the machines people believe. They're men and women obeying orders. The silverclads too. When they see how it is a lot of them will forget their loyalty to Engn, trust me."

"And the wreckers will stop any that try to save Engn," said Diane.

"They might," said Connor. "There *are* thousands of them, all over Engn, but they're disorganized. Once things blow, I think they'll be fleeing right alongside the ironclads."

"And you're sure you want to do this, Connor?" said Diane.

"What do you mean?" Connor looked wary, as if he still hadn't told them everything.

"Well, look at you. You're in charge, you could leave things as they are. You could live like a king here. Press a button to summon the silverclads, blame the Director's death on us and you're in the clear. You could even tell yourself you were doing the right thing. That you were going to fix it all from within."

Connor reached inside his gown and pulled something from a pocket. Something small and metallic. He slipped it onto his finger and held it up to show them.

"You kept your ring," said Diane.

"I did."

"Us, too," said Finn, holding his hand out. It was the first time they'd all worn their rings in years.

"But you're throwing so much away," said Diane. "I wouldn't really blame you. You must be a bit tempted."

"I have been at times. I just looked at him though." Connor indicated the old man with a nod of his head. "I imagined myself ending up like him. Bitter, miserable, friendless. That's no life."

"You could do things differently," said Diane.

Connor shook his head. "You didn't know Finn and me when we were young. I had no one. I mean I had everything I needed but I was alone. My father and everyone were busy all the time. My mother was house-bound. Then one winter's day Finn became my friend. And later on, you. That's all that matters."

"Tell us what to do," said Diane.

"Once I've unlocked the controls, start shutting down systems while I take the time-signal generator offline. Turn all those dials to zero. Got it?"

"Got it," they both said.

Finn watched as Connor picked out the key the Director had shown him from the great bunch and unlocked the control panel. Taking great care, he typed in the code he'd been shown. Tiny incandescent bulbs flickered into life all around the panel as the controls became active.

"Okay," said Connor. "Go."

Almost immediately Finn heard distant alarms: jangling bells and wailing sirens. Connor ignored them. He was busily plucking cables from the time-signal generator, each time disconnecting some distant component in the vast machine, knocking it out of sync with the rest. Finn thought about those wheels, the chains and belts, accelerating faster and faster, beginning to crack and collapse and explode.

"All done," said Diane.

"Me too," said Finn, turning a final dial.

They turned around to face one another.

"That's it then," said Finn. "We did it. We actually did it."

Connor glanced at the controls around him, then back at the two of them. He nodded his head. "Everything is failing now. You two should go. Make for the tunnel. I'll meet you outside."

"No," said Finn. "We'll go together."

"I have to stay here a little longer. The automated

mechanisms are clever. They'll try to correct themselves. I'll stay here and make sure they don't. I'll catch you up easily. You're both injured and you'll move slowly."

A great muffled boom from outside reverberated through the thick walls. Something vast exploding or falling over. More bells and sirens wailed now.

"There's no need," said Finn. "Everything is falling apart."

"There's one more thing I have to do."

"What?"

"I'll explain later," said Connor. "Here, take this with you." He pulled a small lever beneath one of viewing orbs. A rod of silvery metal like those Finn had seen stored in the metal drawers slid out of the device. Connor handed it to Finn.

"What is it?" asked Finn.

"It will come in useful," said Connor. "In case … in case I don't get chance to explain."

"What do you mean?"

"Hopefully nothing. Hurry, I'll catch you up."

"But what do we do with it?"

"It'll be obvious." Connor gripped Finn's arm. "But Finn, remember what it was all for, yes? Why we did this. Promise me. You must remember what it was all for. I can't say more. Even here and now there might be people watching."

"But I don't…"

"Go on," said Connor. He released his grip on Finn and turned his attention back on the controls. "You have to go now, while you can."

"We'll see you back outside," said Finn.

Connor nodded, not looking at them.

They stepped over the body of the old Director and out of the control room. Retracing their steps through the deserted building, they emerged into the night air. It was no longer dark. The sky blazed orange and yellow. The air tasted bitter with the acrid tang of ash. Finn could hear, or feel, a deep whining rumble in the walls and the floor beneath his feet. With each passing moment it grew louder, as if something vast and terrible was approaching.

Holding hands, moving as quickly as they could, they headed back to the tunnel. Figures hurried to and fro past them, some clutching papers. No one paid them any attention. The ground shook again and again.

They were passing the Sanatorium when Nathaniel burst out of the doors. His eyes were wild as he stared up into the sky. He sank to his knees. Finn had seen a similar expression on a panicked horse that had once charged up the lane back home. A look of uncomprehending terror.

Finn grabbed him and shook him to get his attention. "Nathaniel. Listen to me. You're all right. You're going to be all right."

But Nathaniel wouldn't or couldn't hear. He clutched at his own clothing now, looking around in alarm for somewhere to run to.

"Nathaniel," said Finn, all but shouting into his face, "do you know where Shireen is?"

That caught his attention at least. "Shireen?"

"Yes. Do you know where she is? Can you find her?"

"I … I know where she is. The silverclads. But I can't rescue her. I don't have the authority. And in any case, the world is ending."

"Nathaniel, forget about authority," said Finn. "We have to rescue her. We're going to get out through the tunnel. Do you understand?"

"Tunnel?"

"Yes, the tunnel," shouted Finn. "You know where it is."

"Old stories. Fantasies. I don't believe such things."

"Then it's just as well Shireen does. We have to save her. She needs us. She needs you."

"She does?"

"Yes. Come on, there isn't much time. Show us where she is."

Nathaniel looked more certain of himself now he'd been given some orders to follow. "No. If we all go, they'll be suspicious. They might recognize you. I'll go alone. Perhaps I can override their orders."

Finn glanced at Diane. Did he trust Nathaniel to do this? "And you'll take her to the tunnel?"

Nathaniel looked troubled. "If that's what she wants, yes. I won't try and stop her."

Finn grasped Nathaniel's shoulder. "Then hurry. Get her out before it all blows up. Understand? We'll see you outside."

Questions formed on Nathaniel's lips. Then he appeared to make up his mind. He turned and raced away into the darkness.

"Let's get to the tunnel," said Diane. "If anyone can rescue her, he can."

They reached the room they had first come to without further hindrance. Inside it, the same woman worked away on the same mechanism, disassembled on her bench.

"Come on," Finn said to her. "Leave that. You must get out of Engn. Everything's being destroyed."

The woman glanced up with one eye. "You two again. Haven't they cured you yet?"

"You can hear the alarms, surely? You can feel the explosions through the walls. You have to get out."

The woman smiled a sad little smile. "But there is no *out* is there?" She spoke slowly, as if to a child. "I explained that before, do you remember? Even if Engn is coming to an end, there isn't any *other world* we can escape to."

"No, you can. Really. Follow us."

The woman shook her head. "I have to get this working."

"Leave her," said Diane. "We have to go."

The two of them ran from the room, back down the stone passageway to the tunnel entrance.

They were both badly out of breath. Finn began to imagine the door wouldn't be there; that Nathaniel had been correct all along. That he really had invented the world outside. He could see only stone walls ahead of him, dimly lit by electric bulbs, flickering now. What would he do if he came to a dead end and there were no steps down to the tunnel?

Then, around a final corner, the passageway ended and there were the stairs. They clambered down. At the bottom, in the gloom, was the ancient rotting door. They barged it open, crouched inside, and began to crawl.

As they scrambled forwards, Finn could feel the destruction of Engn in the ground around him. The earth shook and boomed and shook, sending cascades of soil onto his head. He wished they'd brought a light. Soil and dust filled his mouth. He could no longer hear Diane behind him. But he didn't dare stop. There was nothing he could but grind on through the darkness.

XXXVI

The tunnel entrance smoked like the muzzle of a musket as Finn and then Diane flopped out of it. Although it was the middle of the night, the sky was as bright as midday: a raging red and orange that cast deep shadows around them. Flames from the fires of Engn. Clutching each other, spluttering and coughing, they began to scramble up the side of the pit.

Diane made it to the top first and hauled Finn up after her. They stood beneath the walls. The air was ash and smoke. The ground shook and shivered beneath them. A great ball of flame boiled off from the machine into the night sky, its heat scorching on Finn's face. All through the long crawl the insistent whining sound had grown in intensity and pitch, as if something were spinning faster and faster. Now, out in the open air, it screamed and thundered at the same time.

"We have to get away!" Diane shouted.

"Did you hear anyone behind us in the tunnel?" Finn shouted back. They had to help Shireen and Connor.

Diane shook her head. Finn looked back down into the pit. There was no sign of anyone else emerging.

"I'm going back down!" he called. "See if anyone is coming." He slid and skidded down the slope, slowing himself by grasping the boughs of the scrubby bushes. Back at the entrance he stooped and put his head into the tunnel to listen. Soil and stones showered down upon him. He could hear nothing but the screaming noise.

"Shireen!" he shouted into the tunnel. "Connor! We're outside!" He coughed some more from the effort of shouting and then, when he'd recovered, repeated himself, bellowing as loud as he could.

He had his head and shoulders fully inside the tunnel, so he didn't hear the sound of someone descending the slope. He knew nothing until a hand reached in to grasp his shoulder.

"Finn! You're safe!" His father stood there, the red light from the sky flaming in his eyes. Once again, he hugged Finn to him.

"We did it!" Finn replied, having to shout into his father's ear to be heard. "Connor and Diane and me. We did it!"

"Did you see Shireen?"

"Yes! She should be coming through the tunnel."

"Then you get out of the way," his father shouted back. "I'll wait for her."

A booming explosion from Engn lit up the world. Even sheltered in the dip Finn felt the blast on his face. They did need to get away, but they couldn't leave Shireen and Connor behind.

"No, we'll wait too. We…"

At that moment, an unseen hand grasped him by the ankle. Finn shouted out and tried to leap away, terrified someone was trying to pull him back into the tunnel.

His father, however, was on his knees, grasping the hand, pulling it free from the earth. A person emerged in a rush of soil and rubble, nearly toppling down the slope.

For a moment Finn couldn't see who it was. Then there was a gasp, and another bear-like embrace, and Finn knew his sister had escaped, too.

Someone else worked their way down the slope, then, silhouetted against the burning sky. Their mother. She clutched both Finn and Shireen close. For that brief moment it was just the four of them, together for the first time since the day fourteen years earlier when the ironclads had come for Shireen.

"Connor," said Finn. He knelt down to reach inside the tunnel. There was someone else there, feeling their way forwards, only their eyes and a searching, scrabbling hand visible.

But it wasn't Connor. Coughing and spitting, it was Nathaniel who emerged from the tunnel. He slumped forwards as he came out and rolled down the slope to land among the shattered boulders.

Between them, they manhandled him up the slippery slope to ground level. Regaining his balance, he stood for a moment on the lip of the pit, taking in the scene around him – the walls of Engn, the plain stretching off into an unknown distance. Then he fell back to the ground and covered his head with his arms. Shireen knelt beside him, her hand on his back.

"We have to get away," his father bellowed. "It's not safe this close."

"No!" replied Finn. "We have to wait for Connor."

The insistent whining, thundering noise reached a sudden crescendo then cut out. A vast silence rolled across the plain. Everyone stopped and looked up expectantly, even Nathaniel from his place on the ground. Nobody spoke or moved.

The huge concussion sent them all sprawling to the ground when it hit them. Finn felt it in his ribcage as much as in his ears. The ground writhed and shook. Looking upwards over the walls, he could see the towers and wheels collapsing. Falling vertically downwards. The pillars of rock had given way. Engn was falling into its own abyss.

"Run!" his father shouted.

This time Finn didn't object. How far did the caverns spread underground? Half carrying, half dragging Nathaniel, they raced from the walls. Finn imagined the ground opening up behind them, a crack in the ground pursuing them. He didn't dare look back.

They ran and tripped and scrambled while the vast explosion thundered on behind them. When they could run no farther, they stopped, all of them wide-eyed, labouring for breath. Fires raged all through the machine now, illuminating great clouds of oily smoke that roiled through the air.

A figure ran towards them through the darkness, screaming wildly, just a black shape against the fires. At first Finn thought it was someone coming to assault them, or someone screaming in terrible pain. But the person – a man – ran straight by, not stopping, and his cries were cries of uncontained euphoria. Whoever they were, they had escaped Engn and were running and screaming simply because they could.

They began to see others, emerging from the cracked and broken walls, fleeing through the gates. A great tide of people spilling out onto the plain, their faces lit up by the fires. Between explosions, sounds of cheering and whoops of delight filled the air. Some people staggered around, bemused. Others danced and skipped and hugged. One or two even turned back and began to hack at the walls as if to destroy what still stood of the machine.

"Where should we go?" said Finn. "There'll be thousands of people out here soon and we need to find Connor. Perhaps he escaped by another route."

"The line-of-sight tower," said Diane. "There's a better view from up there and it's an obvious landmark."

Finn nodded. "Okay."

Half an hour later, the top of the line-of-sight tower became visible over a rise in the ground, its Engn-facing side picked out in orange from the fires. As they'd done before, Finn and Diane climbed the ladder and pushed open the trapdoor. One after another, the six of them pulled themselves up. Inside, it was immediately obvious that no line-of-sight messages were coming from Engn. The bank of 'scopes facing that way were all dark. But lights flickered in thirty or forty of the incoming ports. Word had got out already. People would be able to hear and feel the explosions for hundreds of miles around.

The tower was cramped for the six of them. Finn cleared away all the 'scopes pointing towards Engn to give people room to sit or lie down. "See if you can spot Connor through the ports," he said. "Scan around with a 'scope."

"What are you going to do?" asked Diane.

"I'm going to talk to Mrs. Megrim. Send her word of what's happened. She can tell everyone else. People need to know."

While the others felt around for a place to lie on the floor or kneeled to peer through one of the ports, Finn set to work. Would Mrs. Megrim be in the Switch House? Surely, she would be after hearing the explosions. Not bothering to encrypt the message, he began to type.

The reply, when it came, was swift. Three words. *Tom and Rory?* Finn glanced over towards the others, still peering out through the ports. He typed his reply. *We're still looking. Lots of people escaping.*

It was all he could say. It struck him it was entirely possible both Tom and Rory were dead. Killed in the destruction of the machine. Because of him. The thought made him sag to his knees and hold his head in his hands. Had they really been right to do what they'd done? His chest felt tight from the bad air he'd breathed. He suddenly felt very weary.

"Finn." His mother knelt down beside him, put her arm around him. "Are you okay?"

"Yes. Can't quite believe what we've done. I just hope

Connor got out. Connor and everyone else."

"He stayed inside?"

"He told us to get out. Said he'd follow. There was something he had to do first."

"Then I'd believe him. You of all people should believe him."

"Yes. I know. Still, I don't see how he could have."

"Well. There's nothing more we can do now. Let's all try and get some sleep and see how things look in the morning."

It seemed impossible he'd be able to sleep, but she was right. They needed the morning light. He nodded his head in the darkness. The distant roaring of the fires of Engn continued, punctuated by the occasional *crump* of something exploding, or the metallic crash of collapsing ironwork.

Finn lay down, still tasting the smoke and dust of Engn in his mouth. The others, his family, lay down around him. Eventually he drifted into a half sleep, waking again and again, unable to understand where he was. The only illumination was the glow of the fires through the open ports, staring at him like banks of red eyes. At one point in the night another huge blast rocked the tower. In the darkness, it felt like the tower was whipping backwards and forwards far enough to touch the ground. The sensation reminded him of some memory, but he couldn't recall what.

The following day dawned bright a few hours later. The sun picked its way through the distant mountain peaks and began to fully illuminate the scene of destruction.

Engn was a smouldering ruin. Great swathes of smoke drifted over it, like its own private rain clouds. Here and there wheels and towers were still standing, but the destruction continued as new explosions ripped through the machine. Through a 'scope, Finn picked out the dome from the window of which the Director had once beckoned to him. A great bite had been taken out of it, as if some blast from within had ripped through it.

People continued to flood out. Many walked away from the walls and out onto the plain, spanning out in all directions. Others stood or sat around in groups, as if they still couldn't believe what they were seeing. While his parents went off for supplies, Finn studied the crowds through the 'scopes. He watched as people searched through the jostling crowds for loved ones. Each time two were reunited, he felt a little better about what they'd done.

At one point he picked out an old man hobbling forwards to greet his toad-like son, a master no longer, just plain Owyn. A gaggle of workers walked along behind him, unsure of where to go or what to do. Finn watched as they sat down on the ground. He picked out Tanner and the woman he'd sat next to in the Valve Hall three years earlier, but he didn't recognize any of the others. Later, as his gaze swept across the crowds, Finn thought he glimpsed the clock-winder, the old Director, pushing his way through the throng. Finn's heart thumped in his chest. But when he tried to find the man again, there was no sign of him.

Finn made his way across the floor of the tower to peer through one of the 'scopes that pointed towards the mountains. People were already heading that way, off into the purple distance. Perhaps Connor was among them. Finn searched for nearly an hour but saw no one he recognized.

"Finn."

It was Nathaniel, standing over him in the pale darkness. Nathaniel seemed a little happier in the enclosed space of the line-of-sight tower. More like his old self. His knelt down on the ground. "Finn, I wanted to apologize. For everything. For not believing you. I thought you were mad. I mean, I *knew* you were. You had to be. Only you weren't."

"It's okay. You weren't to know."

"All those stories you told me. They were true, weren't

they?"

"Yeah."

"And all those years," said Nathaniel, sounding as if he was trying to understand it. "Shireen kept it all secret, too. All that time I thought I was so wise, so clever. But I didn't know anything."

"It's not your fault," said Finn.

"I was born in there, you see," said Nathaniel. He clearly felt the need to explain. "Engn was all I knew. I was brought up to know there wasn't an outside world. The machine was everything. But it was a lie all along."

Finn took his gaze from the eyepiece and looked at Nathaniel, his features picked out by the beams of light from the ports. They were all victims, weren't they? Even the masters. Even Nathaniel. Even the Director himself, lonely and bitter. What was the point of it all?

"The thing is," said Nathaniel, whispering now. "Now I don't know what to do. I don't know where to go. I don't know how to live. The world is so vast. I mean, those mountains in the distance. They must be enormous."

"They are."

"I've lived such a small life," said Nathaniel. "And now there's all this. Out there. I have to make up for all that lost time. I thought I understood the world, sitting there in the Sanatorium, reading all the old papers. But I didn't know anything."

"You tried to do the right thing," said Finn. "That's more than most people."

"I'm glad you think so, Finn. But still, I don't know what to do now. I don't know how to start."

"I think it's obvious what you have to do," said Finn.

"It is?"

"The valley. Our home. That's where we'll go now. Shireen, too. You have to come with us. With her."

"With Shireen?"

"Don't you see? There's nothing to come between you now."

"You'd let me come with you?"

Finn smiled. "I imagine Shireen will insist on it."

Nathaniel touched Finn on the forearm. "Thank you, Finn."

"For what?"

"For everything. For letting me come. And for Engn. I would have spent the rest of my life in there. Never knowing, never understanding."

Finn sighed. "You were safe, though. And happy enough. Perhaps it would have been better to leave everything as it was. How many people haven't got out? How many have been killed?"

Nathaniel was silent for a moment. "I don't know," he said finally. "I can only speak for myself. The truth is this new world frightens me, but I'm glad you did what you did. I'll always be grateful to you."

"Finn!" It was Diane, calling to him from across the room. "I think I see someone."

Finn scrambled over to peer through the 'scope Diane had been using. "Where? I don't see him."

"Not Connor. It looks like Tom."

"Yes, I see him. He's walking with a group of others. He must have escaped the mines after all. They all must have."

"Can you tell who the others are?"

"No. They're in the shadows. Wait. Yes. Ah. I see."

"What?"

"It's not Tom. It's his twin brother, Rory. I recognize some of the people with him, too. There's Ciara and Aelth."

"I'll go and get him," said Diane. "Tell him where we are."

"I'll go," said Finn.

"No. I'll go. You need to tell Mrs. Megrim one of her sons at least is alive."

After he'd sent the line-of-sight, Finn clambered down the ladder to meet Rory and the others. Rory looked thinner than he remembered, but he grinned as he approached.

"Finn!"

"You survived," said Finn. "I thought they'd catch you for sure."

"They nearly did. But I had friends at the Drop Tower to cover for me. It's more amazing you survived."

"Tom helped me."

"Tom?"

"He was there. In the mines. He kept me alive. But I haven't seen him since I escaped. I haven't seen anyone from down there. I'm sorry. I would have got him out if I could."

Rory put a hand on Finn's shoulder. "I know you would."

"I've spoken to your mother," said Finn. "Sent her a message to say you're alive. Come and talk to her yourself. She's sitting in the Switch House back home."

"You've got the line-of-sight working?"

"The lines into Engn are dead, but we can send messages back home from here."

Rory turned to Ciara and the others. "We should tell everyone, let them know they can talk to their loved ones via the towers. Let's put the word out."

Ciara stepped forwards. She came up to Finn and squeezed his arm. "I'm glad you're alive. What you did – it was incredible."

"Where is Maeve?" asked Finn. "Or Lud, or whatever her real name is. Didn't she come with you?"

"She and the others have stayed inside," said Ciara.

"Why?"

"She said it was to make sure the destruction is complete," said Aelth. "It's strange, though. It was like she didn't want to leave."

"What happened after I was taken?" asked Finn. "Was anyone else punished for the fire?"

"No," said Ciara. "That master vouched for us, said we

weren't involved."

"Connor?"

"That's him. He saved us."

"I'm glad."

"Do you know what happened to him?" asked Ciara.

Finn shook his head. "No. I wish I did."

They spent all that day and the following working the line-of-sight. Having helped Mrs. Megrim herself, Shireen was able to operate the devices nearly as quickly as Finn. The others helped too, punching in messages or delivering responses to those gathering beneath the tower. No one minded having to wait. People talked and laughed, or just lay on the grass with their eyes closed. One or two people had fashioned musical instruments, blowing through lengths of pipe or banging on old pots. They sang ragged songs for the waiting lines, each performance being met with a roar of delight. Others entertained the crowds by juggling or performing acts of acrobatics. When he wasn't working on the 'scopes, Finn loved to walk among them all, watching and listening.

Some of the people sending messages via the line-of-sight left disappointed, their loved ones no longer alive or not answering. But most of the communications were messages of purest delight. Finn loved to watch those people, too, their faces lighting up as they read words from home.

By the third day the gathering of people beneath the tower had reduced to a trickle. It was the same at all the towers. Ciara and Aelth had left, hand in hand, leaving Rory behind. One or two people still picked their way from the ruins. Scattered groups of people remained on the plain, as if they intended to stay by the ruins of Engn. Some of them had been there so long it was their home, now. Finn even noticed one or two people creeping back inside once the worst of the fires had died down. Searching for loved ones, or maybe just food and shelter. But by now most people had left, walking away from Engn alone or in groups, fanning out in all directions across the grass plain.

Diane came over to kneel beside him as the sun started to dip behind the shattered machine.

"I underestimated him, didn't I? Connor, I mean," she said.

"I think a lot of people did."

"Do you think he knew? That he wouldn't be able to get out?"

Finn sighed. "Perhaps. Whatever it was he was up to, I think he knew he might not make it."

"What do you think it was?"

"Don't know. I suppose it doesn't matter now."

They sat in silence for a time then, Finn watching the vast plume of smoke fanning upwards into the sky. "Do you think they'll ever rebuild it?" he asked.

"Only if we let them," Diane replied. "But it won't happen in our lifetimes. Nor our children's."

"Our children?"

Diane didn't reply.

"What will you do now?" Finn asked. "Where will you go?"

"Back to the valley. See my family. After that I was thinking of coming north again. Up to see you. If you're okay with that."

Finn clutched her hand and leaned his head on her shoulder.

They waited one more night before agreeing no one else

was coming out. Tom had died in the mines. Connor, last Director of Engn, had been killed somewhere in the Directory, perhaps trying to escape, perhaps still in the Panopticon. Finn wondered if the ex-masters and ironclads knew what had happened, knew what Connor had done. It barely mattered now. Let them think what they wanted.

"Are you ready to go?" His father sat at the hatchway, his legs on the ladder. The others were back down on the ground, lifting bags and sacks onto their backs, supplies for the journey.

"I'll send one more message to Mrs. Megrim," said Finn.

"We'll be waiting for you."

"Okay."

"Finn, I'm sorry about Connor."

"Yeah."

"I wish I'd done what you did thirty years ago. So you didn't have to. I can't tell you how proud of you I am, Finn." His father climbed down the ladder to leave him alone.

Finn sat at the line-of-sight 'scope and began to type. He didn't want to have to tell Mrs. Megrim, but it had to be done. They were coming home. There was no sign of Tom. There was no sign of Connor. Mrs. Megrim, he knew, would relay the message to Connor's parents.

When he'd transmitted, he sat alone in the silence of the hut, awaiting a reply. He was just beginning to think the message had got lost when the light in the 'scope began to flicker.

Come home safely, boy. We'll be waiting for you all.

Closing the hatch behind him he climbed down the ladder. Halfway down he paused to survey the smouldering, broken ruins, thinking about everything that had happened there.

On the ground, he turned away from Engn for the last time. Then the seven of them began to walk, across the grass for the valley and woods of home.

Engn II – The Clockwork War

The wheels of the great machine turn again…

Three years after the destruction of Engn, Finn is awoken by a shattering earthquake. As the people of the valley flee the ruins, rumours circulate that the machinery of Engn is working once more. Finn is haunted by the thought that Connor desperately needed him to do something. Uncovering buried secrets, Finn sees he has to return to the wreckage of Engn to find the answers to his questions.

To him, the events of the Clockwork War are history, but he learns that others are still fighting the ancient battle. For them, the machinery of Engn and its mysterious purpose are at the heart of everything.

Diane refuses to come with him, thinking he needs to put the past behind him. But then Engn's line-of-sight signals start to broadcast again…

ABOUT THE AUTHOR

Simon Kewin was born on the misty Isle of Man but now lives deep in the English countryside. He writes fantasy, science fiction and some things that can't make their minds up. He is the author of over 100 published short stories as well as a growing number of novels.

To find out about his other books, go to:

www.simonkewin.co.uk

Sign up for his newsletter and you'll be the first to know when he has new books out. There are some fine sci/fi and fantasy books to download for free as thanks.